Temporally
Out of Order

Other Anthologies Edited by
Patricia Bray & Joshua Palmatier

After Hours: Tales from the Ur-Bar
The Modern Fae's Guide to Surviving Humanity
Clockwork Universe: Steampunk vs Aliens

Temporally
Out of Order

Edited by

Joshua Palmatier
&
Patricia Bray

Zombies Need Brains LLC
www.zombiesneedbrains.com

Interior Design (ebook): April Steenburgh
Interior Design (print): C. Lennox
Cover Design by C. Lennox
Cover Art "Temporally Out of Order" by Justin Adams

ZNB Book Collectors #2

Kickstarter Edition Printing, July 2015
First Printing, August 2015

Print ISBN-10: 1940709024
Print ISBN-13: 978-1940709024

Ebook ISBN-10: 1940709032
Ebook ISBN-13: 978-1940709031

Printed in the U.S.A.

Copyrights

Table of Contents

Introduction
by Joshua Palmatier   1

"Reading Lists"
by Seanan McGuire   2

"Salamander Bites"
by Elektra Hammond   12

"Black and White"
by David B. Coe   24

"Dinosaur Stew"
by Chuck Rothman   46

"Not All Is As It Seems"
by Faith Hunter   58

"Batting Out of Order"
by Edmund R. Schubert   79

"Grand Tour"
by Steve Ruskin   93

"'A' is for Alacrity, Astronauts, and Grief"
by Sofie Bird   114

"The Spiel of the Glocken"
by Laura Resnick   134

"The Passing Bell"
by Amy Griswold   149

"Destination Ahead"
by Laura Anne Gilman   159

"Where There's Smoke"
by Susan Jett   179

"Alien Time Warp"
by Gini Koch   192

"Cell Service"
by Christopher Barili   212

"Temporally Full"
by Stephen Leigh   227

"Notes and Queries"
by Juliet E. McKenna   242

"Temporally Out of Odor: A Fragrant Fable"
by Jeremy Sim   254

About the Authors   272

About the Editors   277

Acknowledgements   279

Signature Page

Patricia Bray, editor:

_____

Joshua Palmatier, editor:

_____

Seanan McGuire:

_____

Elektra Hammond:

_____

David B. Coe:

_____

Chuck Rothman:

_____

Faith Hunter:

_____

Edmund R. Schubert:

_____

Steve Ruskin:

_____

Sofie Bird:

_____

Laura Resnick:

_____

Amy Griswold:

_____

Laura Anne Gilman:

_____

Susan Jett:

_____

Gini Koch:

_____

Christopher Barili:

_____

Stephen Leigh:

_____

Juliet E. McKenna:

_____

Jeremy Sim:

_____

Justin Adams, artist:

_____

Introduction

While traveling to a convention, waiting for a connecting flight at an airport, I sat across from a bank of pay telephones in the terminal. One of the telephones had a note attached to it: "Temporally Out of Order." Obviously it was a typo, but as I sat there I began to wonder… If I picked up the receiver, who could I call? Could I dial my father, who'd died when I was eighteen, perhaps talk to him one last time? What about my grandfather? Or perhaps I could talk to my future self, find out what mistakes I'd made in the next few years, maybe attempt to avoid them.

And then I began to think, what other everyday objects could somehow behave "temporally" out of order? What kind of stories could evolve out of such a situation? How would such an object change your life, either for good or bad, and what would the repercussions be?

I decided to throw the idea out there, to see what kinds of stories would pop up. This anthology is the culmination. Seventeen authors used their imaginations and took gadgets—some every day and ordinary, others … not so much—and let them run temporally wild. We hope you enjoy them.

And maybe next time, when that phone rings oddly or your computer acts weird, you should look at it askance and ask yourself whether it's really out of order

… or perhaps only temporally out of order.

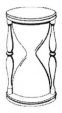

READING LISTS
by Seanan McGuire

Megan Halprin was forty-seven years old when she got her first library card. She didn't particularly want it, all things being equal: she'd never been much of a reader, and she didn't have the time to waste on books. But her employer had been very clear. Either she needed to bring her reading up to at least a ninth grade level, or she was going to be looking for another job. With the economy in the shitter—no pun intended—even janitorial jobs were thin on the ground. It wasn't her fault the damn chemical cleaners were so complicated. How was she supposed to know that mixing them improperly would fill the halls with toxic smoke? It wasn't on her. It was on the people who didn't bother to make things simple.

But that hadn't held any water with management. "Remedial reading classes or the unemployment line," was the order, and she was almost fifty years old, for God's sake! She wasn't going to go out and pound the pavement if there was any possible way for her to avoid it. Checking out a library book and doing a report on it was a requirement for graduation, and there wasn't any way around it. So here she was, with a goddamn library card in her name. She didn't even know why they bothered calling them "library cards" anymore. It was just an app on her phone, authorizing her to take books home. As if she'd ever want to do that again after she had passed her class.

"Goddamn waste of time," she muttered uncomfortably, and looked uneasily around the library's cavernous main room.

Megan Halprin was almost too scared to breathe.

Bit by bit, she inched down the main hall, eyeing the brightly-lit rooms with their intimidating piles of books and periodicals. She'd been briefly hopeful when she heard that most libraries had lots of magazine subscriptions, but then her teacher had said "No reports on the latest issue of *Us Weekly*," and all her hopes had been dashed. It was a book or nothing, and nothing wasn't an option.

It wouldn't have been so bad if there hadn't been so many *people*. They were everywhere, holding books, looking at shelves, looking at *her*. No matter what she tried to pick for her report, there would be people there, judging her, knowing that she didn't read as well as they did. They'd think she was stupid. They'd think she was old and useless and didn't belong.

She continued down the hall, looking for a room that didn't have so damn many people in it. There had to be something. There had to be some little corner of this damn library that no one cared about.

She nearly missed the door.

It was closed, which was unusual: all the other doors she'd seen had been open. There was a piece of paper taped to it— "Temporally out of order."

"They work at a library and they can't even spell," muttered Megan. How could a room be out of order? It had to be some sort of library joke. She tried the knob and the door swung open, revealing a small, surprisingly well-lit room packed with books. Best yet, there were no people there. It was, at long last, an empty space.

Megan slipped inside and closed the door behind herself, moving toward the nearest shelf. Fiction, non-fiction, how-to manuals, she didn't care: all she cared about was getting a book and getting out of the library.

"Can I help you with something?"

The voice was female, pleasant, and probably didn't deserve to be answered with a brief shriek of surprise. Megan whirled to find herself facing a smiling, hazel-eyed blonde with a name tag pinned to her breast. A librarian. Of course there would be a librarian. A librarian named "Holly," because why not be as cutesy about things as possible?

"This room closed?" Megan asked, once she had her breath

back.

"Not at all," said the librarian. "We've just been having some mild causality issues. Can I help you find a book?"

Megan didn't know what "causality issues" were, and she wasn't about to ask. "I need something to read. No big words. I'm just looking for something quick and easy." Her cheeks stung a bit as they reddened. She hated admitting that she wasn't the best reader. But this was a librarian. Librarians probably dealt with people who just wanted something relaxing all the time.

"I have just the thing." The librarian smiled, turned to a nearby shelf, and pulled off a book with a bright orange cover. She offered it to Megan, who took it cautiously.

"*Forty Things to Do Before You're Forty,*" she read, sounding the words out carefully and feeling a small ping of triumph when she didn't have to hesitate at all to figure out what something said. Then she laughed roughly. "I probably should've read this eight years ago, when it could have done me some good."

"Do you want it anyway?" asked the librarian.

"Since you can't give it to me eight years ago, sure," said Megan. "It's a book, and that's really all I need right now."

"Great," said the librarian. "Let's get you scanned and on your way." She turned, heading for the circulation desk. It was a little odd that such a small room would have its own desk, but Megan didn't question it much. Everything about the library was odd, or at least new, to her.

The librarian took the book away and ran it under the computer while Megan pulled up the library app on her phone. The computer beeped. Megan's phone beeped. She looked at the display, and her eyes went wide.

"What the hell does this thing mean, I have a book that's more than five years overdue?" she demanded. "I just got this card today!"

"Five years is when the system stops tracking how overdue something is. It looks like a glitch," said the librarian, her mouth drawing down into a moue of displeasure. "I'm so sorry about this. Look, why don't you go and grab something to eat, and then come back here? I'll fix it. Trust me."

Megan frowned, but couldn't think of a good reason not to take the librarian's advice. "I'll be right back," she said, and started for the door.

"I'll be here," said the librarian.

Megan stepped out into the hall, and disappeared.

oOo

Megan Halprin was thirty-eight years old when she got her first library card. She'd been putting it off for years—she didn't like admitting that she'd dropped out of high school; it felt too much like saying she hadn't been able to hack it, when really she'd just been bored and unequipped for all that damn homework—but the new management of her building had promised her a promotion if she could just bring her reading up to snuff. Janitorial work was nothing to be ashamed of. At the same time, the idea of getting to a desk job someday, where she could tell *other* people to go and mop up spills while she sat on her butt and let her feet recover from the last ten years? Damn, that was a nice idea.

So now here she was, standing in the library, fresh from her first Adult Literacy class, and she had no idea where to go. There seemed to be people everywhere, and while she didn't mind other people so much, she really didn't feel like sharing her first careful exploration of the library with folks who wouldn't understand why she looked so confused, or why she was clutching her phone—loaded with one of the new library card apps that were all the rage these days—quite so tightly. She thought she might have preferred to get one of the physical cards after all, even though that was a five dollar materials charge. It would have been nice to have something a little smaller to hold onto.

Slowly, she began moving through the library, trying to look like she was going somewhere in specific, when really she was just going wherever she wound up. When she saw the closed door with the sign taped to it, she paused only long enough to be sure that the sign didn't say "private" or "no admittance"—it didn't—before opening the door and stepping through into the small, book-lined room on the other side.

"Hello!"

Megan turned. There was a smiling woman standing behind a circulation desk. It looked a little out of place here; weren't the circulation desks supposed to be out in the more general-use parts of the library? But the woman's smile was very bright, and she was wearing a name tag. She must be a librarian.

"Hello," said Megan. "Is this room open to the public?"

"Oh, absolutely," said the librarian—"Holly," according to her name tag. "We're just experiencing some causality issues. You're Megan Halprin, right?"

Megan stared. "How do you know my name?"

"The system alerted me when it scanned your card into the library," said the librarian. "It's a new feature. I have your book." She reached under the counter and produced a book with a bright orange cover. *Forty Things to Do Before You're Forty*, proclaimed the title.

"Oh," said Megan. "Um, yes, that does look like something I'd ... but is there some sort of recommendations system?" She wasn't entirely comfortable with the idea of the library profiling her likely reading tastes. She wasn't even sure she *had* reading tastes as such.

"No, my system says you put a hold on it last week." The librarian looked from the book to Megan before offering, "Maybe we have someone else with the same name coming to this branch. Well, since the computer thinks it's yours, would you like to check it out anyway?"

"Sure," said Megan. "Can I ... can I get more than one?"

"Of course," said the librarian. "What can I help you find?"

Forty Things to Do Before You're Forty checked out just fine, but Megan's second book—a travel guide to Alaska, which she had always intended to visit—came up as five years overdue.

"Go grab a cup of coffee and then come back," suggested the librarian. "I'm sure it's a simple fix."

"All right," said Megan, and left, *Forty Things to Do Before You're Forty* tucked safely under her arm.

oOo

Megan Halprin was thirty-three years old when she got her first library card. She had never been a recreational reader—strictly instruction manuals and self-help books—but if she was going to make it past supervisor with the cleaning company she worked for, she needed to learn how to relax. Reading seemed like an easy, effective, and best of all, economical way to let her hair down a little bit.

Most of the rooms at the library were full of people, which didn't really suit her much: she wouldn't have gone into janitorial services if she liked dealing with people day in and day out. So she wandered the halls and browsed the reading rooms until she found a little door with a sign claiming it was somehow out of order. Unable to resist, she tried the knob. The door swung open.

The woman behind the desk—Holly—smiled. "Hello," she said. "Are you here to pick up that book about Alaska?"

Megan blinked. "Excuse me?" She stepped into the room as she spoke. She didn't have much experience with libraries, but what little she had told her that it was impolite to shout.

"Alaska." Holly produced a travel guide from beneath the counter. "You're Megan Halprin, yes? I have a hold on this in your name."

Megan had been considering a trip to Alaska for years. It was an easy cruise, according to everyone she knew who'd taken it, and it wasn't even supposed to be that expensive. Talk about relaxing: two weeks all-inclusive in a floating hotel seemed about perfect. "Yes, that's mine," she said, suddenly making up her mind. "Do you have internet here?"

"We do," said Holly. "Would you like me to show you how to use the public access terminals?"

"Yes, please."

An hour later, Megan had all the information she could possibly have needed about Alaskan cruises, what they cost, and when the best times to book were. Some of the cruises were even in her price range, if she was willing to scrimp and save for the next six months or so. Something she had always assumed was outside of her grasp might not be that impossible after all.

"Thank you for all your help," she said, turning to the librarian.

Holly—whose name tag identified her as part of the library's archive corrections department—smiled. "That's what I'm here for," she said. "Was there anything else you had been meaning to look into, and just didn't have the time for?"

Didn't have the ... but that was a fair description, wasn't it? Megan had been dreaming of Alaska for years. She'd just never been willing to make the time. Much like she'd never made the time to go back for her GED. "Do you have study guides?" she asked.

Holly's smile widened. "Let me show you."

The book on preparing for your General Educational Development Test came up as four years overdue. The librarian suggested she come back later, after the system glitch had been repaired. Megan agreed and, still clutching her book on Alaska, stepped out the door, where she promptly disappeared.

oOo

Megan Halprin was twenty-nine years old when she got her first library card, on the recommendation of her GED prep instructor. "Read more and you'll get more comfortable with reading," was Mr. Milton's suggestion, and since she wanted to pass the class, she'd agreed to go to the library and sign up. There was an app available, even, to stand in for her library card. It only cost $1.99, and the proceeds went to pay for library upkeep. She'd shrugged and swiped her credit stick. Might as well be a good patron from the outset, right?

Most of the carrels and study areas seemed to be in use. Regular library visitors probably got there early to make sure they'd be able to snag the prime spots. Megan wandered until she saw a closed door. "Temporally out of order," she read, after a moment. "Cute." Then she turned the knob, and stuck her head inside.

The librarian behind the circulation desk smiled like the sun. "Hi," she said. "Megan, right? I'm Holly Littlejohn. I have a study guide for you."

Megan blinked.

This time, before she checked out, she picked up a beginner's guide to personal computing. She liked her job with the housecleaning service, but she was pretty sure she could figure out spreadsheets and move into clerical work, if she just took the time. Maybe there would be a computer unit in the GED prep.

The book came back five years overdue. Megan left.

oOo

Meg Halprin was twenty-four years old when she got her first library card. She collected her book on personal computing, and got a weird error message on a book about deferred college admissions. The librarian suggested she step out for a cup of coffee.

oOo

Megan was nineteen when she got her first library card. The librarian in the weird little private room she found had a book on deferred college admissions already waiting for her. She found a book about computer programming for beginners that— ironically—couldn't be checked out, since it was already five years overdue.

She promised to come back for it later. The librarian watched her go, and smiled.

"Earlier," she said, and turned back to her book.

oOo

Meg was fourteen when she finally decided to get a library card. Middle school had been a slog, and she was sure high school was going to be even worse. Access to more books might help. Besides, she'd heard that the library had books on programming that were up to date and even counted for high school credit.

She found a room that wasn't filled with "helpful" adults who wanted to approve her reading choices before she could decide whether she really wanted to make them. She found the book she was looking for. She also found a book about calculus for preteens that she thought looked pretty cool. It scanned as already overdue.

"Why does that happen?" she asked, scowling at the book, and then at the librarian.

"Well, there are a lot of reasons," said the woman—Miss Littlejohn, according to her name tag. One more "helpful" adult in a world that was just full of them. "Mostly, it's a matter of causality being broken in this room. You know, that's the first time you've asked me that question?"

Meg blinked. "What?"

"Never mind."

"No, really. I don't understand." Meg hated it when adults talked like they were smarter than she was. She couldn't wait to be a grownup, and be able to answer all her own questions. "I'm old enough to have a library card. That means I'm old enough to understand how it works."

Miss Littlejohn looked weirdly amused. "My apologies," she said. "Every book has a unique footprint in our system, and sometimes the computers try to backtrack when someone checks them out. So they go, for example, 'Oh, someone who's reading *Programming for Beginners* probably read *Middle School Mathletics: Calculus* five years ago.' And then they show the second book as overdue. Are you sure you want it? You have a long reading list ahead of you already. Although I'm going to bet you don't need a few of them anymore."

Meg bristled. "I'm sure."

"All right," said the librarian. "Go get a soda and come right back."

Meg went.

oOo

Meg was nine when she convinced her mom that she was ready for her first adult library card. She had been looking for the children's library, flush with the excitement of being able to get *any book she wanted*, when she made a wrong turn and wound up in front of a door marked "out of order." Not just any "out of order": *temporally* out of order, which didn't make sense.

"Can I help you?" The voice was kind, mellow, and adult. Meg turned to see a librarian standing beside her. The woman was pretty, in that adult sort of way, with long blonde hair and a friendly face. Her nametag said she was Miss Littlejohn. It was a funny name.

"What's in there?" Meg asked, pointing to the door. "Time can't be out of order."

"Not usually," agreed the librarian, cheerfully. "Come on. Let me help you find a book."

They turned, together, and walked away.

The door stayed closed.

SALAMANDER BITES
by Elektra Hammond

Steve checked the next ticket up and groaned—it was marked "Chef's Choice," and the server had written "VIP" across the top. Someone out front thought this customer was a reviewer or food blogger. Their meal needed to be *perfect*.

It was just over a year and a half since they'd combined his cooking expertise and his girlfriend Carrie's business skills to open *With Wine*, and now he was running his kitchen with a skeleton crew, working himself to exhaustion.

He sighed as he assembled the ingredients for a classic escargot starter that had been a specialty at *Avec le Vin*, the famous French restaurant where he'd learned to cook, preoccupied with trying to decide what would be an appropriate entrée to follow up with.

He turned to the Salamander, a high temp broiler that looked like an open-front toaster oven on steroids. He put in the jazzed-up snails and, distracted, moved too close. There was a nasty sizzle, and a second later his arm stung with intense pain. He sputtered a curse as he stared at a narrow crescent of skin starting to tighten next to a nearly identical old scar.

"Problem, Chef?" said Marco, from across the room.

"Burned myself. Hurts like a sonuva*bitch*. Don't get too close to the lower right corner on the Salamander. Damn thing bites."

He took a brief moment to check the oven, noting the offending area was on the Salamander's metal front leg: a dent had left a raised area on the far end. It was only a hazard to those passing too near in the tight kitchen. It was an odd place for an almost invisible protrusion; the Salamander at *Avec* had had a very similar one, courtesy of an altercation with a cast-iron pan wielded by a very annoyed chef. *Better to take out a complaint on a piece of kitchen equipment than to yell at an unhappy customer ...*

He pulled out the starter, plated it, and sent it out to the dining room. A nagging worry made him glance back at the prep station. The spices were conspicuously absent. *Damn!* What a time to let distraction push him into making a beginner's error. But it was too late to fix it now.

He looked at the empty pan, which seemed more oval than when he had put it in the Salamander, then shook his head. He must be imagining things.

In between managing his small staff, and inspecting every dish before it went out to the dining room, he personally prepared Coquille Saint Jacques for the VIP's main course, being extra careful before giving it a quick pass through the Salamander to melt the cheese perfectly. He plated it with care, then handed it off.

"Chef, the guy at table eight loved the escargot. He said it was seasoned to perfection."

"Good to hear," Steve said, thinking he couldn't possibly be a critic if he hadn't noticed the lack of seasoning. "Better get this out before it gets cold."

The work in the kitchen finally eased up, so Steve took his time preparing dessert, a fresh fruit tart with Grand Marnier sabayon. He cut up strawberries, blueberries, raspberries, pears, peaches, kiwis, and oranges. He whipped up the Grand Marnier-flavored sauce, coated the fruit with it, arranged it in a tart shell, and heated it up in the Salamander to give it just a bit of a crust. He sent it out to the dining room.

He'd sent a request via one of the servers asking Carrie to come back to the kitchen, but she'd never materialized. *Couldn't someone cover the hostess station for* two minutes *when he needed her help?* He slapped a bandage on his arm, which was starting to blister, no thanks to her, and went out to talk to the customer.

Steve gestured at the empty chair at table eight. "May I?"

"Please do, Stephen," said the man seated there in softly

accented English, his dark beard obscuring his familiar face.

Steve started. For a moment, he was back in *Avec* working his ass off as Chef Étienne taught him the wonders of French cuisine. Never a minute's rest. But no, this man was too young and his accent wasn't nearly as thick. After a few seconds, he had it—the grandson who helped out on the occasional weekend.

"Pierre! What brings you to my restaurant?"

As Steve settled into the chair, Pierre said, "Happenstance. A new French restaurant in town. How could I resist?"

"I hope it was worth your time."

"A meal of delights. I don't believe my *grandpère* could have done better. Your Escargots á la Bourguignonne was perfection."

"Glad you liked it," Steve said automatically, as he desperately tried to figure out how Pierre had utterly failed to notice the missing spices. "Not everybody does. We've been getting murdered by reviews. I work my butt off cooking, and some critic comes in and says that the food is 'okay' or 'lacks complexity.' We're barely scraping by. We need a break. Soon."

"I am just one man, and I must needs be honest, but perhaps I can do for you something, Stephen. I will think on it."

"Thanks, man. Every little bit, you know. Hey, Carrie!" He waved at his girlfriend as she passed by.

"Carrie, this is Pierre. His grandfather was Chef Étienne—*the* Chef Étienne I've told you about. The chef who taught me to *really* cook. Pierre, my partner Carrie."

"Nice to meet you," said Carrie.

"The pleasure, it is mine," said Pierre, with a bow of his head. "Carrie? Surely that is not your given name …"

"Carolina," said Carrie, with a half-smile and a little giggle.

"A lovely name, Carolina," Pierre replied, taking her hand and kissing it.

Steve watched the exchange, glad to see Carrie flirting with Pierre a little. If he *was* going to review the restaurant, a little female attention would surely help. *Maybe there was a way to get them dancing ...*

"Your grandfather, how is he?" asked Carrie.

Damn. Hadn't he told her about the old man's breakdown?

"My *grandpère* is not well, I'm afraid. He never recovered

from closing the restaurant—cooking was his life."

"I'm so sorry," Carrie said, softly.

Pierre shrugged.

They chatted for a bit, then the bartender waved Carrie over to answer a question. A few moments later, Steve excused himself from Pierre, hoping the meal had been enough to turn *With Wine*'s luck around.

He was unfocused during clean up, again thinking back to working at *Avec*. It had been one of the hottest tickets in town back then, but he'd left after customers starting complaining that the house specialties didn't taste as good. He'd worried he would be blamed. Once he was gone, though, he'd heard a series of bad reviews had sent the restaurant into a downward spiral. Eighteen months later it closed its doors for good.

Steve came back to the present as he finished putting things away.

"Marco, did you notice these pans don't stack right?" he asked, examining the pans for dents. There were none.

"No, that's odd. They did yesterday."

Steve spent a few minutes puzzling over the pans, but he was too tired to care. He had a kitchen to clean up.

The next night the restaurant was packed. Steve was struggling to keep on top of all the orders without yelling at his sous chefs, Marco and Joe. He sliced onions and tried to calculate—how many days like this before he could justify more staff? But *where* had the people come from?

"Steve, look at this," Carrie had slipped into the kitchen while he was daydreaming about success, and now held her iPad in front of him.

He pushed it away. "I'm too busy cooking. Later."

"Now," she insisted, getting into his personal space.

The tone of her voice drew him up cold. He glanced at her iPad. A blog with the title "Ville Gastronomie ~ Fine Dining in the City" was displayed, with the top entry labeled "*With Wine*." He read as much to get Carrie to leave him alone as out of curiosity:

Chef Stephen has mastered classic French cuisine. Eating at With Wine *reminded me of the very best of times at my* grandpère *'s table. I look forward to returning there.*

Carrie said, "The whole review is stellar. And there are a ton of comments—people saying they want to eat here. I think that's why we're so popular tonight. Got to go!"

As the night wore on, dishes were popped in and out of the Salamander constantly, to brown them attractively or melt cheese on top. Reports coming back from the dining room were positive, which kept the mood in the frantic kitchen from going sour.

After clean up, more of the pans didn't nest properly. When Steve peered at them closely, they were a different brand then the ones he had purchased, and a slightly different shape. *Hadn't Avec used that brand?* Both Marco and Joe denied any knowledge of switched out pans, and he wondered where the hell they'd come from …

The next day, the prior night's momentum brought Steve in a bit early to get dinner prep going and he had the kitchen to himself. He grabbed a standard pan and started making Coq Au Vin—it had a long cook time. He slipped it into the Salamander to simmer, then saw the bacon sitting on his cutting board. Another rookie mistake. He pulled the pan back out, intending to add in the bacon, and opened it.

He stared.

The dish in the pan was completely cooked and ready to be served. And it visibly included bacon, despite the uncut bacon clearly sitting on his station. He tasted it. It was amazing. Complex layers of flavor, smokiness, earthiness, with tender, perfectly cooked chicken. The seasoning was worthy of Chef Étienne on his best day.

Something very strange was going on. A memory surfaced, and Steve poured himself a glass of red wine, swirling it in the glass as he sipped and tried to recall. A day at *Avec*, before he moved on, trying to distance himself from a doomed restaurant whose executive chef was showing signs of losing it. A customer had complained that their Coq Au Vin had no bacon. And was under-seasoned.

He drank some more wine, finishing the glass and pouring another.

He deliberately took another standard pan and placed a filet of sole in it. He covered it in fish stock and grated some cheese over it. Into the Salamander it went.

Out came a dish that looked and smelled delectable. He tasted it. Filet of Sole Mornay. Both pans were rounded and not the same brand he'd been cooking with.

He sat down and thought for a few minutes as an unpleasant smile slid onto his face.

He was in the bar when Carrie came in for work a little while later, drinking yet another glass of wine. "Carrie, where did you get the Salamander? It's used, right?"

Carrie tilted her head a little to the right, frowning, with that look she got when she was unhappy with something he was doing. "*You* took care of getting the Salamander. That's the broiler, right? I handled procurement for front of house, you took care of the kitchen."

"It was in the kitchen the first day after we had everything cleaned up—I assumed you'd gotten it."

"Nope, Steve, that one's on you. Is it working okay? Do we need another one?"

"It works just … fine. No need to mess with it. It's just that I burned myself on it yesterday and I think it's the Salamander we used at *Avec*. Funny that it found its way here."

oOo

It had been a year of growing success for the restaurant, as a few superb reviews had brought the naysayers back in to give *With Wine* another try. Those reviews, with comments like "hit its stride as one of the city's top eateries" and "a can't miss destination for anyone who likes classic French food with innovative seasoning" were filling the restaurant every night. They were solidly in the black and considering expansion.

Marco pitched his voice too low for anyone else to hear. "Steve, where did you find those new line cooks? They know nothing about French food. Or any food, really."

Steve whispered back, "So train them."

"I'm trying."

Steve looked at the stove, where a Béarnaise sauce sat

halfway completed, getting lumpy. "Who's responsible for this?"

One of the new cooks turned around. "Mine, Chef."

"Throw it away and start it again."

"Right away, Chef."

"Who showed you how to do this?"

"Marco did, Chef."

Steve could feel his face getting hotter. "Marco, you know a Béarnaise must be whisked constantly."

Marco said, "I was prepping starters, Chef. My fault."

"Don't let it happen again."

"No, Chef," said Marco, his eyes down.

Steve was finishing set up as the restaurant's opening time approached. He smelled burning, and looked up to see another pan of Béarnaise, this one smoking.

"Marco! Burning. On the stove."

"Yes, Chef."

With the larger kitchen staff, and subsequently more crowded prep area, Steve had to actually cook, and he was frustrated. It wasn't worth putting much effort into. He'd taste the dishes coming out of the Salamander and they were perfect every time, no matter what went it. It took the fun, the passion, out of it. He knew he should replace the Salamander, but a nagging fear remained that he just couldn't produce dishes as good as what was coming out of that oven. So he went through the motions.

At the end of shift, Marco tapped Steve on the shoulder. "Chef?"

"What?"

"I work hard. My cousin Joe works hard. We can't have you yelling at us all night in the kitchen just because the new kids *you* hired need to be trained."

Steve felt his annoyance at the whole situation come to a head. "It's my restaurant. I'll yell at you when you screw up if I want to."

Marco looked at him and shook his head slowly. He took off his apron and said, "Then I quit."

"So do I," said Joe.

"You can't do that!"

"Yes, we can," said Marco, as they walked out.

Steve stared at the new line cooks, "What are *you* looking at? Get back to cleaning up."

It's great to be on top, Steve thought, with no enthusiasm at all to keep on cooking.

oOo

Beginning of another short-handed shift. Desperate to save some time, Steve glanced around and, while no one was watching, put a couple of pieces of filet of sole and fish stock in a pan and rough grated some cheese on top. He tossed it in the Salamander. Two minutes later, he pulled it out. The dish was a mess … just a jumble of toasted ingredients.

Shit. Now he was really in the weeds.

He threw more ingredients into the pan, trying to convince himself that it hadn't been enough to trigger the Salamander. But deep inside, he knew. He put the pan into the oven, but the result was just what he feared. A disaster.

He forced himself to concentrate and cook the dish properly, from scratch, before popping it in the Salamander to melt the cheese. He plated it and sent it out to the dining room, trying to figure out what was going on.

He stopped and looked at the burns on his arm. *Did the Salamander need another offering?* He shivered at the thought.

All shift he cooked, snapping at the improperly trained sous chefs, at the even newer line cooks, working harder than he had in ages. Dishes were sent back to the kitchen with complaints they were undercooked, overcooked, or over-seasoned. After over a year, he'd become dependent on the Salamander to make his food for him, and he'd lost the knack. *If he'd ever had it.* The day stretched on.

When the dinner service was finally done, Steve sent Carrie home without him. He opened a bottle of his favorite red wine and drank a glass, then another, slowly sucking down the whole bottle while working up his nerve. He rolled up his sleeve, walked over to the Salamander, and, before he could back out, pressed his arm against the raised area on the right corner, slowly counting to ten.

The burn hurt like hell.

He forced himself to put together a pan of fish and grated cheese and slid it into the Salamander. He tapped his foot waiting for it to finish, the skin on his arm's third burn blistering. When he couldn't wait any longer, he pulled it out.

A gooey, overcooked mess.

He sat in a corner in the kitchen and got very, very drunk, stumbling home just before dawn

Later, Steve sipped black coffee to banish his hangover while he tried to explain to Carrie. He looked down, anywhere but at her. He was halfway through his second cup when he finally said, "There's something I need to tell you. That night Pierre reviewed us, the review that started everything ... I think that's when it started."

"When what started?"

"When I put food in the Salamander, it came out ... different."

"Different ... how?"

"The pans, for one thing. When I looked at them later, they were a different brand. And the food—the food was *perfect*. Even when I forgot an ingredient. One night there was a mix up in the kitchen and we used sugar instead of salt for about an hour in all the starters—it didn't matter. Anything that went through the Salamander came out tasting fantastic."

"You weren't *cooking* the food?"

"I was sort of cooking it. Some of it. I didn't figure that out right away. Stuff from the Salamander was just coming out *better* somehow. Then I realized I just needed to put in enough ingredients to somehow trigger the right dish to come out."

"Steve, you're not making sense. Pierre wrote that review eighteen months ago. The dishes he ate—were you cooking the food or not?"

Steve's brain hung on the phrase *eighteen months. Avec* had gone into a decline it never recovered from that lasted for *eighteen months.* Chef Étienne's specialties stopped tasting right ...

He looked at his freshly bandaged arm and shook his head.

"Steve. Steve!" Carrie's perky voice intruded. "Didn't it

bother you that you weren't cooking the food?"

"Yes. No. At first. I *was* cooking, kinda. It was just another tool. I mean, if I've got a blender, should I be whisking soups by hand?"

"Steve, this sounds crazy. Don't get me wrong—I'm glad you've gotten it off your chest. Can I see the Salamander do ... whatever it does?"

"It's *over*. Yesterday, it just stopped. I tried everything to get it to work, but it'll never work again. *Avec* is closed."

"*Avec*? It's been closed for years."

"I thought the Salamander was magic—but it's not. It's the same oven I burned myself on at *Avec la Vin*, just before their food got, well, not so good. Somehow, in some screwed up way, it's been pulling the dishes from *Avec*. Through time." Steve started to talk low and fast, trying to get it all out. "The bad reviews Chef Étienne got were for *my food*. The food I cooked here, at *With Wine*. It somehow got swapped back to *Avec*. But after eighteen months—"

"—*Avec* closed," Carrie finished, staring at him. "Do you really think that's possible?"

"I don't know. But today I worked my butt off cooking. And food kept getting sent back to the kitchen—I don't know what went wrong."

"We can fix this. You're a great chef. We'll work it out." Carrie's voice was calm, soothing.

"I don't need to 'work it out.' I know how to cook." Steve got up and stomped out of the apartment. She would never understand. *Had he been responsible for the failure of* Avec? There was a cold feeling at the pit of his stomach when he thought about the future of *With Wine*.

oOo

Steve let himself into the restaurant to prep for dinner, and poured himself a glass of wine. Lately, it made the work easier. Over the last month, he'd come to dread coming to work. Carrie's bitchy side had come out, constantly checking up on him, pushing the sous chefs to double-check everything he did.

He was in charge of the kitchen, not her. In the last month, since the Salamander had stopped doing its thing, there'd been bad reviews. Critics were speculating that the original chef had left. Business had dropped off.

Carrie'd moved out last week. He tried to make himself care, but in truth he was glad to see her go. She never let up, whining about losing her investment if the restaurant went under.

The dinner service went pretty smoothly. The restaurant wasn't crowded—it was never crowded anymore—and only a few plates were sent back with complaints.

The next day, Steve came in early to work on a brandy cream sauce, trying to get the seasoning and texture right. The night's special was pork chops, but the sauce kept breaking, while the chops were undercooked. Or overcooked.

In the middle of the chaos, Carrie stepped into the kitchen.

"Steve, can you find some time for me after closing tonight? We need to *talk*."

"*Fine.* I'll make time."

At least she left the kitchen and let him work. His staff was starting to arrive. He gave up on the sauce and cooked the chops in butter and garlic. They were *not* a popular special.

After closing, they talked over coffee for a long time in the kitchen, cavernous and echoing now that the staff had gone home.

"Steve, it's come to this. We're chafing at each other, and it's hurting the restaurant. Either buy me out and I'll leave; or I'll buy you out, but you'll have to go."

He thought about it for half a second—he'd been itching to leave since the Salamander's mojo had failed—then said, "It's yours. I want a bank check for my half of the investment tomorrow."

"You know that's not possible."

"As soon as you can make it happen then."

He walked out without looking back, confident no one working in that kitchen could do half the job he did.

oOo

Three months later, Steve walked past *With Wine*. He'd just quit his job at a high end steakhouse, and was wondering if Carrie would re-hire him. The restaurant was full, with people queued up outside. Carrie stood next to the hostess, looking relaxed and animated, chatting with the customers. The day's menu was posted, with Chef de Cuisine Étienne Morel across the top.

Above the bar, on a shelf, the Salamander sat, disconnected. A few climbing plants were sitting on it, vines twining in and about it.

Steve turned around and walked away for good.

BLACK AND WHITE
by David B. Coe

Jessie stepped into her grandfather's office the way she might have slipped into a crypt.

Even now, a grown woman come to sort through a dead man's effects, she felt ill at ease alone in this room. It didn't matter that Nana had sent her in here to sort through the boxes of old photographs stored in his closet; Grampa's office had always been hallowed ground. During her childhood, when she and her cousins descended on Nana and Grampa's house, they were free to roam wherever they wished. Nana's kitchen was their common room, the upstairs bedrooms and closets and hallways their castles, caves, and haunted houses.

Only Grampa's office remained off-limits.

"Grampa's working in there," Nana would tell them. "You leave him be."

As a little girl, Jessie hadn't known what to make of this. She pictured him sitting at his desk, solemn and intent, poring over papers she couldn't quite see, or perhaps speaking on the phone with important men. Men like him. On those few occasions when she was permitted to enter the office, she found it both exciting and slightly disappointing, the thrill of being with him in his special place tempered by the realization that his refuge was not all that different from the dry, colorless offices of other adults she knew.

She didn't remember his desk appearing quite so disheveled, or the volumes on his bookshelves sitting so haphazardly. The photos on the walls, however, hadn't changed much over the years. Some had faded, a few hung off kilter, but the images remained the same, comforting in their familiarity.

And the camera sat where it always had, on the shelf behind his desk, where he could reach it without getting up.

A Nikon "F" series SLR in silver and black. Made in 1959, it and its siblings were the first of their kind. Single lens reflex cameras dominated the photography market now and had for more than half a century. All of them traced their lineage back to this camera. It looked clunky and antiquated–nothing like the sleek digital SLRs she used–and it bore scratches and small dents that bespoke a lifetime of use. Still, she couldn't help but admire its stolid utility, so much like that of the man who had used it to capture the world. She walked to the shelf, her eyes never leaving that old camera and the fifty millimeter lens mounted on it. She didn't touch it of course. This was Grampa's camera. At least it had been. It was hers now, if she wanted it.

"He'd have wanted you to take all that equipment of his," Nana had told her when she arrived in Berry's Bluff for the funeral.

That would take some getting used to.

Jessie stared at it for another moment and even went so far as to reach out toward it, only pausing when her hand hovered just above the viewfinder.

No, not yet.

Instead, she opened a window to let in fresh air, and then went to the closet and dug out his boxes of photos. There must have been thirty of them, one heavier than the next. Odd that images made of light and imagination could weigh so much.

The meticulousness that Jessie remembered from the Grampa of her youth–and that she no longer saw in the office–persisted in his cataloging of the photos. Each box was marked with a range of dates: "October 1964-May 1966," "April 1972-June 1973," and so forth. Those notations bracketed births and birthdays, anniversaries and deaths, wars and elections and assassinations. But for this purpose–for the organization of Daniel Stratton's professional life–the dates themselves were enough.

She opened the first box, the earliest that she could find, and began to work her way through the photos. Nana wanted her to cull the "worthless" shots and keep only those of value. But

Jessie knew from the start that this would be impossible. There wasn't a worthless photo here. She meandered through the collection, marveling at his eye, the deceptive simplicity of his compositions. She was a professional photographer, just as he had been, and yet nothing like him at all. She ran her own business: portraits in her home studio, weddings, showers, parties, and the occasional corporate event on location. On occasion, magazines hired her for stories, but those assignments were the exceptions.

Grampa, though, had worked for the Berry's Bluff *Herald*, and had sold work to several regional papers with far larger circulations. Some of his photos had been picked up by AP and UPI. He'd been featured in exhibits and published in at least two dozen books. Daniel Stratton might not have been a household name, but he was a pro. More often than not, Jessie felt like a pretender.

Not that Grampa had ever made her feel that way. From the time she was eleven and started to ask questions about photography, he had nurtured her interest. He bought Jessie her first camera, showed her how to load it and use the controls, and taught her to see the world through a viewfinder.

"You have a fine eye," he'd say, looking through her photos. "And you're careful. A good photographer takes the time to get her settings right."

He never warmed to digital photography.

"Film slows you down," he told her once. "It demands precision. Digital is too easy. It makes you sloppy, wasteful. You screw up one, you get it right the next time. That might be taking pictures, but it sure as hell isn't photography."

She smiled at the memory.

That first afternoon in the office, she spent hours poring over his work. Outside the sky darkened lazily, the way it does in late summer in the South. At one point Nana called her for supper, but she wasn't hungry and kept working, accompanied by the drone of katydids and the distant cries of nighthawks.

The next morning, Nana apologized to her.

"I didn't mean to make you work so hard, sweetie. How late were you up last night?"

"Not that late." A lie. Jessie hadn't gone to bed until after two. "And I don't mind it. But there are so many images I can't identify. His work belongs in a library, but first we should be able to assign a date and place to every photo."

"Well, Dan did that. It's all in his journals."

Jessie gaped. "He kept journals?"

"Oh, yes. I think they're in the attic. He wouldn't put his pictures up there because of the heat and such. But the journals should be up there."

The words were barely out of Nana's mouth before Jessie was scrambling up the pulldown ladder into the attic. She found it much as she remembered, in easy disarray. The stifling air still smelled of dust, mold, and bat piss, of summer and hide-and-seek and the sweet hint of an approaching thunderstorm.

It didn't take her long to find the journals, in a pair of boxes marked with Grampa's neat scrawl.

She carried them down to the office, pulled one out, and opened it, hands trembling with excitement. It took her some time to figure out Grampa's notations, but once she did she was struck by the logic of his system. He listed every photo by roll number, but provided as well location, subject, aperture, shutter speed, and any special notes on the image capture or development: "Pushed film speed to 400," "Extra burn to deepen shadows," "Darken skies for whole shoot."

With the journal in her lap, she returned to the rolls she'd looked at the previous day, matching the entries to photos. When she found duplicates of images she especially liked, she set them aside to frame, either for herself or for her cousins.

Late that day, she noticed that some photos weren't where they were supposed to be. She wondered if they were missing, or had merely been missorted.

oOo

They buried Grampa the next day, the service and reception leaving Jessie no time to go through the boxes. But the morning after, she was back at it. She worked well into the night, slept a few hours, and worked another full day. When at last she finished, she had a list of several shoots mentioned in the journal but absent from the boxes.

That night at dinner, she asked Nana if she knew why some photos might be missing from the collection.

"No," Nana said, spooning potato salad onto her plate. "I can't imagine why. Dan never threw anything away. Are you sure you didn't miss them?"

"I'm sure. We're missing five days in all. I searched everywhere in the office."

Nana had reached for the salad bowl, but she stopped now, staring at Jessie. "From when, exactly?"

"The three I remember were from August and September 1962. And two others were from a couple of years before that. 1960, I think."

"Well, no wonder," Jessie's mother said. "You're talking about pictures from more than fifty years ago. There are bound to be a few missing."

Nana nodded, picking up the salad tongs and serving herself. "Patty's right. A lot can happen in fifty years." But she didn't look Jessie in the eye as she said this, and though it might have been a trick of the light, Jessie thought her grandmother's cheeks lost some of their color.

She said no more about the photos at dinner, but that night an idea came to her, one she thought her grandfather would have liked.

"Did you mean it when you said that Grampa's equipment is mine if I want it?" she asked Nana over breakfast the next morning.

"Of course," Nana said. "Your Grampa was always so proud that you'd followed him into the business. There's no one else he'd rather have using all that stuff."

"Even the camera?"

Nana's eyebrows went up. "Well, yes. But I didn't think you'd want that old thing, with all those fancy new cameras y'all use today."

"Are you kidding? It's a treasure, not to mention a collector's item."

Nana beamed, her eyes welling. "Then it's yours, sweetie. He wouldn't have wanted it any other way."

Jessie took a breath, wondering how her grandmother would respond to what she intended to say next. "If it's all right with you, I'd like to use the camera today. Several of the shoots missing from the boxes were done right here in town. I was thinking that I might take his journal with me and try to recreate them. If you don't mind, that is."

"Why should I mind?" Nana asked, with what sounded like genuine enthusiasm. "That's a lovely idea. If there's no film in the camera, there should be a few rolls in Grampa's desk. He always kept them in the top right drawer."

The camera was empty, but as Nana said, there were several rolls of Kodak black and white film in that top drawer, and none of them expired for at least another year. Jessie grabbed two rolls, loaded one, and stuck the other in her pocket. She also retrieved her grandfather's light meter from the desk.

She drove into town, parked, and walked to the square, the journal in her camera bag, the light meter in hand, and the camera hanging around her neck.

She couldn't have asked for a better day. A few passing storms during the night had taken the edge off the heat and cleared away the usual summer haze. A light wind blew, and plump, cottony clouds dotted a deep blue sky. She halted in the center of the square, retrieved the journal, and read the first entry.

"Roll 147, ASA 200. #1, Stuart Park. F8, 1/125."

She laughed at the coincidence. She was in the middle of Stuart Park, facing the statue. Towering oaks shaded much of the grass, and if she composed the shot carefully enough, she could include not only the statue and trees, but also the façade of the courthouse behind it. She tucked the journal back into her bag and began her shoot.

Grampa exposed only two rolls that day in 1962. With her digital camera, Jessie could have captured as many images in fifteen minutes. But she slowed down her usual process, composing and setting her exposures with exquisite care, as he would have. His descriptions of subject matter were vague– "Courthouse, north side, and passerby," "Davis Plaque," "Courthouse steps and group"–which meant that Jessie had to decide for herself how best to frame each shot. It was good practice; it forced her to be creative, to push herself beyond the simple point and click she resorted to at weddings and corporate picnics. She couldn't remember the last time she had enjoyed a shoot so much.

She returned to Nana's house several hours later, feeling almost giddy with anticipation. After grabbing a quick bite to eat, she went down to the darkroom Grampa had constructed in the basement. As soon as she entered, the smell hit her: darkroom chemicals; pungent, acid, like vinegar on steroids, and yet as welcome as the memory of Grampa's cologne.

Until that moment, it hadn't occurred to her to wonder if she would find enough supplies there to develop the rolls she shot. She needn't have worried. Grampa had left her ample amounts of developer and fixer, and more than enough paper for her prints.

It had been years since she'd last developed her own film, but she could hear Grampa's voice in her head, walking her through each step. As always, loading the film onto reels for processing took forever. Mixing her chemicals, on the other hand, came as naturally as making her morning coffee. Eventually, after perhaps two hours, she had her negatives hung for drying. She left the darkroom and climbed the stairs to the kitchen.

The sun had set, though the last light of day still silvered the windows. The kitchen smelled of roasted meat, and the dishwasher hummed and sloshed. Nana sat at the table working on the crossword from that day's paper. She turned at the sound of Jessie's footsteps.

"You're still up," she said, sounding surprised. "Your mom and I assumed you'd gone to bed before dinner. We would have called you."

"It's all right. I wasn't hungry. I've been down in the darkroom."

"All this time? You must be starved, you poor thing." She set the paper aside and stood. "Let me fix you some food."

"I can get it."

"Nonsense. You rest." She paused beside Jessie, inhaled and smiled. "That brings back memories. Dan would come up from that darkroom smelling just like you do now." She swallowed, dabbed at her eyes with a shaking hand.

Jessie put her arms around her.

"He'd like that you were using all his things," Nana said, sniffling. "He didn't get to do much these last few months."

"Well, he left it all set up for me. The chemicals and paper–it was all there."

Nana pulled away and swiped at her eyes again. "Good. Then use them all up. No sense letting them go to waste."

She warmed up some pork and green beans, and then sat while Jessie ate. They talked about trifles: what a lovely day it had been, how much new construction there was in the neighborhoods around town, where Nana liked to shop now that the old supermarket had been torn down. It wasn't until Jessie had gotten up to rinse her plate that she raised once more the matter of the missing prints.

"Is there anywhere else Grampa might have stored photos?" she asked.

"Anywhere else? I thought you found all those boxes in his office closet."

"I found the boxes, but I still haven't found those missing ones."

Nana's expression darkened. "Not this again."

"I thought maybe he had missorted them," Jessie said. "But I've been through everything in that closet and they're not there. So then I thought—"

"That's where he kept all his pictures!" her grandmother said, sounding so cross it actually frightened Jessie. "If they're not there, then they don't exist!"

"But he mentions them in the journal, and he never would have thrown any photos away."

"Is that right?" Nana asked, eyes blazing in the dim light of the kitchen. "So now you think you knew my husband better'n I did?"

Jessie blinked. "No! I never—"

"Those pictures are gone!" She looked away, a frown creasing her brow. "Or they never were there in the first place. Whatever the case, I don't want to hear about them again. You understand me?"

"Yes, ma'am," Jessie said. She hadn't "ma'am-ed" her grandmother in ten years, but at that moment, she couldn't imagine addressing her any other way. "I'm going to check on my prints from today's shoot."

She crossed to the cellar stairs.

"Jessie, honey, wait."

Jessie turned to face her.

"I'm sorry. This is all ..." She shrugged. "I miss him, is all. It's hard sometimes."

"I know." Jessie returned to the table and gave Nana a quick hug. "I'll see you in the morning."

"All right. Good night, sweetie. I love you."

Jessie descended the stairway once more, her thoughts churning. She had been insensitive, she realized, bugging her grandmother about something as unimportant as a few missing photos so soon after Grampa's death. It was selfish of her. Yes, Nana's reaction had been strange, overwrought. But she and Grampa had been married for over fifty years. Contemplating life without him must have terrified her. Jessie wouldn't mention the photos or his camera to her again.

She stepped back into the darkroom, and tried to put their exchange out of her mind, a task made easier by her eagerness to see how the photos had turned out. She took down the negatives, gave them a cursory examination to make sure the exposures looked right, and switched on the enlarger.

Making prints had always been her favorite part of this process. It was like tasting a meal after taking all day to prepare it. She mixed more solutions, set up her trays, fixed the first negative in the carrier, and focused the image.

She noticed immediately that the photo appeared lighter than she remembered the scene being, and she wondered if she had overexposed it. She tried to compensate for this in the developing process, but only when she finally rinsed the finished print did she realize that the exposure wasn't the problem.

The image simply looked wrong.

It was the same scene: Stuart Park, the statue and oak trees, with the courthouse façade in the background.

But there was too much sky. The trees were smaller than they should have been; significantly smaller. The statue looked the same, as did the building in the distance, but this was not at all the park she had seen earlier in the day.

Puzzled, she hung this print to dry and moved on to the next one, a photo of Davis Hall from the street. But as she focused the lens for this second exposure, eyeing the negative through the loupe, she saw that this one wasn't right either. The people she could make out in the negative looked nothing like those she had seen that day in the square.

She made the print, her work sloppier this time, more rushed. She didn't care. Who were those people? Who dressed like that anymore? Who wore their hair that way? Several of the men wore dark suits and thin dark ties; others were in trousers and short sleeved dress shirts. But she couldn't find anyone in jeans or shorts. And every woman she saw was wearing a dress or skirt.

Then Jessie noticed the cars, and her knees buckled. She braced herself on the counter to keep from falling to the floor, but her heart labored in her chest and her breath came shallow and quick.

The cars.

She might as well have been looking at a still from a movie set. Every car in the photo had that clunky look of autos from the late '50s and early '60s. A few had long, sharp fins on the rear. Most were more contoured, with the round, flat headlights that gave cars of that era an aspect of wide-eyed innocence. The pickups–all of them–had domed hoods, flat grills, and low beds. They looked nothing like the pickups she had seen driving to and from town.

Had one of those antique car clubs been in Berry's Bluff today? Surely she would have noticed if every car on the street had been vintage instead of modern. Unless her work with the camera had so absorbed her that she was oblivious to everything around her.

She hunched over the carrier and centered the third image on the strip of negatives, and doing even that much made her breath catch. She glanced at the journal, remembering this shot from earlier in the day. She had wondered about it: The north face of the courthouse was essentially solid brick, except for a pair of metal doors that looked like they hadn't been used in years. It had seemed an oddly prosaic subject for her grandfather, who never wasted a photo.

The image she pulled from the fixer bath, however, was anything but prosaic. Looking at it, she felt her stomach knot.

An African-American man stood by the building, gazing toward the camera, wary and ill at ease. He wore a suit jacket and tie, a beat up pork pie hat. And above him, mounted in between those same metal doors, which in the photo stood open, hung a sign reading, "Colored only."

"What the hell?" she whispered in the red light of the darkroom.

Obviously that hadn't been there today. The film had to have been previously exposed. What other explanation made any sense? But fifty years ago? No film, not even professional quality black and white, lasted so long. It would have long since fogged. These images were as sharp and clear as Jessie would have expected from new exposures.

She picked up the canister from which she had extracted the film. She'd checked the expiration date on the box earlier in the day, but maybe she had misread this one. The canister itself bore no date, but she had seen old rolls of film, and had used film cameras for half her life. This canister was new, made of black plastic and bright yellow metal. Film from the early 60s didn't look like this.

What the hell?

She rushed the rest of her developing, but she no longer cared about the quality of the prints. She just wanted to see what else was on the roll.

Images of the statue and the Davis Building plaque appeared much as she expected they would, and yet not entirely. The perspective on the statue wasn't quite as she remembered; the plaque had been in dappled sunlight when she took the photo, and yet in the image the sunlight was complete, without any shadow at all.

Because the trees weren't as tall then.

Jessie shook her head at the thought. None of this made any sense.

On the second roll of film, she found more pictures of that north side of the courthouse, each one with different groups or individuals standing outside the "Colored only" restrooms or walking by the building. Some showed only African-American men, women, and children; in others whites and African-Americans walked side-by-side. And yet she could see from their facial expressions, particularly those of the white pedestrians, that proximity didn't breed intimacy. The two races, it seemed, moved in different though adjacent worlds.

But in all of them, the clothes of those on the sidewalk and street were appropriate to another era, just like the cars in the background.

The last photo on that second roll had been the hardest to recreate. "Courthouse steps and group." She hadn't known to what group Grampa referred, so she had snapped a shot of the steps with foot traffic in front of it. Using a slow shutter speed and narrow aperture, and bracing the camera on a parking meter, she had hoped to blur the people while keeping the stairway in clear focus. She had looked forward to seeing the resulting image.

But this photo was nothing like what she shot. Nothing at all.

The steps of the building were crowded with a group of people, obviously posing for the photo. There were perhaps thirty of them, men in suits and ties, women in fine dresses and white gloves, all of them smiling. They stood with their bodies angled toward the center of the stairway, those on the right turned slightly to the left, those on the left facing right. Every person in the photo was white.

But that wasn't what drew the short, sharp breath from Jessie.

On the second step from the bottom, a bit to the right of center, stood Nana. Jessie grabbed the loupe to look more closely, but she was sure. She had seen plenty of photos of her grandmother as a young woman. The loose curls of her light brown hair, the round face, wide-set eyes, and bow-shaped mouth: There was no mistaking her.

Jessie straightened, grabbing hold of the still-wet print, fully intending to go upstairs and ask her grandmother about the image. Who were these people, and what was she doing with them? But she stopped herself, remembering Nana's cross words in the kitchen. Only a short while before, Jessie had chided herself for forgetting how fragile her grandmother was right now. The last thing Nana needed were more questions about Grampa's photos.

And who else could have taken this one? Jessie hadn't been alive when it was shot. Somehow, these old images had found their way onto new rolls of film. Perhaps her grandfather hadn't lost the missing photos. Maybe he had given them away, and before doing so he had captured images of the photos themselves. It wasn't the best technique; if he still had the negatives he should have printed new ones. But it was possible that he had been unable to find the negatives and so had resorted to this.

Jessie pulled from her camera bag another of the rolls she had found in Grampa's desk drawer earlier in the day, one she hadn't yet used. Holding it in her hand, she hesitated. It was late, and what she had in mind would take some time. It might also waste a perfectly good roll of film. But she had to know.

She mixed more chemicals, switched off the safe light, and pried open the canister to remove the film.

The processing didn't take as long this time, but she needn't have bothered. The film was blank, as it should have been if it hadn't yet been exposed. She could try the others, but did she really want to waste more of her grandfather's film? Was it possible that she had chosen to load in the camera the only two rolls he had used before his death?

Maybe. What else could explain what she had seen? Frustrated, confused, troubled by the images she had developed, Jessie left the darkroom and climbed the stairs to her room.

oOo

She slept poorly, her mind filled with questions and theories, some of them so implausible it should have been enough to make her laugh out loud. But none of this struck her as funny.

In the morning, she took the camera into town again, but this time she brought along her digital point and shoot as well. And rather than using her grandfather's film she stopped by Pellman's

Camera near the square.

Mister Pellman was reading the *Herald* when she walked in, but upon seeing her he put down the paper and stood.

"Jessie! It's good to see you. I was so sorry to hear about your Grampa. That was a lovely service the other day."

"Yes, sir, it was. Thank you for coming."

"I wouldn't have missed it."

She walked to the counter and leaned across to give him a hug. He looked just as she remembered. Tall, lanky, with neat silver hair and a long, angular face. There may have been a few more lines around his mouth and eyes, but Jessie had thought him old twenty years ago. She wouldn't have dared guess his age. "What can I do for you?"

"I need some film," she said. "T-Max 400."

He nodded and turned to a shelf mounted on the wall beside the cash register. "How many do you want?"

"How many do you have?"

He grimaced. "Too many. With your Grampa gone, I don't expect I'll be ordering any more. He was the only person in town who used black and white. He was just about the only one who used any film at all." He gestured at the display case, which was filled with digital cameras. "These are all anybody wants anymore."

He pulled down eight boxes and set them on the counter. "That's all of them. I can order more if you want, but they'll take a few days to get here."

"No, that's plenty," she said, setting a credit card on the counter. "Thank you." As he rang up her total, she asked, "Did Grampa ever say anything to you about the film he bought ... behaving strangely?"

He paused and frowned, his pale eyes on her. "Whaddya mean? Strangely how?"

She shrugged, looked down at the counter. "I don't know. Did he ever mention that his images didn't come out quite the way he expected them to?"

"Well, his vision wasn't so good near the end. He had some trouble focusing, and he tended to overexpose more than he did in his heyday. Is that the sort of thing you mean?"

"No, I was …" She forced a smile, feeling self-conscious. "Never mind. It's probably just that I'm not used to his camera."

"That could be. Those old 'F's can be temperamental sometimes. Keep at it. You'll get a feel for it."

Once he had run her card, Jessie gathered the film and dropped it in her bag. "Thank you, Mister Pellman. It's good to see you again."

"You, too, Jessie. Take care. Give my regards to your mom and your Gramma."

"Yes, sir, I will."

She left the store and returned to the town square where, according to her grandfather's journal, he shot the second set of missing photos about two weeks after he shot the first. Again, this shoot consisted of two rolls. Grampa's notations, however, made replicating these new images a good deal more difficult.

"March, Magnolia Street." "March, corner of Magnolia and Pine." "March, Walnut Street."

Jessie didn't know what "march" her grandfather referred to, but a part of her–a foolish part, a crazy part–thought it likely that this wouldn't matter. She might not know, but the camera would.

She loaded the first roll and started to snap photos, following the progression of the march as documented in her grandfather's notes. She chose not to worry about the modern cars gliding along the streets, or the pedestrians who filled the crosswalks. But every photo she took with the old film camera, she also took with her digital. When she finished at the square, she drove to another part of town, where her grandfather had worked on the day of the third missing shoot. Here he had exposed only one roll, and so she did the same, the implication of this location leaving her uneasy.

Once again when she finished, she headed back to Nana's house, greeted her grandmother, mother, and cousins in the most perfunctory way, and retreated to the darkroom.

As soon as she saw the first of the developed negatives, she knew that it had happened again. She had taken photos of random passing cars and people. Those were the images that showed up on the view screen of her digital camera.

The negatives showed something else entirely.

She rushed the printing of the enlargements, not caring if they were off-center or crooked.

The first showed what appeared to be the vanguard of a parade. Marchers walked seven abreast, the two men on either end carrying American flags. Next to them walked two more men, each carrying the Confederate battle flag, the so-called Stars and Bars. And in the middle, three women held up a long white banner that read, "Berry's Bluff, White Citizen's Council."

Behind them the street was choked with demonstrators–men, women and children–all of them white. Many carried signs, although Jessie couldn't make out what they said. Others in the march carried smaller Confederate flags.

Subsequent photos showed the same procession from different angles, and now Jessie could read the signs, though doing so made her want to cry. "No Racial Integration of Berry's Bluff Schools." "Race Mixing is Communism." "Negroes Belong Back in Africa." One little boy–he couldn't have been more than seven or eight years old–held a sign that read, "We Want Our School to Stay White," and a young girl, about the same age, held another one: "I Don't Want To Go To School With Negroes."

Jessie made herself look at them all, though she winced at every new slur, and could hardly believe how many people seemed to have turned out for the march. She had read about citizen's councils in college, while taking a course on the history of the Civil Rights Movement. They had been active in towns and cities across the South and also in some Northern states. Why had it never occurred to her that Berry's Bluff would have had one, too?

Jessie knew what she was looking for. She didn't want to see it, yet she scrutinized every photo. And when at last she saw her grandmother in one, a soft sob escaped her.

Nana carried no sign–a small mercy–but she walked next to a woman who carried one.

"Save Berry's Bluff From Integration."

Nana wore a light colored skirt and a white, short-sleeve button-down blouse. A lock of curled hair hung over her brow and she was laughing and looking at her companion, as if the woman with the sign had said something hilarious. She looked young and pretty and alive, and Jessie had never been so ashamed of her, of both of them. She loved Nana, and she had revered Grampa. These photos felt like the worst sort of betrayal.

Setting these prints aside, Jessie took up the images from the third roll, the one that replicated the next of her grandfather's missing shoots. But in this one, the images on her digital camera and those from the negatives were identical.

She didn't understand. Unless the shoots had to be done separately, as they had been originally. She would go back tomorrow and try again.

Jessie left the darkroom and ascended the stairs to the kitchen. Nana sat at the table with her crossword.

"There you are," she said, turning at the sound of Jessie's steps. "Your mom was looking for you."

"Okay," Jessie said. "I'll ... I'll go find her."

"You don't look well, sweetie. Are you all right?"

"I'm fine."

Nana frowned. "You probably haven't eaten all day. Let me get you something."

Jessie shook her head. "I'm really not hungry. I'll go find Mom."

She practically ran from the kitchen, feeling like a child, feeling like a coward. But she couldn't look Nana in the eye. Not yet. Not until she had seen it all.

She found her mother out on the porch, reading.

"Where have you been all day?" her mother asked, setting the book in her lap.

"I took Grampa's camera back into town," she said, sighing the words. "And just now I was down in the darkroom."

"Seems like you're a little obsessed with that camera."

"It ... takes some interesting photos."

"Well, your Grampa certainly loved it. Took it with him everywhere."

"What do you remember about growing up here?"

Her mother shrugged. "I remember my friends, your uncles, your grandmother and grandfather." She gazed out over the yard, the evening light making her eyes shine. "I always loved this house."

"Do you remember what it was like in town? Were their racial problems?"

Her mom gave a small shake of her head, her brow furrowing in a way that reminded Jessie of Nana. "Not that I recall. Oh, don't get me wrong. I'm sure there was plenty of that in this town. Nana probably remembers. But by the time I was old enough to understand those things, it was mostly settled. At least here. It was worse in some of the bigger towns and cities. I was lucky. I didn't see much of it."

"Do you know how Nana and Grampa felt about it all?"

Her smile was rueful. "I never asked, because I never really wanted to hear the answer."

"Yeah," Jessie said, staring at her hands. She stood. "Nana said you were looking for me earlier."

"Nothing important. Just hadn't seen you all day."

"Right. Sorry about that. I have one more shoot to do tomorrow. It shouldn't take me long." She kissed her mom's forehead. "Good night."

"Good night, hon. Sleep well."

oOo

She didn't, of course. She hardly slept at all. The sun had barely cleared the horizon when she rose, dressed, and headed out again with the camera and Grampa's journal. She didn't bother with the digital this time.

Once, maybe ten years ago, her mother had taken her to Berry's Bluff High School. Jessie had feigned indifference, of course. What teenaged girl wouldn't have? But she had been fascinated, just the same. How odd to imagine her mother as a sixteen year-old, sitting in class, trying out for the cheerleading squad, flirting with boys. She couldn't remember now if she had imagined her mother with friends both white and African-American, or just white. She wanted to believe that she had pictured her in an integrated school, but she wasn't certain.

Jessie aimed her camera and clicked the shutter as Grampa's journal instructed, but whatever joy she had derived from that first shoot two days before was gone now, replaced with a sense of dull dread and a dark resolve to see this exercise to its end.

The school wouldn't open for another week, but she didn't linger there. She drove back to the house and took the camera down to the darkroom.

Scenes like those she found on this last roll lurked in every history textbook, every website dedicated to the story of school desegregation. Young blacks walking into brick buildings, surrounded by armed men–police officers in this case–and heckled by angry whites, adults and children. The African-American teens in Grampa's photos appeared terrified, and who could blame them? Most of the white students wore expressions of amusement, but the grown-ups ... they looked vicious, their faces contorted with fury, mouths open in shouts of vile epithets.

At the center of it all stood Nana. Like those around her, she was enraged, defiant, filled with hate. And it appeared to Jessie that one photo caught her in the act of spitting on a young black woman. Jessie didn't want to believe this, but she could see spittle flying and she could tell from the girl's posture that she was flinching.

Enough.

Jessie took the print and stomped up the stairs.

Nana stood near the kitchen sink, rinsing the carafe from her coffee maker.

"Good morning, sweetie. You were up—"

Jessie slapped the photo down on the counter, the sound making her grandmother jump.

"Explain this!"

Nana gaped at the print, her mouth open, her cheeks as white as porcelain.

"Explain it! That's you, isn't it? That's you, spitting on that poor girl!"

"Where did you get that?" Nana asked in a whisper. "We got rid of those. We burned them years ago. The negatives, too."

"Never mind where I—"

"*Where did you get it?*"

Jessie's turn to jump. "The camera. It ... I don't know how, but it's been recreating Grampa's old pictures. The school, the Citizen's Council march. All of it. I've seen all of it."

"That's impossible."

"No, it's not," Jessie said, her composure returning, and with it her anger. She jabbed the photo with a rigid finger. "There's your proof."

Nana's gaze fell to the print once more. She reached out toward it, but stopped herself before she touched it, her hand trembling.

"How could you, Nana?" Jessie asked, her voice low. "Abusing those children that way. And Grampa snapping pictures of you doing it, like you were some kind of hero."

"We were young." She looked up, her eyes finding Jessie's. "I know that's no excuse, but it's true. We were newlyweds, starting to think about raising kids of our own. And we were scared and so stupid. We just wanted things to stay the same."

"But you knew it was wrong. You had to know."

"You'd think, wouldn't you?" Nana said. "It seems obvious now. Truly it does." It came out as a plea. "I want you to believe that. We both realized long ago how wrong we had been, how terrible ..." She did touch the photo then, though only the very edge. "What awful things we did. Your Grampa knew, and I know it, too. That's why we got rid of the pictures. We were ... mortified, and we didn't want any of you to know, not your cousins, or your mother, or the children you'll have some day. We didn't want you to see that we'd been involved in all that."

"There were other photos missing. From two years earlier. They weren't taken here, but it was the same thing, wasn't it?"

"Do you remember where they were taken?" Her grandmother asked this in a way that made Jessie think she already knew the location.

Jessie closed her eyes, trying to remember. "College Junction," she said at last. She opened her eyes once more to find Nana watching her.

"That's right."

"The integration of the university."

"Yes. We'd graduated only a couple of years before, and it had been all-white then. A group of us went, all of us alums. We had a grand time; we treated it like a big party. Until we got there, and then it was a lot like that day at the high school."

Jessie picked up the print again and stared at it. The look on her grandmother's face would remain with her for a long time. And she would never think of her grandfather the same way.

"I know you're angry with us," Nana said. "You're ashamed, and I understand why. But that—" She pointed at the photo. "We're not like that anymore. I swear to God we're not. We haven't been for a long time."

Before Jessie could answer, she heard her mother calling for her.

Nana's eyes widened and she raised a still-trembling hand to her mouth. "Please," she said, breathing the word. "She doesn't know."

A part of her felt her mother *should* know. This was as much her family's history as it was Jessie's. But she also knew that as horrible as it had been for her to see Nana in Grampa's photos, it would be worse by far for her mother.

As her mom appeared in the doorway, Jessie turned slightly, using her body to shield the print from her view. She folded the photo in half and slipped it onto her pocket.

"There you are. Didn't you hear me calling?"

Jessie faced her and nodded. "I'm sorry. We were just ... I was telling Nana that I need to get going. I've been away from home and my work for too long."

Her mom gave a little frown. "I'm sorry to hear that. I feel like I didn't get to spend any time with you."

"I know. It's my fault. I spent too much time with that old camera."

"You should take it with you," Nana said.

"I don't think so." Jessie reached out and gave her grandmother's hand a squeeze to soften this. "I have all the cameras I need, and Grampa's things belong here with you."

Nana nodded, her eyes brimming with tears. "It'll be here if you change your mind."

Jessie left her mother and grandmother in the kitchen, and returned to the darkroom one last time. The negatives and photos she had made over the past few days were everywhere.

"I'm not going to destroy them," she said aloud, as if her Grampa might hear. "I'm not going to make it that easy for you."

She also knew, though, that she wouldn't show them to anyone else, at least not now. Out of deference to Nana and the memory of her grandfather, she would keep them hidden from the rest of the family. But eventually they would go to a museum or library somewhere. That was where they belonged: in a place where others could see them and maybe learn from them.

Which meant that eventually she would take up that old Nikon "F" series SLR again. Her Grampa's other lost photos still waited for her in College Junction.

DINOSAUR STEW
by Chuck Rothman

Kevin Nagle picked up the plate from the table and licked the last of it clean.

"Kevin!" said Toni. "You know better than that!"

He set down the plate, gravy on his nose. "Mom, that stew was great!"

Toni was startled. She couldn't remember the last time one of the boys had complimented her cooking. "Well, thank you. But that's no excuse for—"

"Yeah, mom. It's great," said Colin.

She hadn't had both boys praise her cooking since they'd learned how to talk. "It's just the usual crockpot stew."

"Dinosaur stew," said Colin.

People say that dinosaurs lived in the Jurassic period or the Cretaceous age, but they certainly thrived at the age of seven. Colin had dinosaur sheets, dinosaur underwear, dinosaur LEGO, and dinosaur Halloween costumes. Kevin, older by five years, had outgrown all that and was more interested in dinosaur games for his computer, dinosaur figurines, and posters of Tyrannosauri eyeing him hungrily while he slept.

Toni hated dinosaurs, even as a child. She remembered going to *Dinosaurs Alive* and coming back terrified. "It's not dinosaur," she said.

"How do you know?"

"It tastes like beef," said Toni. "Dinosaur tastes like chicken."

"How do you *know*?" Kevin asked. It was his favorite question.

"*Everything* tastes like chicken," said Toni.

"It's not chicken," said Colin, "but it's really good."

oOo

The pot roast was a simple recipe: chuck roast, onions, and cream of mushroom soup. She had made it dozens of times before.

"It tastes different," Kevin said.

"Better?" Toni asked hopefully. "Like the stew last week?"

"Dinosaur stew!" said Colin. He had taken to using the phrase and then giggling as though it were the funniest joke in the world.

"Well, at least this time—" She paused. There was something in the meat that her fork couldn't spear. Gingerly, she pulled it out.

It was a tooth, sharp and about four inches long.

"Dinosaur tooth!" said Colin.

"Not everything has to do with dinosaurs," Toni snapped.

Kevin gave her a funny look, then took it. He examined it closely, rubbing the meat and gravy off with a paper napkin. "It can't be from a dinosaur," he said with the gravity of his age. "It's made of bone, not rock."

Toni looked at her bowl. "I think I'm going to be sick."

"It's been in the pot all day," Kevin pointed out. "Any germs are dead."

"That's not comforting," said Toni.

Kevin turned the tooth over.

Toni didn't like it–too sharp, too big. She was sure it wasn't there when she put it in the pot. And she didn't want to see the creature it belonged to.

"Dinosaur tooth!"

"Colin!" snapped Toni. "That's enough."

"I'll show you," said Colin and walked away.

"Come right back here! You weren't excused!" Toni shouted after him, glad to have something else to think about.

Kevin kept examining the tooth. "Did you see this before?"

"No! It wasn't there when I put everything together."

"Well," said Keven thoughtfully. "If it wasn't the meat, it must have been the crockpot."

"For Pete's sake, Kevin. How could it be the crockpot? It only cooks what's inside it." A suspicion snuck up on her. "Did *you* do anything with it?"

Kevin didn't look her in the eye. "What could I have done? I wouldn't waste a perfectly good dinosaur tooth in a stew!"

"Well, *someone* had to have done *something* to turn chuck roast into brontosaurus."

"Apatosaurus, not Brontosaurus," said Colin, who loved correcting her on that point. "It's Brontosaurus again," said Kevin.

Colin ignored him. He had returned with one of the dozens of dinosaur books he had on his shelves. "And look at this."

It was a photograph of a tooth, looking just like the one that lay on the kitchen table. The caption spelled out everything, the ink on the page leaving no doubt.

"Tooth of a velociraptor," it said.

oOo

"I'm not using it again," said Toni.

"Ah, mom!" said Kevin. "It'd be cool."

"Cool? The last thing I want is to put in a chicken and have a pterodactyl take its place!"

"Pterodon," said Colin.

Toni ignored it. "I'm not going to eat million-year-old meat!"

"We already have," piped up Colin.

"Colin," Toni said. "Please go to your room."

"I want more dinosaur! I liked it."

He hadn't taken more than four bites, but, to be honest, that was more than he usually ate. "We can discuss it later," she said. "Go to your room. Look up ... I don't know ... what sort of dinosaur you want to eat next."

"I can choose?" said Colin.

Toni knew enough not to give him a blank check. "We can discuss it. Now go."

Colin hurried off.

"We can buy a hamster," said Kevin thoughtfully.

"We're not cooking hamster!"

"Ah, mom," said Kevin in his "you're no fun" voice.

"You stay away from that crockpot," Toni said, unplugging it and putting it up in the highest shelf. "And that's final."

oOo

The next day was a hard one: working, picking up Colin at school, spending far too much time getting groceries. She was beat when she got home.

The crockpot was on.

"Kevin!" she shouted.

He came out of the living room. "What, mom?"

She pointed at the crockpot. "Who did this?"

He scrambled over, ignoring her question. "Cool!"

She set down her bag and peered through the glass lid. She saw one pale gray oval the size of her fist. It pulsed slightly as she watched.

She glanced at the controls. It was on the "Keep Warm" setting, not hot enough to cook anything.

"What did you do?"

"You never said I couldn't," said Kevin.

He's going to grow up to be a lawyer, isn't he? Toni thought. "How did you set it up?"

He looked at her with the level of disdain only a twelve-year-old could give to his mother when she didn't understand. "I'm not a baby, mom. I can plug things in."

She made a mental note about not thinking of him as a two-year-old, then asked, "What did you put in there?"

"An egg," said Kevin proudly.

"An egg? Like from a chicken?"

"What other eggs do we have? I wanted to see if it could hatch. I thought that 'keep warm' would make it an incubator."

"You can't—" She let her protest die. Where this crockpot was concerned, she wasn't sure what it couldn't do.

There was a tapping sound from the pot.

"It's hatching!" said Kevin. "We can see it soon."

oOo

Colin returned from soccer practice at six. "How long does it take for a dinosaur egg to hatch?" Kevin asked as soon as he got in the door.

"I don't know," said Colin. "How long does it take a dinosaur egg to hatch?"

"It's not a riddle, Colin." Toni had spent the past few hours watching Kevin staring at the crockpot like it was the best TV show in the world. "There's an egg in here."

"What do you mean?" Colin asked, moving for a better look.

Kevin filled him in.

"This is great!" said Colin.

"Having a prehistoric creature running around the house is not my definition of 'great,'" said Toni. "What if it tries to eat us? It might be a tyrannosaurus!"

"Oh, mom," said Kevin, filling the words with a boatload of scorn. "It's too small."

"That's not very comforting," Toni said.

"Look," said Kevin. "We can show it to people. It'd be neat." He peered into the pot. "It's hatched!"

Toni looked. The creature standing blinking in the pot was the same size as a baby chick, but instead of down, there was dark brown leathery skin. The head had a bony crest that it wore like a hat, and instead of wings, there were two forward-placed arms, tipped with claws. It looked up at them through the glass lid with curiosity, then made a sound like a pleading "meep."

"What is it?" she asked.

"I don't know," said Kevin. He reached for the lid.

"Don't let it out!" Toni said.

Kevin ignored her, removing the lid and picking up the creature. "If he stays there, he might cook."

"It might bite you, Kevin."

Kevin cradled the tiny dinosaur in his hand. "Doesn't look like he has teeth. He's cute."

"Can we keep him, mom?" Colin asked.

"Are you crazy?" Toni asked. "This isn't a stray cat! This is … well, I don't know what it is, but we're not keeping it."

Kevin couldn't take his eyes off the creature. "Come on,

mom. He's harmless. See?"

He held it up to her. She shied away, and the creature gave a little screech like something out of a cartoon. It cowered into Kevin's chest. "Oh, you scared him."

"I'm not concerned about its feelings right now."

"I think he bonded to me. Birds do that. Maybe dinosaurs do, too."

The little creature looked Toni right in the eye and gave a pleading little "meep."

oOo

Toni watched the little dinosaur exploring the kitchen, pecking at pieces of dirt with its beak like a chicken in a barnyard. She wondered what would happen once it started to poop.

"I think he's a Microceratus," said Kevin. He had gone to the computer and searched with Colin for the past half hour.

"I don't care if it's Michael Jackson," Toni said.

"That's a great name for him!" Colin said.

"That wasn't a suggestion! We can't keep it. We need to get it out of here."

"Oh, mom," said Colin, his tone colored gray with disappointment.

"I don't think he'll be any trouble," Kevin said.

"Kevin, we discussed this. We had to agree if we got a pet."

"But Mom, these are *dinosaurs*! They're herbivores, too. Not dangerous at all."

"How big does it get?"

"Maybe the size of a duck."

"If you're right about it."

"Then I can e-mail the college. They probably have paleontologists there."

"I don't want it here," said Toni.

Kevin tore himself away from looking at the animals. "So what do you think we should do? Kill him?"

That was going too far. She didn't trust the little creature, but she didn't want to kill it. "I don't know."

"So it's the college."

"They're not going to believe you."

"They will when I send pictures." He had his phone out in a moment, snapping merrily.

Michael pecked at Toni's foot. She knew she had lost this battle. Maybe the paleontologist would be on her side.

oOo

The next day was Saturday. It wasn't Aaron's weekend with the kids, but she still hoped to be able to sleep in.

The doorbell rang at 8:00 a.m.

They'd set up the boys' old playpen in the sunporch, covering it with newspapers. Kevin put down a head of lettuce, and Colin added a bowl of water. Its squawking kept Toni up, so when she heard the sound of the bell, she wasn't in the best of moods.

Two men were in the doorway. They were they type of person that she would call "burly"—about six feet tall and built like a sumo wrestler. They each wore a Hawaiian shirt, a straw hat, sandals, and shorts. Neither was her image of a college professor.

"Mrs. Nagle? We saw your son's e-mail. Please let us in."

"And your name is?"

"I'm Darley Goldolphin." He nodded to his friend. "He's Turk Byerly."

"'Turk?' How does a college professor have the name of 'Turk?'"

"It's a long story," said Darley. "Now, may we see the Compsognathus?"

"The what?"

"The dinosaur."

"I thought they were micro-somethings."

"Microceratus. It's a common mistake."

"Common? People see these things often?"

Darley exchanged a glance with Turk that shouted "We're up to something." "Well, just at paleontological conferences."

She didn't have to see his nose grow to know he was lying. "What's the difference between the two types?" Toni asked.

"Compsognathus are meat eaters."

"What!" Damn Kevin and his assurances. "Come in! It's that way," she pointed, not wanting to get any nearer than she had to.

"Who are they?" came Kevin's voice. He had come down the stairs.

"From the college," Toni said. "And as for your herbivores-"

"That's not Dr. Hayes."

"Hayes?"

"The guy I e-mailed. His picture was on the website. Where do you think—?"

He was interrupted by the sound of screeching, like a crow spotting a stalking cat. Kevin and Toni looked at each other, then rushed to the porch.

The two men were grabbing for the dinosaur like lobsters grabbing a butterfly: badly. Turk held up a metal hamster cage and held the door open. Michael kept skittering away to the opposite side of the playpen.

"What are you doing?" Kevin asked.

"Protecting you," said Turk, not looking up. "She's cute now, but can be pretty nasty when she get bigger."

"She? How did you know that? And how did you find out we had it?" Toni asked.

"Well," said Turk. "It's not like we read every e-mail sent to paleontologists just to check it out."

"You don't?"

Turk looked panicked. "Darley?"

Darley sighed at Turk's word. "All right. No use being coy. Yes, this has happened before. We're from—well, I can't tell you and it doesn't matter anyway. But we're protecting you here. Let us do our job. Aha!" He said, finally grabbing Michael by the tail.

It screeched.

Toni may have hated having the little creature, but she couldn't stand the sound of pain. "Stop that!" she said, and, surprising herself, jumped on Darley's back.

He was startled for a moment, then shook her off. "Look, lady, she may be a pet to you, but she's a danger to us all. Do you know what sort of diseases she might have?"

"Do you?"

"Believe me, you don't want to know."

"So you *don't* know?"

Darley sighed. He dropped Michael into Turk's cage. "Just let us do our job. Now, where did she come from?"

"The Cretaceous," Kevin said.

"You're being cute, kid. I'll ignore it this time and ask again. Where did she come from?"

Toni may not have liked the dinosaur in her house, but she liked these two troglodytes less. "The food processor."

Turk shut the door of the cage. "Is she telling the truth?" he asked Darley.

Darley considered. "Probably not. There was that case in Kansas City, but it's more likely the crockpot. Where is it?"

"I'm not telling you," said Toni.

"Why bother asking?" Turk said, lifting the cage, Michael still screaming. "It's in the kitchen. Take care of it." He headed toward the door, Darley for the kitchen.

"Are you going to let him do that?" Kevin asked.

"What can I do?" said Toni. "They're probably going to wipe our minds and make us forget all about this."

"No," said Darley, returning with their crockpot. "Talk all you want. Who's gonna believe you? But that reminds me," he reached into his shirt pocket. "Here," he said, handing her a card.

"What's this?"

"Gift card for Wal-Mart," Darley said. "$39.95. You can get a really nice replacement that doesn't have any *factory defects*, if you know what I mean."

"Shit!" it was Turk outside. "Darley! Get here now!"

"Sorry folks. Sounds important. But, really, you're better off without it."

"Now!" Turk shouted. "And kid, when I get my hands on you—"

"Kid?" said Toni. "Colin!"

She rushed out the door. Turk was on the front walk, being attacked by a tyrannosaur. Toni recognized the previous year's Halloween costume.

Colin only growled. He flashed the teeth (realistic, of course;

Colin had insisted) in Turk's face, looking ready to bite him.

Turk raised a hand to fend him off and tried to move the cage as a shield.

Kevin had taken action, too. He knocked the cage away from Turk. It fell to the walk and he was on it, stomping on the cheap metal like he was Godzilla.

He may not have been a giant Japanese monster, but a hamster cage doesn't know that. The metal bent under the onslaught, breaking just as Turk pulled Kevin off it.

Colin had crouched down behind the man as though the attack had been planned. Turk tripped over him, then fell back and toppled into Darley, who dropped the crockpot with a crash.

The cage was open.

"Run, Michael, run!" shouted Colin.

The little dinosaur either heard his words or was scared to death by the ruckus. She darted off, vanishing into the woods behind the house.

"Shit," said Darley. "We'd better find her, or the paperwork will be ferocious."

"I must say," said Toni, "you are the most inept government agents I've ever seen."

The two men picked themselves up off the sidewalk. "It's our first job," said Darley.

"I never would have guessed. Is it really carnivorous?"

"Certainly. We wouldn't lie to you about that."

"Yes, you would. You'd lie to us about anything."

Darley was about to argue, but shrugged. "Fair point. Turk, let's try to find that dinosaur."

"Should we get back-up?" Turk asked.

"And explain how this happened? No." Darley turned to Toni. "Those kids of yours are a handful."

"Try living with them every day."

Darley nodded and headed off to follow the trail.

oOo

Colin stared sullenly into his bowl of Cap'n Crunch. He had had the same hurt look for the past week.

"I'm certain she'll be fine," said Toni.

Colin looked up. "What if they caught her?"

"Then she'll be well taken care of."

"What if they didn't?"

"She's a dinosaur. She knows how to survive. And the woods have plenty of food." She hated having to repeat the platitudes, but it was best to shield them from the truth for now.

Kevin came down. He said nothing, sat down listlessly, and stared at his empty bowl.

It was time to bring out the big gun.

"All right," Toni said. "I had meant to hold off on this, but I see I can't." She went to the closet and took out a box.

Colin looked up, with his "I'm not taking that bribe" expression. Then he saw the box.

A helicopter.

Colin's eyes regained their brightness. "For me?"

"For the two of you," Toni said. The gift card had come in handy.

Kevin looked up and, at the sight of the box, said, "Does it fly?"

Toni smiled. "It's radio controlled. Now, there are only two rules."

At the word "rules," their enthusiasm waned. "What are they?" Kevin asked suspiciously.

"Don't fly it inside. And you have to share."

The two boys weighed the decision. "All right," Kevin said gravely.

"Good. Now finish your cereal and you can try it."

"I'm finished!" said Colin, shoveling spoonfuls into his mouth.

"Not before me!" said Kevin.

It was a photo finish—impressive because of Colin's head start. In a few minutes, they had the toy out of the box and were heading for the driveway.

Toni waited. The kitchen's quiet was soothing.

She went to the refrigerator and took two baby-cut carrots, then headed for the basement.

In the back of the laundry room, there was a computer paper

box. Toni lifted up the lid.

"Meep?" said Michael.

"Quiet," said Toni. She dropped the carrots into the box. Michael scampered over to nip at them.

She had come back the night she had hatched. "Bonding," Kevin had said. And like a cat, Michael bonded to the one person who didn't want to have anything to do with her.

She watched as Michael chewed up the carrot. Herbivore, definitely.

"Now, keep quiet," Toni said. "Let this be our little secret."

It would remain so: she knew from experience that neither Kevin nor Colin would venture anywhere near the laundry.

It was nice to have another female around the house.

NOT ALL IS AS IT SEEMS
A Story from the World of Jane Yellowrock
by Faith Hunter

*Author's Note: This short story takes place (in the JY timeline) after **Broken Soul** and before **Dark Heir**.*

I didn't like moonless nights. Even with the protective ward up over the house and grounds, I felt isolated and vulnerable, not that I'd ever tell Big Evan. After years of struggling, his business had recently taken off, the result of an offer from the rich son of a sultan to create astounding and extravagant lighting for his string of casinos and clubs around the world. It required travel, this time back to Brazil for a week, which we all hated, but the gig was profitable enough for us to finally put money aside for the children's educations. And Evan was making a name for himself and his fantastic lighting creations. He was fulfilled and excited. I could live with a little disquiet.

I finished washing dishes, listening to the kids play in their rooms, Angie talking to an imaginary friend or a doll or toy soldier and Little Evan making growling noises as he played with his newest toy bear. He'd picked it out himself, a pink bear with purple nose, paw pads, and eyes. Probably a girl's toy, but no one cared in this household. Our children were being raised to express themselves and their imaginations as every proper, nascent witch should—

The *ding* on the wards interrupted my woolgathering. I dried my hands, spotting two figures standing on the street, side by side, slender males by their body shapes, possibly human, but they could be anything. There was no car by the road, so they had walked, or flown, or run. Or teleported. I studied them, and they didn't move, though they could surely see me outlined in the lighted window. There was no movement, no small shifts of posture or weight distribution, no change in body position at all. I smiled grimly. It was one hour after dusk, the perfect time for vamps to come calling. Not that I ever had vamps come calling. But these two didn't move, exactly the way vampires didn't move, in that whole undead thing. With the Mithran/Witch Accords being planned, there was no way to ignore them or send them on their way.

I picked up the landline phone and held it up for them to see, then pointed at it to indicate I was checking them out. One bowed, an old fashioned and proper bow. The other waved, a modern gesture.

Son of a witch on a switch! I have vamp callers.

I dialed Jane Yellowrock at Yellowrock Securities and went through the electronic procedures to be put through to my best friend. While I waited, I put on a kettle for tea. Even though things had been strained between us, I knew she would take my call. Jane killed rogue-vamps for a living and there was no one better to give me advice. When she answered I said, "Big-cat, I've got vamps in front of the wards and my hubs is out of town."

"Descriptions." That was my pal, economy of, well, of everything.

I gave her the descriptions, and heard her make a call on another line, her voice growing clipped, pointed, and slightly snarly. When she came back on she said, "Lincoln Shaddock sent them on an errand. I wasn't able to find out what kinda errand. I don't like it, though I have no reason to tell you to turn them into fried toads. Your call whether to let them in." Jane sounded ticked off, letting me know that she was not happy that visitors had come calling without her prior approval. I had a feeling it wouldn't happen again. Ever.

Turn them into fried toads was my BFFs way of describing my new death-magics, if used to defend myself. At the simple thought, I felt my powers rise, eager to be let loose, free and destructive. The only problem was that I might not be able to get them back under control. I could kill the ones I loved while trying to defend them. No. Not an option.

I breathed slowly, forcing the magics back down as I stared into the dark, watching the patient-looking vamps. With the accords so close, little moments like this might make a huge difference in vamp/witch relations for years to come. "I'm letting them in."

"Your call," she repeated. "I've sent a message to them that if they hurt you or yours, heads will roll." Jane was a rogue-vampire hunter and the on-again/off-again Enforcer to the biggest, baddest fanghead in the Southeast, so when she said heads would roll, she meant it literally.

"Thanks. Later, Big-cat." I ended the call and set the phone down. I held up one finger so the vamps would understand that I needed a moment, and went to my living room where I prepared three defensive workings and one offensive working. The defensive ones would turn an attacker into fried vamp, which would take a long, painful time to heal, even with access to healing, master-vamp blood. The offensive one would kill them true-dead.

I checked on the children, who were playing together now in Little Evans's room, bear and toy soldiers in some form of Godzilla-bear versus the US army. I closed the door and opened the front door. Night air breezed through, still warm from the day, but holding the bite of deepening night. I took another breath and let it out, thinking, *Bite. Haha.* Nerves. I prepared the easiest defensive *wyrd* spell, dropped the ward with a thought, and waited.

The vamps walked slowly up the drive, not moving with vamp speed, but like humans, which should have put me at ease, but didn't. Nothing a vamp could do could put me at ease, not with Big Evan gone and me with the kids to protect. The vamps stopped a polite three feet from the open doorway and I looked them over. One was wearing jeans, his red hair in a shaggy, mid 80's, style, his hands clasped behind his back. The other had dark brown hair cut short, wore a suit and tie, and looked like a lawyer at first glance. Until I looked down at his hands. They were calloused (strange among vamps) and stained with dye or ink—a working man's hands, not the smooth hands of most dilettante vamps, letting humans do everything for them. Something about the man's hands set me at ease and I nodded once.

The suited one bowed slightly again, something military in the action, and offered me his full titles, in the formal way of vampires who want to parley. "Jerel D. Heritage, at your services, ma'am. Of Clan Dufresnee, turned in 1785 by Charles Dufresnee, in Providence, and brought South when Dufresnee acquired the Raleigh/Durham area. Currently stationed with Clan Shaddock of Asheville."

The other vamp said, "Holly, turned by the love of my life in 1982, and now serving with my mistress, Amy, under Clan Shaddock." Unassuming history, no last name, making him very young as vampires went. More interesting, he was ordinary looking, until he smiled, a fangless, human smile, but one that transformed him into a beautiful man. I knew why Amy, whoever she was, had turned him. It was that smile. He tilted his head in a less formal bow than Jerel's and yet somehow turned it into a graceful gesture. "We come in peace," he said, the smile of greeting morphing into true humor.

Jerel looked like a fighter and a gentleman from his own age, a bit stiff, too formal for modern custom, yet the kind of man who stood by his word. Holly looked like a dancer and a poet. Yet, possibly, Holly might be the more dangerous of the two because he looked so unvampily kind. Looks can be deceiving.

Reluctantly, I said, "Molly Everhart Trueblood, earth witch of the Everhart witches. I grant safety in my home to guests who come in peace."

The two seemed to think about my words before they carefully stepped in. They took chairs in my great room, the space and furniture sized for Big Evan, oversized leather couches and recliners and lots of wood. The smaller vamps looked like Angie Baby's dolls in the chairs. The one in the suit—Jerel—said, "We come at the request of the Master of the City of Asheville, to ask if you recently came into possession of a teapot."

My brows went up and I barely managed not to laugh. This visit by vampires was about a *teapot*? I said, "I drink black China tea with Jane Yellowrock, *my friend*," I enunciated carefully, to remind them that I had friends in high vamp places, "is here to visit. I prepare herbal teas as needed for health. I have *several* teapots. None recently acquired."

"We received a call from the Enforcer's partner, Alex Younger, while we awaited your response to our visit," Jerel said. "No insult was intended in our unannounced arrival. Please allow me to explain.

"The Master of the City, Lincoln Shaddock, was turned in 1864. When he was freed from the devoveo—the madness that assaults our minds after we are turned—the first thing he did was visit his wife, though this was strongly opposed by his master. The year was 1874, and his wife had remarried. The meeting was … unfortunate."

"I'll bet," I said.

Holly smiled and Jerel frowned before going on. "The teapot we seek was his wife's. It is a redware, hand-thrown, English-styled piece, salt-glazed in the local tradition, and painted with a yellow daisy."

"I see," I said, not seeing at all. My powers, my death-magics, had begun to roil as he spoke. I held on to them with effort, trying to balance my waning earth magic with my growing death-magic. "Again. I have acquired no teapot in the last few months and certainly not one like you described."

"May we," Jerel took a breath and his face twisted in what I might have assumed was human distaste, had I not known he drank blood for sustenance, "inspect your kitchen?" he asked.

I stood in surprise and said, "No. You may not."

Angie Baby burst from behind the door opening and down the two steps into the great room, shouting, "You can't have him! You can't!" Child-fast, she whirled, strawberry blond hair streaming behind her, and ran through the house. The door to her room slammed.

My mouth slowly closed; I hadn't been aware that it hung open. Everything—every single thing—had just changed. "Will you do me the kindness of waiting here while I speak with my eldest?" I asked, carefully. When they both nodded, as unsure as I was, I added, "There is a kettle of hot water on the stove. Tea is in the tin beside it. Please make yourselves at home in my kitchen. And if you take the opportunity to search for the teapot you desire, I assure you, it isn't there."

Jerel said, just as carefully, "As I recall, children are … difficult, at times."

"Yes. I'll return as soon as I know what's going on." They nodded and I followed my daughter to her room. When I was still several feet away, I heard the sound of furniture moving and realized that Angelina was barricading her door. My eldest, possibly the only preadolescent witch with two witch genes on the face of the Earth, was hiding something. Something important. Something dangerous. Something that could hurt her? Had bespelled her?

I didn't bother with simple responses. I unleashed the spell I had prepared for the vampires and blew her door off the hinges. It was a restricted spell, releasing and containing any debris, intended to toss vamps off my property, but not injure them. Much. Angie's door shuddered, tilted in from the top, and fell forward to rest upright against my daughter's bed.

Big Evan would have some new things in his "honey do" jar when he got home.

Angie was standing at the foot of the bed, fists on her hips, and shouted, "You broke my door!"

"Yes. I did," I said as I crawled over the mess of the door, the bed, the toy box, and into the room. Except for tears and an out-poked bottom lip, Angie Baby looked alright, no streams of black magic wafting off her, no dark manacles. Standing with my hands on my hips I demanded, "Young lady, what is going on?"

"George is *mine*. He came to *me*," she shouted, arms out wide, her face red, tears streaking her cheeks. "They can't have him!" She was positively furious. I struggled not to smile at the picture she presented; she needed only a sword and blue paint to look like a Celtic warrior princess, and something about her stance made me feel inordinately proud. My baby was defending something, not bespelled.

I sat on the foot of the bed and laced my fingers together. From behind me, my familiar—not that I had a familiar; no witches have familiars—leaped into the room and stalked across the bed, purring. I said, "Tell me about George."

Angie's eyes narrowed with suspicion, but when I didn't do anything more frightening, she opened her toy box and removed a teapot. It was redware, made from local red-brown clay and glazed in red-brown, except for the yellow daisy on the front. Angie cuddled the teapot like a doll in both arms. And I had never seen it before, which pricked all my protective instincts again. "How did you get it," I asked. "Did you buy it with your allowance? Did someone give it to you?"

"No," Angie said, crossly. "It showed up in my toy box this morning. Like poof." *Like poof* meant like a spell. Like magic. "Its name is George. It loves me."

"May I hold it for a moment? Please?"

Angle scowled but passed the teapot to me. It tingled in my hands like an active working, a spell still strong. Worse, it felt … alive somehow. As if it quivered in terror. I handed it back to my daughter who petted the teapot and said, "It's okay Georgie. I got you now. It's okay."

"Angie Baby, do you remember the time KitKit disappeared? We looked and looked and then we found her at Mrs. Simpson's place, down the hill?" Angie's scowl was back and, if possible, was meaner. "She was lapping up milk from a bowl and Mrs. Simpson was mincing salmon for her. KitKit had no interest in coming home, but she belonged here, with us. Remember? Mrs. Simpson gave her back to us."

Angie looked down at the teapot, her hair falling forward over it, a tear splashing on the top handle. "But—" She stopped, sniffling. "Okay. But I wanna give George to them myself."

"Okay. Can you be nice?"

"I don't wanna be nice. But …" she sniffled, "I can be nice."

I stood and grabbed up KitKit in one hand and helped Angie over the mess of her broken door with the other. In the great room, Angie, with huge tears racing down her cheeks, walked slowly over to the two vampires. They watched her come with strange lights in their eyes, and I realized that human parents didn't allow their children anywhere near vamps. Human children, and especially witch children, were surely rarities in their lives. Angie stopped about six feet away, inspecting them.

To Jerel, she said, "You're not wearing a sword. You got one?"

"Yes, little witch child. I have a sword."

"Can you use it good? Well?" she corrected before I could. "Can you use it well?"

"I can. I am a swords master as well as a master cabinet maker."

"You get to protect George and fight off the bad guys." To Holly, she said. "Here. George is scared. It needs you to hold it close and pet it. Like this." Angie demonstrated, one hand stroking the pot.

Holly knelt on one knee and extended his hands. Grudgingly, Angie placed the teapot in his hands. Holly gathered it close, holding it as Angie had, and petted it. Angie let out a sob and raced to me, burying her face against my capri-clad thighs.

I pointed to the door and the vampires both bowed, so vampy-formal, and departed, closing the door quietly. I watched and as soon as they reached the end of the drive, I raised the protective wards and pulled Angie to me on the couch. At the door to the hallway, Little Evan was hugging the jamb, crying in sympathy with his big sister. I held out a hand to him, too, and we all four snuggled on the couch, my children, my unfortunate not-familiar, and me.

An hour later, as I was tucking a sleeping Angie back into bed, I heard another ward-ding. I had very bad feeling when I looked out and saw the same two forms at the end of the drive, illuminated by the security light. With trepidation, I went to the toy box and looked inside. The teapot was nestled into a corner.

I knew my daughter was strongly gifted with power, and she was probably capable of calling the pot back to her, but I hadn't felt any kind of magical working in the house or on the grounds. Which meant the teapot had come back on its own or under another's working. It might be a danger to us all. As if it was made of dynamite instead of fired clay, I lifted it from the box and carried it out onto the front lawn, to within four feet of the ward and within six feet of the vamps. Who now looked like what they were—dangerous predators; unhappy, dangerous predators.

"Do you taunt us with the return of our master's teapot?"

Jerel asked.

"No. It came back on its own." Both vamps blinked, the twin gestures too human for the bloodsuckers. "It's heavily spelled, and seems to have a will of its own. I'd like to try an experiment. I'd like to drop the ward, hand you the teapot and see what happens."

"You did not call the teapot back to you?" Jerel asked.

"No. My word is my bond."

Jerel nodded once, the gesture curt.

I dropped the ward, stepped to the vampires, placed the teapot in Jerel's hands this time, and stepped back. The ward snapped back into place. Within thirty seconds, the teapot disappeared. "Not me. Not my magic. Certainly not my daughter's magic." I let derision enter my tone, because no witch's gifts came upon them before they reached puberty. Except Angie's. And that was a secret. A dangerous secret, to be protected as much as my children themselves.

The vamps looked from me to each other, and back. "What do we do now?" Holly asked.

"You will break this spell," Jerel demanded.

"Tell me the tale of the teapot. And how the master of the city knew it had appeared at my house. I'd be very interested in that one."

Holly's eyes went wide, human-wide, not vamped-out. "That never occurred to me. Where did it come from and how did it get here, and how did our master know of it?"

"Right," I said. "You go back to the vamp master and ask him those questions, because if he wants his teapot—or whatever it really is—back, I'll need to know everything to break whatever spell is on it."

"We will be back by midnight," Holly said, excitement in the words.

"Wrong. I have a family and you two have intruded enough on family time tonight. You go back and chat with your master. I'll see you an hour after dusk at Seven Sassy Sister's Herb Shop and Café."

"Your family business," Jerel said, letting me know that my entire extended family could be in danger because of the blasted teapot.

"Tomorrow," I said, and turned my back on the vamps. Secure behind the strongest wards that Big Evan and I could create, I walked slowly back to my house and shut the door on the bloodsuckers. And leaned against it, trembling. I was in so much trouble. I had less than 24 hours to break a spell on a weird teapot that was clearly far more than a teapot. No wonder Lincoln Shaddock wanted it, whatever it really was.

oOo

I got the children off to school in the morning, without letting Angie discover that the teapot had returned to her toy box, and texted my sisters: "911 my house. Hurry soonest after breakfast crowd." They'd all get here as fast as possible. The 911 call was used only for extreme emergencies. Meanwhile, I set four loaves to rise and made salad enough for all of us, all my sisters. There were seven of us, or had been until our eldest had died after turning to the black arts. We were still grieving over that one. Four of us were witches, and the remaining two were human. Four of the youngest were taking classes at various universities and colleges in the area, but they'd get here any way they could after the 911 text. Family always came first.

oOo

Carmen Miranda Everhart Newton, my air witch sister, set her toddler Iseabeal Roisin—pronounced Ish-bale Rosh-een— down at the door. Ishy ran, shouting for the cat, "Kekekeke," her arms raised. The witch twins, Boadacia and Elizabeth, had called in sick for their morning classes and closed the herb shop. Our wholly human sisters, Regan and Amelia, were the last to arrive, having cleaned up the café after the last of the breakfast crowd.

When we were all sitting in my kitchen, the toddlers happily talking to each other in incomprehensible kid-language, I realized how long it had been since we sat like this, working on a magical problem. Since our eldest, Evangelina, had died as a result of consorting with demons. Well, at the hand of my BFF, but that was another story. We were all red-haired, some more blond, some more brown, some of us flaming scarlet. All of us with pale skin that simply couldn't tan. All of us rowdy and chattering and happy to be together again. We had to do this more often. Not the teapot part, just the playing hooky and visiting part.

To capture their attention, I centered the teapot atop the old farmhouse table, then caught them up on the teapot problem, the vamp problem, and the time limit problem. I had been studying the teapot for hours, so I already had some new things to share. "It isn't, strictly speaking, just a teapot. It's both a teapot and not a teapot, the result of a spell, and is magical, in some way, on its own. I can't tell why it keeps coming back here and I can't make it stay away."

"Yeah," the human Regan said. "That whole not having a magic wand really sucks."

"Haha," Liz said, sounding bored with the oft-used banter.

"What I want to do is to raise the wards on the house, make a magic circle, and study it together." I looked at the human sisters. "You two will have to babysit and keep watch. Pull us out if anything strange happens."

"We always get stuck with the babysitting duty," Regan complained.

"Word," Amelia said, sighing her agreement. "Fine. I'll go play with the kiddies." To her sister she said, "If you need help hitting them with a broomstick to break a circle, lemme know. I want in on some of that."

I raised the house wards and my witch sisters made a protective circle around my kitchen table by joining hands. It wasn't as formal as the circle in my herb garden but it was enough to study the current situation. The combined magical power of the Everhart sisters is weighty, intense, and deep. It tingles on the skin, it whispers in the air, and in this case, it made a teapot spill its secrets.

Half an hour after starting, we broke for tea and slices of fresh bread with my homemade peach-hot, untraditional peach preserves with chili peppers. While I put the snack together, Liz said, "His name is George."

"Not he, as in a human he," Cia said, "but a male something."

"He stinks," Carmen said. "A bit like muskrat. Or squirrel. Something rodent-ish."

"I got wet dog out of the scent," I said.

"Whatever he is, he's alive," Liz said.

"And not evil," Cia added. "Trapped. The result of a hex."

"Only a witch could have done a spell that captured a soul with a hex, and a blood-witch at that," Liz said, exasperated. Blood-witches spilled blood to power spells. The bigger the spell, the more blood needed. Human sacrifice had been known to be involved in black magic ceremonies.

As we talked, I passed out plates, butter, the peach-hot, and topped up our mugs. "It feels like wild magic. Something not planned, but the result of something else. As if the incantation is sparking off all over the place."

"Why did it come here?" Cia asked.

"Opposites attract?" Carmen asked. "Your house is free and happy and he isn't?"

"Maybe he thought you could free him?" Liz asked.

"Or the death-magics pulled him in against his will," the human twins said, nearly synchronous, walking into the kitchen together.

"Somebody didn't call us for the eats. Bad sisters," Regan said.

Amelia added, "Right. Evil sisters. And anyway, you left out the death-magic possibility. Maybe it's here to get Molly to do something deadly to it." No one replied and I sat frozen in my chair, my hands cupped around my heated mug.

"What?" Amelia asked, her tone belligerent. "Sis, the witches among us were there when your magic turned on the earth."

"The rest of us saw the garden of death afterwards," Regan added.

"And we all know it's still dead," Amelia said. "Doesn't take a witch to know that nothing will ever grow in that soil again."

"And then there's the whole thing about your familiar keeping you in control," Regan said, the conversation Ping-Ponging as my world skidded around me.

"And about the music spell Big Evan made to keep your magics under control," Amelia said. "Not talking about this is stupid. Gives it power."

Regan said, "My twin is taking her second year of psychology. Pass the cream. Thanks. She's teacher's pet because she can add the witch perspective to the psycho stuff."

Amelia huffed with disgust. "Not psycho stuff. That's rude to people with emotional or mental disorders or illness." Regan rolled her eyes and buttered her bread, taking a big bite.

The time my human sisters argued allowed me to settle. "Okay." The Everharts went still as vamps themselves. Because Amelia was right. It wasn't something we talked about. Ever. And secrets, things hidden, buried, and left to molder in the dark of one's soul did give evil the power to rule. "So," I said, taking a fortifying gulp of tea. "What do you think about the death-magics? Did the teapot come to me to die?"

My sisters all broke into talking at once, suggesting things like meditation and prayer, singing chants, spells to disrupt my death-magic, and suggesting that we simply bust the teapot and see if that would work to free the trapped soul. At that one, the teapot vanished, and appeared instantly back in hiding in my daughter's toy box. Liz dubbed it the teleporting teapot. Then the human sisters cleared the table and started research into Lincoln Shaddock's history, trying to find out about his relationship to witches and the teapot. There was nothing in the standard online databases, but I had an ace in the hole with Jane Yellowrock. She had tons of data on vamps, including Lincoln Shaddock, and she sent it to us, no questions asked. The information she offered confirmed the vamps' story.

Shaddock had been turned after a battle in the Civil War. When he came through the devoveo, he traveled to find his family. His wife had remarried and moved south. She rejected him. According to the data, there was evidence that she was an untrained, unacknowledged witch, not uncommon in those witch-hating times. There was nothing about a teapot, not that it mattered.

By lunchtime, we had a plan. Of sorts.

oOo

We closed the café and the herb shop at dusk, and rearranged the tables so there was an open place in the middle of the café. All of us, children, witches, and humans, stood in the middle, circled around the toy box with its magical teleporting teapot, held hands, warded the space where we would work, and blessed our family line with the simple words, "Good health and happiness. Protection and safety. Wisdom and knowledge used well and for good. Everharts, ever hearts, together, always." Then we broke the circle and the human twins piled our children into my car and headed back to my house. We witches? We waited.

Seven Sassy Sisters was decorated in mountain country chic, with scuffed hardwood floors, bundles of herbs hanging against the back brick wall, tables, and several tall-backed booths, seats upholstered with burgundy faux-leather and the tables covered with burgundy and navy blue check cloths. The kitchen was visible through a serving window. It was comfortable, a place where families and friends could come and get good wholesome food, herbal teas, fresh bread, rolls, and a healing touch if they wanted it. We also served the best coffee and tea in the area. But it wasn't the sort of place that vampires, with their fancy-schmancy, hoity-toity attitudes, would ever come. Until they knocked on the door just after dusk.

This time there were four vamps: Holly, his red hair in a ponytail, Jerel, a blond female vamp wearing a fringed leather vest, jeans covered in bling, and cowboy boots, and Lincoln Shaddock. He bore a striking resemblance to the actor in *Abraham Lincoln, Vampire Hunter*, a beaked-nosed frontiersman but with a clean-shaven chin, tall, rawboned, and rough around the edges. Unlike most vamps who dressed for effect, Shaddock was wearing dark brown jeans and a T-shirt with a light jacket. And an honest-to-God bolo tie with a gold nugget as the clasp.

I took a steadying breath and unlocked the door, stepping back as they filed in and stood in a semicircle on one side of the toy box. The witches stood ranged on the other side. Holly said, "May I present—"

The outer door slammed open and Angie Baby raced inside, strawberry blond curls streaming and tangled, face flushed and sweaty. She had run from … somewhere. She dashed between us, rammed the toy box open, grabbed the teapot, and screamed, "George is mine! He likes me, not you!" And ... she stuck her tongue out at Lincoln Shaddock, the most important master vamp in the Appalachian Mountains.

We were all frozen, my sisters in horror, me in sudden, blinding fear for my child, Jerel with a sword half drawn, Holly with a bemused smile on his face, and Shaddock in ... fury. Utter, encompassing fury. His pale skin flushed with blood, his eyes vamping out, the pupils widening, white sclera flaming scarlet as the capillaries dilated. And his fangs clicked down from the roof of his mouth, the snap the only sound in the dead silent room. Then everything happened at once.

Lincoln pointed a long bony finger at Angie and took a single step toward her.

Moving faster than I could follow, Jerel drew his sword with a soft hiss of steel on leather. Holly stepped toward Angie Baby. Both vamps put themselves between my daughter and the enraged vampire. Jerel pointed his sword at his master's throat. Holly maneuvered, barehanded, his feet rooted and knees bent, clearly much more dangerous than he appeared—a martial art master of some form or other. Or several. Bladed. That was what Jane called it. His body was bladed. He was primed to attack his boss.

Lincoln slowed, but shouted, "Witches deal falsely! We will have our property!"

"Children are sacrosanct, my Lord," Jerel said softly.

"It would pain us to bring you harm," Holly, said, his red ponytail swinging.

"I am not ready to become the MOC, just yet, Honey, but if you hurt that young'un, I'll let 'em take your head," the blond said, which identified her as the heir apparent of the Shaddock Clan, Dacy Mooney. And she too stepped between the vamp and the rest of us. I remembered to breathe and reached for Angie, pulling her close enough for Carmen to activate the ward we had prepared. It closed us in and closed the vamps out. "Take a good cleansing breath, Link," Dacy said. "Relax. Or it will be the last time you lose your temper."

Outside, my van squealed into the lot and stopped hard. The

twins boiled out before the vehicle even stopped rocking, one holding two handguns, the other with a shotgun. "Son of a witch on a switch," I cursed softly.

"I'm not here as the blood-master of my clan," Lincoln Shaddock said with a strong Tennessee/Kentucky accent. "I'm here to regain what I lost."

"We all want to regain what we lost when our humanity left us," Dacy said, "but we got rules and limits. And memories. That has to be enough," she finished, her tone telling how much she had lost and how painful memories could be.

"Children. Are. Sacrosanct," Jerel said his tone adamant, light glinting off the steel of his long-sword.

The twins moved into the room and positioned themselves so they could shoot Shaddock and not one of us. Holly shifted so he could get to Regan and Shaddock both. His face was intent, focused, and troubled. He would kill if he had to. But he clearly didn't want to.

Lincoln blinked and looked at my daughter, cradling a brown and yellow teapot like a pet. His fangs clicked back into his mouth. His eyes paled and lightened, as did his skin. And he blew out a puff of breath as if he really needed to breathe for something other than talking. He looked up to me. "My apologies, ladies. I am … not myself tonight, I haven't been myself ever since I felt the burst of magic. I raced to see if …" he paused and shook his head as if changing what he had been about to say, "but it was only the teapot. But the teapot was better than nothing. Better than the nothing that I had. I ask your forgiveness."

And then he did the strangest thing. The fiercest fanghead in the hills dropped to one knee. The three defending vampires stepped slightly to the side so Lincoln could see us, but not so far that he could get to us if he still wanted. He said to Angie Baby, "I especially beg your forgiveness, little witch child. I was distraught and forgot how frightening my kind can be."

"George is scared of you," Angie said.

Lincoln smiled, a purely human smile, and said, "No. The dog was named George, not the teapot."

Angie narrowed her eyes fiercely. "What kind of dog?"

Lincoln's smile widened. "A Bassett Hound. He was my best, my very best, dog. Ever. I gave him into my Dorothy's keeping before I went off to war. He was ancient and toothless and fierce in protecting her when I appeared that night. Until he caught my scent. There must have been something still of the human scent about me. For he came to me when my Dorothy would not."

"Bassets weren't imported to the US until the late eighteen hundreds," Regan said, her shotgun broken open and resting on a table, her eyes on her tablet.

"Incorrect," Shaddock said, as if a discussion about Bassett Hounds was the purpose of this gathering. As if he hadn't just threatened my baby. "George Washington himself received a pair of Bassets from Lafayette."

"Huh. Yeah. You're right. Legend, unsupported."

"Truth," Lincoln said.

I asked, "What did you hope when you felt the magic last night?"

Shaddock shook his head slowly, in sorrow. "The foolish dreams of an old man. When my Dorothy rejected me, she threw out a ... it was as if I was hit with a bolt of lightning. I never saw the like, not before, not after. When I came to, my wife was gone, along with the teapot she had been holding, and the old dog. Gone and never returned, never seen again. Last evening, I felt the same jolt of power, of lightning, and I ran to the old log cabin, hoping ... hoping foolishly." He shook his head. "Hoping that my Dorothy had come back to me. Somehow."

Dacy Mooney, said, "By all that's holy. That's why you kept that old cabin? Hoping your wife would come back?"

"Tis so, Dacy. Foolish. I know. Foolish." He shook his head. "She returned to her husband. She lived on until her natural death."

"Had you been bleeding, when you woke from your wife's ..." *Temper tantrum* wouldn't work. "... anger?" I asked.

"Yes. I had healed but I could still smell my blood, going sweet and rancid on the air. How did you know?"

Because wild magic did this. And wild magic is even stronger with blood, I thought, though I didn't share this with Shaddock. Carefully, feeling my way, I said, "There is a spirit trapped in this teapot. It isn't human. It's possible, maybe, that the dog's soul is stuck in the teapot and it is tied to your blood."

"George doesn't like you," Angie Baby said. "Weeell, he likes you, but he's mad at you." Her eyes went wide. "He's pooping on your pillow!"

Lincoln dropped to the floor, sitting on a level with my baby, eye to eye, on the far side of the ward. He looked awestruck, if vamps could look struck with awe. "I went away for a week," he said, "to do business in town, to register to fight in a war I never wanted. George was but a few months old. When I returned he raced to our marriage bed and he ..." Lincoln's smile went wide. "He defecated on my pillow." Lincoln's eyes rested on the teapot in Angie's arms. "Oh, my God. It's George." He held out his hands, beseeching. "I never wanted to leave you. Never. War was never my desire."

Angie scowled so hard she looked like that Celtic warrior, fierce and unyielding. My baby was going to grow up ... a warrior. A true warrior. Pride filled me. I said, "Angie? What do you think?"

Still scowling, Angie walked to the edge of the ward and I quickly dropped it. For all I knew, my powerful child could walk straight to them with no ill effect, but I didn't want that to get around, if so. Grudgingly, she placed the teapot in Lincoln's outstretched hands and he gathered the brown and yellow teapot close, stroking it, murmuring, "I am so sorry. I beg your forgiveness. And yours, little witch child. Most earnestly." To me he said, "I owe you and yours a boon, whatever you may want, at a time of your choosing. If it is within my power to provide, it shall be yours. "

I wasn't holding my breath for that. "Angie, go to your Aunt Regan." My daughter walked around Lincoln, sitting on the shop floor, cuddling a teapot, and took her aunt's hand, her face long and woebegone. I was pretty sure Regan hissed a threat to beat her black and blue if she ever jumped out of a moving car again. And then hugged her fiercely. I'd deal with my daughter later. For now, we still had vampires in my family business and vamps still drank blood. Dangerous, even if they did look cute and defenseless sitting on the floor.

"Ummm," I said. "We may have a way to free George." If it really was the spirit of a dog stuck inside the stoneware teapot. "But we need the teapot back for a bit." Without hesitation, Shaddock placed it on the toy box and took a step back to the tables and chairs that we had placed along the wall. Holly pulled out a chair and Link sat, his eyes never leaving the teapot.

It was a wild magic spell, somehow tied to Shaddock, for him to have felt the reappearance after so many years. I didn't ask where the teapot had been, but I had a bad feeling that Dorothy's wild magic had knocked it out of its own timeline and into the future a century and a half or so. The four of us witches stood at the four cardinal points, circled around the toy box, hands clasped. As eldest, I took north, even with my magic so damaged and me having to rein in my death-magics beneath fierce will.

Together, we said the words to an old family spell, softly chanting. The *wyrd* spell was originally meant to heal that which had been wounded by black-magic. "*Cneasaigh, cneasaigh a bháis ar maos in fhuil,*" we said together. The rough translation, from Scots Gaelic: "Heal, heal, that which is soaked in blood."

We chanted the words over and over as our power rose. And rose. I closed my eyes, feeling my sister's magic flow through me and through the floor, into the earth. Fecund and rich and potent. Power. Life. And when our massed magics were meshed and full, we directed the working, like a pin, a pick, an awl, directly at the teapot.

It shattered.

Pieces flew through the air, and beyond the circle, breaking it. The power that we had been using blazed up and out in a *poof* of heated air and broken stoneware. We ducked. Shattered pottery crashed into the floor and walls. And into Lincoln Shaddock's bony knees.

The vamps reacted faster than I could see, racing at us, weapons to hand. Ready to kill.

"George!" Angie Baby shouted, and broke free from a dumbfounded Regan to throw herself at the multicolored, long-eared, dog standing on the toy box. He licked her face and nuzzled her. And then he turned to stare at Lincoln. He sniffed, smelling, tasting the air, redolent with the ozone of burned power and vampire blood.

"Son of a witch," Carmen muttered. "It worked."

George slowly dropped his front paws off the box and waddled to his old master, to Lincoln, licking the trace of blood off Lincoln's bleeding knees.

"Son of a witch," Carmen muttered again. "It really worked."

Lincoln Shaddock dropped again to the floor and pulled George into his arms. He was crying, purely human tears, and the old dog licked them from his cheeks. Lincoln chuckled and rubbed the Basset behind the ears. "You are a sight for sore eyes, you are, old boy. Good old boy. Good George."

It was the first major working we had done as a family since we lost our coven leader and big sister. Tears fell down my face in joy and delight and excitement. My earth magics weren't what they had been before. But they weren't dead. Not yet.

oOo

One week later, to the day, there came a knock on the wards. Holly and Jerel stood there, in the dusky night, waiting patiently. Carrying KitKit, I went to the front door and dropped the wards. When the vamps reached the porch, Jerel bowed again, stiffly formal, and opened a folded note. Vamps have great night vision and when he read, I had no doubt he could see the words.

"Lincoln Shaddock, Blood Master of Clan Shaddock, does not forget his promise of a boon to Molly Everhart Trueblood and to Angelina, her daughter. But he offers this small token of thanks, for the memories and humanity gifted by the child and her tender care of his beloved dog, George."

Holly knelt and set a small bundle on the grass at the bottom of the low porch. "He is from a line of champions. And his name is George."

From behind me, Angie squealed and threw herself off the porch and directly at the Bassett puppy. The two tumbled across the night-damp grass and rolled, the puppy licking her face. In my arms, KitKit struggled and scratched and hissed, and made a twisting, leaping, flying movement out of my arms, over my shoulder and back inside. The puppy, seeing the movement raced after, managing to trip over his huge paws, and step on his own ear, sending him flying. Angie, to my horror, whirled and threw herself into Holly's arms for a hug that left him shocked and motionless on his knees, and then into Jerel's knees for another hug. And then she was gone, inside, chasing after the pets. Oh dear. I had a dog. Big Evan would be home tomorrow and … we had a Bassett.

Before he stood, Holly removed something from his pocket and handed it to me. "Final thanks," he said, backing away, "but not a boon."

I looked down at my hand and saw what looked like a diamond. Payment for an old dog was a diamond? A *diamond*? When I looked up, the vamps had gone, disappeared into the shadows. I closed the door and reset the wards. And went to check on my enlarged family.

Big Evan would have a cow.

BATTING OUT OF ORDER
by Edmund R. Schubert

Fifteen-year-old Jerome Howard leaned against the small wooden desk in the bedroom of his family's Brooklyn apartment. The lamp to his right pushed back the darkness and illuminated the lone, baffling baseball card that lay before him—at least visually. In all other ways the card remained a dark mystery.

At the base of the lamp sat the rest of the holographic cards, the full set from 2049, stacked tall and neat. Instead of arranging the cards in numerical order, Jerome had grouped the players into their respective teams: the New York Mets on top, then the Baltimore Orioles, then the New Orleans Dodgers, starting with his favorite teams and descending to those he had no interest in.

To the left of the stack, directly in front of him, rested the baseball card that had foretold his doom: card #874, Frank Ryan; pitcher; New York Mets. The card's voice-over had said that in ten years Jerome would suffer permanent brain damage at Ryan's hands.

There had to be some way to find out if that card was … was … what? Defective? A joke?

An impossible, unwelcome messenger from the future?

Jerome weighed the idea of sneaking back into his father's room and using his 3-D nano-printer to create another set of cards, wishing there were a way to print singles. Maybe another Ryan card might tell him something more helpful, more hopeful. But the program he'd downloaded didn't allow for that. It was the full set or nothing.

Earlier that day he'd watched his father install a fresh cartridge of nanites into the family's 3-D nano-printer and then print a replacement for his broken geniusphone, so Jerome knew there were nanites to spare. The question was, could he get away with printing a whole new 1,048-card set without his father catching him? It had been risky enough to do once. Nanite cartridges were expensive and his ex-Navy father was notoriously tight-fisted—a dangerous combination.

On the one hand, the idea of brain damage was terrifying—especially if it was going to happen by the time he'd celebrated his 25th birthday. Jerome was as good a student as he was an athlete and he'd quickly calculated that was barely one-quarter of his expected lifespan.

On the other hand, even news of his semi-impending doom wasn't enough to squash the excitement of the fact that the card had said he was going to be a Major League baseball player. *A Major Leaguer!* He'd dreamt of playing professional ball ever since his mother put a first-baseman's mitt on his tiny hand on his second birthday. He'd immediately grabbed a huge hunk of cake with the glove, and his mother crowed hysterically at the sight of icing all over the webbing, even as his father barked in his most commanding, military voice about damaging the leather. It was the beginning of the baseball dream.

Of course, Jerome had no actual memory of the event, but his grandfather had taken a holo-vid of the party and Jerome watched it so often that it felt like one.

His mother was gone now, his parents long ago separated for reasons he didn't know. That's why he watched those holo-vids as often as he did. He hadn't seen his mother in a decade.

So he'd make it to the bigs. An All-Star no less. At least, that's what the card had said, right before adding that his promising career would be cut short by a fastball to the temple.

But how could the card know what would happen? Was he even the Jerome 'Cal' Howard the card referred to?

That last question was the easiest to guess at. Jerome's all-time favorite player was Cal Ripken, the Iron Man, whose record of 2,632 consecutive-games-played was over fifty years old and still standing. Jerome had always planned on calling himself 'Cal' in honor of his hero if he ever broke into the Majors—and how many "Jerome 'Cal' Howards" could there be?

So the card was talking about him. It had to be.

And the rest? The bigger questions? *Death* by fastball would have been better; at least that would be quick and clean and truly over with. But brain-damaged? How badly? How long did he have to live with it? Jerome could imagine more options that were horrifying than ones that weren't.

Jerome snuck down the hall and peered into the living room where his father was watching baseball on the wall. The Dodgers were playing the Astros, the biggest rivalry in the Gulf of Mexico Division. His dad became a big Dodgers fan while stationed outside of New Orleans for three years.

Just above his dad's new geniusphone a holographic image of a cartoon balding man in a toga said, "Pizza pizza, delivery in twelve point five minutes." His father disconnected the call by swatting away the image with an openhanded swipe like he was snatching a fly out of midair.

No, Jerome thought. He'd better not try printing out another set of cards right now. His father would be too alert listening for the approaching pizza-oven truck. Those trucks didn't ever want to stop rolling, so if you met them by the curb, delivery was free; if they had to wait for you for more than thirty seconds it was a huge extra charge. The Howard family wasn't poor, but they also didn't pay extra charges. Jerome's father saw to that.

Jerome returned to his room. To the card.

It lay there, inert, looking like an ordinary piece of plasticardboard with an old-fashioned color photograph printed on the front. Jerome picked it up and studied it.

It weighed next to nothing, was slick on both sides, and was artificially impregnated with the scent of bubblegum for a retro smell to match the 2-D retro look. The stats listed on the back were pretty standard.

• 2046: Games, 23; Innings, 132; Wins, 6; Losses 9, Strikeouts, 144, ERA 3.55
• 2047: Games, 26; Innings, 147; Wins, 9; Losses 14, Strikeouts, 171, ERA 5.42
• 2048: Games, 29; Innings, 208; Wins, 10; Losses 11, Strikeouts, 195, ERA 4.33

And that was that. It was this year's set, 2049, and Ryan had been pitching for three full seasons. He'd come up rapidly through the Mets farm system because of his 100-mph fastball, but he lost more games than he won because that fastball was his only pitch. If he couldn't effectively move it around the strike zone, a lot of hitters would launch it out of the stadium. The announcers had even taken to calling them 'Home Ryans' because of their frequency. He could ring up the strike-outs, but strike-outs alone didn't win games.

Jerome gripped card #874 between his thumb and forefinger and accidentally slapped it down on the desk harder than necessary. The embedded nanites required only the slightest impact to activate, but Jerome knew what was coming and was anxious about it.

As the nanites worked their digital voodoo, a full-color 3-D hologram of Frank Ryan sprang to life above the card.

Holographic Ryan nodded to an invisible catcher and went into his wind-up while a voice-over announcer called the play—just as it had the first time Jerome activated the card. And just as had happened the first time—and the second, and the third—as Ryan reached full extension, the card glitched, white static and digital square blue sparks flying above his desk like a miniature fireworks display. Jerome didn't flinch this time; he knew the square sparks were coming. This time he studied them, trying to figure out what was happening.

But he didn't understand what occurred this time any more than previously. The square blue sparks were too bright to look at for long, and when they subsided, a haggard and clearly older Ryan stood on the mound, halfheartedly doffing his cap to an invisible but adoring crowd. Through the cheers, Jerome heard the announcer:

"After several years of mediocrity as a starter, Frank Ryan was converted into one of the most dominant relievers in baseball history. But early in 2059, his seventh year as a reliever, Ryan put a fastball into the temple of 2058's Rookie of the Year and one-time All-Star, Jerome 'Cal' Howard. Unable to shake off the effects of causing permanent brain damage and ending the promising young slugger's career, Ryan once again became ineffective and announced his retirement before the end of the 2059 season. Who knows what records the fireballer might have broken if not for that one ill-fated pitch."

The voice stopped, the hologram collapsed, and the card sat in plasticardboard silence. Jerome stared at it, Ryan's flat, unblinking eyes returning his gaze.

Impulsively Jerome grabbed a fistful of other cards—Mets players all—and slapped down one after another after another onto the desk, watching as they sprang to life. All projected as they normally did; all delivered last season's information: 2048. Most modern holocards gave stats for the current year, updated daily through the nanite's online link as the season progressed. Not using this year's data was intended to be part of the set's retro feel, but the idea hadn't been well-received by fans—they were too accustomed to immediate updates—which is why Jerome had been able to download the program so cheaply.

More than anything else, right now he regretted buying the stupid program, because the more he watched this one particular card, the more convinced he became that the story it told was real. But what was he supposed to do? How was he supposed to react? Could he change it, stop it? What if he simply chose not to play baseball?

Jerome tried to slow this tornado of thoughts; he was getting swept away by their negativity.

Consider the possibilities, he told himself. Even if he played only one season, it would be worth millions of dollars. That would set his father and sister up for life. His father could finally stop worrying about money and his sister could go to any college she wanted, instead of the community college their dad always talked about.

And his mother …

He hadn't seen her since she left ten years ago, but she'd been an even bigger baseball fan than his father. That's where his parents had met, the baseball stadium; she was sitting near third base, his father was making extra cash by working the radar gun behind home plate. He'd abandoned his position and talked to her for two full innings before realizing how much time had passed and how much trouble he was going to be in.

His father had lost the job, but he'd always said it was worth it.

Maybe if Jerome played professionally, she might come to see him. Maybe he could arrange for his dad and sister to be there that day, too. Just, you know … coincidentally.

Yeah, right. And all he had to do was find a way to live through the next ten years, every day knowing that a fastball was going to turn him into a vegetable. Jerome wished he could be that noble, but he was too human to embrace such a fate. He was a fifteen-year-old kid, for cripes sake, not Captain America. He could imagine himself too vividly as a drooling, vacant-eyed *thing*, shuffling down the hall of some white-painted, semi-sterile institution, surrounded by other patients who were as likely to walk face-first into a wall as they were to find and operate a doorknob.

God, what an image. And now that he'd thought it, he couldn't get it out of his mind.

No! This wasn't fair! And he wouldn't believe it! He couldn't. It was a defective card made with defective nanites spewed out by a defective printer, telling him about a defective pitcher for a defective team that hadn't won a World Series since 1986. Nineteen freakin' eighty-six! Even the Cubs had finally won a World Series. But the Mets? The Amazingly Futile Mets? Two-thirds of a century of nothing.

No, Jerome would not accept this.

He walked out of his room and was partway down the worn linoleum-lined hallway when his father came in the front door with their pizza. "Kids! Dinner."

With that pronouncement, his eleven-year-old sister, Eliza, exploded from her room. She ran past him, rounding the corner and flying into the living room just ahead of their pizza-bearing father. She launched herself into his decrepit recliner with glee, shouting, "Mine!"

It was their weekly Saturday-night ritual, the one thing they still did from before mom had left them. The rest of the year they ate hot dogs and spaghetti and frozen lasagnas, but during baseball season, Saturday night meant pizza and baseball. Eliza in dad's chair. Dad cross-legged, leaning against the couch, slice in hand, grousing about losing his chair in a voice that no one could take seriously. For just a few hours things almost felt normal again, even if mom wasn't pacing back and forth behind the chair, coaching the game in perpetual motion.

But Jerome couldn't embrace the moment. He couldn't get this beanball madness out of his head, and now that his wheels were turning, there were other things clamoring for attention as well.

"Dad?" Jerome said. "Why did mom leave? Why don't we see her anymore?"

Dad paused, slice halfway to his mouth.

He lowered the slice.

Then he raised it again and took a large bite—like he did every time one of his children asked that question. He would chew that mouthful of pizza until it was cheese-flavored paste before he so much as acknowledged the issue. The look of sadness on his father's face was unmistakable, but it changed nothing. It never did.

"I'm not feeling so good," Jerome announced sharply. "I'm gonna go to my room and lay down."

Jerome stalked back down the hall, fuming, but not to his room; to his father's. Forget him. If he couldn't answer one simple question, Jerome wasn't going to worry about pinching pennies. He was going to print another set of baseball cards and find out what happened in the future. Jerome couldn't say why, but every instinct told him that was the key: finding another card that could tell him more about what had happened. Or was going to happen. Or … whatever.

Inside his father's room, he closed the door and went straight to the printer, hitting the power button. It hummed and whirred. He heard the familiar *zzt-tik-zzt* of the priming nanite-cartridge. He heard the nozzle emerge from its housing and center itself over top of the print zone.

He heard the doorknob of the bedroom door slowly turning.

Crap!

He dove for the power button, praying it would shut down quieter and faster than it powered up, knowing full well that wasn't how it worked.

The printer's digital voice spoke, even as his father entered the room.

"Cancelling print operation. Are you sure? Press enter to confirm."

"Yeah," said his father. "You sure?" His tone was calm, even, and measured—which meant he was *really* pissed. "I came to check on you, to see if you were alright. I guess I won't need to take your temperature."

"Dad," Jerome said. "Let me explain."

"Not interested."

"But dad, this is really important."

"I'm sure it is. And you can tell me all about it next week, but until then you're going to be in your room. If you're not at school, you'll be sitting at your desk pondering the meaning of words like 'privacy' and 'respect.'"

"But dad—"

"Your room. Now. Not another word." He pointed down the hall. "Unless you want to make it two weeks."

"But dad!"

His father stepped forward. "Two weeks it is, then." He never raised his voice; he just grabbed Jerome with one hand by the collar and with the other by the back of the belt. Jerome stood nearly six feet tall and weighed 175 pounds. His ex-Navy father hoisted him like an inflatable doll and dragged him bodily down the hall, his stockinged feet scraping the floor all the way.

Standing him up in the bedroom's doorway, his father patted him on the head. "See you in two weeks, kiddo."

Jerome bit his tongue and stepped across the threshold, closing the door behind him. He couldn't remember the last time he'd felt so disrespected, so like a child. But he wasn't a child; he was fifteen, nearly a man. A man who was going to play professional baseball—if only for one season.

He leaned against the door, listening as his father walked away. He wanted to rage, to tantrum, to scream at the injustice. But if his father heard so much as a peep, he'd be stuck in this room for the rest of his life.

He strode across the room, a hurricane building inside of him. *Two weeks!*

As he neared his desk, his first impulse was to grab the chair and throw it against the wall.

Too noisy. He'd get into even more trouble.

He prowled to one side of the room, then the other, then back to the desk again.

He looked at the lamp, immediately rejecting the idea of hitting it. That's when his eye fell on the tall, neat stack of cards under the lamp. The neatness offended him, and with a sidearm swing he launched them into the air. They fluttered up and out like a flock of pigeons.

It wasn't as satisfying as smashing the chair, but it was something.

But the relative silence lasted only a second or two. As the cards hit the wall, then the floor, the nanites activated, and one by one, baseball cards flared to life, holograms popping up, baseball players swinging at pitches and throwing them, fielding grounders and diving into the stands after pop-ups.

And one card, somewhere amongst them all—one card in an army of holographic baseball players—glitched, sending up a miniature fireworks display of square blue sparks and white static.

But before Jerome could identify which one, the fireworks ended.

His eyes flashed instantly to his desk, but the Ryan card sat precisely where he'd left it. Unmoved. Unglitched. Unsparked.

On the floor, hundreds of voice-over announcers yammered over each other, demanding his attention, describing deeds heroic and mundane. Then just as quickly as it began, the cards fell silent again.

The room lingered in suspended tension.

Something in the back of Jerome's mind told him he should be worried about his father hearing the racket the cards had made, but a larger piece of him focused on the place where the cards had fallen. He had no way of knowing which one had sparked, but his eyes locked onto the general area where the lightshow had come from. It might take a few minutes to find the right card, but it was only a matter of time.

He went to the spot, to the pile, to the cards scattered at the

base of the wall. Picked a fistful of them up and threw one down.
Normal.

He threw another.

Not yet. Jerome remained calm and focused.

Finally, the thirteenth card—that was the one. Lucky thirteen.

He hadn't bothered to look at what was pictured on the front;
he'd just flung it. Of all things, it turned out to be a team card.
The Baltimore Orioles. Under normal circumstances Jerome
skipped the team cards; they were useless and uninteresting.

When this card hit the floor, a hologram of Orioles Park at
New Camden Yards came to life before his eyes—literally; it was
a time-lapse holo-vid of the construction of the team's new
stadium. But before it was half-completed, the now familiar
display of glitch-static-squarespark occurred. It ended with a
transition to an interior shot of the stadium, focused at home
plate.

The faces of the trio holding court there were instantly
recognizable, but they weren't baseball players. It was his family.

His sister Eliza, grown and beautiful. She was standing on the
left. His father, as imposing as ever, stood on the right. And in
the center was a figure he knew instantly from grandfather's
holo-vids: his mother.

She sat in a wheel chair, her torso entombed in some kind of
awkward-looking metal and plastic brace.

Dad and Eliza flanked her, each with one hand on her
shoulder, and there was a baseball nestled in her lap. The three of
them had the oddest expression on their faces, as if they'd been
simultaneously laughing and crying from their very core.

The voice-announcer began: "After the tragic loss of the
popular young first baseman Jerome 'Cal' Howard in a freak
accident on Opening Day, the Orioles dedicated the remainder of
the 2059 season to his memory, winning the World Series in his
honor. The notoriously divided, argumentative team came
together in swift and unexpected fashion, and, defying all pre-
season predictions, ended up winning 120 games against only 64
losses and sweeping all four rounds of the playoffs. In a moving,
impromptu ceremony, Howard's family was brought onto the
field immediately following the game's final out, with the game

ball passed around among teammates who took turns inscribing it to the family."

Jerome ... was stunned.

He didn't know what to think.

He picked up the team card and studied it. It looked and felt exactly like the rest of the cards, including the Frank Ryan card which had set this whole nightmare in motion.

He considered throwing it down again, watching it again, but he didn't need to. The whole thing was emblazoned in his memory as thoroughly as if he'd watched it a thousand times; as thoroughly as the holo-vid his grandfather had taken of his second birthday party.

Jerome went to the door of his bedroom and opened it. He walked down the hall to where his father and Eliza were still watching the game.

The minute his father saw him, irritation flooded the man's face like Noah's worst nightmare. He popped to his feet, pizza falling upside-down onto the carpet, words ready to fly from his mouth like hornets. But Jerome spoke first, softly, just barely audible over the game on the wall.

"How bad is it?" he said. "Is it just her legs or is it full paralysis?"

The flames dimmed in his father's eyes for the briefest of seconds, and Jerome knew the answer.

"Was she in a wheelchair when she left?" Jerome continued. "Or did that come later? I bet it was later. I think I would've remembered."

And like a Frank Ryan fastball down the middle of the plate, the pieces grooved into place for Jerome. His mother's absence. His father's tight-fistedness with money. His father simultaneously clinging to their Saturday night pizza-and-baseball ritual, yet steadfastly refusing to talk about their mother.

Suddenly it all made sense.

"She's in a home someplace, isn't she? She's embarrassed to see us, and you're letting her hide."

"She's not hiding!" his father snapped, finally breaking his silence. "She's ... she's ..."

"Are you secretly visiting her?" Jerome took a sudden, angry step into the living room, closing the distance and jabbing a finger into his father's immense chest. "Are you seeing her without us?"

His father exploded, backhanding Jerome across his face, shouting, "*She won't let me!*"

As if in slow motion, Jerome felt his body lift up, off the floor and drift backward. And as he fell, the oddest thought crossed his mind. *I wonder if this is what it will feel like when that baseball gets me ...*

He hit the ground, but it wasn't so bad. It hurt—but he could handle it.

Eliza sprang from the recliner. "Daddy, no!" She threw herself over top of Jerome, shielding his body with her own.

Their father stepped back, horrified at what he'd done, yet barely able to contain the torrent of emotions that coursed through him. He put his hand over his mouth, unblinking, lost in thought. "It's what she wants," he said. "She wants to be left alone."

Jerome rolled onto his back. Blood ran down his nose as Eliza climbed off him.

"Does she always get what she wants?" Jerome asked. He put a tentative finger to his bloody nose, then blotted it with his sleeve.

"Yes. Yes, she does."

"Well, at least someone does."

Jerome bolted down the hall to his room, but before he could get through the doorway Eliza materialized right behind him.

"It's not dad's fault," she said gently.

Jerome stepped back, startled. "What?"

Eliza pushed him into his room, looking over her shoulder for their father. "You're supposed to be in your room," she said. "Two weeks. Remember?" Jerome always grew uncomfortable with how quickly she became protective over him. He was supposed to be the big brother, not the other way around. Yet here she was, looking out for him. Again.

Eliza said, "It's not dad's fault that mom's gone."

"Who said anything about fault? I just want to know what happened."

His sister shook her head. "If you're going to be mad at anybody, be mad at me. It's probably my fault."

"What are you talking about?"

"Think about it; she left right after I was born. Something must have gone wrong with the pregnancy. A complication or something."

Jerome was taken aback. "How long have you been thinking this? I can't believe you're blaming yourself ..."

Eliza rolled her eyes. "Doofus. I only found out five minutes ago that she's in a wheelchair. How did you figure that out, anyway?"

Jerome didn't know what to say, but before he could even think, Eliza went surprisingly quickly to a dark, brooding place.

"Still, mom did leave right after I was born."

"So you *have* been blaming yourself."

Eliza's gaze wandered the room, looking at everything except her brother. She shrugged a tiny shrug. "Who else could it be?"

Jerome didn't know. But that was kind of the point; they *couldn't* know.

Except in this case, he did. He knew. Not how it began, but how he could make it end well. End right for Eliza.

He embraced it. It was time for him to be the big brother that he should have been all along. He owed it to her.

Jerome hugged his sister. "It's going to be okay," he said. "I promise."

Eliza squeezed him back. She didn't say a word, but somehow, the longer she squeezed, the more it felt as if her hug were saying, *If you say so.*

Jerome took a deep breath, let go of his sister, and went to his closet. He got out his two favorite bats, one wooden and one carbon-fiber composite; then he put on his Orioles cap, the one his father gave him for Christmas two years ago but he'd never worn.

And he walked out of his bedroom.

Down the hall.

Through the living room and up to the apartment's main door.

And as he put his left hand on the door knob, two bats propped on his right shoulder, his father barked, "Where the devil do you think you're going? You're so grounded that a dozen Harrier drones couldn't get you off the flight deck. Do not even think about opening that door."

Jerome stopped. After tonight he'd probably be grounded for more like two months than two weeks, but at this moment he had to act. If he didn't take this first step, right now, he might still chicken out.

He looked back.

"I need you to trust me, dad," he said. "You can ground me for the rest of the year if you want, but for just this one night you need to trust me. There's an indoor batting cage that's open late, and I have to practice. I've got a lot of work to do."

Jerome looked hopefully at his dad, feeling the tightness from the dried blood around his nostril and upper lip even as he tried to put on his bravest smile.

Dad studied him: his new O's cap, his resolute eyes, his bloodied nose. And he softened. "You've never defied me before. Not like this."

"Nothing has ever been this important."

"Nothing?"

Jerome shook his head.

"And someday you'll tell me what this is all about?"

Jerome shrugged, and the baseball bats rose and fell with his shoulders. He said, "I think someday, when the time is right, you'll know. You'll look back on tonight and it'll be like a fastball down the center of the plate. When that happens, hit a home run for me, okay? One perfect shot that brings everybody home again."

Dad nodded like he understood what Jerome was asking him to do. Exactly how he'd pull all the pieces together wasn't something Jerome would ever know for sure—because it wouldn't happen until after he was gone.

But he could live with the uncertainty.

In fact, he kind of preferred it that way.

GRAND TOUR
by Steve Ruskin

Late October, 1845
Whitechapel, London

"What exactly ... is that?" Madame Magnin eyed the device lying on the table before her.

"A *camera lucida*," said John Foxx.

Magnin inclined her head slightly, raising her eyebrows.

"Ah," said Foxx. "It's an optical device, you see. For drawing. This small prism here, atop this stem, it projects an image of whatever is before it downward upon a flat surface. Then the image can be traced."

Magnin blinked.

"On paper."

She blinked again.

"By me. I'm an artist, you see."

Foxx was already uncomfortable in the tiny room, with its sagging ceiling and yellowed, peeling wallpaper. A séance! A fool's errand more likely, and a costly one at that.

But it was what Harriet had asked of him.

"You set it up like this," Foxx said, assuming an explanation might help the medium with whatever it was she was going to do. He stood the device upright on the velvet-covered table, its spindly shadow scattered different directions by the candles guttering in tarnished sconces. Small and portable, around ten inches high, the *camera lucida* was nothing more than a thin brass rod with a flat, stable base at the bottom and a prism affixed to the top. Both the base and the prism were attached to the rod by hinges so they could be adjusted to different angles, allowing the prism to be positioned beneath the user's eyes, which Foxx now did.

"As I adjust the prism to the proper angle and look down with my right eye, just so, past the edge of the prism, an image of whatever is in front of me—which currently is you, sitting across the table—is reflected downward onto the surface of the table. If I had my paper and pencils, well, I could simply trace the image on the paper, making a perfect copy. Of you, right now as we sit here. Or St. Paul's cathedral if I were sitting on a bench in New Change street. Or Parliament—"

Magnin suddenly waved her hands in front of her face and turned away. "Please! Not my image ... my spirit. Please, no images."

"Of course, I'm sorry. I only meant to demonstrate ..." Foxx trailed off, returning the *camera lucida* to the middle of the table and laying it on its side.

The room smelled of sweat and smoke and, faintly, of gin. Perhaps Madame Magnin managed a quick tipple before his appointment. It would hardly have surprised him.

"And your woman, this was hers? She could use this?" The medium was skeptical. "Remember, I require an object that was *hers*. Perhaps you have a handkerchief ... ?"

"We shared the *camera lucida*," Foxx replied. "Harriet was quite competent with it. I ... I have nothing else of hers." This last admission pained him. Harriet had scrimped to buy him the *camera lucida* as a wedding gift—selling many of her own personal effects—so he could sketch landscapes, which he would later use as studies for landscape paintings.

Someday. When they could afford a studio. And paint.

Magnin sighed. "Then it will have to do. Come, place your hands in mine. We begin. Now, what questions do you have for your Harriet?"

"I have only one."

"Ah, of course. 'Are you with the Lord?' That is the first—"

"No."

"'Are you in heaven?' That's very much the same."

"No, um—"

"'Are you well? Are you lonely? Have you located grandpa and Aunt Bertie?'"

"No, I—"

Then she smiled, winking. "Ah! Of course. 'Are your carnal desires—'"

"No!" exclaimed Foxx, red faced.

"What then? What is it you wish to ask of your departed Harriet?"

"I ... I ..." he stammered, disbelieving his own words even as he spoke them. "I want to know if she's ready to go to Italy."

oOo

The coach to Dover was bumpy and cold, a mail wagon and a poorly maintained one at that. With what little money he'd had left it was all he could afford, wanting to save what he could for his not-so-Grand Tour.

He bought passage on a paddle steamer to Calais. It was a postal ship, and he transferred to it along with the mail from the coach like so much portage. At sea, Foxx was left to fend for himself on the shelterless deck as the little craft struggled across the heaving waves of the English Channel. A cold, miserable passage.

Paris, of course, was denied him. That great city was the traditional first stop of any Grand Tour itinerary, where wealthy English travelers would begin their cultural holiday polishing their French, touring the Louvre, maybe learning how to fence or dance. But Foxx had neither the money nor the time for that kind of dalliance. He was bound for Italy, and directly.

So he spent his three hours in Paris, between his arrival and departure, negotiating for sour wine, day old-bread, and hardened cheese. Fare for the rest of his journey.

It wasn't until he was on the overland coach through southern France that he reflected on what had happened during the séance. He had heard those rituals were supposed to involve spinning tables and ghostly knocking. But his had not. Perhaps he had been shortchanged?

Madame Magnin had gone into a trance, swaying and

muttering, and after only a few minutes sat bolt upright, her dark skin suddenly pale, and blurted out, "Yes! Your Harriet said yes. And ..." the medium seemed as if she were trying to recall a dream "... she says you must bring ... *that*."

She pointed a crooked finger at the *camera lucida*. Foxx glanced at it and noticed it was, unaccountably, standing upright. He was sure he had laid it on its side.

But that could be easily explained. A sleight of Magnin's hand. A parlor trick for dramatic effect. Easy to accomplish in the darkness with his attention directed elsewhere.

And that was the entirety of the affair. Magnin waved him away, declaring the séance over. "Her spirit is strong, Mr. Foxx. Take your seeing device and go." Foxx felt the medium watching his every move as he folded the base and prism of the *camera lucida* inward on their hinges—collapsing the apparatus so that it was barely longer than his own hand—and placed it into its small, cloth-lined wooden carrying case. Then he slipped the case into his coat pocket and was back out in the street.

What had he expected? It was all nonsense, and dramatic nonsense at that. Magnin, whose shop was little more than a closet tucked down some nameless Whitechapel alley, had been recommended not because of her reputation for conducting effective séances but because of her reputation for conducting them inexpensively.

Foxx was convinced she was a crackpot.

But Harriet had been so adamant that he try to contact her before he left for Italy. To let her know he was ready to go. The séance had been Harriet's wish; she had left him money for it, and so he had obliged.

Money wasted, he was sure. Harriet left him all she had, but it wasn't much, the small remainder of her job teaching history and classics at a school for well-to-do girls.

"You will be a fine artist, John!" she had told him, and not because she was naïve and in love. No. She had an eye for art, although history was her passion, and after all Foxx had trained at the Royal Academy. That's where they had met, one day when she was touring a new exhibition with her students and he was painting in one of the nearby galleries.

They fell in love, and married.

Their dream was to take the Grand Tour through Italy, that rite of passage that any member of the nobility or landed gentry undertook in the pursuit of the art and culture of Western civilization.

But they were commoners, with only her meager salary and his occasional commission—a portrait here and there. They would have to consider themselves fortunate to spend a month abroad, maybe two, so Foxx could visit the home of the Renaissance masters, see their works first hand, study their techniques, sketch the landscapes. And then he and Harriet would return to England, penniless but happy, and start their lives.

But soon after they were married, before they could even think of taking their Tour, Harriet grew ill. And did not improve.

When she knew she had only a short time left she made Foxx promise that he would go to Italy without her. He protested and wept and said he could never go alone but she smiled beatifically and promised she would join him, hovering like an angel above him, guiding him as Beatrice did Dante, showing him things no one but they could see. He was too distraught to say no to her sweet, moribund madness, and too grieved after she was gone to not keep his promise.

He patted his pocket and felt the thin padded case with the *camera lucida* inside.

It was all he had left of her now.

oOo

Florence in early November was pleasantly cool, nearly deserted (at least by other Englishmen), and completely glorious. The late Autumn daylight was flat and soft as the sun swept ever lower toward the winter solstice, turning the city's labyrinth of stucco walls to golden caramel and its *terra cotta* roofs to molten copper.

Foxx walked around Florence for an entire day—not sketching, just getting his bearings—finding his way with an outdated guidebook he had bought before he left London. He crossed the river Arno at every bridge and wandered through small sunlit *piazzas*. Tall *palazzos* announced the former wealth of the Medici family, their terraces climbing to dizzying heights down from which, as night fell and windows glowed, came a gentle shower of music and conversation.

The next day he climbed a nearby hill with his portable drawing table and looked down on the city. Florence from above was dotted with gardens and clusters of finger-like cypress trees. The city's cathedral dominated the view—Brunelleschi's great dome rising out of the mists like a ruddy egg. He thought about the Renaissance, and how magnificent it would have been to live in Florence, to be patronized by the Medici as were Botticelli, Leonardo, and Michelangelo.

By a little stone wall at the side of an ancient, cobbled road he unfolded his table, unpacked pencils and paper, and began to frame his scene. How he wished Harriet had been there with him. She had an eye for perspective, for middle distance and foreground placement.

The morning sun was just hitting the Arno, making its surface shimmer, as he adjusted the prism of the *camera lucida* on its brass stem. Just below him on the road a peasant appeared, stopping to water his cattle at a roadside spring.

Foxx peered through the prism. *Not quite.* Tweaked the brass rod. *Better.* The peasant was in frame—good, very bucolic. But the top of the cathedral was still ... *no.* He adjusted the prism again.

Perfect! The entire scene, just so.

The image the *camera lucida* projected was crisp and airy, almost as if looking through a magic lens onto a fairy world. Sharp lines, ethereal colors. Of course, he would sketch in lead pencil. But the dynamic image was a joy to behold while he did.

He started at the top, the sky with its scudding clouds. Then down to the horizon of distant Tuscan hills. Over the course of fifteen minutes he traced the scene: the cathedral center-right, the Arno snaking away bottom left, the tower of the Palazzo Vecchio dead center. He finished his drawing at the bottom, as was his habit, penciling in the foreground trees and the road up which he had walked.

Finally he sketched the peasant and cows. Superb. He could

turn this scene into a beautiful landscape someday. When he could afford paint. And canvas.

Absorbed in his last few strokes he did not hear the approaching feet or the stamp of hooves. Suddenly a procession entered the scene. There, superimposed on his pencil-grey road, came some sort of costume parade. Its participants were dressed as if they were contemporaries of Michelangelo, all Renaissance frippery—flat, broad velvet caps, elaborate shoulders, silken doublets with puffed-out sleeves. Tight trousers, low shoes. At the head of the parade a marcher carried a banner: a yellow shield with five red orbs and one blue one.

He had seen that symbol everywhere around Florence. The Medici crest. Perhaps the parade was some commemoration of that great dynasty.

Now a military guard tramped by. Four abreast, they held long halberds in their mailed mitts, wore red- and white-striped sleeves and pants beneath metal breastplates. A bright spectacle, even though they were clearly hardened soldiers—scarred faces, muscle-knotted bodies.

Foxx had not looked up from the *camera lucida* when the parade came by for fear of losing his perspective as he drew. Sketching rapidly, he added a few of the costumed marchers as they passed, before finally setting down his pencil and looking up to observe the parade directly.

But nothing was there. The road was empty save for the peasant, now dozing, and his lolling cattle.

Foxx gaped in disbelief, and looked back down through the prism. As he did so the parade reappeared, filing past him on his sketched-in road as if he had never looked away.

It was then he realized they were moving silently, like ghosts. He heard nothing, when he should have heard the stamp of feet and clank of armor.

He looked up again.

Nothing.

This is madness! Like a cuckoo, Foxx's head bobbed up and down, looking up at nothing, then down again at the continuing procession.

He closed his eyes and rubbed them, convinced he was

hallucinating. He opened them, and looked up.

The road was empty, the peasant snoring loudly.

But through the lens of his prism the parade seemed to be reaching a climax as heralds with trumpets—which he quite distinctly could *not* hear—marched by. And behind them—he *had* to be hallucinating—loped an African giraffe, muzzled and led by long cords, resignedly following his handlers along the road toward Florence.

Foxx sketched like a madman, convinced now that he might in fact be one.

After the giraffe came an opulent gilded carriage, drawn by four cream-white horses. Inside rode a dour man with coiffed brown hair and a hooked nose, staring magisterially down upon the city below him. Then came one final platoon of soldiers before the road was once again empty, save for the sleeping peasant and lolling cattle.

Madness!

"I say!" Foxx called to the peasant below him. "*Mi scusi! Mi scusi, signore!*"

The peasant opened a bleary eye.

"I say, did you see the parade? The one that just passed by?"

The peasant simply shrugged his shoulders. Foxx ran over to the man, gesticulating in the exaggerated manner that tourists use when trying to convey anything more complicated than "hello" in a language they do not speak.

"Parade! Did you see a *parade?*" Foxx shouted, even though he was now standing directly before the peasant. Foxx marched back and forth, swinging his arms, kicking out his legs and pretending to play the trumpet. "Parade!" he yelled, even louder.

This merely caused the peasant to burst into laughter.

"*Parata!*" the man howled. "*Parata! L'idiota Inglese vuole una parata!*" Then he rolled back over, chuckling, and fell asleep again.

Foxx returned to his table and stared at his sketch. He had captured the banners, the soldiers, the heralds, the giraffe, and then the carriage with its scowling occupant. And although the parade had been much longer than what he had drawn, it was accurate enough.

With great care, as if it was somehow possessed, he rolled up his sketch, tied it with a ribbon, and made his way slowly back down to Florence, shaking his head.

oOo

Later that evening he sat at an inn nibbling fresh bread and waiting for his stew (the least expensive item on the bill of fare). He unrolled the sketch and set it gingerly on the table, watching it nervously as if the parade might suddenly begin anew.

When the stew was placed before him—an earthenware bowl full of potatoes and onions floating in thick gravy—the waiter stared over Foxx's shoulder for a minute and then said, in good but halting English, "Is very nice. Good *immaginazione*! Look just like *Lorenzo il Magnifico*. And his *giraffa*. Just like the Vecchio painting."

"Which painting?" Foxx asked, surprised.

"In the Lorenzo room, Vecchio palace. You get your idea from this painting, yes? When Lorenzo marches into Florence with his *giraffa*? Very good."

The next morning Foxx was first in line when the Vecchio opened. It had been Florence's town hall since it had been built by the Medici family centuries ago and still contained frescos worthy of a dedicated museum. Someone pointed him to Lorenzo the Magnificent's room. Craning his neck to look upward he saw, painted in a massive fresco high atop the arched ceiling, the very same man, and the very same giraffe, that had marched past him the previous morning.

He walked outside to the broad flagstone expanse of the *Piazza della Signoria* and consulted his guidebook.

Lorenzo died in 1492.

oOo

He left Florence two days later, after trying and failing to recapture the parade from the same spot on the road. Each time he finished drawing the scene ... nothing happened. No parade.

And then it was time to move on.

Foxx had no itinerary other than to travel Italy until his money ran out, sketching picturesque scenes that he would someday paint, God willing, back in London.

In Pisa, he made a sketch of the town's famous tower with its off-kilter angle. Just as he was putting the last lines on the teetering tower and the nearby cathedral of the *Piazza del Duomo* the scene changed, revealing something unseen.

He watched as a man, beard flowing over the collar of his knee-length coat, dropped balls and other objects of various sizes from high atop the tower. Another man on the ground—an assistant?—made notes, a quill in one hand and sheaf of papers in the other. This assistant occasionally looked upward as if to yell something to the man on the tower.

Foxx grinned. It had to be.

Galileo!

He had just read about Galileo and his experiments in his guidebook.

He sketched the man into his scene, Galileo leaning out over the tower's precarious balcony. Foxx drew two round wooden balls the man had dropped, one rather large and the other quite small, just before they hit the ground ... together.

On the island of Sicily, Foxx climbed the smoking slopes of Mount Etna. He sketched the city of Catania far below, with its neoclassical buildings and Roman ruins, and the spreading blue waters of the Mediterranean beyond. As he outlined the last spiny cactus in the lower foreground, the prism suddenly darkened, filling with ash and fire. Lava poured in a fiery stream just to the right of where he sat and he almost fell backwards in fear, until he looked away from the *camera lucida* and saw that the mountainside was quite free from lava, the air around him clear and cool.

Looking back down through the prism into the apocalypse that was Etna erupting, he gasped as a group of men climbing up out of Catania, shovels and poles in hand. Sketching frantically, Foxx drew as the men hacked holes in the sides of the lava's hardening channel, diverting the flow away from their city ... until another group, from a small village towards which the lava was now heading, rushed up and chased off the Catanians. And soon the lava was flowing once more toward Catania.

Foxx knew the city was doomed, even before he reread his guidebook: "... Catania was destroyed in the eruption of 1669, most of its twenty-thousand inhabitants killed..."

A few days later Foxx was sketching the plains of Cannae, the site of the brutal defeat of the Roman army in 216 BC. Harriet had loved teaching her students about it; he suspected it was because the arrogant Roman army got crushed so soundly by a smaller but smarter force.

After he finished penciling in the nearby farmhouses, the peaceful scene suddenly became a nightmare as Hannibal the Carthaginian, outnumbered and far from his African home, outmaneuvered and utterly destroyed the defending Roman army. Foxx frantically sketched the charging Roman cavalry and their heedless destruction at the hands of Hannibal's well-positioned infantry. He drew severed limbs and broken spears and bloodied helmets, piles of bodies stacked like hillocks. He had never sketched so rapidly in his life, and it was all he could do to not leap aside every time a riderless horse or wounded soldier ran past him as he watched the carnage through the prism.

So it went as Foxx zig-zagged across Italy, the *camera lucida* showing him the impossible as he sketched his way toward Rome, where he would spend the remainder of his time until the money was gone—just as he and Harriet had planned.

oOo

Rome in mid-December was a city gone dormant: bare trees, few tourists. Foxx walked quiet streets, a rough woolen scarf around his neck to stave off the chill.

Now comfortable with whatever the *camera lucida* revealed to him, he drew images of a bygone Rome with abandon: Senators taking their baths; merchants selling olives from huge clay pots; dark-skinned Africans and red-haired Gaels being sold in the slave markets, their wrists and ankles in chains; crusaders passing through on their way to the Holy Land; the great dome going up, brick-by-brick, over St. Peters. Whatever period of time he concentrated on as he drew was what came alive through the prism when his sketch was finished.

One cold afternoon he sat sketching the Colosseum. He had just traced the rounded walls with their stacked arches when the *camera lucida* showed him throngs of Romans, milling about and waiting to see the day's combat. Some were well-to-do citizens, most were plebians, poor and restless—the mobs Emperor Vespasian had built the Colosseum to mollify.

Foxx was sketching the Romans filing into the arena when a tall gladiator swaggered up out of the stone tunnels from beneath the Colosseum. The giant man walked along the flagstone street while the gathered crowd cheered, at least visibly. Foxx could, of course, hear nothing.

The gladiator's strutting brought him near where Foxx sat, giving him a close-up view of the polished iron helmet pushed back on the fighter's broad forehead. Foxx drew in the man's leather and iron armor, the greaves strapped around his thick calves, the sandals on his feet. He could almost smell the dust and sweat as his pencil flicked and scratched, his memory capturing and filling in the details even after the gladiator disappeared back underneath the Colosseum.

A breeze twirled leaves around the legs of his drawing table as he sketched, and it was then, from the corner of his downcast eyes—out from beyond the perspective of the prism—that Foxx caught sight of the toes of a pair of fine leather boots.

He had grown used to people looking over his shoulder while he drew. Most only stared for a minute before moving on, occasionally commenting on his clever historical embellishments.

But today these boots stayed. Three minutes. Five. Then ten. Foxx was absorbed with the gladiator and soon forgot about the observer.

When he finally put down the pencil, the boots shuffled and a voice said, "I say. Very sorry to disturb, but that's quite remarkable."

Foxx looked up.

The man was tall, about his own age. English—his accent conveyed breeding and wealth. He was dressed expensively, an ivory-topped cane in one hand, a well-tailored coat over his shoulders.

"Thank you."

"Your speculations on the attire of the ancient Roman citizenry, and that gladiator, seem quite specific," the man said, indicating the sketch. "An educated guess? Perhaps based on the displays in the museums?"

"Something like that."

"Well, an impressive drawing, accurate or not. You've a good imagination, and a great hand. I wonder ..."

The man trailed off, scanning the exterior of the Colosseum. Foxx followed his eyes and saw a young boy, small wooden sword in hand, running back and forth among the arches. The child was engaged in mock combat with unseen adversaries.

"That's my son," the man said, a note of sadness in his voice. "He's recently lost his mother. He's been inconsolable, so I thought a trip to Rome might do us both some good. Warmer climate, exploring the ruins. Oscar—that's his name—is fascinated with the Romans. Anything to do with their battles and armor and weapons. Mark my words, someday he'll either be teaching classics at Oxford or developing strategy at the Royal Military College. He's obsessed. But at least it keeps his mind off of ..."

Foxx said nothing, letting the man talk. The late afternoon sun spread long shadows across the cobbles and a distant church bell tolled. Otherwise the streets were quiet, a few Romans hurrying home, or to mass.

The man continued. "We return to London in a few days. Oscar has wanted a souvenir of our trip, something unique. Do you perhaps do commissions? Something like your sketch there. He would be thrilled, as would I."

"Commissions?" said Foxx, surprised.

"I'll pay you, of course," the man continued quickly, misinterpreting Foxx's reaction. "Would five guineas do it?"

Foxx nearly choked. "F-f-five?" he stammered. That could keep him in Rome for another two months.

"Dear me, I'm sorry. That must be terribly insulting. Your sketches certainly are unique, and well contrived. I do hope I have not offended you, Mr. ... ?"

"Foxx. John Foxx."

"Mr. Foxx. Shall we say ten guineas, then? I hope that is more acceptable."

Foxx nodded, stunned, and the man extended his hand.

"Settled, then. I'm Clifford Rotham. Pleasure to meet you, Mr. Foxx."

"Clifford Rotham? Earl of Lowestoft?" Foxx said, stunned once more.

"Yes, yes," the man said. "But that matters not here, eh, Mr. Foxx? I'm just a father, trying to secure some measure of happiness for his son."

Then he turned toward the Colosseum. "Oscar! Come here please."

The boy disengaged from imaginary combat and walked toward them, sulking at being brought back to reality. Foxx knew all too well how that felt, and thought perhaps he could do something about it.

"Oscar, this is Mr. Foxx. What do you think of his drawing here?"

The boy stared down at the strutting gladiator and his scowl disappeared. "Brilliant!" he beamed. "Can he do one for me? Please, papa?"

"How about," Foxx said, an idea forming, "I do one *of* you?"

oOo

The sketch of the boy fighting inside the Colosseum had been easy enough to manage, even in the fading daylight. They made their way inside the arena, and while Foxx set up the *camera lucida* and sketched the interior from the perspective of a spectator in the stands, the boy and his father, following Foxx's instruction, found a flat spot down on the floor, careful to avoid the areas that had collapsed over the centuries.

By the time the boy was in position Foxx had finished his sketch. He thought of the gladiator and the Colosseum—to Foxx's eyes at least—came alive. Colored banners streamed from the highest arches, canopies hung over long poles for shade, and bare-chested drummers beat giant sideways drums. The crowds were thick, the seats nearly full. Foxx could imagine the tremendous noise of such a spectacle.

Down on the arena floor, two gladiators—chained together at their waists and each bearing a short sword and small, round shield—battled a half-starved bear. The bear eventually lost, but not before delivering a nasty gash to the leg of one of his attackers.

Then the gladiator that Foxx had drawn earlier appeared from behind two wooden doors, and the crowd stood to cheer. He was far bigger than the two who had just killed the bear, and he was their next challenge. Though Foxx could not hear the crowd, he knew they were rooting for this lone champion, who raised a long spear over his head and pumped his arms.

The boy, Oscar, was juxtaposed over this scene in Foxx's prism. Foxx called down to the boy to act like he was in combat with a gladiator. The boy started posturing, shouting, "How's this, Mr. Foxx? Shall I jab, or swing wide?"

"Whatever you like!" Foxx called back, and drew the boy—attacking aggressively here, parrying there—so that little Oscar appeared to be battling the champion in different locations across the arena floor.

The lone gladiator, strong and swift as he was, should have defeated the two smaller combatants. But to Foxx's surprise the pair eventually overcame him, by clever use of the chain that bound them together to trip him up and their swords to finish him off. As they stood over the fallen champion's body, Foxx called down to Oscar.

"Stand over there. No, there! Yes, good. Now, lift your foot and bend your knee just so. Excellent!" And he drew the boy, foot atop the fallen champion, sword raised high.

Oscar was beside himself with the finished sketch, delighted to see himself drawn as an ancient gladiator—attacking, feinting, parrying, and finally victorious over a much larger foe.

His father was even more pleased.

"He hasn't smiled this much since before his mother passed," he said as he pressed the payment into Foxx's hand.

Ten guineas, as agreed, plus one extra.

"For his happiness," the Earl said. And then, as if an afterthought, he handed Foxx a small card. "If you'll be in Rome next summer, please send word to me at this address in London. I'll be sure to recommend you to those in my circle who will be making the Tour. If you do other Roman scenes—you know, the baths for the ladies, chariot races for the men—with your artistic skill, and a copy of Tacitus or Gibbon ... why, Mr. Foxx, you could be a very wealthy man!"

They disappeared into the late December evening, the sketch rolled under the Earl's arm and Oscar swiping emphatically at invisible foes.

oOo

December became January, which passed into February. With the money from the Earl's commission, and frugal living, Foxx could afford to remain in Rome through summer.

He rented a small room near the Pantheon and spent his days sketching.

He mastered the trick behind whatever it was that made the *camera lucida* open a vista onto the past. All he had to do was draw the scene before him, and *then* think about some known historical event that occurred there. The more detailed his thoughts, the more specific the scene would be. And then, as if someone pulled back a curtain, the past came alive before him.

Tacitus and Gibbon, indeed! He found second-hand English copies of *The Histories* and *The Decline and Fall of the Roman Empire*, read everything he could on the Renaissance masters, and daily congratulated himself for having paid such close attention to Harriet's fervent historical discussions.

One glorious April morning during Holy Week, when the trees on Palatine Hill were a riot of pink blossoms and Rome was filled with pilgrims, he convinced a priest at the Vatican to let him into the Sistine Chapel between morning Mass and afternoon Vespers. After sketching the silent, gorgeous chamber he thought of Michelangelo, high on his scaffold, dabbing at the ceiling.

And then, through the prism, the chapel was suddenly filled with rickety wooden platforms. On the topmost stood the master himself, painting his fresco. From down below Foxx watched as the artist's arm reached up and spread wet plaster, then applied a few strokes from his brush before it dried. Inch by inch, a small section of one of the Renaissance's most celebrated frescos was painted before his eyes.

Foxx also learned with regret that once he observed a scene, he could not go back and observe it again. So it was. But with all of history at his disposal, he never seemed to run out of material. And so he adopted Rome as his own even as the city, and the rest of the Italian peninsula, grew restless. There were rumors of revolution, that the great patriot Giuseppe Garibaldi might even return from South America to lead the fight to unify Italy's various kingdoms into a single state.

Meanwhile his money dwindled. In March Foxx had sent a short letter to the Earl in London, politely reminding him of their meeting, and informing him that during the coming tourist season Foxx would be doing sketches daily at the Colosseum, in the Forum, in front of St. Peters, and elsewhere around Rome. Foxx included his address, hoped for the best, and eventually forgot about the letter until late May, when a small package arrived.

It was a copy of *Murray's Hand-Book for Travelers in Italy, 1846*—a small red book, sized to fit in a coat pocket, freshly printed. A white card was inserted near the middle, and when Foxx opened it to that page he found a section of text had been circled in thick, black ink.

... As to souvenirs of Rome, the Earl of Lowestoft reports that a certain expatriate sketch artist, by the name of Foxx, does remarkable drawings with his camera lucida *in which tourists are inserted into imagined recreations of past events. We have observed a drawing that this Mr. Foxx has done of the Honourable Oscar Rotham, the Earl's son, and it is truly remarkable, casting the boy in the likeness of a gladiator engaged in combat within the Colosseum itself! Such fanciful historical sketches would make wonderful souvenirs for the traveler who already has enough of the olive-wood carvings and leaded-glass religious baubles that constitute the usual Roman momentos. Mr. Foxx can be found sketching in the vicinity of the major attractions of Rome, or can be hired for commissions directly at his studio near the Pantheon ...*

The bookmark was another of the Earl's calling cards. On the back was a short message:

Good luck, Mr. Foxx! —C. Rotham

He smiled. June was just around the corner. The days were lengthening, and already the first English accents could be heard calling through the streets of Rome.

Foxx hurried out to buy more paper.

oOo

November, 1851
Mayfair, London

Foxx's Historical Artworks was a small place on Cork Street, just north of the Burlington Arcade and a two-minute walk from the Royal Academy of Art. It had a small shop in front, where light from tall windows fell upon display tables stacked with books and woodcuts, and a private studio in the back. The little bell on the front door chimed as someone stepped in off the sidewalk.

Foxx's assistant, George, stood to greet the customer while Foxx himself, back in the studio, finished inscribing copies of his latest folio book, *Historical Sketches, Vol. 18: The Late Italian Renaissance Reimagined.*

When the London publishers saw samples of his work coming up out of Italy in 1846, and learned of his growing popularity among wealthy vacationing nobles, they outbid each other for themed volumes of his sketches, which Foxx sent to London from his studio in Rome. *Renaissance Italy Revealed* was an instant bestseller, and was followed by other wildly popular works, some now into their fourth or fifth printing: *Florence Through the Ages, Rome During the Time of the Apostles,* and *Leonardo in his Studio.* And although no one was willing to admit it openly, Foxx's *Techniques of Michelangelo,* though never an official part of the curriculum of the Royal Academy, was secretly read and reread by the faculty and students alike.

By the end of his first summer doing souvenir sketches in

Rome, he was as much a tourist attraction as were the Trevi Fountain or the Spanish Steps. But in June of that year Rome had a new Pope, Pius IX, whom Italian patriots believed would support their unification efforts. Tensions heightened all over Italy and by the following summer of 1847 the tourists were far fewer. Foxx read the writing on the wall; before the revolutions broke out in January, 1848, he left Italy and took his *camera lucida* north of the Alps.

Other bestsellers soon followed: *The Construction of Chartres Cathedral, Paris and the Court of Louis XIV*, and *Famous Battles of the Thirty Years War*. Even as the revolutions of 1848 spread out of Italy and engulfed Europe, Foxx traveled and sketched, careful to avoid the areas where the uprisings were most destructive. He eventually returned to London in 1851.

Thus six years passed and Foxx became a minor celebrity. His display in the Fine Art Courts of the Crystal Palace at London's Great Exhibition that year was constantly filled with visitors. Prince Albert came through and shook his hand, and after that every English family with a claim to noble blood wanted a Foxx historical portrait—showing them triumphant on the fields of Agincourt, or looking grave and solemn at the signing of the Magna Carta. Those who could not afford a private sitting gladly settled for one of his limited-edition "historical recreations"—Wellington at Waterloo, Nelson at Trafalgar. Military victories were perennial favorites. But the gruesome posthumous beheading of Oliver Cromwell's corpse was, somewhat disturbingly, far and away his best seller.

Money, in short, was no longer an issue. If only Harriet were with him now. She would be so pleased. But Foxx had been discouraged as of late, spending all his time satisfying London's desire for fanciful historical "reimaginings," while neglecting his own desire to paint.

He looked around his studio, saw the blank canvases he had purchased and the many tubes of paint sitting unopened on shelves.

Do not complain, he reminded himself. He had been given a great gift: enough wealth to be comfortable along with fame for his masterful, if "fanciful," artistic skill.

Yet even now, his work with the *camera lucida* was not coming along as readily as before. It was as if the clarity and intensity of the historical scenes themselves were fading with his lack of interest.

"Mr. Foxx?" It was George, appearing from the front of the shop. "There is a woman here to see you. She claims to have met you many years ago. A Madame Magnin? Funny old bird."

Foxx started. "Yes, of course. Please, send her back."

A minute later the old woman shuffled into the studio slowly, flicking a cane ahead of her with each step, *tik-tik-tik*.

"Ah, Mr. Foxx," she said, looking around. "This is a nice place, quite fancy."

"Thank you." Foxx motioned for her to sit down on the cushioned chair next to his, but she shook her head.

"It has been many years, Madame. How can I help you?"

"I have a message, Mr. Foxx."

"From whom?"

"Your Harriet."

Foxx paled.

"She visited me. She said you have been harder to see lately. Distant. She said I was to speak to you. I've come across London. It is a long walk from Whitechapel to Mayfair, Mr. Foxx."

"What ... what is the message?"

"You must leave the past behind now. It is time for your future. That thing," she pointed to the *camera lucida*, "has served its purpose. Now you must paint."

She turned and began to shuffle out again.

"Wait!" said Foxx, chasing her. "That's the message? Just ... paint?"

"Yes."

It felt incomplete, anticlimactic. Foxx tried to stall her. "But ... Harriet! She is well? She is happy? She is ... with the Lord?"

Magnin smiled, still shuffling forward, *tik-tik-tik*. "Ah! That's usually the first question, you know."

When her hand was on the doorknob at the front of the shop, Foxx remembered his manners and pulled a crown from his pocket, offering it to her. She shook her head.

"Please," protested Foxx. "For your troubles."

"The messages are not troubles," she said, pushing his hand away. "They are gifts."

Then she walked out the door and disappeared into the crowds on Burlington Arcade.

Suddenly, from the studio, there was a shout and the sound of something breaking. A distraught George appeared, a bent brass rod and broken prism in his hand.

"I'm … I'm sorry, Mr. Foxx! I bumped the table when I was moving the books you signed. It must have fallen off!" He looked desperate. "Please, take it out of my wages!"

Foxx took the broken pieces of the *camera lucida* and stared at them for a moment. Then he patted George on the shoulder.

"A simple accident, George. Don't upset yourself. This day is nearly over anyway. Why don't you lock up and go home. I'd like to spend a little time alone." Foxx eyed the stack of large, empty canvases in the corner of the studio. "Although perhaps, before you go, you can help me lift one of those onto an easel?"

"Of course, Mr. Foxx," said George eagerly. "Anything you say, sir!"

When George had gone, Foxx set the pieces of the *camera lucida* on a shelf and began to open tubes of paint, one by one.

'A' IS FOR ALACRITY, ASTRONAUTS, AND GRIEF
by Sofie Bird

Becca hadn't even meant to show Sam the typewriter. It had sat in the crate in the attic with the other things she and Julie had played with as children that their mother, Candice, hadn't gotten rid of yet. Becca had flown in to Heathrow, thrown her bag on the lower bunk of her childhood room and driven to the hospital to collect her nephew from Candice's arms.

She'd had to turn her face away from Julie's battered face on the bed, unable to look at the tubes and bruises and swelling. The doctor's prognosis had stuttered through static.

You know she's not in there anymore. Becca hadn't dared say the words. *There's a reason they offered to up the morphine, they just can't say it. She might wake up, but she's not coming back.*

Work had given her two weeks' bereavement leave. A luxury, with the project already overdue. She'd used up two days just getting here, walked out on salvaging six years with Rick with four words that had burned into her mouth like acid. *My sister is dying.*

Now she couldn't even look at her.

Candice had sat haggard in the only chair next to the bed, Sam hunched and silent in her lap. When Becca lifted him from Candice's strong grasp, neither of them stirred. She'd driven Sam back to the house in silence and trawled through the attic for something for him to do while she worked out how in the hell you explained to a seven-year-old about comas and car accidents and orphans.

It would be different if Sam's father were alive. If Candice had had anyone else to call but the daughter who'd crossed oceans to get away from her. Candice had barely said a word since that phone call, not even when Becca had hired a car against her instructions after twenty-six hours on a plane.

It would be okay. It would all be okay. Becca hugged her elbows like they could fill the hole in her stomach. *Julie's not going to wake up, how can that be okay?*

Because she's not going to wake up. You won't have to stay here. You can just say goodbye and go home, like you planned. She sank her teeth into her cheek and forced the admission from her mind. She had more important things to deal with.

Sam was solemn, and for once not full of questions. A dozen platitudes rose in her throat and withered. Julie's weekly Skype calls aside, the last time he'd seen her, he'd been a toddler at his father's funeral. She was the aunt who appeared when parents died.

Becca flinched. *She hasn't.*

You can't tell him differently. It wouldn't be fair.

He sat at the crate, hunched in on himself, and poked the old typewriter buttons. He hadn't even lifted it out. Armed with a cup of earl grey and a chocolate biscuit, Becca sat next to him and waited.

"I'm writing a letter to Mum," he said flatly. "But the letters don't come out right."

Becca leaned over; the typewriter produced the same gibberish she remembered from her childhood.

It had driven her father to distraction. His last unsolvable riddle: a perfectly normal, working, ordinary typewriter that wrote alien hieroglyphics. He'd kept it in pride of place in the lounge to puzzle out with his two girls, and taken it apart three times, even the electronic pieces and the 80's-era solar-cells. *What is it we do when we don't know something?* She smiled at his voice in her head.

But I can't puzzle this one out, Dad. I can't fix it. I just want her to go, to be peaceful and I hate myself for that. She squeezed the biscuit so hard it shattered, gazing down at the typewriter and its printed nonsense like it was a talisman.

Candice had packed it away after he died, along with all of his things, like he'd never lived here at all.

Sam stroked the yellowed paper standing stiff from the rollers.

"How many letters can it make?" he asked.

"How many do you think? Can you work it out?" Becca brushed biscuit crumbs from his hair while he screwed up his face.

"Twenty-six?"

"Come on, that's a guess. You can work it out."

This was met with silence. He peered at the paper, at the keys, fingers opening and closing individually.

"Forty... Fifty ... eight."

"Including the numbers and all the commas and things?"

More silence while his finger hovered over each of the number and punctuation keys.

"Eighty ... six?"

"There you go."

Sam shook his head, blonde curls shivering like Julie's pixie-cut did. Used to. "But it makes more than eighty-six different letters."

Becca pressed her lips, her mother's "that's impossible" dismissal pent up behind them. Julie had said he was bright. Even if you doubled the keys, there seemed to be far more printed letters than the typewriter could physically type, none of them familiar. She released her breath with a smile.

"Your mother and I used to pretend it was a message from someone far away," she said. "It's what made me become a programmer, trying to figure out puzzles like that. We kept everything it printed in that binder, there. Maybe you can figure it out."

Sam lifted the almost-full three-ring binder, flipped it open. Becca's eyes stung at the sight of Julie's margin notes, the backwards 'a's she used to write as a child, and she ruffled Sam's hair.

oOo

The hospital ward echoed with clicks and hums and machine-driven breaths. Julie lay, too bruised and too still, with Candice curled over her.

"Mum! Guess what I found!" Sam burst in, a hurricane of enthusiasm.

Candice glared, barely shifting from over her daughter. "Hush, sweetling. Your mummy is sleeping, she needs to get better."

"But I want to tell her about the codes! It'll make her feel better, it's really interesting!" He shook Julie's shoulder gently. "Mum, I have to show you something."

"No!" Candice slapped his hands away and fussed over the tubes Sam had minutely disturbed. "You mustn't touch, Mummy is very fragile," she snapped. "Nurse!"

"But"—Sam's voice squeaked—"Mum always feels better when I hug her. She said so."

Becca wrapped her arm around Sam's shoulder, squeezing him while she tried to swallow the cannonball in her throat. "You can give her lots of hugs when she wakes up, okay?" She rubbed the crown of his head like her father used to do. "We just need to be careful of the tubes and things, mate. They're very important."

Sam snivelled. "They look uncomfortable."

"It's okay, she's asleep, she can't feel them. Why don't you tell her what you found?"

"You said she's sleeping, she won't hear me."

"She'll hear you in her dreams, love." Becca shot a look at Candice, who still crouched over Julie like she was shielding her, and hardened her voice. "The doctors said it's good for her to hear things." She lifted Sam onto the foot of the bed and pulled the typewriter pages from her bag. Candice snatched the papers and waved them under Becca's nose.

"Not your father's nonsense again! Nothing but broken junk."

"It's a code!" Sam grabbed at the paper. "Someone is sending coded messages and we have to work them out!"

Candice sucked in her breath, and arranged a honeyed smile. "I know you want your Mummy to get better, because you love her very much," she said softly. "You want to help look after her, don't you?" She curled one arm around his shoulders, easing him off the bed. "She needs you to be a big boy so you can help her. Can you do that for her?"

Sam nodded mutely, clearly confused about where code investigation fell in the spectrum of "being a big boy."

Becca stepped forward. "Mum—"

Candice's head whipped up, and the sweetness vanished from her face. "I don't want to hear any more of it. You're under my roof. You'll put that thing away when you get home. Or better yet, throw it out."

Becca clenched her jaw, but couldn't find a retort. Candice had always hated Dad's obsessions. It didn't matter what it was: if she didn't understand it, it wasn't allowed.

Candice lowered her voice theatrically. "Julie needs *him* right now while she gets better, not silly distractions."

"I thought it was interesting," Sam mumbled.

"It's just broken, my sweetling. There are more important things right now."

oOo

Sam barely said two words the whole drive home. He hunched in the back seat, hugging his knees and smearing ink-stained tears across his cheeks.

"Careful with those," Becca joked, nodding to the pile of crumpled typewriter paper she'd retrieved from Candice before they left. "You don't know what they say, yet. It could be important."

He didn't reply. To him, she was still just a face from a laptop. *What did Dad do when I was this upset?* He loved his puzzles, his what-ifs. Sometimes he'd be so engrossed he'd forget to eat, chewing pen lids into scraps until Candice dragged him down to dinner. Becca smiled to herself, then clenched her cheek muscles in place.

What if Julie does wake up? Even just some of her, she might still be Julie.

I can't live with Candice again.

Nine days left. Then she had to be on a plane home. *Or not.* She shook her head. *Focus on Sam.* His smile made Julie's fate— and her own—less terrifying. Besides, Julie had named her godmother. He was Becca's responsibility, now.

"You know what you need to do?" she asked in her best detective voice as they pulled up at the Earl's Court Road traffic light. "We need more data. For instance, there are more letters than keys. So does each key match a certain set of letters? Is there a pattern?"

Sam frowned. "I don't know," he said huskily.

"You don't know?" Becca turned and gaped at him, mock-aghast. "Well, what is it we do, when we don't know something?" Sam shook his head mutely. Becca mimicked her father's exuberance: "We find out!"

The slightest of smiles tweaked Sam's cheek. Becca leaned between the front seats and whispered. "I won't tell her if you won't."

Becca blurred through the morning and afternoon cleaning walls and light switches and other things that didn't need cleaning, to the plunks of Sam on the typewriter in the living room. Until—

"Auntie! I figured it out! And it's *talking* to me!"

Becca raced in, half-expecting he'd taken it apart.

Sam sat in the living room surrounded by open books of dense text, studiously writing in his Buzz Lightyear notebook.

"What do you mean, kiddo?" Becca peered over his shoulder.

"You said I should work out whether the same keys make the same symbols—they don't," he announced, in a tone like he was receiving the Nobel Prize. "So I thought it might be random, but it's not. I counted one hundred and twenty-seven different letters, and there are patterns. Lots of patterns."

Becca remembered to close her mouth. She and Julie had played with this for months as kids. How had they never noticed that? And Sam had, all by himself?

"So I looked through Dad's old books Mum kept, they tell you how to crack codes, by looking for patterns and how many letters and whether the patterns are big or small, and—" he ran out of breath and gulped air. "There was one where it's not based on letters but on sounds. Fo-somethings."

"Phonemes," Becca murmured, half-entranced. She flipped through the books next to Sam—cryptography books. His father had been Military Intelligence. Julie had never said doing what, only that he'd had a knack for languages and numbers.

"That's why there are so many letters. It's writing out exactly what he said, how it sounded. And then it started talking to me."

"Now Sam," Becca heard her mother's tone in her voice and winced.

"I'm not lying! Look!" He pushed his notebook under her face. Becca frowned at the jumble of English words.

"It's backwards," Sam said helpfully. "The words, I mean. They started at the end of the message."

"Why is it backwards?"

"Why is it writing in an alien language?"

"Point made." She took the notebook. "Uncle Sam," she murmured, reading backwards. "I guess Uncle Sam came through after all, I can see the shuttles flying." A grin spread over her face at the beautifully impossible—her father's grin. "That's not you, Sam. That's what people sometimes call America, like it's a big brother. I think he's a soldier or something."

"Like Dad, in Afghanistan?"

Becca caught her breath. *Careful.*

"I don't think this is your father, sweetheart."

How do you know? It could be.

"Is he in trouble?"

The phone rang.

Digging her mobile out of her jeans, Becca silently thanked the universe for the reprieve. "Could be, but it sounds like reinforcements have arrived. Hello?"

"Ms. Willoway? This is Cromwell Intensive Care."

The world paused. Becca sank onto a plate on the coffee table, legs quivering.

"Your sister is awake."

oOo

"She's going to be fine," Candice's insistence shrilled across Julie's vacant stare.

"It's brain damage, Mum," Becca whispered. "You can't *make* it better. It doesn't just heal like a broken bone. You don't know if she's still *in* there."

Candice rounded on Becca. "Of course she is! She just needs rest. We'll take her home this afternoon, we'll get her better."

Becca frowned. "Straight from the ICU? Don't they want to keep her for observation or rehab?"

"I insisted. She needs her family, not faceless caretakers. They'll send a physio-nurse to check on her twice a day. They gave me a list of things... . I can manage, just like with your father, when he went."

Candice really does love her. And you. And Sam.

Becca stared at the vacant woman who looked like her sister. Julie's eyes followed people when they spoke, and she moved her lips as spittle slowly slipped out the corner of her mouth. Gone, though, was the laugh, the flash-in-the-pan grin, the need to be into everything, understanding everything, the intensity when she listened like she was reading off the back of your skull. Gone was the banter which wound up offending people as often as not, the wit that invented codenames for Candice's tactics in their Skype calls. Gone, even, was the bitter resignation at returning to Candice's clutches a widow, Sam in tow, and that steel-eyed determination to climb free again. Nothing in this stranger's face was Julie.

Becca crumpled against the bed, but the tears wouldn't come.

Candice wrapped an arm around her shoulders, pressing her into her perfumed jacket, and soothed the nape of her neck. "She's going to be fine. You'll see," she murmured in her soft voice, the motherly voice from Becca's childhood fevers. She pulled a tissue from her purse and gently blotted at Becca's dry cheeks.

"Sam shouldn't see her like this." Becca glanced out the window where Sam quietly wrote a letter to the lost soldier who might be his father.

"She's his mother. He'll love her whatever she looks like."

"Except she doesn't really look like she loves *him*, now. He won't understand—"

"He should know she does," Candice said sharply. "She needs him. She won't get better without him to come back to. So no more of that nonsense. I know you gave into him. Head full of fluff just like your father. Soon as we get home, you're putting that thing back in the attic where it belongs."

Back in control. Becca opened her mouth to protest, to explain the new wonder. *She just lost her daughter, whatever she says. She needs this.* Instead, she said, "Yes, Mum."

Why do I keep excusing her?

Candice nodded. "We may as well get it over with, then." She opened the ICU door and beckoned Sam inside. "You can say hello, now, sweetling. She's coming home with us this afternoon."

Sam bounded in, pulled up short.

"Mum?" The lost tone in his voice sank like a knife in Becca's ribs.

"It's okay, mate," Becca murmured. "Her brain is bruised, so it's hard for her to move. But you can still tell her all about the soldier." Becca shot a hard look at Candice. "She'd like that."

Candice raised her eyebrow, but said nothing.

oOo

The typewriter disappeared into the attic to make way in the living room for Julie, her equipment, and pills. Sam sat beside her on the fold-out bed with his notebook, filling the otherwise silent room with his theories until Candice snapped.

"No more nonsense, that's enough!" She snatched his notebook up. "Your mother needs rest and care, not silliness and running about."

"Mum," Becca said, clearing plates from dinner.

Candice spun on her heel. "And you, as bad as your father, nothing but a waste of time and energy, leaving the work to everyone else."

Sam started to cry. Becca opened her mouth, but Candice cut her off with words from twenty years ago: "Don't start with me, young madam."

"He needs this. He's seven years old!"

"Old enough to grow up. You both are. Other people are more important than nonsense!"

"Oh, like 'she's going to be fine,' that kind of nonsense?" The words shot out of Becca's mouth before she could stop them.

She stepped forward, hand stretched out as if she could snatch them back.

Candice's face paled, her mouth an 'o' of shock, two pink spots of fury in her cheeks. "How *dare* you talk back to me." Her voice dropped to a growl. Becca flinched. Candice snatched up the gravy boat, marching into the kitchen with notebook and gravy.

"Mum," Becca began, but Candice didn't pause. "Mum, I didn't mean it, I—"

Candice threw the notebook in the bin, dumped the gravy on top of it, and slammed the boat in after so hard it shattered. She turned to Becca, hand half-raised for a slap. Clenching the plates to stop them rattling in her hands, Becca fought not to flinch again. Sam hugged his knees, heels slipping off the edge of the seat, and Candice seemed to suddenly remember him. The hand dropped to rub his shoulders.

"It's time for bed, sweetling," she said. "In the morning, you'll see this was for the best, for your mother."

Sam slunk off to Becca's old room. Becca glared in the silence.

"You shouldn't have taken it out on him," Becca said softly.

Candice stiffened and whipped the tea towel off the rack. "You know not to answer back."

oOo

Sam didn't appear for breakfast. Becca checked every cupboard she'd hidden in as a toddler, the ivy behind the house that Julie had always made her cubby, under every piece of furniture she could lift or wriggle into, even up the apricot tree in the rain. No Sam.

"Why would he do this?" Candice fumed. "Doesn't he know how hard things are already?" She all but wrenched the cupboard door off its hinges. "This is what I'm talking about, running away instead of learning to cope!"

"He *was* coping, in his own way. Not everybody has to cope your way!" Becca shot back.

Candice sucked in a breath in shock. Becca plunged ahead,

using anger as courage.

"Why did you have to destroy his notebook?" she shouted. "Why do you always have to *win*?"

The slap came out of nowhere. Becca reeled against the wall, her cheek on fire.

"I raised you better than that," Candice spat.

"*Dad* raised me. You just controlled me. There's a difference."

Candice raised her hand for another slap, but Becca swatted it down and shoved past her into the cluttered hallway. "Check the street!" she shouted before Candice could follow. She barged into her room and snatched her bag from under the bed. *I can do it. I'll just leave. It's my life. I'll fix things with Rick, go to work, drinks with the guys, live my life. I love Julie, but I'm not helping her here.* Becca shoved her clothes in the bag with numb hands. She'd find Sam, and then she'd …

What? Leave him here? She squeezed her eyes shut, fighting against the nausea that clawed up her throat.

She couldn't leave him here.

Years stretched out in front of her like a prison sentence. Starting over *again*, no job, no friends. Facing Candice alone, without backup. Without Julie.

Dragging at air, she squeezed her fingers around her wrists, ran for the bathroom to be sick—

And tripped over a bucket, landing on a fire poker.

The hell are a bucket and fire poker doing in the hallway? Massaging her jarred ankle, Becca rolled onto her back and stared up at the ceiling, where the attic ladder pull-cord swung slowly.

A shifting thump came from the ceiling. Becca smiled despite herself. She'd discounted the attic ladder as out of his reach. But standing on a bucket to twirl the ladder cord around a fire poker and pull the ladder down—that sounded like her father's grandson. Becca eased the stairs down and crept into the attic.

Sam stared at a box, almost ravenous, scribbling on the backs of envelopes. As she approached, the typewriter clicks came, muffled—he'd wrapped her dad's old shirts around the machine to quiet it. Becca couldn't stifle the grin. He frantically pressed a key over and over, scribbling as he went.

Becca sat, but he didn't look up.

"Grandma's mad at me," he whispered.

"Grandma's worried about your Mum."

"Are you mad at me?"

Becca hugged him close. "What've you got there?" She pointed at the envelopes.

Sam bit his lip. "She took my notebook, but ... I'd already gotten pretty good at remembering the codes. I was working on remembering the rest." He cringed slightly, breath held.

Becca looked over his scrawl. The patterns held steady, three symbols to a phoneme. "Do you remember how you figured them out?" She sifted in the attic piles for some pieces of card and a pen. "Let me show you how to make a decoder ring."

Sam grinned.

"So how's our soldier doing?"

"Someone's chasing him. He almost got caught near Yoorannis but that's when the shuttles showed up."

"Near where?" Becca peered at the envelopes in the dim light of the attic window. Sam pointed, and she squinted harder. "Yoor ... Uranus. It's a planet."

"Like in space?" Sam's eyes widened. "He's a space soldier?"

"Maybe an astronaut. He must be clever, sending the message out."

"He did what you said, asked what he didn't know," Sam pointed to another section, then frowned. "If he's in space, then ... it's not my Dad."

Becca sighed and squeezed Sam close.

Feet slammed on the attic stairs. Candice's head rose from the floor, her face like ice. She glanced at them, and Becca was nine years old again with her new dress covered in mud. She clutched Sam, leaning between him and her mother.

Candice loomed down. "I don't understand what you're doing, when you know how much Julie needs you. But if you can't do it yourself ..." She hefted up the typewriter, crate and all, and carried it over to the attic window. Becca watched, her legs refusing to move, as Candice opened the window and dumped the crate through it into the rain. Sam shuddered at every thump and ping of metal as the crate and its contents burst apart on their front lawn.

"I put your bag away." Her consonants could have cut steel. "When you have realised there are more important things, I'll be in the living room, looking after my daughter." She stalked down the stairs. Becca's face burned.

Sam shivered. "Does Mum think I don't love her?"

"No, mate," Becca rubbed his arms as if to warm him, or perhaps herself. "Your Mum knows how much you love her." Her voice sounded hollow, even to her.

oOo

Becca lay awake on her childhood bed, studying the scrawl on the bottom of Julie's bunk. Sam slept, the rise and fall of his breath like a tiny piston, but sleep eluded Becca.

The pre-dawn birdsong niggled. They were the wrong birds. She missed the magpie warble, the cackle of Kookaburras as they hunted worms for their young.

Who would raise Sam? Her? Her mother? No, Becca had made too many hard choices to break that cycle, she had to spare him that. But how could she take him away from Julie? Rick would never sign on for a kid, he didn't even want a dog. And Candice couldn't care for Julie on her own, not even with a physio-nurse visiting.

Was this her life, now? Walled in with Candice by guilt? Caring for the body of a sister she'd never see again? Becca bit down on her cheek until she tasted blood.

What would Dad do?

Figure it out. Find what you're missing. Build your decoder.

Typewriter pieces sprang forward in her mind. Where had that astronaut come from? How did he contact her?

You're just distracting yourself from the problem. She winced at her mother's voice in her head. If she stayed here, she'd turn into Candice.

She had to leave. They both did. Julie would want what was best for her son, even if that didn't include her. Becca'd find a school nearby, ask work for flexible hours. Her friends would visit, and Rick... She'd work something out with Rick. He'd come around, he'd like Sam. She'd make it work.

Becca swung her legs out from the covers and felt for a torch. The only dressing gown she could find in the dark was Sam's blue Thomas the Tank Engine one that barely covered her hips, but it would have to do. She eased open the dresser that held Sam's clothes and quietly bundled them into his backpack. Candice had hidden hers somewhere. She'd buy a new laptop when she got home. If she didn't go now, she might lose her nerve. She'd put his backpack in the car, then come back for him.

Becca crept down the hallway, past her sister's laboured breathing. In her head, Candice's voice cursed her: *selfish child.* Becca held her breath and slipped the latch on the front door.

The rain had lifted, leaving a pre-dawn sogginess that clogged the air. Becca tip-toed out to the car, the mud squelching through her toes. Shoes. She should get some shoes when she got Sam. She eased the car door shut, and turned back to the house.

The typewriter still lay in pieces on the grass near the bins. Sam would need it. As if it could somehow fill the void of what she was taking him from.

He's already lost her.

Not the point.

She picked over the remains, laying out letter-levers and keys in a sad little row. She couldn't put it back together again; most of it was a twisted mess. She held the 'A' in her hand, its long arm bent from impact and twisted in the ribbon. Broken, like her sister, never to be whole. Her ink-purple fingers blurred as hot tears wet her cheeks and neck, and sobs pulled up from her gut. She curled over her chest, squeezing the broken pieces in her hand until her palm cramped, sobbing so hard her stomach ached.

Her mother *had* been right. She'd just been hiding behind the puzzle. Becca stared down at the ink marks in her hand, drained.

A clear symbol sat on her palm where the A had rested. It wasn't an 'A'. Slowly, hand shaking, Becca pressed the A key through the ribbon into her palm.

Another symbol.

Electricity surged through her blood stream. She sifted

through the rubble. The decoder had disintegrated in the rain, but—but Sam's notebook might be salvageable. Trying not to breathe, she flipped the lid off the garbage bin and rummaged inside, dug out the gravy-sodden notebook and wiped the worst of the mess off with the mountain of used tissues.

The gravy had eaten half of Sam's notes, but with her laptop, she could re-translate it with ocular character recognition. Give it a dictionary and the translations from the notebook, it could take educated guesses at the rest. She could figure it out, finish it for him.

One problem: Candice had her laptop.

Conviction wavered under Candice's imaginary glare.

You could just leave it. You're taking him away from everything, he's probably not going to care. You could just slink away, like always. Because she scares you. Your own mother scares you.

Fist closed around the 'A' key, Becca marched inside.

She found her carry-on bag stuffed in Candice's wardrobe and lugged it halfway to the hall before the lights flicked on. Candice stood in her vermillion dressing gown, one raised hand gripping a leather belt.

"I thought you were ..." she began, expression foggy. She glanced at Becca, then the bag, hardened her gaze and drew herself up, setting her face into battle-mode. She let the silence play out, the seconds battering at Becca's walls like artillery.

"I deserve better than this. So does your sister."

Becca flinched as the words shot through to her gut. "It's not about you." Her voice whined like a child's.

Candice strode towards her, the belt swinging ominously. "She needs you. You can't run away because you don't feel like dealing with it. You don't get to pretend anymore while someone else cleans up the mess."

The bag slipped down Becca's arm like a weight fixing her in place and her mind narrowed to the words, to Candice's voice, struggling to gain an edge.

Candice loomed within striking distance. "Your sister understood that," she said. "We had our differences, but she worked hard for her family, for her son. She buried her husband while you ran off to your koalas. And now she needs you, and you're leaving it to everyone else, like you always do. Leaving us behind."

Shaking her head mutely, Becca tried to drum up words, thoughts, anything.

Candice leaned close. "You selfish child. Always, no matter what I did. She's not the one who deserved this."

Sickening heat flooded up from Becca's belly, swallowing her.

Candice's eyes glinted in triumph. "Were you even going to say goodbye to Sam? Or are you leaving that to me as well, to explain why you're abandoning him."

Sam.

Becca found an edge. *Protect Sam.* She clutched it like a spear, lifted her chin, locked eyes with Candice. "I'm taking him with me," she snarled.

Candice reared back, mouth open.

Drawing her anger from her voice, Becca pulled herself straight. "I gave up every friend I had to move away. My sister. My job. My possessions. I didn't *run* away, I made a calculated choice. I paid a price." She took a deep breath, chin thrust out like she could push the words out and not hear them. "It was worth leaving everything behind to be free of you."

Silence again, but this time it couldn't touch her. Her blood surged like ice through her chest.

"How dare you," Candice breathed. "You ungrateful—"

"I'm just being honest with you," Becca shot back. "Without the nonsense, just like you wanted. Without pretending this is okay." *I can do this. I can stand up to her. I can protect him.* "Because it's not. You are toxic, and if you want to get anywhere near Sam, things are going to have to change."

Candice brandished the belt. "You can't take him away from me. From Julie."

Becca snatched it out of her hands. "I'm his legal guardian. Anyone can see she's not fit for motherhood." She took a deep breath and leaned close enough to smell the laundry soap on her mother's gown. "I will miss her until my heart stops, but it would have been kinder to everyone, especially her, if you had just let her go."

Becca re-shouldered the bag. "I'll bring Sam to you to say goodbye."

oOo

Sam had mumbled groggy goodbyes. Becca had tried to wake him, but the boy just wanted to sleep, so she'd tucked him in the car with her carry-on and the remains of the typewriter and driven to the airport to wait for their standby flight. He slept the whole way, and barely woke when she piloted him to an empty gate lounge. Becca sat in the row next to him and rifled through her bag for her jeans and jumper to drag on.

He should be with his mother.

I can't leave him with Candice.

She scrabbled faster through socks, underwear and camisoles. No jeans.

Candice wouldn't hurt him.

She'd control him.

Deciding this for him isn't control? You can't be a parent. This isn't your life.

Hands shaking, she dragged the jumper out of its tangle with a t-shirt and her headphones. She must have left the jeans at Candice's. She tied the jumper around her hips.

I'd be better than she would. Julie would want this.

Would she? Would Sam? Or is this just what you want?

This was ridiculous. She'd *made* the decision. She wasn't going to unmake it. She shoved the escaping underwear back in, hauled the laptop out and set it up on the table with the typewriter pieces and the gravy-sodden notebook. Her fingers jittered on the keys. Sometimes distractions were necessary.

The program took less time than she'd expected. Components just *fit*, like something guided her code, pulling it into a prototype effortlessly. She could almost smell her father's aftershave on the keyboard.

Gripped with a frenzy, she snatched some napkins from the table, hammered the broken key through the ribbon onto them as fast as she could and held them up to the webcam, tapping the keyboard impotently while the program churned up the translation. Next to her, Sam rolled on his bag in his sleep, curling around it.

There it was: the astronaut's team had been colonising Titan when unfriendly ships arrived from outside the system. He stole one and escaped, largely by jabbing everything to see what it did, and broadcast his distress call until the American shuttles turned up.

Sam was right, this guy had her father's attitude. Poke it with a stick. Never let ignorance or fear stand in the way of trying.

Don't let her beat that out of you again.

Dawn crept over the horizon of the runway. Becca's hands ached. The program struggled with words not in the dictionary, and she paused to decipher them by hand.

"Dear Grandma and Grandpa,

I don't know how this'll reach you, I think their tech latches onto whatever it can. I set the ship to do a data dump at the end of this transmission; hopefully there's something Uncle Sam can use. I'm taking a lot on faith, you know, with your stories. Tell Mum I love her, and say hi to Uncle Sam."

Becca frowned. Was Uncle Sam actually a person?

There was an address before the message, like a letter: Rebecca Willoway and Michael Oaks, 275 Tempus Terrace.

Her name. Candice's address.

Becca hugged the laptop to herself and pressed the 'A' key a few more times against the last napkin. It wrote 'A'. She wasn't surprised.

But it couldn't be her, if it was "Uncle" Sam. Sam would be a cousin to any grandchild of hers. And she wasn't staying here.

Except Sam was *her* son, now. If she had any other children, he'd be more brother to them than anything else.

The dawn sun soaked through the window into her spine with the realisation, sickeningly warm. Becca slumped as her life collapsed back inside the walls of Candice's rule.

Even if you believe in magic typewriters from the future, it doesn't mean that future's going to happen.

No, but it's possible. I hadn't thought of that. I hadn't thought something good might come of it.

The warmth roiled in her chest.

It's not possible, because you're taking Sam away from that. For his own good.

Maybe I just don't want to give up my life. My friends, Rick.

You're doing the right thing for Sam.

Am I, though? Or am I just doing the easy thing for me?

The thought slammed down like stone. Becca shut the lid of the laptop, fighting the urge to curl up around her knees.

Forget the stupid typewriter a minute. What's best for him? That's my job, now. That's what Julie wanted.

The plastic seat squeaked softly—Becca stopped herself from rocking.

I stood up to her once. I can stand up to her again. Maybe I could make some happiness here.

She unfolded herself from the seat and stoked Sam's hair from his face.

He deserves to have his mother—his real mother—in his life.

You'll have to keep fighting for it. Keep fighting her, every moment.

oOo

In the carport of Candice's house, Becca gathered the last of the scrawled-on napkins from the back seat. Sam, finally awake, had scampered off to tell the whole thing to Julie as soon as the engine had stopped. Hands full, Becca flicked the door closed with her knee as another car pulled up in the drive.

A young man in blue scrubs and coiffed black hair stepped out, hospital-branded duffel bag slung across one muscular shoulder. He gave her a wave, smile gracing perfect cheekbones, and Becca was suddenly acutely aware that she stood in the front garden wearing a tied-on jumper and a child's dressing gown, hands clutching stained napkins and sticky with gravy, face still swollen with tears.

"How're you doing?" he called out with a rich burr from one of the southern states of America. He held out his hand. "Oakes, Michael Oakes. I'm your sister's physio-nurse."

"Oh, yes. They—they said." Becca stammered, trying to wind

the robe more tightly against herself. "I'm sorry, it's been a bit of a night. Michael, was it?" Belatedly, she offered her hand to shake, still full of napkins. His warm fingers wrapped over hers securely. A small scar bisected his left eyebrow, giving him a permanent inquisitive expression. He didn't even flinch at the gravy.

"Oakes, yes. It's okay. It's like that." He stepped closer, professional manner softening for a moment. "It gets easier, I promise."

Becca looked back down at the address on the napkins. "Are you sure?" she said, not entirely to him.

He smiled again, and extended his arm to lead her toward the house. "Trust me," he said. "We'll figure it out."

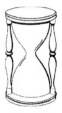

THE SPIEL OF THE GLOCKEN
by Laura Resnick

I first suspected something was amiss when I exited the coffee shop on Greenup Street and was knocked down by a herd of bison.

As I stepped out of the shop, I heard the city's clock tower chiming in the distance—and then, *bam!*, a smelly thousand-pound beast came out of nowhere and ran right into me. I hit the ground so hard that I couldn't breathe, and I instinctively curled up into a fetal position, arms shielding my head, when I saw more hooves coming at me and more massive, shaggy bodies lumbering above me. After a few moments of shock, confusion, and terror, I realized the buffalo might not all be polite enough to keep stepping over me rather than *on* me, so I somehow managed to throw myself out of their path and halfway back into the coffee shop, collapsing on the threshold.

"Oh, my God! Are you okay?" the barista cried.

Stronger than she looked, she dragged me the rest of the way through the door, slammed it shut, then knelt beside my prone body and briefly checked me for injuries.

"Are you hurt?"

"N ... no." I gasped for air as I shook my head. "Wh ... wha ... what ..."

"What's going *on*?" She rose to her feet and looked through the glass door, out at the street where the buffalo still roamed.

Panting in reaction, I rolled over to watch the spectacle of those enormous beasts pounding thunderously on the pavement as they headed downhill toward the Ohio River. There were dozens of them. We stared in stunned silence, watching them dash past the coffee shop.

A buffalo stampede really wasn't the sort of thing that happened in Covington, Kentucky.

Well, not *anymore*, I mean. Once upon a time, sure, the section of the river that separates us from Cincinnati wasn't nearly as deep as it is now. Bison herds used to ford the Ohio River here, heading north to Ohio State in time for the college football season—or perhaps, as some people claim, migrating to fresh grazing grounds. (I'm an IT guy. I can fix your computer, but I'm fuzzy on the habits of wild nomadic beasts.) Native Americans would hunt them here, since the water slowed them down enough to make them easy prey. Down on the riverfront, a couple of blocks from this spot, there was a mural of that scene painted on the flood wall.

But it must be centuries since buffalo had stampeded down this street on their way to the river. In fact, the last time something like this had happened, there probably hadn't *been* a street.

"Where did they come from?" the barista asked in bewilderment after the last bison finally trotted past and the building stopped shaking. "And where are they going?"

"Good questions," I said breathlessly.

I could still hear their thundering hooves, though they were past us now. So why hadn't I heard a thing as they approached? It was almost as if they'd simply popped into existence a scant moment before I collided with them.

I crawled to the door. Still on my hands and knees, too shaken to try standing up yet, I peered through the glass, wondering who was crazy enough to run a herd of bison through these narrow, crowded streets.

"Are those buffalo being loaded onto a river barge or something?" the barista wondered, still standing at the window and looking north toward the river.

"I hope so." Surely the bison would drown if they tried to ford the river these days, what with water depth and current.

"Shouldn't there be cowboys or herders?" she asked, glancing down at me. "Someone in charge of them?"

I looked up at her—and instantly regretted my decision to

stay on all fours. The barista was pretty, vivacious, and sexy, and she was the reason I had recently been coming daily to this shop for my morning cup of carry-out, even though it meant a detour of several blocks on my walk to work.

And crouching on my hands and knees in lingering fear was not how I wanted to present myself, now that we were talking for the first time.

I started to get up off the floor, felt dizzy, and almost keeled over.

She grabbed me before I fell and hauled me over to a chair. "You should sit down."

"Thanks." I felt embarrassed.

She went behind the coffee bar, then came back a moment later with a glass of water. "Here, drink this."

We were alone, which was unusual. In truth, a *lot* of guys came here for their morning coffee. A few of them ... well, no, almost all of them were smoother than me and way ahead of my game. They talked and flirted with her, and a couple of them had asked her out. I hadn't heard her say "yes" to anyone yet, but they were working on it.

In fact, I'd been getting up earlier this past week because I was trying to get here before those other guys poured through the door, so I'd have a chance to talk to her. But the last couple of days, including today, I'd been the first one here, arriving right after she opened the shop ... and I *still* hadn't worked up the nerve to talk to her.

I took a gulp of the water she'd just given me. "Thanks," I said again. "I appreciate it, um ..."

I realized I'd been coming here regularly for three weeks without even managing to learn her name—or managing to speak in complete sentences.

She went back to the window and looked outside again. "It looks like it's safe to go out there now and see what's happening."

While I sat in clumsy silence, trying to think of a more engaging response than telling her I wasn't ready for that, she opened the door and stuck her head outside. Then she looked over her shoulder at me. "Can you watch the shop for a couple of minutes? I want to go find out what's going on."

"Uh, sure. Okay."

The clock tower in Mainstrasse, a neighborhood a few blocks away, started chiming again as she exited, and then the door closed behind her. Watching her go, I supposed that as long as we were behind the herd now, rather than in its path, she would be all right.

A nanosecond later, I was proved wrong.

"Watch out!" I shouted as I shot to my feet and dived for the door while a sword-waving guy on a horse galloped straight past the shop window.

I opened the door in time to hear the barista's stifled scream as the waving sword barely missed her head. She fell to her knees to avoid the blade, and the horseman rode on, not even glancing at her, never mind stopping to apologize.

"Hey! What do you think you're *doing*?" I shouted after him. And then I asked her, "Are you okay?"

While I was helping her rise, I heard a rumbling, thundering noise behind me that suddenly seemed to fill the whole street. Still holding onto the girl, I turned around and saw an army column heading straight for us—foot soldiers with bayonets, officers on horseback, a canon on wheels. ... They were moving along at a brisk clip, filling the street, and they seemed no more worried about trampling us than the bison or the horseman had been.

"Get inside!" I shouted.

But the barista was well ahead of me, already dragging me through the door, which she slammed shut behind us.

Dozens of armed men marched right past us a split second later, followed by hundreds more.

"That's the Union Army," I said blankly, recognizing the uniforms and the weapons of the era. "Is there a Civil War reenactment or something going on today?"

As I said this, I realized that the sword-waving guy on horseback had been wearing the gray uniform of a Confederate officer.

Her eyes widened. "Oh, you mean they're reenacting the story about that guy?"

"What guy?"

The Union Army was still marching past the coffee shop. A historical parade through the city streets seemed as out of place here on a regular weekday morning as, oh, a buffalo herd.

"I took that local ghost tour at Halloween," she said. "You know the one I mean?"

I didn't, but I nodded. "Uh-huh."

"And I learned a lot about the city's history. Such as, when the Union Army crossed the river to occupy Covington, it totally surprised a Confederate officer who was visiting a wealthy family here at the time, in one of those old mansions down the street—well, they're old *now*." She continued, "So the guy ran out back, hopped on his horse, and rode it straight through the house and out the front window, then went galloping down the street—a feat that his ghost still reenacts on dark nights—and he didn't stop until he reached New Orleans."

I suspected there was a fair bit of hyperbole in that story, but it accounted (in a manner of speaking) for a Confederate officer galloping down the street and a battalion of Union soldiers marching behind him.

"Okay, I guess they're replaying that scene," I said with a nod. "But it doesn't explain the buffalo."

"This all must have something to do with the bicentennial," she said. "I know the committee has been planning all kinds of activities. It's always getting mentioned in the local news."

Founded in 1815, Covington was celebrating its 200th birthday this year. I hadn't really paid much attention, though I knew there were "big things" in the works.

"I don't remember the news mentioning *this*," I said.

"It didn't." She shook her head. "They really ought to warn people before filling the streets with hundreds of armed guys, a galloping horse, and buffalo. Don't you think?"

"Definitely."

"Oh, well. Since they're here, why don't we go outside and watch?" she said, mustering some enthusiasm. "This seems like a pretty big deal."

That sounded like she was inviting me—me!—to join her, so I agreed, even though I was due at work soon.

And since she had just asked me out, sort of, I worked up the courage to ask her name.

"Jeff," she said.

"Jeff?"

"Uh-huh."

I wanted to say it was a pretty name, but since it wasn't, I asked, "Is that short for something?"

"Jeffrey."

"Really?" When she didn't respond, I said, "Oh."

I started to feel like maybe I'd been doing better when I was too nervous to talk to her.

"And you?" she asked.

"Huh?"

"What's your name?"

"Oh!" I probably should have realized she'd ask. "Aristhosthenes."

An understandable reluctance to introduce myself to people is one of the reasons I'm shy. I waited for the inevitable questions.

"Oh, right. Like the ancient astronomer," said the barista. "Cool."

"Wow. No one *ever*—"

"I think I'll lock the door," Jeff said. "In case we want to follow the parade or go see what else is going on out there."

I followed her outside, where we stood on the sidewalk, our backs pressed against the shop window, and watched the parade that filled the street. The "soldiers" marching past us looked deadly serious, not very clean—and, to my surprise, they stank.

Jeff wrinkled her nose. "Is that them? Or is it the sewers?"

The odor had a tinge of Covington's aged sewer system toward the end of a heat wave, but I thought the smell of unwashed sweat emanating from the costumed men was pretty unmistakable.

"It's them," I said, raising my voice to be heard above the racket of their marching feet and wagon wheels. "Reenacting the *smell* of a nineteenth century army on the move seems a little obsessive."

And that's when things got *really* strange. As I was finishing my sentence (now that I had learned to speak in complete sentences around Jeff), the entire battalion—or brigade, or whatever it was … simply disappeared.

Hundreds of men, a number of horses, equipment, weapons, wagons … all vanished in an instant and without a trace. It was as quick and complete as a light being switched off.

"Whoa!" Jeff reached out and clutched my arm.

My jaw hanging open, I covered her hand with mine and clutched, too.

In the distance, we heard the chimes of the clock tower ringing.

I looked around and saw other people on the street who seemed just as stunned as we were. Ordinary people dressed in regular twenty-first century clothing.

"Aristhosthenes, what's going *on*?" Jeff croaked.

"I don't know," I said faintly.

A woman across the street who was looking toward the river suddenly dropped her purse, screamed, turned around, and ran off—still screaming. I was staring after her when I heard the menacing trumpeting of an enraged animal coming from the direction she'd been looking, followed by the heavy *thud-thud-thud* of thundering footsteps.

I whirled around as Jeff gasped loudly and tightened her grip on my arm until it hurt. And then I saw what she saw. Coming uphill toward us, trotting rapidly along Greenup Street, was a woolly mammoth.

And it looked very angry.

"*Inside*," I said urgently, reaching for the door handle. "Jeff, let's get inside. Now!"

I turned and rattled the handle, but the door remained closed. I pulled harder on it. "Urngh!"

"Oh, *no*, I locked it," Jeff said breathlessly. She pushed past me, her hands shaking as she pulled her key out of her pocket.

Thud-thud-thud.

"Hurry," I urged.

She was frantically trying to shove the key into the lock but kept missing her mark.

The other people in the street were screaming and fleeing, some going inside the buildings, others running off in all directions.

The beast trumpeted again, and the sound seemed to run straight through my bone marrow. I couldn't believe how loud it was.

I also couldn't believe the *size of* that thing. It was enormous, and those tusks looked like they could take out the army column that had just vanished. As it bore down on us, its tonnage making the street tremble with every heavy step, Jeff panicked and dropped her key.

"God damn it!" She stooped down to grab it, but I realized we'd run out of time.

"Come on!" I grabbed her hand and ran for it.

This, as it turned out, was a bad plan.

I only realized too late that we had no hope of outrunning a wild animal that was twenty times our size (this is a rough estimate, since I was fleeing for my life at the time) and in much better condition than we were—or, rather, than *I* was. I supposed Jeff worked out or did some jogging, since she quickly pulled way ahead of me. Adrenaline is an amazing chemical, but it can't make up for a lifestyle of sitting in front of computers and drinking too much caffeine, and I was already panting hard and feeling fatigued when I reached the next corner.

"Aristhosthenes!" Jeff cried, looking over her shoulder. "Come *on*!"

I saw her slowing down as she realized I was far behind her. "No! Go! *Go!*" I didn't want her to become woolly mammoth rubble just because I had all the athletic prowess of overcooked broccoli.

"*SCREEEEEEEEECH!*" The hairy monster was right behind me now.

"*Noooo!*" Jeff was standing stock still now, staring at me in horror.

"Run!" I shouted—a second before I tripped and fell.

Thud-thud-thud.

The ground shook, and then I felt a heavy gust of hot animal breath on my legs.

Chime, chime, chime, chime ...

I thought the chimes of the clock tower were the last sound

I'd ever hear, besides my bones breaking and my own screams.

But instead, I heard the *toot-toot* of a horn as a vintage car puttered past me, driving up the street. *Really* vintage, like something from a hundred years ago.

Still lying on the sidewalk, I craned my neck a little to watch it, wondering why the driver—wearing goggles and a spiffy hat—didn't seem bothered by the sight of a woolly mammoth killing me on Greenup Street.

"Aristhosthenes!"

I heard footsteps running toward me, then saw Jeff's sensible shoes only inches from my nose.

"It happened again!" she cried while hauling me off the pavement. "That—that—*whatever* that thing was, it disappeared! Just vanished!"

"Woolly mammoth," I said hoarsely.

"No, it couldn't be," she said with certainty. "They're extinct."

"Even so, that's what it was." It looked just liked every drawing of one that I'd ever seen.

"How is that possible? And what was it doing running loose on Greenup Street?"

"I don't know," I said in a daze, leaning on her, since I wasn't ready to stand alone on my shaking legs yet. "What the *hell* is going on around here?"

Another horseless carriage drove past us. A very large piece of paper flew off the car seat, floated briefly on the air, and then fluttered to lie on the pavement near us. It was the front page of a newspaper, and the headline read: *Titanic Sinks Four Hours After Hitting Iceberg.*

The clock tower chimed again.

Jeff and I flinched as a gunshot rang out. We crouched down and watched as a stag with an impressive set of antlers ran past us. Looking further down the street, we saw a guy dressed like Daniel Boone uncork his powder horn and set about priming and reloading his musket.

"A herd of wild buffalo heading for the river ..." I said slowly, thinking of the mural portrayal on the flood wall. "It predates European settlement of this region."

"And a woolly mammoth goes back even farther," Jeff said.

"But those cars are early twentieth century, and the *Titanic* sank in 1912."

"The Union Army occupied Covington in 1862," said Jeff. "I learned that on the ghost tour."

The pioneer strode past us, oblivious to our existence as he stalked his wild prey.

"So what exactly are we saying?"

"I think we're saying that guy might not just *look* like Simon Kenton," she said. "He might actually *be* Simon Kenton."

"Who?"

Jeff looked at me. "How can you not know who Simon Kenton was? There's a statue of him three blocks from my shop. This county is named after him."

"I was thinking Daniel Boone."

"No, that's the next county over."

"No, I mean I was thinking this guy looks like Daniel Boone."

"Oh." She nodded. "Right."

"So … are we saying that all these things are exactly what they seem to be—from another time?"

"That woolly mammoth did not escape from the Cincinnati Zoo," Jeff said with certainty. "And those Union soldiers were not sucked up into the sky by the mother ship." She paused and added, "Well, not as far as I saw, anyhow."

"So either you and I are both crazy and have entirely imagined all this, or else …"

"Or else?"

"There must be some sort of weird—*really* weird—temporal distortion going on here."

"Wow." Jeff shook her head. "This shit's fucked up."

"That's another way of putting it," I agreed. "This isn't my field. What we really need, I think, is a theoretical physicist."

"But there's never a theoretical physicist around when you need one, is there?"

I noticed she rolled her eyes when she said that.

Chime, chime, chime …

The frontiersman, his musket, and the stag disappeared from

the city street. Several African-Americans, all dressed in very humble Victorian clothing, bustled past us, whispering to each other, looking furtive and anxious.

Jeff snapped her fingers. "Underground Railroad!"

"Did you learn that on your ghost tour?"

She nodded. "If escaping slaves could get across the river, then they were in a Northern state and free." She frowned and added darkly, "Unless the slave catchers caught up with them."

"There was no bridge until after the Civil War." The year of 1867 was plainly inscribed on the Roebling Bridge, the first one built in this region, which I drove across every time I went to Cincinnati. "They must have needed boats to escape."

"The tour guide told us the river often froze over in those days. So they could walk across it in winter."

I shuddered, imagining the risk. "I wouldn't want to have to try that. But I guess they had no choice."

The clock tower chimed again, the fleeing slaves vanished, and a large group of nuns in full traditional habit appeared out of thin air and walked sedately past us. As anyone who spent more than five minutes here knew, Covington was heavily settled by German Catholics.

"The time period changes every time the clock tower chimes," I said. "Did you notice that?"

"I notice that it's been ringing like crazy, that's for sure," Jeff replied. "It must be broken."

"And every time it rings, it seems to act as some sort of temporal TV dial that's turning randomly through the centuries, giving us glimpse after glimpse of what once was here."

"This could get *really* out of hand," Jeff said. "We need to fix that clock!"

"We might be able to find a theoretical physicist at University of Cincinnati," I said hopefully.

"Oh, for God's sake, Aristhosthenes, we need to do something *now* and for *real*, not desert Covington in its time of need while we go in search of a theorist!" She turned and marched west. "I'm heading for the clock tower! I can't force you to come with me, of course, but I would *hope* that you—"

"I'm coming, I'm coming," I assured her.

She had a point, I thought, as the chimes rang again and a group of Shawnee Indians from some previous century ran past us, clearly intent on serious business. We saw other current-day citizens like us, and most of them were screaming, running around in confused circles, leaning out of windows and laughing maniacally, crying, or trying to hide under parked cars as temporal rift after rift disoriented and terrified them with each new peal of the clock tower chimes. This situation was spiraling into chaos so fast, the city might not even *be* here anymore by the time we found and secured the help of someone with more expertise on temporal phenomena than either of us had (which was none at all).

We approached Mainstrasse at a brisk pace. I was panting and feeling the burn; Jeff wasn't even slightly flushed, never mind breathing hard.

Mainstrasse is the most picturesque area of Covington, a nostalgic tribute to the German villages that the immigrants in this city left behind in the Old World. Nineteenth century townhouses and attractive brick buildings line a broad and very long village green. The neighborhood is a mix of private homes, restaurants, bars, and businesses.

Some of the most visible features of Mainstrasse, though, are recent renditions of a traditional German setting. The Goose Girl Fountain, which was inspired by the Grimm fairy tale and sits in the center of Mainstrasse, was erected in the early 1980s. (Almost every year, usually during Oktoberfest, some joker sneaks bubble bath into the fountain.) And the other prominent example of recent nostalgia evoking a magical past is the clock tower, also built around that time. Inspired by a medieval clock tower in Munich, it rises high above the park that lies at the end of the village green.

A combination of narration, music, and motorized figurines in the bell tower recount the story of the Pied Piper of Hamelin every hour. The tower also features a glockenspiel with chimes that ring-in and ring-out the hours, day in and day out.

But now our glocken seemed to be broken and spieling all over the place. Maybe a reality-altering crisis was the inevitable consequence of deliberately building a fairy tale clock tower and then failing to maintain it properly, and perhaps the city should have thought this through before committing such folly. But it was too late now for such reflections to be constructive, and Jeff said (when I hung back a little, admitting that I'm afraid of heights) that *we* had to do something about it, since most of the city currently seemed to be crazed with fear or paralytic with shock.

While we hovered at the base of the clock tower discussing this, Jeff picked the lock on the gate that opened onto the stairs which ascended up to the bell tower. I was contemplating this ascension with some dismay when the chimes rang again, and then we heard what sounded like an epic quantity of water roaring toward us.

"What's that?" Jeff asked with a frown.

I had a dark feeling I knew, even before I looked north and saw the rising water rushing through the narrow streets. "Oh, dear God, it's the flood of 1937."

"But there's a huge flood wall," she protested.

"Not in 1937, there wasn't! Come on, Jeff, up—*up!*"

I pushed her ahead of me and raced up the steep, narrow, curving metal staircase behind her, my fear of heights submerged by my newfound fear of drowning in a flood that had occurred almost eighty years earlier.

"How can this be happening?" Jeff wondered.

"How can *any* of it be happening?" I gave her another push. "Keep moving! The river rose so high that neighborhoods twenty blocks south of here were underwater!" I'd seen photos of the devastation.

As we reached the bell tower, the glockenspiel chimed again, switching the temporal dial to yet another channel.

"Oh, thank God," said Jeff. "Imagine if the whole flood had played out all over again."

"I don't want to imagine it," I said sincerely.

"What's happening now?" she asked, looking down at the town below.

I gazed east and replied, "It looks like John Roebling is about halfway through building the bridge, so I guess it's soon after the Civil War." Roebling, who would go on to build the more famous

Brooklyn Bridge, had designed the suspension bridge over the Ohio River that was still in use in our time.

"Let's put a stop to this mess before someone who doesn't know what's going on drives across it," Jeff said firmly.

The chimes of the clock tower's glockenspiel used to be played manually, but I saw that they had long since been programmed to play electronically.

"Didn't you say you're an IT guy?" Jeff asked, looking at the electrical system with me.

"Yes. You remember that?" I was surprised and pleased. I'd mumbled this information two weeks ago, while paying for my coffee, when she'd asked me where I worked.

"So can you reprogram this thing?"

"I can do better than that."

I pulled the plug.

"That's it?" Jeff said incredulously.

"No power, no chimes," I said. "Now let's see if it worked."

We went back to the railing and looked out over the city.

"The bridge is back!" Jeff said with relief. "*All* of it."

And there had been no chime to signal another temporal shift. In cutting the power supply to the glockenspiel, I had somehow bypassed or eliminated whatever strange time-keeping power had gone haywire in the town's clock tower, and thus the temporal continuum reverted to its standard flow.

Let this be a lesson to people who want to install fairy tale devices in their modern cities. It doesn't work out well.

Jeff and I continued to watch anxiously over our city for some time, but there were no more disturbances in the city's normal one-way time flow. The crisis was past.

"We need to put an 'Out of Order' sign on the glockenspiel before we go," I said "And then have a talk with the mayor, to make sure no one plugs it back in."

She nodded. "I suppose I should go check on my coffee shop. Who knows what's happened to it, what with the woolly mammoth, the Civil War, and the flood?"

As she turned toward the stairs, I said, "Um, Jeff, I was wondering …"

"Yes?"

Go for it, I thought. *Would you just go for it, already?*

"Would you maybe, um, think about going out with me some time?"

She hesitated for such a long moment that my stomach sank, and I wished to God I hadn't spoken up after all.

Then she said, "Before I say yes, Aristhosthenes—"

"You're thinking of saying *yes*?" I blurted with enough enthusiasm to make her fall back a step.

"There's something you should know. I'm a transgender woman." Seeing my puzzled expression, Jeff added, "I was born with male genitalia, but I identify as a woman."

"Oh! Um ... have you still *got* the male genitalia?"

"Yes." Jeff waited. "Is that a problem?"

I thought it over.

The barista was pretty, vivacious, and sexy, and I had been getting up ridiculously early all week in hope of having a moment alone with her. She was brave and reliable and had convinced me to help her save our city from a mad glockenspiel and temporal disaster.

"No, not a problem," I said. "Will you have dinner with me on Friday, Jeff?"

She smiled. "Yes, Aristhosthenes, I will.

THE PASSING BELL
by Amy Griswold

My hired horse threw a shoe between Bristol and Bath, and by the time the wearying business of getting another nailed on was complete the shadows were growing long and the wind was sharpening its knives.

"It's kind of you to put me up," I said, jingling pennies in my pocket to encourage such generosity. In a town so small it had neither pub nor inn, I considered myself fortunate to be offered the chance to sleep in the blacksmith's loft.

"Glad to, if you've got the coin," the blacksmith said. "Only the missus is particular in her way about knowing something about strangers who are going to sleep under her roof. What's your name, and what's your age, and what's your trade, good man? For she'll ask me all three."

"Rob Tar is my name, and my age is twenty and six," I said. "And I'm an able seaman aboard the *Red Boar* out of Bristol. My girl Minnie lives in Bath, and I'm on my way to keep her company a while until we sail again. I've never claimed to be a good man, but I'll be no trouble to you, and I can pay you for supper and bed." In fact I had three months' pay, most of it stuffed down my shirt to pose less temptation to thieves. "Will that satisfy your lady?"

"It should," Mister Smith said, with a sheepish sort of shuffle that would have looked more at home on a boy than a big man with biceps like hams. "You understand, she's a particular sort of woman." He seemed to notice for the first time that his dogs were circling me suspiciously, as if waiting for the cue to set their teeth into an intruder. "Get by, dogs, we've a guest tonight."

He led me into a kitchen where a warm fire was glowing and went aside to speak with the presumed mistress of the house, a young wife but hardly a merry one, her dun hair matching her dun dress so that she looked faded, as if washed too many times. I was beginning to get some feeling back into my feet when she came over with bread and salt fish.

"That ought to do for a sailor," she said, and I nodded polite thanks, though in truth I'd eaten enough fish while at sea that I'd have preferred the toughest fowl or most dubious of hams. "If you'd come a week ago, we'd have had nothing for you but pork."

"Too bad," I said, and tried not to think about crisp bacon.

At that moment, a dull music split the air, the heavy tolling of a steeple-bell. It rang twice, paused, rang twice again, and then began a doleful series of strokes. It was the death knell, and I put on my most solemn face, thinking how awkward it was to be a stranger in a small town at such a time. "Who do you suppose has died?"

"I expect no one yet," Mister Smith said. His wife said nothing, only stood with her mouth pressed tight together, listening to the tolling bell. In a small town such as this, I could well believe they kept up the old custom of ringing the bell as soon as the parson heard news of a death, but to ring it before the death seemed perverse.

"Surely there aren't any hangings here," I said. A condemned prisoner was the only sort of man I could think of whose death might be predicted with certainty beforehand. "I suppose if someone's lying deathly ill …"

"We'll know by morning," Mister Smith said. "The bell never lies, you see—" He broke off abruptly as the bell finally came to the end of its dull refrain and seemed at a loss for how to go on.

"Twenty-six," Mistress Smith said, and when I turned at her tone I saw that her face had turned gray with some strong emotion I didn't understand. "Nine strokes to tell a man, and twenty-six to tell his age. Don't tell me I miscounted."

"I'm sure you didn't," the smith said. He twisted the leather of his apron in his hands, looking from one of us to the other. "It might be best if you found your bed now."

"The hour is growing late," I said, because I misliked his wife's expression, and had developed aboard ship a keen sense of how the wind was blowing.

The man picked up a lantern and led me back out into the chill dooryard. The ladder up to the loft above the forge was rickety, and he held the lantern to light my way. "You mustn't mind my wife," he said. "Our troubles here are nothing to do with you."

Well, only the most incurious of born lubbers could have refrained from asking the question after that. "What did she mean about the bell?"

"There's somewhat wrong with our church bell," Smith said. "The parson rings it in the ordinary way after every death in the town, but you can hear it all through town the night before."

It took me a moment to parse that. "You mean the bell rings before someone dies?"

"The bell sounds before someone dies, but the parson doesn't ring it until after. It's been that way as long as anyone in town can remember. You mustn't think we're entirely ungrateful; when it tolls for your old uncle, you can go round and see him beforehand and say your farewells, you see? But it's hard when it tolls for a child, or a man in his prime with little chance of passing away peacefully in his bed."

The light from the lantern shifted, as if his hand were less than steady on its handle. Outside its circle of light, black branches bent against a dark sky that was beginning to spit frigid rain. "This wouldn't be a tale spun to frighten travelers, would it?" I asked. "For I've heard them all in my time."

"I swear it's the plain truth," Smith said. "And it's a bad night for traveling, but I'll understand if you'd rather be on your way." He paused a moment and then added, "It might be for the best. You heard what the bell told."

"I'm willing to take the chance," I said. "I've heard more frightening stories than this."

"It's no more than the truth," the man said, but with resignation, as if he were used to skepticism from strangers. He hung up the lantern, and turned abruptly to go. "Your horse is shod and I've got your coins for the night's lodging, so I expect

we're square, and there's no more that needs to be said." He
tramped out, leaving me to ascend the ladder in no mood to settle
down easily to sleep.

I shivered for a while under the thin horse blanket spread over
an equally thin pallet, and then realized that the forge and the
kitchen of the house shared a common chimney that went up the
opposite wall. I made my way over to it, hoping to warm my
hands at least, and I heard the mutter of voices through the wall.
After a bare moment's hesitation, I pressed my ear unashamed to
the stones, having long profited from such caution.

"Give me the hatchet," I heard Mistress Smith say, and was
abruptly glad I hadn't balked at eavesdropping.

"You don't need the hatchet," Mister Smith said. "I mean to
leave it in the good Lord's hands."

"You mean you don't mean to lift a hand yourself to save
your life, when it's you or that stranger who'll die tonight. Well,
you needn't get your hands dirty if you scruple to it. Just you give
me the hatchet, and tell anyone who asks that you slept sound."

"And what do you mean to say, when the town watch comes
knocking?"

"Old Bill? I'll tell him that I woke at a noise in the courtyard,
and came out to see men running away. He'll set up a hue and cry
that will take the rest of the night. You'll see." There was a
feverish certainty to her voice. "All you need do is leave it all to
me."

"I won't have it, I tell you."

"I don't care what you will and won't have. You're not much
of a man, it seems, but you're my man, and I don't mean to
wager your life on the toss of a coin. Give me the hatchet, and
don't you set foot outside until I come back."

I had only a few moments to escape. I had a knife, which I
took up now, and the cover of darkness on my side. For all that,
my heart was pounding in my chest; I've never been a brawler,
nor been much in the habit of fighting with women. I made for
the ladder, but before I reached it I heard the sound of footsteps
below.

"Do you lie comfortably?" Mistress Smith's voice rose up.

I thought of feigning snores, but lacked confidence in my

own dramatic skills. "Quite comfortably," I called back down. "I've everything a man could want."

"I thought I'd bring you a hot drink," she said. "A bit of a toddy to take the chill from the air. Do come down and drink it before it gets cold."

"It's very kind," I said, putting my back to the loft wall and hoping that a swung hatchet wouldn't go through it. "But I never touch the demon drink, not since I got religion."

"A sailor who's an abstainer?" she said. "I never heard of such."

"It's true all the same," I said. "It pleases my girl, you understand."

"I've a blanket for you at least," she said. "And you can come in with me and fetch a cup of hot milk."

"Thank you kindly, but I'll lodge where I am." I held my breath, and heard the ladder creak as she put her foot on it. It creaked twice more, and then her head and shoulders appeared framed in the doorway and light glinted off the hatchet blade.

I kicked her square in the bosom, though I'm not proud to say it, and knocked her and the ladder both down from the loft. I swung down after her, seeing her sprawled in the straw, unhurt but struggling to rise, and went for the hatchet.

She grasped it as well, her hands clawing at mine, raking them with her fingernails.

"Will you give over!" I tried to shoulder her away. "You're wrong in what you think. I'm no man of twenty-six."

"You claim now you were lying?" Her face was close enough to mine as we struggled that I could smell her breath. "There's a strange habit, for a man to tell lies about his age to everyone he meets."

Her grip on the hatchet loosened as she spoke, and I tightened my own. "So it would be," I said. "But I'm no man, and that was the lie I told. That and the bit about the drink, which I admit is a besetting vice. I put on breeches to go to sea, but I'm a woman all the same underneath them, and never more glad of it than today." I forebore to add that my girl was glad of it too, as I felt under the circumstances it would be taken as cheek.

She laughed in my face. "That's a nasty lie to save your

skin."

"I'll prove it if you like," I said. "If you'll give over your attempt to chop me up for firewood long enough."

At that moment, her husband came in, and I shoved her toward him, hoping that he'd catch the hatchet out of her hands. He plucked it away from her with his left hand and tossed it aside, but as he let her go I saw that he had a cleaver in his right hand. I saw the bulging of his shoulders and thought I must know what a chicken felt like at butchering time.

"It came on me that it was wrong to leave the missus to do what must be done," he said.

"I'll swear any oath you like, my mother named me Kate," I said, and reached for the top button of my shirt.

"A wicked wench who'll dress up as a man can't complain if she's buried as one," the woman said, and I saw a look pass between her and her husband that made my heart sink. "What the parson doesn't know won't hurt him."

"I'm sorry to have to do it," Mister Smith told me, but he was lifting the cleaver, and I turned tail and ran.

I heard the clamor of dogs barking behind me, and rethought in a hurry my initial plan to make for the road out of town. I looked about for a tree to climb, and saw none. There was a stone wall at the end of the lane, though, and I went pelting toward it with what sounded like a whole Bedlam of dogs baying at my heels.

They leapt snarling as I scrambled up the wall, but any sailor, lad or lass, can climb like a monkey, and I reached the top of the wall and dropped down on the other side. I was in a little churchyard, but before I could slip away over the wall on the other side, the parson came out to see what was the matter with the dogs, who were still howling in a perfect fury. Though he wore spectacles balanced on his narrow nose, he also had a heavy stick in his hand and looked as if he were willing to use it.

"The blacksmith set his dogs on me," I blurted out. "I swear to you I'm no thief."

The parson didn't loosen his grip on the stick. "I don't believe Mister Smith is in the habit of setting his dogs on innocent strangers."

"It's on account of the bell, the passing bell," I said, and couldn't help looking up at the tower that threw its shadow over us both. The bell tower was just a rickety little thing by the measure of city churches, but the pool of gloom it cast over the churchyard seemed heavy and dark. "His wife put him up to it, for she thinks it's either him or me who'll die tonight."

The parson came forward a little, then, and looked me up and down through his spectacles. "I never knew the blacksmith's age," he said, as if speaking as much to himself as to me. "I try not to know, you see. But in a town so small, it's hard not to be aware …" He shook his head, and there was something closed in his expression. "I think I had better see you out the gate," he said.

"The dogs are still out there," I pointed out.

"That's really not my concern."

"And you a parson."

"I can't stop what's to come," he said. "You must understand that, you must see. I've tried, sometimes, when I knew. There was a girl, a child of thirteen … I sat up with her all night, in the church, and we prayed together. She wept, and I told her to have faith, that the Lord would protect her. And an hour before morning her fear overcame her, and she rose to flee. I caught hold of her, I demanded she stay, I promised she would be safe. I struggled with her. And she fell, and her head struck the altar steps. And God was silent."

He reached out and caught hold of my collar to march me toward the gates. My hand rested on my knife, and then I took it away again, not sure if I could bring myself to stab a man of the cloth, even to make my escape.

"I don't see why you can't just resolve not to ring the bell anymore," I said. "If you don't ring it in the morning …"

"I did not ring it that night," he said, still marching me along, as if by thrusting me out the gates he could banish the memory. "I sat on the altar steps in misery, and at the first light, I heard the bell tolling. It was little Johnnie Boots, the choirboy, who had taken it into his head to ring the bell for me as a kindness, since, as he said, I must have been taken ill."

He paused before the high wooden gate, and outside I heard an eager chorus of barks, and then the even more ominous growling of dogs who see their aim in sight. "There are some who have called for us to take down the bell," he said. I silently cheered on "some," whoever they might be. "But it is the Lord who put this curse on us, and when he judges us free of sin, he will take it away again. When we have been made clean." His knuckles were white on his stick, and his eyes were on the horizon, as if he saw some horror there I couldn't see. "I have prayed, but of course my sinner's prayers have not been answered," he said. "Pray now, and perhaps yours will be heard as mine have not been."

I put my hands together, although I had done precious little praying of any kind since I'd taken up my present life. It sat badly with me to beg for my life anyway, like a craven captain pleading for quarter on his knees. *Dear Lord, I've been a wicked woman but a good seaman*, I said silently. *You've winked at my deceit, and let me live when better men have died. If you care for wicked women, as I've heard you did in life, show me one more trick to save my skin.*

The parson was reaching for the gate, and I blurted out, "A moment more!"

"You've had time for your prayers."

"A moment to wish my girl goodbye," I said, and drew out the locket I carried. It was a little tin thing with a half-penny sketch inside, but the boy who drew it had caught Minnie's laughing eyes, and it was worth a fortune in gold to me. She'd scolded me for going back to the sea, though it was my wages that kept her all the time I was away, and told me at some length that if I drowned she wouldn't have a single prayer said for my worthless wayward soul.

"You've had that as well," the parson said, and reached for the latch on the gate. I reached again for my knife, wondering if I could stick him without hurting him too much, and what the townsmen would do to me if they caught me after that. Being hanged for stabbing a parson seemed even worse than being hacked apart for nothing.

And then I had it, all at once, like a breath of wind snapping open a slack sail. "One thing more!" I demanded. "I had a traveling companion on the road, another sailor who took ill and died by the wayside. I buried him as best I could, but I'd be easier in my mind if the passing bell were rung for him. His name was Tom, and I know his age as well, for he told me at the end he was born twenty-six years ago to the day."

The parson stood staring at me for a long moment. "Do you expect me for one moment to believe such a story?"

"Is it any of your business to doubt it?" I asked, and reached into my coat to draw out my purse. "If I had come to you a week ago, would you have questioned whether there was a man named Tom or a roadside grave?"

"I would not," he admitted. I held out my purse to him, and while I'd like to believe he took it in pure gratitude for the escape I offered him, I can't say that its weight didn't figure in his decision as well.

"Then go on and ring the passing bell for poor old Tom," I said. "For I think I have worn out my welcome in this town, or at least it has worn out its welcome with me, and I am eager to be on the road again."

I followed him to the foot of the tower stairs, and watched him ascend. I waited until the sound of his steps told me he had gone a full turn of the stairs, and then started up after him, keeping my own steps quiet.

Even after everything that had happened, I was not entirely prepared for what I saw when I mounted to the bell tower; the parson was heaving on the bell-rope, his back to me, and the bell was heaving as well, the clapper slamming into its sides hard enough that I could see its tremor, but no sound came from the bell, no sound at all. The only sound was the wind, keening through the wide openings on all sides of the tower like a crying dog.

I waited, breath held, until the bell made its final swing and the parson released the bellrope. I scrambled around him, evading his surprised attempt to catch me back, and clambered up onto the beams that held the bell in place. The bell was an old one, and held only by thick ropes, not by a heavy chain; it was the work of a moment to hack the stiff ropes in two.

There was a clamor like brazen hounds baying in hell as the bell came crashing down. It tumbled out the open side of the bell tower, clattering for a moment on its edge and then plunging toward the earth.

"They do say the Lord helps those as help themselves," I said, jumping down. The parson crossed himself and backed away from me.

"There's some devil in you, and I'm not sure whether to try to cast it out or thank you for what you've done," he said.

"Call it payment for all the hospitality I've had in this town," I said. "But now I must be away." I took off down the stairs at a run, and plunged out into the open air.

I stopped short when I saw the bell lying fallen on the churchyard stones. It was cracked and split, crumpled like the body of Mister Smith, who lay fallen beneath it, with his dogs circling round him, cringing now and whimpering.

The parson came out after me, and made the sign of the cross over the dead blacksmith in silence. "He was a good man," he said after a while.

"I expect he was," I said.

"You mustn't blame yourself."

"Nor will I," I said, for it seemed the blacksmith had been doomed from the time the bell first sounded, and at least now the bell had rung its last. "But can I have my purse back, then? I expect I can find a man to ring the passing bell for my old mate Tom somewhere considerably nearer home."

The parson gave me a look as he handed it over that I suppose I well deserved, but what can I say? I've never claimed to be a good man, but I am Minnie's best girl, and she'd been waiting patiently for me to bring her home my pay, and to come back to her safely from the sea.

DESTINATION AHEAD
by Laura Anne Gilman

We'd been driving nearly ten hours, two dogs and a kid asleep in the back seat, when I realized the GPS was lying.

"Babe?" I kept my voice even, controlled: no need for alarm and for god's sake don't take this as a personal accusation, but...

There was a sigh, and then, "Yeah, I know." I heard a click and a rustle: the sound of a map being pulled from the glove compartment. God only knew how old that map was, it had probably migrated over from the old car with all our other junk. But even an out-of-date map would still have highways and byways on it; maybe ones that the GPS hadn't been programmed with. Cartographers are more careful than programmers.

"Huh. We should have turned left back there." Jack waved a vague hand that could have meant back there at the last tree, or back there an hour ago.

I glanced at the GPS, still showing a blithe green line going forward, then looked back at the road. The disturbingly empty, unfamiliar road. Damn it. Jack's mom had moved to a new house a few months ago and this was our first chance to visit, but despite punching the new address in the moment we pulled out of our driveway, this didn't look right.

Mom wasn't the most social of creatures, but she wasn't the sort to live out in the middle of nowhere Pennsyltucky. And she'd have mentioned it if she'd made such a drastic change, right?

I tried to remember when I'd last seen something familiar. We'd stopped at a gas station to let the dogs do their thing, and I'd managed not to bitch at Jack for something, I didn't even remember what, just that I'd had to bite my tongue to keep from saying something to him. But that had been nearly half an hour ago. How had we gone from strip mall gas station to this utter emptiness in half an hour? The GPS had claimed that there was a shorter route that would avoid traffic, so we'd gotten off at that exit and stayed on the county road, rather than getting back on the highway, but even a county road should have something along it, right? We hadn't been living in the city that long...

"Want me to call, tell her we're running late?"

"Yeah, probably. Who knows how long this'll take to sort out."

He pulled his phone from the charger, swiping the screen awake. "And perfect, no signal." Jack sighed. "At least the pack's still asleep."

A glance into the rear view mirror showed me two dachshund and an eight-year-old, curled up and using each other as pillows. Letting them run around in the back yard until nearly midnight last night had been a stroke of genius. Keep them up, wear them out, and wake 'em up early: the secret to a peaceful road trip.

The female voice I was starting to hate informed us: "In one mile, turn left."

There was a rustle of the paper map, folding and unfolding, and Jack sighed again. I felt my muscles tense, and forced them to relax. He wasn't doing it to irritate me; that was just how he was. I knew that. "There's no left exit or veer on this map for like ten miles," he said. "Your GPS is cracked."

"Now it's my GPS?" I shouldn't have said that—we tried not to fight, not even play-fight—in front of the kid. "So what do you suggest, oh navigator?"

"Finding another gas station and asking them."

"You realize that might get you kicked out of the husbands club?"

"I'll risk it."

"Only problem with that is, I don't see a gas station anywhere. We haven't even seen an exit sign in miles." We hadn't seen any signs, actually. I guess out here, they figured you knew where you were and where you were going? "Should I ask the lady in the box?"

"Yeah, 'cause I'm sure her directions will be so much better finding a gas station versus finding my mom's place. Sondra, where is the nearest gas station?"

There was a pause, then the GPS's generated voice came back: "Calculating… "

Then nothing.

"Sondra? Nearest gas station?"

"No gas station within calculating distance."

Jack folded the map with irritating sloppiness. "Oh that's just great. Nobody out here needs gas? They all have electric cars? Where did my mom end up, planet of the incredibly wealthy senior citizens?"

"If she did, we need to renegotiate that prenup."

"Hah. In your dreams. I just—"

Whatever Jack was going to say was lost when the suspension suddenly burped, and the wheels rattled off pavement and onto what sounded—and felt—like gravel. I gripped the steering wheel and blinked at the road ahead of us, which had suddenly lost its reassuring high-speed-friendly asphalt. "The hell?"

"Dads?" The munchkin was awake. "Are we lost?"

Again? hung heavy in the air, even if the munchkin didn't say it. Our kid was way too perceptive for our own good.

"Nope," Jack said immediately. "Your dad's taking us on a long-way-around shortcut."

Again, again hung in the air, loudly unspoken.

"You two can get out and walk, if you'd like," I offered. "Me and the dogs will be just fine without you."

Maxine shot me a grin, so much like Jack's it still made my heart squeeze to see it. "Walking, we'll probably get there first."

There isn't much sass like an eight-year-old's sass.

The GPS decided that was a good moment to interrupt. "Turn left in one hundred yards."

"Idiot voice, there isn't… " Except there was, a dirt road appearing to the left a hundred yards ahead that I'd have sworn wasn't there before. I'd've sworn the entire road was paved a few minutes before, too, though, and we were clearly on gravel now.

"Mom did say the house was part of an estate built on an old farm," Jack said slowly. "Maybe this is a back entrance?"

"I don't think this is such a good idea," I said, letting the car idle just before the turn. There was nobody else visible on the road, but I kept my attention split between the rear view mirror and the road ahead, just in case.

"If we go back to where the gas station was, we're going to add at least an hour's travel time." We'd already been in the car too long for everyone's comfort. "Afraid your car can't handle a dirt road?"

"You really want to get stuck out here with a broken axle?" I shot Jack a sideways glance that wasn't quite a glare.

"I don't want to get stuck out here at all." There was just a wedge of ice in the words, layered out of kidshot, a fight just waiting to break out. I drummed my fingers on the wheel, then hit the gas, bypassing the first road to stay on the equally unfamiliar but at least partially paved main road.

"Recalculating." I was really starting to hate whoever they'd modeled that voice on.

Maxine leaned forward, her arms resting on the back of my seat. Next to her, the dogs shifted in their sleep.

"Max, sit back, put your seatbelt back on." Jack was using his dad-voice, the one he brought out when he thought I was too wound-up to be allowed to say anything.

"Daaaad."

"Now, Maxine," I added.

I loved my husband. And my kid. And even the dogs. I was less fond of them all together, after too many hours in the car. I felt no shame in admitting that. I just kept it between my teeth, and dealt with the ulcers after the fact.

Sondra told us, "Go five hundred yards and turn left."

"What drugs are you on, machine?" I muttered, then glanced at the display, then down the road again. "Seriously?"

Jack glanced at me, then at my hands. I consciously eased them off the wheel a little, wincing as they uncramped. "It wants us to go left. Maybe we should go left?"

"Maybe you should let me do the driving?" I sniped before I could stop myself.

"Maybe you should have taken a better dump before we left the house?"

I could tell Jack regretted the words the minute they left his

mouth. We'd sworn to always call each other on bad behavior—
it'd been part of our wedding vows, for Christ's sake. But all it
had taken was Maxine bursting into tears after one of our fights,
and we'd agreed to clamp down on the blunt speaking.

I exhaled, a tight whistling noise. "Fine. I'll take a left, right
by the ... are those goats?"

A small herd of goats, in fact. Grazing on the verge next to
the road, a few of them lifting their heads to look curiously as the
car pulled up, then—as though someone'd thrown a switch—then
turned and ran off, hooves kicking up clods of dirt in their wake.

"You'd think they'd never seen a car before."

"This far out in the middle of nowhere, maybe they haven't."
I glanced back, but Maxine was occupied with her tablet, the
dogs curled on either side of her. Good. The last thing we needed
was a meltdown over why hadn't the goats stayed and why
couldn't she pet them.

The road was dirt, but it felt like it was pretty smooth: no
worries about the car's alignment . I stared out the window,
hoping to see some sign of civilization. At this point, even a
grungy gas station would be a welcome oasis.

"Jack."

"Hmmm?"

"Is that what I think it is?"

Sondra's voice confirmed it: "Destination ahead."

Jack let out a "poh" sound, the way he started doing after
Max was born and he stopped swearing out loud. "That's not my
mom's house."

Except it was, kind of. The lines of the building, the massive
stones set in the corners, even the slant of the roof were similar to
the photos she'd sent us. But his mom had spent a fortune
replacing the slate roof when she bought it, as well as the
windows. The windows in this building were ... ancient was too
kind a word for them. And ...

"There are goats outside," Jack said.

Goats, and a cow. Not right up next to the house, but closer
than his mom would ever allow anything not a cat to get near her.

"Cool!" Max had heard us, and was bouncing on her seat, and
therefore so were the dogs, awake now and leaping up to slobber

all over the windows.

"Don't let the dogs out," Jack said sternly, as I pulled to the side of the road and cut the engine. "Whoever animals these are, they're not going to appreciate Mutt and Jeff chasing after them."

Max slumped back into the seat. "Where are we?"

The GPS answered her. "You have arrived at your destination."

I shook my head. "The hell we have."

As though in response, the GPS blinked, then displayed the "lost signal" icon, and went blank.

Before Max could demand I put a quarter in the swear jar, someone came out of the building, shooing the goats away. They scattered, leaping into the air like they had springs on their heels, and the woman—it was a woman, tall and broad at the shoulder, wearing a long skirt and a shawl over her arms—turned, as though suddenly realizing we were there—

And screamed and ran back into the building.

"The fuck?" I joked about the car being an eco-monstrosity, but it hadn't ever gotten that kind of reaction before.

"Seriously," Jack said. "What the hell?"

"Dads!" The two of us together was too much for Max to ignore, goats or no. "Quarter in the jar!"

"When we get home," Jack said. Then, lower voiced, "If we ever get home."

I couldn't deal with him right now, not him and the kid, and the dogs, and… "Maybe they'll know how to get back to the main road, assuming I can peel our hostess off whatever ceiling she's flipped onto. Stay here."

I got out of the car, shutting off a one-sided discussion from the munchkin on if the goats would like dogs or not, and eyed the house dubiously. It didn't look like it was going to fall down any time soon, but it sure as hell hadn't been modernized anytime in this century. An impressive garden sprawled out on the other side of the lot, filled with a bunch of green leafy things I couldn't recognize. And, other than an equally ramshackle barn-like building further off, there wasn't anything else in sight.

"If this is a prank, I'm going to skin someone alive and wear them as a raincoat." It was a good threat, but I couldn't think of anyone who could have pulled this off. Rewiring the GPS, sure. Between the two of us we know a dozen people who not only could do it, but would, and there were another handful of people who'd know someone who could do it for them. But the rest of it? It would take Koch-level money to screw with the landscape like this—removing the buildings, adding goats?

"We were in a car crash. I'm in ICU, having one seriously whackadoodle surgery-dream." I reached the door, studying the sturdy, weathered wood that looked even worse up-close.

The sound of the car's horn jolted me, and I waved a hand back at the car to tell them to keep their damn pants on, then knocked three times on the door, trying to be both authoritative and unthreatening.

There was a sound from inside the house, but the door didn't open. So much for country hospitality.

"Oh come on, all I want to do is get directions! I'm stepping away from the door, okay? I'm not a threat, I'm just lost."

Silence, and then the sound of someone on the other side of the door. But I wasn't expecting to have to look down when the door finally slid open a hand-span. Looking back at me was a kid, maybe ten, sure as hell not eleven. Pale blond hair, wide blue eyes: he looked like he should be auditioning for a role as some stereotyped cherub, not staring at me like I was a monster come to eat him.

"What do you want?" He was trying to sound tough, but it didn't quite come across, considering his voice hadn't broken yet.

"Directions, kid. That's all. We're trying to get to my mother-in-law's, and we're lost." No need to say mom's house looked a lot like this one; odds were back then they were building a bunch the same, like all the cookie-cutter duplexes back in the Fifties. This one clearly hadn't gotten any updating: they were probably poor as dirt. I had a couple of twenties in my wallet, that'd be more than fair payment for directions back to civilization.

Wide blue eyes narrowed suspiciously. "There're none of your kind here."

My kind? Oh, great. "Look, kid, just tell me how to get back to the highway, and I'll be out of your hair." I didn't know if sending Jack over to deal with him would make things better or worse. If the kid'd been raised a racist, odds were he was a homophobe too, no matter how whitebread Jack was.

Blue-eyes scowled at me, but I was pretty good at reading kid, and I didn't think it was anger or fear or even hatred. More … puzzlement. Like I'd said something that confused him.

He wasn't the only one confused. Landscapes that made no sense, a look-alike house that was a hundred years past-due on an update, dirt roads where there should be a highway, GPS systems that went haywire and then crapped out and not a single sign of civilization anywhere. If I were a paranoid person, or the kind to get fanciful, I'd swear …

Oh.

No.

I was pretty sure I stopped breathing there for a minute, and I probably looked a proper lunatic, standing there with my foot in the door so the boy didn't close it on me, my hand on the doorframe and my jaw doing a fair impersonation of, well, a slack-jawed idiot. If so, the kid didn't call me on it, just stood there like he was waiting for me to turn around and go away.

Jack calls me stubborn, but I prefer to think of it as logic-driven. If the evidence says X, then X is probably the answer, however much current science refutes the possibility.

"Son," and he didn't even blink at me calling him that, no matter how much he might not want "'my kind'" standing in his doorway. "Son, what year is this?"

oOo

Max was still talking, but I tuned her out. Something was wrong. I could see it in Shan's stance, the way he leaned in, then leaned back. Whoever he was talking to was blocked by the door, but they clearly weren't friendly, or were giving him shit about something.

Shit. I should have gone, not him. Shan's got a chip on his shoulder, not huge, but sometimes he pisses people off without realizing it. Not that I'm any model of diplomacy, but …

"What's wrong with dad?"

"Nothing. You know he hates asking for directions, that's

all."

Max snorted, a wet, sarcastic sound she'd totally inherited from me. "So do you. We get lost all the time."

Truth. That was why we'd—I'd—bought the damn GPS in the first place, much good it had done us.

One of the dogs whined, and a quick look over the back seat showed that all three of them were getting antsy. Just what we needed. "Can you take them for a quick walk? Not too far, stay near the car. And stay away from the goats."

The dogs were energetic, but low enough to the ground that the kidlet could handle them, and even if they ran away, there weren't any other cars in the area to worry about. Just goats and a cow. Did cows kick? The only thing I knew about cows was that they produced milk.

I looked back at Shan to see a young boy now standing in the doorway, and my husband stalking back to the car with an expression on his face I'd never seen, and couldn't read.

He was coming to my side of the car, so I rolled down the window. "What's up?"

"Jack-o. I don't think we're in Kansas anymore."

"We're in Pennsylvania." My logic was wasted on him. His eyes were a little too wide and his hands, where they rested on the sill, were shaking slightly. "Shan, what's going on? What did that kid say to you?"

"It's 1849."

"What?" I hadn't heard him right. Or something. "You just said—"

"It's 1849, yeah. That's what the kid says. And he's seriously wigged out by me, and the car—that's why the woman ran, they have no fucking clue what it is."

I shook my head. "Are you listening to yourself? That's—"

"Check your phone."

"What?" But I reached down to grab my cell phone. I didn't expect it to have signal, and it didn't. I held it up as though to say "And … ?" when I realized it wasn't telling me it didn't have a signal—the display was dead. Completely. Even though I'd just finished charging it.

"Mine too." He touched his pocket. "Not like we don't have

signal, like there's no signal anywhere to get."

Was he fucking with me? Was this a prank? If so it wasn't funny … but no. I remembered the way he'd been, driving here, the escalating irritation and frustration. He wasn't that good an actor. He wasn't a good actor at all. He was freaked out, and dangerously close to losing his cool.

"You're trying to tell me that, according to that kid," and I lifted my chin in the direction of the house, "we took a left turn at Albuquerque and ended up over a hundred years in the past?"

The Bugs Bunny reference was enough. Shan's faint uptick of a grin mellowed the slightly panicked look still in his eyes. "Hope to hell you got a warranty on that GPS, lover, because it's seriously borked."

oOo

I took more convincing than Shan, but no matter how I poked around, I couldn't find any way to convince myself this was a prank.

The sullen-eyed kid was named Elias, and his mother was Mercy, a misnomer if ever there'd been one. She wanted nothing to do with any of us, or the car, no matter how often her son tried to get closer to sneak a peek. She kept yanking him back by the collar of his shirt. And they insisted that the year was 1849. June 11th 1849. The same day it had been that morning, just nearly two hundred years ago.

I tried to remember local history from that time, and came up blank, but one thing that was obvious was that homosexual couples—especially mixed race homosexual couples with a kid—weren't on the "happy to see you" list.

It was Max who wore mother Mercy down, or at least softened her to less than stone. Me she gave side-eyes to, which might or might not have been a step up from the way she ignored Shan entirely, like the color of his skin might rub off on her. But Max did the trick.

"God wouldn't forgive me if I turned away a child in need," she said, square and stern with the bulk of her house to protect her, arms crossed over her apron and a squint-eyed frown on her face, "but you stay away from me and mine."

"Lady, with pleasure," I muttered, turning on my heel to stalk back to the car. I'd rather sleep outside with the goats than under a roof with a bitch like her. I'd throw everyone back in the car and drive off, if I could see anywhere to drive too. Grass, a couple of plowed fields, and trees in the distance, that was about it. Philadelphia was just a few hours' drive away, but our phones, tablets, car—not a single one of them was showing an erg of power.

We were stuck. And if it really *was* 1849 ...

Shan, the map spread out on the hood of the car, had come to the same conclusion: this was our destination, for now.

Max had the dogs on the leash, keeping them away from the small herd of goats, and Elias was inching closer, clearly wanting to pet them but afraid of what his mother might say if she saw him. My stomach rumbled unpleasantly, reminding me of the dinner we weren't getting at my mother's house, and making me wonder about what kind of meal we could expect from Mother Mercy.

"Oh god," I said, my eyes going wide. "Coffee. Do you think she'll make us coffee?"

Shan looked up from the map then. "That's what's freaking you out about all of this? Seriously?"

"No. Fuck no. But it's the only thing I can wrap my brain around right now, okay?"

We paused a moment, ready to butt heads for lack of anything else to do, until the sound of Max's laugh reached us both, forcing us to relax. Not in front of the kid, don't lose your cool in front of the kid: our mantra for too long for even this to break it.

Shan folded the map and put it back in the glove compartment and we spent the next few hours trying to keep Max and the dogs occupied, making it into as much of an adventure-game as we could. Later on, as dusk was falling, Elias brought us out a simple dinner—a thick, pea-laden soup and dark bread—and then came back with a few rough blankets and a rolled-up tarp, dropping them and then backing off again. He wouldn't meet our eyes, but he couldn't stop staring at the car.

Well, that made sense. Two strangers, one of them with dark

skin, was excitement of a normal sort. A car—never mind it was a dirt-common Toyota—was something else entirely.

"How does your vehicle move?" Elias might be a racist prat-in-training, but he was still a kid, with a kid's curiosity. But trying to explain an internal combustion engine to someone with no understanding of … well, anything, was beyond both of us. I reached down to scratch my leg where something had bitten me, and sifted my brain, trying to find something that would work.

"You ever see a water wheel?" Shan, keeping a safe distance from the kid so that Mother Mercy wouldn't come out swinging a rolling pin, made a gesture with his hands that was probably supposed to be the movement of a wheel. "Like a mill would use?"

Elias nodded.

"We have something similar to that inside the … the vehicle. The wheel turns, and that makes the outer wheels turn."

As explanations went, it wasn't too bad a handwave. So long as Elias didn't ask how we got water to flow inside the car... We were all three running on blank-eyed acceptance of the shit we couldn't deny, at this point, I guessed. Elias was either going to grow up the most open-minded futurist of his century, or he was going to convince himself it was all a delusion when we finally went home.

Assuming we got home.

On that thought, I picked up the blankets and gave our offspring a gentle nudge with my foot. "Maxine! Help me find a place to set up camp, okay?"

We'd better get settled before night fell. I had the feeling it got pretty damn dark out here.

oOo

Jack and the kidlet took to sleeping in the rough like it was the best thing ever. Neither of them had been scouts—well, Jack hadn't, and kidlet was too young yet. But I had horrible memories of rain-sogged sleeping bags and having to pee in the woods, and none of it had left camping with any romantic glow. Camping out under an oilskin tarp, rolled in scratchy wool blankets that smelled of goat, wasn't creating any, either.

To be fair, pretty much everything smelled of goat. And after a while, it wasn't that bad.

After forty-eight hours of that crap, I would have killed someone for a hot shower and a safety razor, though.

"Maybe if we—"

"Just … stop, all right?" I put a hand up, feeling the tension shiver in my body like a physical pain. "We don't know anything, so anything we suggest is just … crap." We'd spent the past two days trying to hammer out some way to get home, exploring on foot as far as we could, hoping to find … I don't know, a signpost or a portal or a magical wardrobe. Nothing except grass and goats, and a woman who ignored us when she had to be outside, yanking her son out of our reach whenever we started talking.

I just couldn't do it anymore. The tension was going to snap soon, and I knew what happened then. I wasn't going to start yelling. I wasn't going to let Jack start yelling. We weren't going to do that to Max.

"So what, accept that we're stuck here, make the best of it?"

"Maybe." I felt the urge to shrug and—knowing it would just set Jack off again—repressed it, staring out across the grassy expanse.

"You're giving up?"

"I'm not giving up." I could feel my control stretching and snapping; why did Jack always have to *push*?

"Don't turn away from me, Shan, damn it—"

"Dads?" Max ran up to us, her hair a mess and a grin a mile wide on her face. "Dads, Elias said there's goats being born but we have to go over the hill. Can I go? Can I?"

I looked at Elias, who was standing off to the side, slightly diffident, his hands shoved into his pockets, the dogs seated at his heels. The poor kid was just lonely as hell out here, without anyone his own age to play with.

I waited, but for once, Jack didn't seem to have an opinion on the subject. Or he was biting his own cheek trying not to let the argument continue while Max was standing there.

"Yeah, all right." The kid'd been good, accepting this as

some unexpected adventure, trusting us to figure things out. How much trouble could they get into, going over the hill? And Max had already seen puppies being born, so it wasn't like Elias would be exposing her to something new, without appropriate parental supervision …

Or we were going to parenting hell. Shit.

Max looked at me, then past my hip at where I presumed Jack was still standing. "You come with?"

I knew that voice. She knew we were fighting, even though we hadn't raised our voices. She'd come over here not to get permission, but to interrupt us. Shit.

"You go on," Jack said, his voice tight. "It's okay, Max."

Max's face scrunched up, like she was going to argue, or cry.

About two years ago, we realized that our arguments had been stressing her out, so we'd stopped, cold turkey. Except, I was starting to figure out, our not-fighting was stressing her out, too.

"Ah, hell," I said, forcing the air out of my lungs so I didn't say the other things that had been building there. "Jack, you ever see goats being born?"

His chin rested on my shoulder, just sharp enough to dig, his breath warm on my ear. "You know she's going to want to bring one home," he said, but there was laughter in the words now, not just anger, and I thought a goat kid might not be such a price to pay, for that.

oOo

Shan was curled on his side, a frown creasing his forehead, his breathing slow and steady, and I studied my husband with a sense of odd wonder. Despite the hard ground underneath us, he hadn't slept so peacefully in the past six years. I was tempted to cuddle in closer, but the pressure in my bladder reminded me that I had to walk a distance to the outhouse, rather than a few paces into the master bathroom.

The memory of that bathroom, with hot water on demand and towels that didn't scrape the skin off, and … god, what I wouldn't do for central heat and water pressure and a fully stocked fridge. And a takeout menu. I may or may not have had a wet dream about pizza last night. Although I didn't think I was ever going to eat goat curry again. Not with the memory of tiny little goatlings—kids—in Max's arms, still damp from the afterbirth their mother had groomed off them, already full of squirm and bounce.

"All right," I told the squirrel staring at me from a nearby rock. "So maybe this hasn't been *entirely* a horrible no good very bad experience."

I rolled out from under the blanket, leaving Shan curling more tightly into the warmth, and noticed that Max was awake, sitting quietly on a rock with the dogs flanking her, tiny curled tails wagging slightly, the three of them watching the first glimmers of daylight peeking over the trees. When had Max gotten old enough to wake up before dawn, to take care of the dogs without reminding, to need time by herself? Where had the warm bundle I'd held in my arms, newborn and helpless, gone to?

I went off to do my business, and came back to sit with her, the morning dew soaking through my jeans. I'd gone three days straight without a shower, and I felt disgusting, but at the same time, sitting next to my daughter, watching the sun rise over an empty field, there was also a strange nub of ... not contentment, exactly. Calm. That was what I was feeling.

It had been so long, I almost didn't recognize it.

"Are we stuck here, dad?"

"No." I said it, and I believed it. I had to believe it. This moment might be peaceful, but this wasn't our world. For Max's sake—for our own sake. I couldn't let her grow up here, and I couldn't let us grow old here, having to hide what we were, who we were to each other. "We'll get back."

Max leaned against my side, and I wrapped my arm across her shoulders, and we listened to her dad snoring behind us, and watched as the sun rose over the green horizon and the dew dried around us.

"How?" Max asked, when the dogs finally had enough of sitting quietly, and started to tussle with each other in the dirt.

I kissed the top of her head and respected this growing-up

child enough to be honest. "We're trying to figure out how, kiddo. We're trying to figure out how."

oOo

When Shan finally rolled out of the blankets, we'd already had breakfast, saving him some on the tray. I'd even saved him some coffee, which he took with a tight smile of thanks. He was angry at himself for sleeping in, I could tell; he thought he'd screwed up somehow, leaving me to deal with things, and a few days ago I might have agreed. But that quiet time with Max—knowing that Shan needed his sleep ... maybe not everything had to be shared equally. Not all the time.

After breakfast, at Max's urging, we wandered back over the hill to the wooden shed, so she could check on the baby goats and their momma. She ran ahead, arms pumping, feet practically skimming over the grass.

Shan took my hand as we walked, and I pressed my thumb into the flesh of his palm, a thing we'd started when we were first dating, a quiet way of saying "I'm here. It's okay," without being too obviously reassuring.

"Not quite the getaway we had scheduled," I said, and saw him swallow a laugh.

"Yeah." He tipped his head against my shoulder, a companionable thunk. "But if I knew tomorrow we'd wake up and we'd be home, I'd say this had been a pretty damn good weekend. Except you were right, your daughter is going to want a goat for her next birthday. Goatherd was not the career I'd had in mind for her."

"She's worried we're stuck here."

Shan frowned at the sight of Max surrounded by the small herd of goats, the shorter dogs weaving in and out of hooved legs like they'd been doing it all their lives. "We're going to have to start thinking about that possibility, yeah. And if we are, Jack, you and Max could—"

"Shut up. Just ... shut up, okay? No. We're not going anywhere without you." My voice rose, and Max's head turned like a radar on high alert, abandoning the goats to zero in on us.

"Shit." I forced my voice lower. "Look, Shan, I know you've got issues, god knows I know, but you can't control everything."

"I can't control a damn thing, obviously. Not even a fucking road trip." He'd dropped my hand, taken a step away, raised his own voice. I knew what was happening, could feel it happening, but couldn't find the words to smooth it over. The past few days—the past few years—had all been about making sure everything went smoothly for Max, but the idea that Shan would walk away from us or expect us to walk away from him? Fuck him.

"So fucking don't," I shouted, furious. "Jesus, you think this is fun for me? You think I enjoy knowing my mom's probably out of her mind, worrying about us? That the moment we try to leave here, we're going to have to deal with the way people will look at us, what they'll think, what they'll say—what they'll do? And then you start talking about abandoning us, for our own good?"

Shan opened his mouth, and if I'd been less pissed I'd've laughed at how much he looked like a fish. "Damn it I—"

And then Max was running toward us, skidding to a stop a few paces away, eyes wide and tawny skin flushed with anxiety. "It's okay, munchkin," I said, forcing my voice to a calm, even tone. "Everything's fine."

She frowned at us, round eyes now narrowing dubiously. "Don't. Dads, don't."

"Don't what?" Shan went down on one knee to reassure her, but Max pushed him away.

"I hate it when you do that. I like it better when you and dad yell at each other, not when you're all tight-faced and quiet. You touch more after. And you laugh more, too. The dogs like it better, too."

"They do, huh?" I said, amused. "Not sure any parenting handbook is gonna agree with you, kid."

"Well, maybe they should." Max's voice cracked, but her chin had a defiant jut to it that said she wasn't going to budge on this. "Because I'm right."

"So we should try yelling and panicking and waving our hands a lot?" Shan stood up, turning to glare at me like this was somehow my fault.

I flexed my own jaw back and forth, feeling the anger still rumbling under my skin, knowing I wasn't mad at Shan, and he wasn't mad at me, not really. Probably. "Maybe? Because not-yelling wasn't doing the job either, obviously." Some days it seemed like we spent more time trying to avoid problems than plowing through them. "I think we've agreed, we're pretty much at the flailing and panicking stage anyway."

Shan hacked out a dry laugh, then sighed. "Yeah, what the hell. Okay, Max: next time we'll have a huge screaming match, everyone can join in, then we hug it out. That good by you?"

Max beamed at us like we'd just won dads of the year award, then tore back to play with the goats, like that was all it took to set her world to rights.

It wasn't that easy. Nothing was ever that easy. But we could try.

"Your kid's not a dummy," Shan said.

"Our kid," I said. "You and me and her." I reached out again and took his hand in mine. "Let's go look at baby goats."

oOo

The goats were cute, and Jack and I both—firmly, as a unit—denied Max's request to adopt one.

"You already have two dogs," I told her. "That's enough."

It felt easy, relaxed. It wasn't. I could feel the tension in myself, in Jack, even in Max. Her words had kicked open a box we thought we'd closed, and neither of us was comfortable looking inside. Yelling stressed the munchkin, but it turned out not-yelling was stressing us, and *that* was stressing her too. Maybe having the box open would be better than trying to keep it shut. Maybe.

Mercy was watching us when we got back. Not staring, nothing so direct or aggressive, just watching. Somewhere between the attention of a hawk and the paranoid awareness of a rabbit. Her arms were folded across her stomach, and her scarf was over her head, as though blocking herself off from being seen in return.

"Your vehicle," she said when we passed close enough to be shouted at. "It's making a noise."

Everything—my fight with Jack, the things Max had said—got shoved to the side as I got behind the car, turning off the alarm and staring at the GPS display, now with full bells and lights.

"Recalculating."

"How the—" Jack was standing by my open door, looking between me and the dash.

"I don't know. Shut up." We held our breath as the GPS blinked at us, then displayed a route. Max had her hands full keeping the dogs under control, their stumpy tails wagging with our excitement.

"You think we can trust it?" I asked.

"How the hell should I know?" I looked over: Jack was biting his lip; three days of uncertainty against the memory of how it had screwed us over the last time weighing in his eyes. "No," I said. "I don't think we can trust it. I know damn well we can't trust it, it got us here. But it's what got us here. So odds are it's what will get us out."

"You're still on the magical time-traveling GPS theory?"

My "fuck you" had more heat to it than I would have allowed, before. "Until you come up with a better theory ..." I let the words trail off, and raised an eyebrow, waiting. He nodded, and I reached for the keys we'd left in the ignition, turning them cautiously, half-afraid of what might happen.

The car started, making Elias—who had come within several feet of the car—jump back with a startled shout. I could empathize: my heart was racing, too.

"Sorry," I called out, but left the engine running. If I turned it off again, who knew if it would start back up again?

The GPS's faux-human voice told us, "Route plotted. Estimated time of arrival: ten minutes."

"Get the dogs in the damned car," Jack snapped at Max, the same uncertainty and urgency I felt clearly drumming in him, too.

"But—" Max looked over her shoulder, not at the dogs, but at Elias, and I felt a pang of guilt.

"Get them in the damn car now, don't give it a chance to

change its mind!" Given permission to yell, Jack took full advantage, and Max and the dogs tumbled without further hesitation, abandoning everything we'd dragged to our makeshift camp. He raised a hand to wave goodbye to Elias, whose mother pulled him closer in a protective hug. Elias, poor kid, didn't dare wave back.

I hesitated. "How do we know it's going to take us back to our time?"

"We don't. But look," and Jack jutted his chin through the windshield. Past Elias, his eyes wide, his mother's arm around him, pulling him away from the devil-beast vehicle kicking exhaust where there shouldn't ever have been any in this air. Squinting, I could see the faint, foggy outline of other houses where the field and goats had been, a road—a blessed paved road—snaking between them.

"Son of a ..." I still didn't put the car into drive. "Why now? What the hell changed?"

"I'm the one without a theory, remember? Don't know, don't care, okay?" Jack raised his voice again, this time at me. "Jesus, Shan, now's not the time to argue—drive!"

I put the car into gear, and hit the gas.

"Destination ahead," Sondra's voice told me, and I'd swear, she sounded *smug*.

WHERE THERE'S SMOKE
by Susan Jett

"EEEEEEEEeeeeeeeeeee!   EEEEEEEEEeeeeeeeeeeee!
EEEEEEEEEE—"

Jack's thrown shoe connected with the smoke detector, silencing it abruptly. Either he'd managed to hit the reset button—unlikely—or broken the alarm entirely. He flopped back onto his pillow. *So much for getting back my security deposit.* It might be worth it, though, if the thing would quit waking him up at—he checked—"Yep, 2:43am."

This was the third night now and—if the detector hadn't been so old its plastic had turned the same color as Grandpa John's nicotine-stained fingernails—he'd suspect a computer chip had gone wonky. But this thing was way too primitive for a chip. *Just a sensor wired to some demon's larynx*, he thought, rubbing his eyes. Maybe dust was triggering the sensor, or this was just the alarm's inefficient way of reminding him to change the batteries. Though how it could go off at exactly the same time each night without an internal computer was beyond him. And far too much to think about at 2:44 in the morning.

Jack groaned, rolling over so he wouldn't have to see the time. If Neil hadn't told him less than a month ago, in typical Neil-fashion, that trying to maintain their relationship was as hopeless as trying to construct a Theory of Everything, Jack might have called him up. Neil lived downstairs, though since he had grown up in this building, he had an actual view of the park. As a relative newcomer, all Jack had was a view of his neighbor's kitchen window.

If he went downstairs, and if Neil answered the door, they

could talk. And look out Neil's big living room window. If one had to be an insomniac, access to a wide-open, moonlit view seemed only fair. But that was obviously not happening tonight. *As hopeless as the Theory of Everything*, Jack reminded himself. *Whatever the hell that is. No window-gazing tonight—or any other night for that matter. Probably no more sleep, either.*

The smoke detector's light gradually grew stronger, a beady red eye staring at him in the darkness. *I just stunned the damned thing. And now it's healing itself. How else could it regain enough strength to wake me up again tomorrow night?* Jack squeezed his eyes shut. *Tomorrow I'll replace the batteries. Or I'll get one of those fancy all-in-one smoke/carbon-monoxide/heat sensing/monitor/nightlight things. Or maybe I'll just buy a new smoke detector from Brothers Hardware that isn't out to ruin my life.*

Not that there's much left of it to ruin.

Neil wouldn't have sneered at him for anthropomorphizing a smoke detector, though wallowing in the emotional mud of their breakup might arouse his contempt. But Neil believed all kinds of weird-ass things—much weirder-ass than a smoke detector out to get someone. It came with being a physicist. The guy was scary-smart; he made Jack feel like an idiot without even trying. For example, no matter how much Neil tried to explain it, Jack had never really understood that business with the Theory of Everything, and Jack wasn't a stupid guy. But even Neil's assumption that everyone was as smart as him had been kind of endearing, once Jack realized Neil made even his grad students feel like idiots.

Jack admitted he might never have given Neil a chance when they'd been in college. Neil might be good-looking in a hot-nerd kind of way—his body was frankly ripped—but he believed some seriously wacked things: time travel, alien abductions, not to mention his bizarre British TV obsession. Jack suspected Neil was hoping to be recognized as a long-lost descendent of the Doctor someday. It was one of the many reasons Jack's friends—his normal friends—said he was better off without Neil. But honestly, being in the same room with the guy was bracing. Like waking up next to Sherlock Holmes, if Sherlock had been more interested in the mysteries of the universe than homicides.

The smoke detector's red eye winked, bringing him back to the present: awake in the middle of the night, alone. *If I were a Time Lord, I'd never stick around for insomnia,* Jack thought. *I'd go back and try to re-do that last fight. Neil's infuriating, but I was being a jerk.*

And with that admission, his inability to sleep was confirmed. He spent the rest of the night squirming and replaying old conversations. He finally decided that he hadn't just been a jerk, he'd been a complete asshole.

oOo

Jack dragged through work the next day. He usually enjoyed his job, and was good at it—when he wasn't nodding off before he could accomplish anything. For want of anything better to do, he watched the YouTube ad for that fancy smoke/carbon monoxide/heat sensor he'd heard about. He actually made a couple of notes regarding the sales video—his own ad team could learn something from these guys. Even knowing it was way more smoke detector than he'd ever need, Jack was tempted, but backed out of the "buy" screen at the very end. A hundred dollars was too much.

For one thing, he'd never be able to justify chucking a shoe at it.

A wet shoe. Trudging home, he winced when rain seeped through his socks only a block from home. *Shouldn't have stopped for the bibimbap.* New York comfort food, Neil called it. The guys at Kim's Diner still asked about him even though it had been more than three weeks since they'd been in together.

Jack didn't mean to punch the seventh floor's button in the elevator; it was just habit. Although, if he thought Neil missed him, Jack would be perfectly willing to be the one who apologized first. *I'll bet he's not eating take-out alone in his apartment tonight.*

But of course no one was there.

Jack's shoulders sagged. He hit the button for his own floor.

The *bibimbap* wasn't quite hot anymore, but it was still filling and familiar. *Almost five years I've been eating there*, Jack realized. He tossed his half-empty bowl into the recycling can and shoved the plastic bag into the cupboard with all the others. He looked around his tiny kitchen and sighed. His life wasn't awful. Smoke detector—and lack of a view—aside, the apartment was fine, and he liked his job, even if it wasn't going to change the world. He had some good friends. But this still wasn't how he'd thought he'd be living at this point in his life.

Armed with a screwdriver and a new battery, he turned. "I'm coming for you, smoke detector." Saying the words out loud made him feel like an idiot. *I don't even have a cat. If I fell off the chair and broke my neck tonight, I wouldn't even make a good cautionary tale.* Jack wondered if he should sneak a cat in, or just admit that he talked to himself.

He climbed up on a kitchen chair, stretching on tiptoes and wishing for about the millionth time that he wasn't so fucking small. *Neil would make short work of this job. Short work—get it?* A cat wouldn't appreciate his puns any more than Neil had. *But at least a cat would notice if I were dead. Eat my eyeballs to mark the sad occasion, maybe.* With a grunt, he twisted the smoke detector off its bracket and levered off the cover. He yanked out the old battery, then hesitated. *I don't even cook in here, and I certainly don't own an iron. Screw it.*

Before he could hear his mother's voice in his head, he snapped the cover back on, admiring the smoke detector's completely darkened sensor light. *Black is the color of a good night's sleep*, he thought smugly. He twisted the alarm back onto its bracket and returned the chair to the kitchen.

From the bed, he glared up at the smoke detector. "Got you, you little bastard," he muttered before falling into a deep sleep.

oOo

"EEEEEEEeeeeeeeeee!   EEEEEEEeeeeeeeee! EEEEEEEEEEEEeeeeeeeeeeee!"

He leapt out of bed, his body tingling with adrenalin. "What the hell?"

He dragged the chair in. Just as he ripped the bracket's screws through the drywall, cursing and blinking powdered gypsum from his eyes, the alarm fell silent. He peered up, looking for stripped wires. *Nope.*

Wearily, he repeated, "What the hell?"

Pulling off the mounting bracket, he checked the empty battery compartment, then tossed both parts onto his nightstand.

If Neil were here, he could confirm that Jack wasn't losing his shit.

Jack glared at the clock, his heart still thundering. *2:48. Two-fucking forty-eight.*

oOo

Morning came too early and after another slow day at work he didn't even notice he'd punched the seventh floor again. Unlike yesterday though, Neil was waiting for the elevator when it stopped. Neil grinned, and Jack felt his mouth stretch in an answering smile that he hoped might somehow make him look cooler than he felt.

"Going down?" Neil asked.

Jack shook his head. "Just getting home. You want to come up?" Jack pulled his hands out of his coat pocket, trying to look a little taller, and both nine-volts fell out. Stooping for them, he said quickly, "Never mind. I didn't mean it like that. It's just … there's something weird going on with my smoke detector that you should see."

He was so tired he didn't immediately understand why Neil started to laugh.

"Dude," Neil said, shaking his head. "That is the worst line I ever heard in my life."

Jack smiled wryly. "But you'll come up and have a look?"

"For a few minutes. It's good to see you, even if you are a terrible conversationalist."

"Yeah, you too."

"Yeah."

Neil stood too close in the elevator. It was all Jack could do not to close his eyes and just breathe in the smell of Neil's soap and shampoo and the cedar-y smell of that hideous handknit sweater Jack had spent last winter ripping out and starting over. The sweater wasn't warm enough to wear outside in this weather, and he certainly wouldn't have been wearing it down to the gym in the basement. It occurred to Jack that Neil might have been coming up even before he'd invited him.

With that thought, he gave in to the impulse, closed his eyes, and, for a minute, everything was all right. Neil's voice cut into his reverie. "We're here, dude. You wanted to show me your, uh, smoke detector?"

But even though his words were obviously aiming for world-weary ennui, Neil sounded, if anything, as shy as Jack suddenly felt. The smoke detector from hell was suddenly the furthest thing from Jack's mind.

oOo

Even if that conversation needed more bourbon than I knew we could drink, Jack decided, *it wasn't as bad as I'd thought it would be.*

He had snapped awake a few moments ago, which should have been annoying. But it was so much easier to stomach being awake in the middle of the night when his sleeplessness hadn't been initiated by a screaming alarm. Or dull regrets. He was glad they'd talked. *And Neil made a lot of good points,* he admitted. *I don't even realize when I'm pushing him too hard, sometimes. But I can work on that. I can do better.*

He looked over at Neil's sleeping face, lit unevenly by streetlights filtering in through his blinds. *The bourbon certainly made the sex funnier. And I think having someone to laugh with was the best part of the night.*

Jack had always liked watching other people sleep. It was soothing, even when he couldn't rest, to be near someone who could. *Actually, having company right now might be the best part of the night. I hate sleeping alone even more than I hate not sleeping.* He smoothed a bit of hair away from Neil's eyes, so it wouldn't flutter with every breath, then glanced past the disabled smoke alarm on his nightstand to his clock. He whispered, "2:43 and all is well. Gotcha, you little bas—"

"EEEEEEEeeeeeeeeee!   EEEEEEEEEEEEeeeeeeeee!
EEEEEEEEEEEeeeeeee!"

Jack threw himself backwards as Neil heaved up, wild-eyed and staring. Reaching past him, Jack grabbed the possessed smoke detector and stuffed it under a pillow, then grated, "This. Is. Not. Possible."

Neil groped for his glasses then flicked on the bedside lamp. He dragged the smoke detector out as soon as it stopped shrilling. Interest tightened his drink-slackened face, and the sight made Jack smile, even though his heart still thumped painfully. He asked, "You're not seriously going to try to figure this out now, are you? It won't start up again until tomorrow night at 2:43. Trust me. This has been going on all week."

Neil's eyes narrowed as he poked at the empty battery compartment. He didn't look at Jack. "Once is annoying, twice is wild coincidence, but three times—and you say it's always at the exact same moment?"

"Actually, this is more like the fifth time …"

"And you're not dying from curiosity? Philistine." But Neil's slightly slurred voice sounded fond, not totally exasperated.

Jack yawned, wincing as his jaw cracked. "Tired Philistine. Exhausted Philistine. Completely drunken Philistine. I'm going back to sleep. How about we figure out the mysteries of the universe tomorrow?"

"If there is a tomorrow. Dude—what if you're trapped in a time loop?"

Without opening his eyes, Jack said, "Like *Groundhog Day*?" He shook his head. "Nothing else has been the same." He thought about the evening they'd just spent together and smiled, before a twinge of irrational fear made him reach for Neil's arm. *I'd better not wake up all alone.*

"So maybe it's the smoke detector that's trapped in a time loop." Neil sounded like he was actually considering this theory.

Jack only opened one eye—to show Neil that he refused to take this seriously, at least not at this time of night. "Then I suppose it's time for a new goddamned smoke detector. It can loop all it wants to at the bottom of the harbor. Which is where we can toss it tomorrow."

"But what if there is no tomorrow?" Now Neil just sounded drunk again.

Jack smiled. "Because my smoke detector has breached the space-time continuum?"

"Are you making fun of me? The world is a mysterious place, dude. Sometimes I don't think you appreciate that."

Three hours ago, Jack might have worried he'd hurt Neil's feelings or overthought things until he managed to convince himself his own feelings should be hurt. But after all the drinking and the talking and the making up he felt certain Neil was only teasing him.

He reached over and took the broken smoke detector out of Neil's hands, setting it gently on the nightstand. Then he flopped back on the pillows and let his arm fall across Neil's bare chest. Feeling more contented than he had in a long time, he murmured, "Totally. I'm totally making fun of you, mysterious dude." His eyes closed as Neil brushed a bit of hair out of his face.

Neil was still stroking his hair when Jack heard him ask, sounding half-asleep, "You want bagels in the morning?"

Jack nodded without opening his eyes and his whole body relaxed into this moment, this universe, this continuum. Time-traveling smoke alarm or not, this was where he was supposed to be. Jack yawned, hugely. "Missed you," he whispered as he drifted toward sleep.

oOo

He smelled toast burning and wondered if Neil was trying to surprise him with breakfast. Neil cooked about as well as he did, but surely it had only been a few minutes since the alarm went off. It couldn't possibly be morning already.

He turned toward the clock on his nightstand, but it was blocked by the shell of the broken smoke detector. *Too much work*, he thought, and almost went back to sleep. *Neil will wake me up when it's ready, and I really need to sleep some of this bourbon out of my system.* But now he was curious—had he really dozed off without realizing? He made a heroic effort, and lifted himself up on one elbow to see the clock.

Jack's eyes stung, and he rubbed at them hard. The numbers were blurred, more orange than red, like he was viewing them through a sepia filter. *2:57? No one makes toast at three in the morning. Not even Neil. And Neil's right here.*

The burned smell was stronger now. Unpleasantly strong. He cleared his throat, and Neil rolled over, burying his face in the pillow. Neil slept like the dead—always had—and he'd had four or five bourbons besides. Feeling a little woozy, Jack shook Neil's arm, then sat up, trying to get his bearings. He immediately wished he hadn't.

He coughed harder this time, hard enough that his head pounded and sparkles of color flashed across the dark bedroom. But when he caught his breath, breathing shallowly to keep from setting himself off again, there were no colors, just smoke swirling overhead, obscuring the dark spot on the ceiling where the smoke detector belonged. He lay back quickly, gagging on the thick air his lungs wanted to expel even though there wasn't any cleaner air to replace it.

The smoke detector.

Smoke.

Fire.

Heart pounding in his ears, he shook Neil again, but the bigger man just groaned and pushed him away feebly with one hand. Now Neil started to cough, gently, little puffs like he was clearing his throat. Jack looked up at the darkening ceiling and shoved hard at Neil's shoulder, starting to panic. They were both going to die, because there was no way he could carry or even drag Neil to safety if he'd truly passed out. The man outweighed him by nearly eighty pounds, and Jack had never been particularly strong for his size.

Goddamn smoke alarm would have woken him up, his mind raged. *It's my fault for taking out the batteries: I might as well have started the fire myself. And now we're going to die. Mom was right.*

"Neil! Get up! There's a fire!"

But Neil just coughed a little, his face still buried under the pillow. The room was still dark; Jack couldn't see any flames, but the smoke was definitely getting thicker. *At least Neil's using my pillow as an air filter. He's smart even when he's unconscious.* A particularly violent coughing fit grabbed Jack by the throat and his stomach tried to empty itself. They couldn't stay here.

Gagging, he crawled out of bed, trying to keep his head low. The air was clearer down here. From the floor, he reached up and grabbed Neil's arm. Bracing his feet on the box-spring, Jack pulled Neil's torso off the bed. Neil thumped onto the floor, then sat up, shouting. Then he coughed, choking convulsively. He knocked the smoke detector down as he groped, still coughing, for his glasses. After he shoved the glasses on his face, they both stared at it.

"Fucking smoke detector," Jack rasped. Saving his breath, Neil tucked the smoke detector under one arm before reaching out for Jack. Gulping a deep breath, they crouched hand in hand, then rushed for the front door. But even before they touched it, they saw black smoke creeping from beneath it. The smoke must be coming from the elevator shafts or the hallway.

"Fire stairs in the kitchen," Jack said, coughing with the effort, and they covered their faces with their elbows and ran. Jack shoved the recycling can out of the way, strewing take-out bowls across the kitchen floor. Congealed egg and *gochujang* splashed across the floor.

Jack couldn't remember the last time he'd opened this door; he forgot it was here most of the time. He reached up to twist the knob on the latch, but the thing was stuck tight. This was so not funny. It felt like the worst of the bad dreams he had endured as a child. Hissing under his breath, he cursed the weakling genes his Grandpa John had given him. But he saved his most virulent curses for the building's goddamn super, who must have bribed the fucking fire inspector who should have insisted on new smoke detectors and verified that everyone's fire doors opened easily, instead of worrying about who had an illegal cat in their apartment. *Thank god I don't have a cat,* his mind gibbered. *That sucker would be hiding and we'd both die from smoke inhalation while I was trying to drag it out from under a bed.*

But of course, even though Jack might not be strong enough to open his own goddamn door, he wasn't alone. And Neil was big, and actually put his gym membership to good use. Neil handed Jack the broken smoke detector—which he apparently planned to rescue—and Jack had an instant to admire Neil's forearms tensing as he used both hands to get a better grip on the knob. Jack looked back at his apartment, wondering what he should try to save, but then more smoke billowed up from under the front door, chasing them into the gray-painted fire stairwell, so they just slammed the door shut behind them. At the bottom of the first flight of stairs, they paused to look up and catch their breath, spitting the sooty taste out of their mouths. Wisps of smoke were already dissipating as they drifted upward. They banged on every door on the way down, even though they could already hear the hallway's alarms going off.

By the time they reached the lobby, sirens heralded the arrival of the fire department. Other residents were beginning to join them in the lobby, managing to look both very sleepy and very worried as they searched for acquaintances in the growing crowd. Jack rasped, "You think everyone got out?"

Neil looked up as if he could see through walls, as if Jack were asking for logic, not reassurance. "I think the fire had to be right beneath your place. Isn't that the floor that the buyers are remodeling?"

Jack nodded absently and then smiled. "Yeah. Been empty for six months already while the workmen do their thing."

"There you go. Someone did their thing wrong. So the flames were contained on an empty floor, and 12-A and -C are over there," he nodded at Jack's next-door neighbors. "And it would have taken a lot longer for a dangerous level of smoke to get to thirteen, so yes. Everyone's likely just fine."

"Damn, I missed you, logic-man." Neil smiled shyly, and Jack confided, "You know, I probably wouldn't have had the nerve to invite you up if not for that damned smoke detector. Well, that and being kind of sleep-deprived."

"And if it hadn't woken us up just a few minutes before the fire—however the hell it managed to do that—all that bourbon might have made us sleep too soundly to wake up in time when we needed to. Dude. That would've sucked. Don't ever let me drink that much again."

Jack smiled crookedly and nodded. "Yeah," he said, "but if

the smoke detector hadn't been malfunctioning in the first place, it would have gone off at the right time."

"Maybe. But—and don't take this the wrong way—I don't think you could have opened that door alone. You need to spend some time at the gym, dude. And haven't you ever heard of WD-40? You need someone to look after you."

"So you think the smoke detector saved me by going off at the wrong time? And therefore making sure you'd be there with me?"

"It went off at exactly the right time. Novikov's self-consistency principle, dude."

"This may come as a surprise to you, but I have no idea what you're talking about."

"Time wants to run along its proper track. You know that, right? When your smoke detector's worldline formed a closed timelike curve—a loop in spacetime, so to speak—it allowed the smoke detector to return to its own past. It had to find a way to right the world—bring things back on track—and this was the only way to do it."

"Wait. So you're saying my smoke detector—this very smoke detector—knows its way around the space-time continuum and altered all this shit just to save us from a crummy apartment fire? I must be pretty damned important."

"Physics doesn't work that way. You're as important as any other particle in the universe—no more, no less. The universe just wants things to happen the way they already did, and something obviously got out of whack and needed correcting. Unless you want to get into paradox theory and different branching realities, and I'd rather not. Because dude, honestly, I think we both just died in most of those. Besides, do you have a better explanation?"

"You're the physicist. I just write ad copy. My point is that it seems rather, um, improbable. Arbitrary." Jack stared hard at the smoke detector, wondering if he would be relieved or creeped out if the thing started glowing red right now.

Neil smiled a little. "The world is a mysterious place, dude. For tonight, that's good enough for me. Of course, I'm still a little bit drunk. Also I'm starving. What time does the bagel place open? Four? Five?"

Two firemen in full gear pushed past them, and he and Neil hurried through the front door to get out of their way. Jack looked up, shielding his eyes; he didn't see flames shooting out any windows. It was chilly, but the gooseflesh rising on his arms wasn't from the cold. *Flames or not, I could have died up there tonight.*

Other residents began straggling out of the lobby too, wearing pajamas and cradling their illegal pets with the same care Neil was showing for the stupid smoke detector. Jack hoped the building superintendent wasn't going to be a dick and make a fuss over a cat or two.

"Bagels," Neil said sharply, snapping him out of his reverie. "I'm starving, dude."

Shrugging, Jack looked up at him. "Even if they'll sell us something at the bakery window, my apartment's going to be trashed, between the smoke and the water."

"I've got a better view anyway. And I think I've still got some of your clothes somewhere. Um, you should just stay with me 'til your place is cleaned up. If you want. You being so important to the universe and all."

"Really?"

In answer, Neil draped one big arm over Jack's shoulders again. Another fire truck pulled in, red lights flashing, as they started walking toward the bagel shop. "The universe is a mysterious place, dude, and it seems to want us to stick together. And don't believe for a second that I mean that as a bad thing." Neil's squeezed Jack's shoulders and lowered his voice. "In fact, I've been thinking of all the money we could save if we just gave up your apartment. What's mine is yours, etcetera." Neil hefted the smoke detector in his free hand. "I'm claiming this, though, and you can't have it back. I'm feeling very sentimentally attached to it, all of a sudden."

Jack nodded happily. "Let's go get some bagels and talk it over," he said, as blithely as he could manage around the lump in his throat. But for the first time since they had met, he thought he knew exactly what Neil meant.

ALIEN TIME WARP
by Gini Koch

Author's Note: For readers of the Alien/Katherine "Kitty" Katt series, this story takes place during the events of **Alien Separation**.

Time is mutable.

That's been shown to me in a mind-shattering way. And I'm not sure I'll ever recover.

Einstein, Hawking, all the scientific greats, they've all tried to figure out time. Maybe some of them *did* figure it out. If they did, I know why they didn't tell anyone. Knowing what I now know about time makes everything meaningless and, at the same time, makes every action, even the minutest action, the most vital thing in the multiverse.

"Chuckie, are you okay? You look … funny." That was Kitty. My best friend. For most of my life, my only real friend. My first big love. Until I'd met Naomi.

I was sure I did look funny. We weren't where we were supposed to be. We should've been on Earth. Instead, we were on an alien planet in the Alpha Centauri system. But that wasn't the real issue. It was *when* we were that was wrong. So very wrong.

"How did we get back here?" Jeff Martini asked. Jeff was Kitty's husband and an alien, from a different planet in this system than we were on right now. But he'd never been here before. None of us had. And yet, we'd been here many times before.

We were high up on a mountain. A very flat mountain. Me,

Kitty, Jeff, Jeff's cousin, Christopher White, sixteen of our people, plus a lot of natives. And yet, at the same time, in both my future and my past, I knew Jeff was being tortured in order to force me to allow our enemies to use my mind to power their mind-connecting machine. Which would, if unchecked, blow my brain out and make me a gibbering idiot in a very short time.

I was chosen for this because I'm the smartest. Which really wasn't fair. Why not turn a moron into a vegetable? Supposedly an idiot would be using less of their brain, meaning more untouched brain for the brain battery I was strapped to. Not that we had any of those along, of course. But then, that's pretty much how my life has been—reasonably good with a lot of unfair thrown in so I don't get cocky.

It was unfair Jeff stole Kitty from me. It was unfair I fell just as deeply in love with his cousin, only to have Naomi killed before we'd been married six months. It was consistently unfair that being the smartest guy around just meant I'd gotten picked on and abused my entire life. But it was really unfair, once my friends risked everything to save me, that a part of me was still trapped in, lucky me, what looked like a time loop.

I saw myself getting rescued, saw us saving the day, saw my friends doing amazing things in order to get me to safety before my mind exploded—just before, really—and yet, we weren't saved and I was still trapped.

Because while I was still in the brain torture contraption, I was also on this mountaintop where we could see for miles. The planet looked the same—a bizarre spiral of colors surrounded by ocean, the only continent on this entire planet.

Making the whole experience a complete mind freak, there was also a giant telescope, hanging right above us, held up by absolutely nothing. That shouldn't have been possible, of course, but there it was. And I knew it was supposed to be there.

There were natives up here with us—creatures who seemed unfazed by the telescope—and they were sentient. That they were sentient was one thing, but that they weren't questioning the giant floating telescope was, frankly, amazing.

But not as amazing as what else I was seeing.

We lived in a multiverse and because of the device strapped

to my head, I could see each universe as it peeled off from the main one. Or at least what I thought was the main one. Maybe there were as many main universes as there were new universes being formed. And I could see them all—past, present, and potential futures—all at the same time.

No wonder God checked out of the day-to-day running of all of this.

I sincerely doubted the people who'd strapped me into this mind expanding device expected that I could see all of time and all the multiverse, too. Whether that meant the damned device was malfunctioning or not was probably the relevant question. But who was I kidding? This was us. Of course it was malfunctioning. Our luck, mine in particular, didn't run any other way.

I was sure the telescope had been stolen from Earth and then, somehow, put back on this planet. It looked just like the telescope that had been stolen right when I'd joined up with the C.I.A., which was less than a decade ago. Only, as I looked at the timeline we were in, *when* we were on the mountaintop, we were thousands of years in the past. And so was this telescope, which hadn't been created yet. And this was possible, not only because I was seeing it, but because whoever was in charge obviously knew how to use time to his or her advantage.

Whoever this being was, I was pretty sure he or she was a bastard.

"I think we need to, ah, take some action," Christopher said. "Because the natives look restless."

We looped. It was as if we stretched out along time itself, went through adventures here, battled in space there, then came back again, right to the top of this mountain. And what I knew and the others didn't was that, when we were on the mountaintop, we were thousands of years in the past from the moment when we'd first arrived. And yet, Jeff and I were being tortured now. Whenever "now" really was.

My head hurt.

While Kitty again asked me if I was okay and Jeff again asked what was going on, I looked for any sign of my life with my wife, any other universe where we might have actually gotten a fair chance. I didn't see any. And that was, possibly, the most unfair part of all. I'd finally moved on from the first love of my life only to have the second one ripped away from me.

I wanted Naomi back. Would it be so wrong, in the grand scheme of all the multiverse, for her and me to be together? I didn't think so. Surely there was some way, some place, where we actually got more than six months of married happiness. Dammit. I *wanted* more than six months with Naomi. I wanted the rest of our lives.

Another loop. I noted again I was both released from the brain torture contraption and yet, at the same time, I was still in it. Meaning I wasn't free at all—I was still a human battery and was just seeing possibilities. Great. So, where were my possibilities with Naomi?

We went back in time again, back to the mountaintop. This time, though, instead of telling us that the natives were restless, Christopher looked up. "Ah, everyone? What happened to the telescope?"

We looked up. Sure enough, the telescope wasn't there anymore. I took a look at the multiverse. This time I saw Naomi. She and I were together again and it was wonderful.

I could see her beautiful face, touch her soft, dark skin, make love to her again. She got pregnant, and we were having a girl. We were both so excited, and everyone else was too. For the first time, I truly felt like I belonged, that I was part of the family, not just Kitty's friend who everyone else was forced to be nice to.

Naomi glowed with pregnancy, and I'd never been so proud and hopeful in my life. I loved this timeline. I wanted it to be real. I wanted to make it real and keep it forever.

But then the world ended horrifically, with the entire galaxy turning into a gigantic black hole that sucked the rest of that universe up. My child was never born, and Naomi and I died, like everyone else, quickly and helplessly. This was definitely not my idea of a happy ending.

Another loop, another change in the timelines I was seeing as we zoomed back and forth along them. Our world was dying earlier and the whole "we end as a black hole" thing was happening quicker. After a point, it didn't even matter if Naomi lived or died—the world ended in the same horrific way, just faster and faster.

We looped again and as we did, I realized that, improbable though it was, without the telescope that shouldn't be here, time was fragmenting. I was the only one who could see it happening, and that meant I was the only one with a chance of fixing the situation. Nice to be important, I guess.

This time, as we looped, I focused on the telescope. We needed it here—meaning I had to do something to get it back. And as I concentrated, the looping slowed, then seemed to stop. I could tell it hadn't, not really, but at the same time, I wasn't with everyone else on an alien planet anymore, being used as a human Cerebro device for our enemies.

I was somewhere else.

oOo

An office. A very messy, cluttered office. With a blackboard in it. I recognized the figures scribbled on that blackboard.

There was a woman. Cleaning lady, I thought, maybe the housekeeper. She wasn't that old, probably around thirty. Pretty. And I could tell by how she was dressed I was somehow in the late 1940's.

She wasn't cleaning, she was studying the blackboard.

I studied it, too. I was sure it was Einstein's work on the generalized theory of gravitation. There had always been debate about it, but as I stared at the blackboard, something seemed off from the formulas I'd memorized when I was in grade school.

The woman cocked her head and moved closer to the blackboard. She put her hand up, then seemed to feel me in the room, because she spun around, looking guilty. "Oh! I'm sorry, I didn't realize you were in here."

"Ah, I didn't mean to startle you." She seemed to recognize me. There wasn't a mirror around so I couldn't look to see if I'd hopped into Einstein's body or someone else's.

She looked guilty. "I know you told me not to disturb anything in here, Professor, but I just can't stop looking at that formula."

She'd called me Professor, so I went with the idea that I'd body hopped somehow. But I didn't know what to say. Went with my training—when in doubt, interrogate. "Why are you looking at it?"

She hung her head. "Because it looks wrong to me. Still. I know you told me yesterday that it was fine, but ..."

I looked around the room, hoping to spot something, anything, that would give me a clue for who she was and who she thought I was. Before I could speak, someone called out. "Elizabeth, I need you for a moment, please." The voice had a German accent, and I'd heard it before, but only in recordings. Now, right now, I was hearing Albert Einstein's voice in reality. I did my best to keep my expression calm.

The woman looked up. "Please don't tell him," she begged me. "I know you're angry with me—"

"No, I'm not. Help him and then come right back. I want you to tell me what you think should be fixed. I ... I think I was wrong yesterday."

Elizabeth nodded, then hurried out of the room. I waited, being careful not to do what I wanted, which was to touch everything, take a scrap of something with me, and go look at Einstein. Me pawing things would undoubtedly make Elizabeth upset or worse, taking anything could upset timelines that were already in a bad state of flux, and Einstein seeing me—whoever Elizabeth and he might think I was—was a bad idea.

She returned quickly. "He just needed some tea and couldn't remember where it was." She smiled. "He's such a dear, isn't he?"

"Yes, he is. So, tell me what you wanted to change."

"I told you before, Professor. You said I was wrong."

Whoever she thought I was probably *had* thought she was wrong. That didn't mean he was right, however. "Yes, but tell me again. Let me hear it fresh."

Elizabeth nodded. "Fine." She went to the blackboard. "This is shown to be E, but, I believe that it should be R." She went on to explain why, and her reasoning was quite sound.

And she was right, at least as far as my memory of the equation confirmed. "What did he say about it?"

"He hasn't looked at this for days." Elizabeth looked worried. "I think he knows it's wrong but has been too close to it to see the fix."

"How did you see it?"

She blushed and looked down again. "I've read all his papers."

"Good. Keep on doing that. Because you're right. Fix it. Match his handwriting if you can."

"You're sure?"

"Positive." I was. I'd been sent back here for a reason, and this reason seemed obvious. If Einstein had this wrong, then many things would be more wrong as time went on, even though this wasn't considered his most definitive theory. "Change it, but don't tell him you've changed it."

She nodded. "I don't want to lose my job."

"That's not why. Either he'll realize it and think he fixed it himself and forgot, or he'll come back to it, see it corrected, and be happy about it. But, either way, I think you need to aim higher. Because if you could see what was wrong with this theory, then you shouldn't be spending your days finding the tea."

Elizabeth smiled. "Thank you. I enjoy working for him. But … maybe someday." She reached her hand out. "Thank you, Professor. We've enjoyed your visit. And thank you for not being angry with me anymore."

I took her hand and gave it a gentle squeeze. "I was having a bad day yesterday. Today it's all much clearer. And you need to use your mind for higher math and science."

"Elizabeth, dear, I cannot find the sugar," Einstein called.

She smiled again. "I'll stay until he knows where the tea and sugar are without me, Professor." She leaned up and gave me a kiss on my cheek, then she hurried out of the room.

As I took one last look around, I felt the pull of the time loop and Einstein's study faded from view.

oOo

I didn't go back to the mountaintop like I'd expected. Instead,

I was on a street in what looked like an old movie version of a big city. Only it looked and smelled real.

I'd landed at the mouth of an alleyway. I took a look behind me—no one and nothing of interest there—so I stepped out and turned right, because why not? There were no cars on the street I could see, but there were lots of horses pulling buggies and similar. However, the way everyone was dressed was more modern than in the 1800's.

There were victory ribbons hanging from the window of a small dress shop. They didn't look brand new, but they weren't ancient, either. I listened—the people were definitely American.

I looked at myself in the reflection of the shop's window—I looked like me, but I was dressed differently. So, if I was body jumping, I could only see myself, not who I was supposed to be. How *Quantum Leap* of whoever was in charge of this, myself included, if it was me doing it somehow.

Kitty was better at fashion than I was. She might've been able to tell the era based on the clothing. I wasn't. The dresses were long and elaborate, but this could mean any time before the 1960's, really. I stopped staring at the dresses—whenever I was, they probably frowned upon men staring at women's clothes.

There was a diner next door and I stepped inside. They had a calendar on the wall—1819. Just after World War 1, which explained the ribbons and clothing, and just before cars became common, which explained their absence.

I looked around. I'd been sent to Einstein's study for a specific reason and to interact with, as near as I could tell, a specific person. But no one in here looked familiar and all that was on the blackboard behind the lunch counter was a listing of the specials of the day.

The pretty hostess asked me if I wanted a booth or the counter. I chose the booth, simply because I had no ideas and figured I could think better if I was alone.

She led me to one in the back. I put my back to the wall to see the rest of the diner. No one looked out of place, or like a scientific genius who needed my presence. Many of the people seemed tired and somewhat beaten—the Roaring Twenties weren't going to show up for a couple more years, and it showed in this diner.

But other than noting that I liked my time better, I had no freaking idea why I was here.

The waitress came over. Also pretty. "Good afternoon, sir. My name is Melissa. May I take your order?"

"Just coffee, please. Black. I may want something more in a bit."

She nodded, smiled, and bustled off.

Melissa returned with my coffee. Then she went to the older man who was in the booth next to mine. His back was to the rest of the restaurant, so he and I faced each other. He looked angry and depressed, but in a very quiet way.

"Mister Ritchey, don't let them get to you," she said, patting the man's shoulder. "Why, you'll just continue your work on your own and show them all."

He grunted. "What, really, is the use? Might as well just stop and raise begonias and make cabinetry. The flowers would be far more pleasant to work with and I'd have cabinets to show for the effort, instead of rudeness and disgrace."

"You'll overcome it. I know you will. There's no one else who has your skill at optics and instrument construction." She patted his shoulder again, refilled his coffee, and moved on.

But now I knew why I was here. I could've kissed Melissa, but, attractive though she was, that would probably get me slapped or arrested in this day and age.

I took my coffee and moved to the seat opposite Ritchey. "I'm sorry to bother you, sir, but I wanted to agree with Melissa. Despite your setback, you shouldn't give up."

He looked up and shot a glare at me. "Just who are you and why are you intruding? Again, I might add."

"I'm a fan." This was true. George Willis Ritchey was one of the main pioneers in giant telescopes. If he didn't continue his work, the likelihood that the giant telescopes our world used to see the galaxy and beyond wouldn't be created. Meaning the telescope on the alien planet would never exist. "And, I'm sorry, but when did I intrude on you before?"

"Yesterday," Ritchey snapped. "Right outside. Told me I was right to be angry and right to show the rest of them that they needed me. Let them suffer without my expertise. Now you're here acting solicitous?"

I really wished I knew whose body I was in. But I didn't, so I'd deal with this the same way I had with Elizabeth. By lying.

"Ah, Melissa spoke to me yesterday. Gave me quite the tongue lashing for not encouraging you."

"Well, she worked with me, at the factory during the War. She's a tad biased."

The factory he referred to was the one that made optical parts for gun sights for the U.S. government, meaning Melissa was highly skilled and, as a woman in that field, all the men at war or not, probably proficient at math, science, and astronomy. And now she was working as a waitress.

"Biased or not, she was right, sir. The world needs your expertise, and the rest of the scientific community needs to see that a minor setback hasn't stopped you. If you keep on, I'm sure, just as Melissa is, that you're going to end up creating great things, greater than anything you have yet."

Ritchey stared at me. "You think so, do you?"

"I know so, sir." He wasn't buying it, I could tell. Time for a bigger, better lie that he'd definitely believe. I heaved a sigh. "Honestly, sir, I was hired by Mister Hale to discourage you. He's jealous of your skills, and wants to keep the glory of the work you've done together for himself. He's afraid of you, sir. Afraid of the great things you might do without him. So," I spread my hands, "he paid me to talk to you yesterday and tell you lies."

Ritchey stared again, but this time there was fire in his eyes. "That ... I can't say what he is but we both know the word I'm holding back, don't we, young man? I appreciate your coming forward. It was a brave thing to do."

"No, sir. This wasn't brave, it was just right. What I did yesterday was cowardly."

Ritchey sat up straight. "I'll be the judge of that. Melissa!" The waitress came rushing over. "I need my bill, and put this young man's coffee on my tab, too, please." He gave me a small smile. "I like you. Are you looking for a job? I could use an assistant."

оеое

Melissa drew in her breath and her hands tightened on the coffeepot and cloth she was holding.

Tempting though it was to stay and work with one of the greatest minds in optics and telescopes, I knew where I belonged, and it wasn't here. But I could do another good deed in the process.

"I'm honored to be asked, but I can't. However, I believe that, if you look to your right, you'll find a young woman who you already know to be more than qualified."

Ritchey seemed surprised by the idea. I was glad Kitty wasn't here—she couldn't have held back a feminist rant of epic proportions in this situation.

"Would you really be interested?" he asked Melissa.

"Yes, sir, more than anything."

"Then it's settled." I stood up and shook Ritchey's hand. "It's been an honor, sir. Make us all proud."

"Thank you," Melissa said softly. She put her hand on my arm. "I honestly can't thank you enough."

"Make sure he never loses the fire, and make sure you don't, either. That'll be thanks enough." I nodded to both of them, then left the diner, without drinking a drop of the coffee. Which was too bad—my head was hurting again and the caffeine would've probably helped.

I headed back to the alleyway and, sure enough, the moment I got there, I felt the pull again. Time to go some time else.

oOo

I landed in a bathroom, in a stall. This was almost normal. I'd gotten used to taking gates—alien tech that looked like airport metal detectors but transported you all over the globe in seconds—and the majority of them were located in men's bathrooms.

I flushed the toilet, just in case, then stepped out. I was alone.

A bathroom meant a mirror. I couldn't see who I was, but I could see what he was wearing, and I was wearing a uniform. I was a three star Lieutenant General in the Marines. Whoever the hell I was, I had a lot of clout. But that also meant I'd be expected to know who I was talking to and what I was talking about. Thank God I loved a challenge.

I left the bathroom to find a young Captain waiting for me. On the plus side, he looked vaguely familiar. But I had no idea what time I was in yet, and he wasn't familiar enough for me to say for sure who he was.

He saluted; I did the same. "This way, sir, they're waiting for you." As he turned I got a glimpse of his nameplate but didn't catch his name. It dawned on me that I hadn't looked at my chest closely enough. I'd have a nameplate on. But looking down at it now would be incredibly obvious, and there were too many people around—many of them civilians—to risk it.

I looked at the civilians out of the sides of my eyes. The clothing was definitely not modern but not old fashioned, either. Haircuts were mostly crew cuts, high and tights, and so forth. None of this was giving me any bet for the exact year we were in, but, lucky me, we passed a photograph of Lyndon Baynes Johnson on the wall. We were in the mid- 1960's, and therefore probably in the midst of the Viet Nam War.

We entered a room I knew—Mission Control. Only there were no spacecraft on the screens. Instead there were a group of people surrounded by what looked like a lot of Top Brass.

And one of those people looked like Jeff Martini.

I managed not to ask Jeff how he'd gotten here, but only because I knew his father, Alfred. Take off several decades and, sure enough, Alfred looked like a younger version of his son. Or looked probably like Jeff had in his early twenties. Or something like that. Bottom line, there were differences and, though they were slight, they were there.

I recognized the other men with him, too. Younger versions of men I knew—Stanley Gower, my father-in-law, and Richard White, the former Supreme Pontifex of Earth's A-Cs and Christopher's father. I recognized them, and I didn't. Because they were young. Incredibly young. Like, early twenties young. Younger than I'd been when I joined the C.I.A. young.

I knew when I was now for certain—at the dawn of Earth's first realization that we weren't alone in the galaxy.

The three A-Cs looked relaxed. They had hyperspeed and

were stronger than any of the humans, so there was no way they were going to be captured. But the people around them looked tense, and, exiled heir to the Alpha Four throne, exiled other more distant heir to the throne, and religious leader or not, the three A-Cs all looked wet behind the ears, meaning they probably hadn't impressed any of the hardened military men that filled this room. If I was a betting man, I'd have said that the A-Cs weren't winning friends and influencing people in terms of sticking around.

"What's our status?" I asked the Captain quietly. The danger in talking was that I had no idea how the person I was "riding" actually spoke. I decided to channel Hollywood and just sound brisk and somewhat pompous. It seemed to work.

"They're waiting on you, sir," he replied in kind. "Your points yesterday were well made." As he turned towards me I finally saw his nameplate—Katt. Katt didn't look like he approved of my points, whatever the hell they'd been.

"I've spent some time … considering options." I thought about his name. I knew a high ranking Marine very well. He was Kitty's uncle. And he'd have been about this age when the A-Cs arrived. "What are your thoughts … Mort?"

Katt looked shocked at the familiarity, but not at the name. Always nice to be right. "I'm sure your thoughts are far more valid than mine, sir."

"Speak freely, man. It's why I asked."

He nodded. "Well then, sir, I think that your concerns about the general population's reactions are well founded and correct. But, at the same time, these people came to our country as refugees, just as most of our ancestors did. They can help us in so many ways, and we can, in turn, help them."

"You don't think they should phone home, do you?"

"Ah, no sir. They can't. They're exiled remember?"

Damn. That phrase wouldn't be around for an easy twenty years. I had to be more careful or I'd screw up the timeline even worse than it might already be. "Sorry, a little joke that wasn't funny. So, what about my suggestions from yesterday do you disagree with the most?" Katt looked worried. "Again, speak freely, man. You'll never get anywhere pussyfooting around."

This was an exact quote that Mortimer Katt had said to me, more than once, when I was growing up.

But it appeared to be the first time he'd heard it. He grinned. "Yes, sir. Well then, I think sending these aliens 'home' isn't the answer. If they leave the solar system, who knows what will happen to them, or us, frankly? And we don't want them going to our enemies. Russia would welcome them in a heartbeat, especially if they knew we'd refused to house them."

So whoever I was, I'd argued to kick the A-Cs to the curb. Other than feeling like a time traveling Forrest Gump, I didn't have enough data to be able to guess who I "was" and no time to do the research.

Based on the last two stops on my time travel tour, my guess was that I was body jumping into someone who'd negatively affected the timeline, meaning that the giant telescope didn't exist and we were headed to the End of All Things. Meaning I had to once again fix things in a way that wouldn't come undone tomorrow. Or whenever this time's tomorrow was.

It'd been easier at the first two stops. But here, I was surrounded by people, and whoever's body I was borrowing was going to have to live with the consequences of whatever I did. Then again, I knew that what had to happen had happened before.

Whoever the hell I was, everyone in the room was looking at me. Meaning they were waiting for my response to the situation.

"Gentlemen, I've had some time to ponder." I took a deep breath and let it out slowly. "It's hard to admit that I might've been wrong ... but I believe I was. These people represent a bold new age for all of us. I still believe the general population should remain unaware of their presence. But they look like us, and as long as the highest security clearances are obtained, they should be able to blend in with us well enough. In bases we keep hidden and secure, of course."

"Are you suggesting that we be prisoners?" Richard asked in a pleasant tone.

"Far from it. I'm suggesting that we protect you and you protect us. A win-win, so to speak."

Richard nodded. "We would appreciate a mutually beneficial relationship. We would also appreciate not being put onto a reservation, so to speak."

"You'll need to become citizens, but still hold your autonomy. You're royalty, are you not?" I asked Alfred.

The three A-Cs looked surprised. So they hadn't played that card yet. "Ah, yes, yes I am," Alfred admitted. "And so is my cousin." He put his hand on Stanley's shoulder.

The reactions in the room were what I'd expected them to be. Instantaneous interest. Americans might've fought for independence from a crown, but we loved royalty in all its forms.

Richard noted the change in the atmosphere and jumped on it. "I'm so sorry that we didn't explain that. Prince Alfred is, understandably, trying to keep a low profile."

Kitty always said that Richard was the best diplomat the A-Cs had. As he smoothly turned the conversation towards the royal situation and also pointed out that the A-Cs had vast scientific and technical knowledge Earthlings didn't, I felt the atmosphere shift towards friendly positivity. Good.

"When will the President meet them?" I asked Katt softly.

"Now that you've approved, sir? Probably tomorrow." Katt cleared his throat. "Do you plan to stay to oversee their acclimation?"

"No. Please arrange for me to leave this evening, if it's possible. However, I'd like you to take charge. Be sure they're treated right, no funny business."

Katt stared at me. "Me, sir?"

"Yes, you. I'm confident you'll do a good job with it." There were advantages to this time hopping thing. I knew Katt would do a good job because he'd already done it. "Besides, you're close to their ages. You'll have that in common."

"Yes, sir. Thank you, sir."

"Make sure the proper orders are filed and all that." I had no idea if this was a good enough order or if, tomorrow or in a few minutes, the real person I was pretending to be would be asking what the hell Katt thought he was doing.

Katt nodded, and was called away by someone else of high rank. I chose this time to turn and leave. No one tried to stop me.

Back to the bathroom. I was about to look in the mirror—to see who I "was" before I went back into the stall to wait to be pulled back, but I never got the chance. The time loop snatched me away the moment the outer door closed.

oOo

I'd expected to go back to the mountaintop now for sure, but that's not where I ended up. I was backstage in a crowded theater and Aerosmith was playing. I was again glad Kitty wasn't here—she'd have rushed the stage and found a way to tackle Steven Tyler, timeline be damned.

Only it wasn't the band as I knew it. There were two guys there who weren't the ones on most of Kitty's albums. Meaning this was the early 80's and the band had lost two key members.

I looked around and, sure enough, 80's fashions filled the audience. Big hair, girls in ties, guys in open shirts with metallic kerchiefs around their necks. I managed not to wince—every era had clothes that looked cool then and didn't look so hot a few years later.

There was a girl next to me, bopping along to the music. Pretty and kind of funky. She reminded me a little bit of Kitty.

"Hey, you ready to see if he's here?" she asked me, as the song ended.

"Who?"

She rolled her eyes. "Come on. 'Becky, I need to talk to Joe Perry. You're tight with all those guys. Can you make it happen?' As if you don't remember that conversation that we had two hours ago?"

"Oh, right. Yes, I'd still like to meet him."

"Then come on, he just got here."

Sure enough, as Becky led me near the back, there was Joe Perry. He looked uncomfortable. Not a surprise. "You going to introduce us?" I asked her.

"Nope." She grinned. "I want to see you sweat."

"Thanks for that." Oh well, no time like the present. I went over to him. I considered what I could say, then figured I'd just cut to the chase. "Going to get the band back together?"

He shook his head. "No, man, I don't think so. We had a good run. Not sure we can handle being back together." He shrugged. "You know how it goes."

I didn't but, more importantly, I knew how Kitty went. Without this band creating *Permanent Vacation*, Kitty wouldn't hear "Dude (Looks Like a Lady)" and without that song, she wouldn't dig through all of Aerosmith's backlist. Without the backlist, Kitty wouldn't have the proof she needed that there were cool guys out there who supported women. And without that spark, without her firm belief that the guys in Aerosmith were, despite any and all rock star activities, feminists, Kitty wouldn't have the same confidence to be a feminist when it definitely wasn't cool anymore. Meaning she wouldn't be, well … Kitty.

"It's like family," I said to Perry. "You fight, and sometimes you hate each other, and maybe you go years without speaking, but when it matters, you pull together. And it matters."

He laughed. "If you say so, but, man, our family's messed up. And I don't know that we matter all that much, I mean, as a group."

"All families are messed up. Look, I know that, if you guys get back together, you're going to be one of the biggest rock bands in the world again. But it takes you and the rest, together. No substitutes. Only the five of you do it right, you and Tyler in particular."

Perry looked at the stage thoughtfully. "Maybe." He shrugged. "I'll think about it."

We listened to the rest of the show. Becky even made me dance with her for a few songs. The show was good, but it wasn't the Aerosmith I knew and I said as much to Perry. "You guys are right together. Not perfect, but right."

He grinned. "Fine, fine, we'll talk about it."

A thought occurred to me. Perry was the only one who didn't seem to think he'd seen me before. "Did we, ah, speak earlier?"

"No." He laughed. "Well, that's wrong. You were hanging around, but I was playing and I didn't hear a word you said."

"Good. It was what I was saying tonight, anyway."

The show ended, and, as the band came offstage, Perry went to Tyler and they started talking. I heaved a sigh of relief and waited. But the tug didn't come.

The idea of being left here in this time period wasn't really appealing. I was already born, so there was no risk of my becoming my own grandfather or something, but still, if I was going to be stuck somewhere, hanging out with the rock stars wasn't really my place or my thing. Kitty would've killed for the opportunity, but I'd rather have stuck with Einstein or Ritchey.

Becky hugged me, but then she went off with the band, and I wasn't invited along. I left the theater and stood on the street. Maybe I'd died, decades from now, back on the alien planet. Maybe my mind was gone and this was the world I was living in now in some way. Who knew what, if anything, the brain-dead saw? There were worse options, especially since I could see, hear, touch, and smell. I could probably taste, too, but there wasn't anything around to eat or drink.

I hoped I'd fixed the timeline. Maybe I hadn't. Maybe I had another destination and the time stream was waiting to see where to send me next. Maybe this was all some sort of bizarre dream. But my luck didn't run that way.

With time to think, I sat on the curb and, as cars and people passed me by, did just that. If I'd fixed the time stream, then the world, and the galaxy, wouldn't end in a horrific implosion. But that meant that things would be as they were, meaning Naomi would still be dead.

She would've loved this trip I'd taken. It would've been something special that would've been ours and ours alone. But there was no more "ours." When it came down to it, the moment I saw what would happen, how many would die if Naomi didn't make the sacrifice she had, I couldn't ask for the time with her again. It was too selfish, too wrong. She'd given up everything to keep our world—our entire universe—safe. I couldn't be less than her and allow it to be ruined, just so I could have one more day of happiness.

I felt something around me, something warm and loving. It felt like a hug. It didn't last long but at the same time, I could somehow still feel it, even when I knew whatever it was had stopped.

But before I could try to figure this out, the pull I'd given up expecting hit me.

oOo

I was back. We were on the mountaintop again, but I didn't feel the pull of the mind expander now. I wasn't sure if this meant I'd been saved in reality or not, though.

However, trapped or not, brain-dead or not, I could tell when we were, and, once again, we were thousands of years in the past.

"Hey, everyone, where's Boz and Turkey? King Benny? Fancy?" Kitty was asking about aliens we'd already met. Only, technically, we hadn't met them yet and wouldn't meet them for thousands of years.

Polite looks of incomprehension or fear were her reply. Kitty forged on. "Look, I realize you don't seem to know us, but we're the Gods. Your Gods."

This was a lie, only not really. I could see what was happening. Kitty was creating a tradition that would shape this world for thousands of years. Because of the time loop.

I opened my mouth to shush her, but pain hit so hard and fast that I slammed my mouth shut. The pain stopped. I decided to be smart and not try to interrupt, while Kitty shared all our God names that we'd been told about thousands of years from now.

Maybe it didn't matter. Maybe it all mattered. Maybe I'd never know.

oOo

We were back. On Earth. Where we belonged. Back *when* we belonged. I could feel it. And as we returned, time straightened itself out in my head. I still remembered everything, including how we'd been transferred back via a technique not unlike the beaming technology in *Star Trek*.

If I tried, I could see time as the mutable thing it was. Later I'd sort through it all. At my leisure, when the fate of the universe wasn't at stake. But as for now, we were all back, where we belonged, us and history, too, and things were right. Not perfect, but right.

The others had felt something wrong, the other humans in

particular, and they were asking about it. But I knew they needed to forget the déjà vu and move on. To live in time the way regular sentient beings did best—one moment after the other, in a linear progression from birth to death.

"It's just a side effect of the transfer," I said reassuringly. "Nothing dangerous or long-lasting. We're home, we're all alive and most of us are reasonably well. Nothing to worry about."

I'm the smart one, so they all listened.

CELL SERVICE
by Chris Barili

Harry Chambers stood back from the shelf in the musty mechanical room, crossed his arms, and thought about which box to go through first. There were about twenty, from shoebox size all the way up to the size of small televisions, and his instructions were clear: get rid of anything that didn't work or wouldn't sell.

In the next room, television news blared, a female anchor speaking in a tone straight from a disaster movie.

"One of the largest coronal mass ejections since the 1859 Carrington Event took place this morning, and has wreaked havoc across the northern half of the United States. Boston reports large-scale cellular outages, LaGuardia reports numerous air traffic control issues, and several small-scale power outages have struck the Northeast."

"Great," Harry muttered. "Why couldn't this have happened the day Celeste called her divorce lawyer?"

His eyes settled on a shoebox on the third shelf, right at eye level. He slid the box off the shelf and flipped the lid off. Inside were five old cell phones, phones they'd held onto for backups. The two oldest were as big as chalkboard erasers, with flimsy antennas that slid from their sheaths, one marked with a silver "H" to show it had been his. Next came a flip phone with a small LCD screen, followed by a slider phone with a slightly larger screen. Finally, an early generation smart phone rolled around in the box.

"One box of trash," Harry said. He put the top back on and dropped the box in the garbage.

He reached for a second box, but before his hand touched the dusty cardboard, a cell phone rang. It was an old-style ring, a pattern of electronic bleeps repeated three times before pausing and repeating. Harry pulled out his smart phone, but its screen stared back blank and gray. Stuffing it back in his pocket, he grabbed the shoebox out of the trash. Sure enough, the one marked with an "H" was ringing.

Something clenched in Harry's gut. That phone had been inactive almost a decade. How was it ringing? The battery should have been long-dead.

He thought about just removing the battery and throwing the phone away. This was insane, impossible. It should have been no more than a paper weight.

And yet it rang again.

Maybe he was losing his mind, but the ringing sounded urgent, as if pleading with him to answer. He had the feeling in the bottom of his stomach that not answering would be the biggest mistake he'd ever make.

Against all logic, he picked up the phone, raised its antenna, and pushed the talk button.

"Hello?"

"Hi, baby!" Celeste's voice sounded chipper, happier than she'd sounded in months. "What you doing right now?"

"Um, just cleaning out the mechanical room. How—"

"Why are you doing that? You should be out getting a bottle of wine, maybe some champagne."

"Champagne?" Harry tried to keep the incredulity out of his voice, but didn't quite succeed. "Why are we celebrating?"

"Don't you remember? Today's the anniversary of the day we met. I thought we'd share a glass and reminisce."

Harry checked the date on his smart phone. Sure enough, she was right. Alarms rang in his mind, his logical brain screaming this was wrong somehow, but Celeste's voice comforted him. She sounded like the old her, the girl he'd fallen in love with, so he decided to take a chance.

"Sure, um, that'd be nice."

She paused.

"Do you remember when you met me?" she asked.

"Of course."

"What made you fall in love with me?"

Harry didn't even have to think about his answer.

"Your eyes," he said. "I knew I could trust you by looking in your big, blue eyes. I could've gazed into those eyes forever."

"Aww, I love when you're romantic. It's so—"

The call ended, the phone beeping once then going dead in his hand. He held it away from his face and stared at it. He pushed the power button, but nothing happened. Even removing and reattaching the battery didn't help.

"Weird," he said. He dropped the phone back in the box. He couldn't explain why the phone had worked, or why the call had gone to it at all. They hadn't had the same number or even the same provider back then.

With a sigh, he slipped the box back on the shelf just as Celeste opened the door upstairs.

oOo

"What the hell are you talking about?" Celeste glared at him, her blue eyes frosted over.

She'd come home grumpy, and Harry should've known better than to bring this up, but he'd been so sure of their talk on the old cell phone.

Now she stood in their dining room, hip thrust to one side, arms crossed—a posture that said she was open to nothing, especially not to him.

"You called me earlier," he said. He raised his hand as if holding a phone. "On the cell phone. You talked about the day we met, and told me to open champagne."

"Have you been drinking?" She placed her hands on her hips, and thrust her chin out like she always did when irritated.

"No, not even a drop. In fact, you didn't even call me on my smart phone. You called me on the old cell phone, the very first one I had. How did you do that?"

She stepped closer, bending forward so she could look into his eyes, like his mother used to do when he was sick. He half expected Celeste to touch his forehead. Instead, she shook her head and turned away. He caught the scent of her shampoo—

vanilla and almond and a subtle hint of coconut. It'd been months since he'd been close enough to smell her. Now it made his heart ache.

"That thing's been dead for years," she said. "There's no way it's still working."

Harry dropped into a chair at the kitchen table, putting his hands in his lap. She was right, of course, she always was. The cell phone couldn't have worked. Yet, he recalled every word of their conversation, still felt the rush of adrenaline as he heard the music back in her voice.

"I'm telling you, Celeste," he said, "I had a conversation with you on that phone today."

"No. You didn't."

Two possibilities occurred to him: either she was lying or he was losing his mind. Celeste valued honesty in all things—she hated liars. So that left crazy, and he didn't feel crazy. Just confused.

No, he'd talked with Celeste—or someone—on the old cell phone. He knew it.

He ran to the basement and brought the shoebox upstairs. He threw off the lid, withdrew the old cell phone, and held down the power button for a count of three.

Nothing happened. Celeste sighed.

He held the button down again, this time counting to five.

Still nothing.

"I've seen enough." Celeste started for the stairs. "Get some sleep. You'll think straighter in the morning."

She left the room, not even waiting for his response.

He hefted the worthless phone in his palm, then dropped it back in the box and shuffled to the guest bedroom.

oOo

Harry trudged up the basement stairs, and across the linoleum that led to the front door. In one hand he carried a trash bag full of junk, in the other the box of cell phones. He managed to open the door and made it to the dumpster in the driveway when a cell phone rang.

It startled him so much he dropped the trash bag, shattering glass inside. He almost dropped the box of cell phones too, but caught it at knee level. He tore the top off and searched for the ringing phone.

He found it quick enough, as the old flip phone vibrated and skittered across the bottom of the box. He flipped it open and looked at the tiny LCD screen. All zeroes scrolled across the window, the words "unknown caller" underneath. He hesitated, again knowing how impossible this was. He pressed talk anyway.

"Celeste?" he asked.

"Harry, do you remember the bridesmaids' dresses I picked out? Oh my God, they were so incredible. They were that periwinkle color, which normally I wouldn't have chosen, but Beth and Connie both had light blue eyes and those dresses made them pop. And they went perfectly with the bouquets, and invitations, and … why aren't you saying anything?"

Harry's throat tightened. Their wedding had been eight years ago, when they'd used this cell phone, so why was she talking about it now? Still, the excitement in her voice—excitement about their marriage—wrapped him in a spell that held him fast.

"I like hearing your voice." It wasn't a lie. Hearing the light, musical quality return to her voice was like finding a diamond lost years ago. "I could listen to it forever."

"Well, that's good, since marriage is forever."

"You're not mad at me anymore?"

"Mad at you? No, I'm not mad. In fact, why don't you get out the video of our wedding. It's not quite our anniversary, but we can sit back and watch it and remember how much fun we had."

The part of his mind that solved problems and graded papers screamed at him, but Harry didn't listen. He'd missed this so much, the feeling that they were one mind in two bodies. It was the emotional intimacy their current marriage lacked. He couldn't let it go.

He nodded as if she could see him through the phone.

"Of course. We can watch as soon as you get home."

"Okay, I'll see you in a few."

He flipped the phone closed, placed it back in the box, and put the lid on as if he were wrapping a Christmas present. He carried the trash bag to the dumpster, dropped it inside, then paused. Shaking his head, he closed the dumpster and carried the shoebox back indoors.

oOo

Harry stepped back from the big screen TV, admiring the picture paused there. Celeste stood in her wedding dress, her hand looped through her father's arm, preparing to walk down the aisle. Her golden hair fell like waves of sunlight past her shoulders, and her eyes sparkled at the camera, lakes of blue.

Her dress had been magnificent, a hand-me-down from her mother, low-cut in the front and even lower in the back. The train was easily six feet long and had to be held up by the flower girl. The image still took his breath away.

He'd had to search for their wedding DVD, and had found it stuffed in the bottom of a drawer between a dusty photo album and some wrinkled napkins bearing their names. Seeing the old video brought back a nostalgic feeling the same way looking at black-and-white photos of his childhood did.

He lowered the lights in the entertainment room, and thought about lighting candles, but decided that was too obvious. He had to take things slow, baby steps, or he might scare Celeste away. So he set the volume at a level that would allow them to talk, and pulled down the blinds on the two basement windows. The scent of buttered popcorn swirled around the room from a bowl he'd put on the couch.

Upstairs, the front door clicked open and Celeste banged inside. Judging by the heaviness of her steps, she carried something, so Harry jogged up the steps to help her.

When he took the shopping bag from her, she stopped in her tracks and stared at him like he was a stranger. When he took her coat to hang it up, she stepped back, put her hands on her hips, and tilted her head to one side.

"Who are you and what did you do with Harry?"

Harry laughed, which seemed to make her even more nervous, as she rolled her eyes and moved to the kitchen. Harry followed her, and leaned against the counter so the sun streaming through the skylight warmed his face.

"I got it ready."

She opened the fridge and stuck her head inside.

"Got what ready?"

"We talked about it on the phone." She pulled her head out of the refrigerator and raised her eyebrows. He sighed. "Come on, I'll show you."

She followed him down to the darkened media room, but as soon as she saw the TV she froze.

"What is this?"

"It's our wedding video," he explained. "You called and told me to set it up."

"We didn't talk on the phone, Harry. But even if we did, I wouldn't ask you to run the video of the biggest mistake I ever made."

Harry had to fight to keep from doubling over like she'd punched him in the gut. He wanted to speak, but the air had left him. Across the room, Celeste still stood, glaring.

"I see what you're doing. This is hard for me too, but reliving old times won't make me fall back in love with you."

"I'm not ... I mean, you said ..."

"Oh Christ, Harry, are you losing your mind? We did not talk on the phone today."

Harry put his hand on the entertainment center to hold himself up.

"But you called me. On the old flip phone this time."

He thought about showing her the caller ID, but remembered it had come up all zeroes. Was he losing his mind? No, even though his mind called it impossible, his heart knew they'd spoken.

"Don't you have any doubts?" he asked her. "We were good once, Celeste. Better than good, we were great. Don't you think—"

"No, I don't think we should keep trying. I don't think we should try to remember, I don't think we should stay together, and I don't think we should try to fall back in love. If you have to try to fall in love, you're doing it wrong."

Harry dropped onto the sofa, spilling the popcorn. He

slouched, as if all the substance had rushed from his body, leaving nothing but a sack of skin draped over the cushions.

Celeste stood, and for a moment he thought he saw something in her eyes. A softening maybe, a moment when the ice chipped away and he saw the oceans of possibilities in her eyes again. And then it fled.

"Pull your head out of your ass, Harry," she said. "You can't change the past."

oOo

Harry leaned back in his office chair, hands behind his head, and propped his feet up on the desk. How many hours had they spent in here together, her balancing the checkbook while he worked on proposals or graded papers?

He dropped his feet to the floor, put his hands on the desk, and resolved to start cleaning out the drawers. In the living room, the TV news continued ranting about the potential damage from the solar flares. He rolled his eyes—everything was a disaster if it meant ratings.

He opened the first desk drawer, a deep one on the left side, just as a cell phone rang. Inside the drawer sat the box of old cell phones, right where he'd put it. He lifted the lid and saw light coming from the slider phone he'd had five years ago. Sighing, he reached inside.

"Celeste, is that you?"

"Of course it's me, silly. Who else would call you on this phone?"

He paused. "What do you mean?"

"Boy you're flaky today, Mr. Chambers." She giggled and Harry's stomach did a flip. "You just got this phone. No one else knows the number yet, so I'm the only one who can call you."

"Oh yeah."

She laughed again, the sound echoing in his mind like a church bell. "As long as you have your wits about you tonight."

"What's tonight?" This time she said nothing, and tension radiated through the phone. "Did I say something wrong?"

"No, not really," she replied. "It's not important."

He hated feeling like he'd hurt her, like he had crushed her laughter.

"It is to you, so I should move it up on my priority list."

Her voice carried a dull edge of sadness this time, making Harry flinch.

"It's not something you just move up your list. We were supposed to start trying tonight. You know ... to get pregnant."

Harry's heart stopped in his chest, and he forced himself to breathe. He remembered this conversation now, recalled the day they'd had it in real life over this phone. And he remembered their unsuccessful efforts to get pregnant, ending in the discovery that he was sterile. Having children would never be in their future.

He didn't know what to say to her now. None of his options made sense. This talk had planted the seeds that eventually grew into the massive, thorny hedge that stood between them. But it had happened five years ago.

In the background, the news anchor droned on.

"Solar flares of this magnitude can disrupt electrical grids, radio transmissions, navigational aids, and cell phone networks. There may be other effects scientists aren't aware of yet, as storms of this magnitude are rare."

"Harry? Harry did you hear me?"

He stood frozen, unable to move, speak, or even lower the phone. He stared straight ahead as it all set in.

He was talking to the past. The solar storm must have caused ... something to make it possible. There was only one way to find out. He would ask Celeste what date it was.

Yet when he opened his mouth, the wrong words came out.

"Sorry, just thinking."

"About what?"

"About making a baby," he lied. "About what great parents we're going to be."

"See?" she said. "It *is* important to you! We'll make an amazing family."

Before he could say anything else, the front door opened and Celeste clattered in. Harry punched the stop button and dropped the phone back in the shoebox, slamming the drawer.

He got to the kitchen as Celeste set a box of chardonnay on the counter. He leaned there with his arms crossed and watched her open the box, readying the spout. When she reached for a cup, he grabbed her hand and pulled her to him.

"I still love you," he said. "I always will."

She eased herself away, avoiding eye contact, and moved to a chair at the table. She sat with her head in her hands, rubbing her temples, and looked up at him through red-lined eyes.

"I don't know what to say," she said. "I loved you once, when we met, even when we got married. But somewhere along the line you changed and I fell out of love with you."

Harry took the chair opposite her.

"When we decided to get divorced," she went on, "I knew what I was doing, what I needed. You were who you were, and I didn't love who you were. But now I'm confused. The last few days you've been different. No ... not different, the same. A little bit of the Harry I fell in love with is peeking through, and I don't know what to think."

"Are you saying you're having second thoughts?"

She looked at the ceiling and let out a deep sigh.

"I don't know what I'm saying. Starting with that misunderstanding about the phone call, it's like you've gone back in time. Like the old Harry is fighting to come out, but he keeps running into a wall and hiding again. Throw in your erratic behavior of late, and I just don't know if this is real."

Harry felt a tickle in his chest, the slightest twinge in his heart. Fearing a heart attack, he grasped at his chest. It took him a moment to realize the unfamiliar feeling was hope.

"Maybe we're rushing into the divorce," he suggested. "We've been together for ten years, what are a few more months gonna hurt?"

Her brow knitted down as she studied his face, cocking her head to the side.

"I guess we could slow things down. I still think we should do it, but maybe we don't need to rush. We could start going out on dates. Maybe, if the old Harry shows up consistently, there's a chance."

This time his heart soared, as if tied to a kite in a strong wind, completely out of his control. An unexpected grin stretched his lips.

She winced. "Don't get your hopes up. This is just a slow-down, not a cancellation."

Still, as she poured herself some wine, Harry felt like he hadn't in years: alive.

oOo

Harry stood in the kitchen, his back to the window, the sun warming his shoulders as he smiled at the picture of Celeste he held before him. The picture had been taken five years ago, before things went south. Her smile radiated, even from the picture, as warm as the sun on his back.

He had the TV on again, the news echoing in the living room. Another anchor talked about the solar storm. It was dying off, he said. Experts predicted less interference, and said things should start working right again.

Harry hoped not.

He'd left the next cell phone, the two-year-old first generation smart phone, on the desk so he'd be sure to hear it ring. Sure enough, as he stood staring at the picture, it rang, an electronic rendering of the song played at their wedding. Harry jogged through the office door, snatched up the phone, and answered it on the second ring.

"Hi Celeste."

"Harry, I'm meeting Carrie for dinner tonight. I'll be home late." Tension vibrated in her voice, as if she were a guitar string plucked in anger. He remembered Carrie, the willowy brunette who'd whisked Celeste away in a torrent of whispers and gossip about him.

"Is everything okay, babe?"

Silence on the other end told him it was not.

"Come on, Celeste. I feel like you're mad at me."

"Is there something to be mad about?"

He hated it when she turned things around on him, made him incriminate himself even when he had no idea what he'd done. What bothered him even more was the sudden shift in mood for this wife from the past. Every other call had been pleasant, flirtatious even. But never irritated, never angry.

"I don't think so," he said. "We haven't spoken all day, so I couldn't have said something to tick you off."

"Were you ever going to tell me?"

"Tell you what? Come on, stop playing games."

"I'm not the one playing games, Harry." She bit off each word as if it were a finger on his hand. "You're the one keeping secrets. Anything you want to tell me about us making a baby?"

Now he knew why she was angry. This had been the beginning of their end.

"How did you find out?" He'd never asked that in real life. In the past.

"That doesn't matter. You didn't tell me for almost three weeks. Were you afraid I'd stop screwing you if we couldn't have a baby?"

"That's not fair," he said. "I knew it would disappoint you, so I was waiting for the right time. This isn't easy for me either, you know? I'm the one who's sterile."

"You must not have been hurting too bad, since you never saw fit to tell me. I would have understood, but you didn't give me the chance. You just kept pretending so I'd keep doing you."

"You really think this is about the sex? It was never about that. I didn't want to hurt you."

Static trampled her reply.

"You're breaking up. Say that again."

She repeated herself, but it wasn't any clearer. The static blasted his ear over everything. He pulled the phone away. Behind him, Celeste cleared her throat. She stood in the doorway, fists on her hips, her eyes blue lasers aimed at him.

"Who is she?" Her voice crackled with ice.

Harry stammered. "It's ... well ... it's no one. How long have you been standing there?"

She leaned against the door frame, crossing her arms. Harry felt a tightness, a life-threatening constriction inside his chest. The strangulation of hope.

"Long enough to hear you tell some woman you're sterile, that it's not about the sex, and that you didn't want to hurt her."

"Celeste, it's not what it seems."

"Really? It seems obvious to me."

He shifted in his chair, suddenly unable to sit still. What could he tell her? What possible explanation could make her believe he'd been talking to her in the past?

Nothing. But he had to try.

"It was you, honey." She narrowed her eyes. "Since the solar storm started, these old cell phones have come to life. Every day a different one has rung. And each day I talk to an old version of you. First it was ten years ago, when we met. Then it was when we got married. Then five years back, now two on this phone."

He held up the old smart phone, but it had gone dead, its screen gravestone gray. He pushed the power button, but nothing happened.

Still, Celeste's expression softened. She lowered her arms and stood, taking a step closer to him.

"Oh God, Harry. What's happened to you? You're talking on dead cell phones to old versions of me?"

He started to reply, but she cut him off with a wave of her hand.

"I was wrong. We're pressing ahead with the divorce. The old you never would've pulled something like this."

As she swept from the room, Harry put his head in his hands. His chest felt like it would cave inward. He put the smart phone in the box and tossed the box in the trash.

oOo

Harry knew something was wrong the minute he stepped in the front door. The quiet of the house seemed unnatural, more like that of a crypt than a home. He eased the door closed, trying to make as little noise as possible, but the plastic bag in his left hand crinkled and announced his arrival.

With a sigh, he trudged the few feet into the kitchen.

Celeste sat at the table, the five cell phones lined up before her. The box of chardonnay sat beside the phones, and a clear plastic cup rested in her hand, half-full of the silver fluid. Her hair looked like she'd walked through a hurricane, and the make up around her eyes had smudged just enough to tell him she'd been crying. In the living room, the TV showed the local news, muted.

He placed the bag on the counter, and started unloading it. He needed time to think. She didn't give him the chance.

"One of them rang."

His head snapped around and he looked her in the eye.

"Are you sure?"

She nodded, took a gulp of wine, and smacked the cup down on the table.

"I went to answer it, but I couldn't. I actually held it in my hand, felt it vibrate, but I couldn't push talk."

He sat across from her, patted her on the knee, and flinched as she jerked away.

"Don't touch me! I don't know what kind of game you're playing, Harry, but I didn't answer the phone and I'm not going to."

"Aren't you curious who's on the other end?"

She shook her head with a little too much emphasis. "It's you, Harry. Trying to trick me!"

Harry stood, paced for a moment, then returned to the chair.

On the living room television, a headline read, "One Last Large Flare."

"We're getting this divorce," she said. "No electronic tricks will change my mind."

He leaned on his elbows, looked her in the eye. "Listen, Celeste. I'm not playing any tricks. If that phone rang, one of us was supposed to answer. Someone is trying to tell us something."

She opened her mouth to respond, but the second of the brick-sized phones rang, its electronic beeps echoing through the kitchen at least ten times louder than normal. Celeste jumped, then slid back in her chair, putting space between herself and the cell phone. Her hands came up in front of her and she shook her head.

"No, I can't!"

"Okay, Celeste," Harry said. He picked up the phone, extended the antenna. "I'll answer."

He pushed the talk button, and held the phone to his ear.

"Hello?"

After a pause, a man said, "Who is this? Why do you have my wife's phone?"

He almost didn't recognize the voice without the vibrations he normally felt when talking. The slight change in pitch due to the electronics didn't help either, but an instant later he realized the voice was his own.

His heart thudded in his chest, the rhythm of hope's drum.

"Um, hold on a second," he said. "She's right here."

He extended the phone to Celeste with a gentle, sympathetic smile. Her eyes were as wide as the plastic cup.

"It's for you." He placed the cell phone on the table beside her, pushed the speaker button, and turned to go. "You're right: we can't change the past. But we can listen to it."

As he strode to the office, Harry smiled.

TEMPORALLY FULL
by Stephen Leigh

Everything around him was oddly familiar and yet strange.

Tom Finnigan hadn't been to Cincinnati in over two decades, not since the day he'd stormed out of his father's house for the last time. In that time, the landscape of the city had undergone a slow alteration. As he drove down the steep incline of Vine Street from the gaslight district in Clifton near the university toward the tall but compact core of downtown Cincinnati, he found himself saying, over and over, "Well, that's new ..." or "That wasn't here before ..." or "There used to be another building there, but it's gone now."

His wife, Cynthia, from the passenger seat, nodded with each remark. "Things change, Tom, especially when you've been away so long. That's what happens when you don't come back."

The mild rebuke in her voice didn't escape him. For over a decade, she'd been gently trying to have him to reconcile with his father, to attempt to heal the rift that had long loomed between them, but he had always resisted.

And now it was too late. His father was dead, would be buried tomorrow, and he hadn't been there for the final illness, when he might have had a chance to talk to the man from whom he'd fled at nineteen years of age. Tom tightened his grip on the steering wheel of their Prius, tightening his lips at the same time.

Too late for regrets. Too late for anything.

He blinked hard, blaming the sun for the moisture that had gathered there.

"This area's called Over The Rhine," he said to Cynthia. "Way back when, Central Parkway–that big intersection up ahead—used to be a canal. The poor German emigrants largely settled on the north side of the canal. So it became 'Over the Rhine.'" Cynthia lifted her head in acknowledgment, staring out the window at the passing storefronts. She had wanted to see his home town, and he had promised that he'd take her downtown to see Fountain Square and the river area before they went to his father's old house to help his sister Shawna pack up things. They passed Central Parkway and moved into the downtown section of the city and its maze of busy one-way streets.

"Dad used to work in that building there," he said, pointing to one of the high-rises ahead of them: an anonymous glass-and-steel edifice like a dozen others they could see. He flipped on the turn signal. "And he always parked in this garage."

He started to pull into the open-sided facility, just a half-dozen slabs of concrete stacked on rusting steel pillars. A large sign sagged against the pillar between the entrance and exit lanes, facing them. **TEMPORALLY FULL**, it declared in large block letters printed on the smeared poster board. He heard Cynthia laugh at the misspelling. "One of your students?" she asked.

"Hah," he said drily. "Very funny."

She laughed again. "Well, I guess we should back out," Cynthia said.

Tom hesitated, looking in his rearview mirror at the constant stream of passing traffic. He shook his head. "Nah, they'll have an open space somewhere. Someone's had to have left since they put the sign up. We can walk down to Fountain Square from here; it's only a block." Cynthia raised her eyebrows but otherwise made no reply. Tom eased the car forward up to the gate. He pressed the button and took the paper tongue that the machine stuck out at him, then went through into the garage as the gate lifted.

The first level of the garage was indeed full, every space taken, and Tom eased the car around the level, then up the ramp to the next. "Doesn't anyone in Cincinnati buy new cars?" Cynthia asked as they circled again.

"What do you mean?" he asked.

"Just look around."

He hadn't been paying much attention to the vehicles

themselves, only searching for an open space between them. Now that his attention had been drawn to them, he saw what Cynthia had noticed. The cars on this level all seemed to be at least several model years old. In fact—as they circled higher in the garage—the cars appeared to be getting increasingly older. "I wonder if there's some kind of antique car show in town," Tom mused. "You're right, there's not a car in here that looks to be newer than the 90s. Look, that's got to be a vintage early 90's Volvo, and, my God, that's a Ford Escort which could have just come off the lot, and there's—"

Tom hit the brakes hard, the Prius coming to a halt. Tom stared at the car outside his side window. He knew exactly what it was: a 1973 Corvette Stingray coupe, fire engine red and pristine, chrome rear bumper, but with that huge protruding nose and the cowl induction domed hood. But what he stared at most was the license plate: 251 GHU, with blue numerals and letters on reflective white and an outline of Ohio used as separator between the two, the motto "The Heart Of It All" in script letters underneath the state name.

"Tom?"

An old plate. Nothing like the ones he'd seen on the cars out on the street, most of which sported an "Ohio Pride" word cloud under a red triangle, and had four numbers, not three. And that plate number ...

"Tom?"

A red 1973 Corvette Stingray coupe had been his father's pride and joy. *"1973 was the year I met your mother. I always wanted one of those cars, but we couldn't afford it back then. Now, I finally can ..."* His father had bought a used 1973 Corvette six months after the death of Tom's mother in 1984, and it seemed—to Tom, anyway—that his father lavished whatever love and attention he had on the car rather than on his equally grief-stricken son and daughter. On his 18th birthday in late 1992, Tom convinced his father to let him borrow the 'Vette; he managed to total it when—with a regrettable lack of attention and too heavy an accelerator foot—he ran a stop light and T-boned a pickup truck in the intersection. His fault entirely, which his father never failed to mention whenever the wreck came up. It had been most telling to Tom that when he called his father to inform him that he'd just been in an accident, the very first thing his father said was "Oh God, how's the car?"

That incident had precipitated one of the too-frequent firestorms between himself and his father. The sad remains of the Corvette had still been sitting in his father's garage, mangled and broken, on the day Tom left, a silent monument to his failure as a son. His father, after his wife's death, always lived from paycheck to paycheck and could only afford liability insurance on a car as expensive as a 'Vette; since the accident was Tom's fault, insurance wasn't going to pay for the extensive necessary repairs.

"Tom!"

Cynthia's half-shout combined with her touch on his shoulder tore him from his reverie. He started. "Sorry," he said. "It's just—" He shook his head. "I think you're right; it was a mistake to come in here. We'll go park in the Fountain Square garage ..."

With a final glare at the Corvette, he put his foot on the accelerator, turning right into the descending ramp toward the waiting exit.

There was no one in the attendant's booth at the exit, and the gate was lifted. Tom was still shaking his head as he drove through.

oOo

Going into the old house on Nansen Street dredged up too many memories, too many of them bitter. The neighborhood had deteriorated over the years, and his father's house was no exception. It evidently hadn't been painted in a decade or more, blisters of the old blue-gray curling away from the wooden siding, revealing yet older coats and even bare wood. He was glad that he and Cynthia had decided to stay at a hotel rather than the old place.

Shawna's car was parked in the drive, and the front door stood open. He wondered how many of the neighbors he remembered still lived here; not many, he guessed. He and Cynthia walked up the cracked sidewalk with grass growing from every crack, up the crumbling cement steps, and into the house. Inside, the house was more cluttered and dirty than it had ever been. *Mom would have been so appalled at this.* The thought arose, unbidden.

"Did you two have a good morning?" Tom's younger sister Shawna Clawson—Clawson was her married name, which she'd kept even though she'd divorced her husband a decade ago—asked as they entered. She looked up from a cardboard box into which she was placing books, DVDs, and old videotapes from the shelving in the living room.

Shawna still lived in Cincinnati. It had been Shawna who had called Tom two days ago. *"I know you and Dad haven't spoken for, well, far too long. I understand. God knows I've fought with the man enough over the years myself. But the cancer's everywhere inside him now, and the doctors say the end could come any time. I thought ... well, I thought you might want to get down here, if only to say goodbye."*

So he'd come, filled with contradictory feelings roiling inside him: guilt and remorse mingling with residual anger and irritation, all tinged with the memories of the near fist-fights he and his father had had in those last days before he'd left, with his hatred of his father's conservatism, bigotry, and fundamentalist religious views. These hitherto unsuspected beliefs seemed to come boiling to the surface—a volcano of grief-fueled bile—after Tom's mother had died.

Tom was ten. The next nine years of his life were ones he'd tried hard to forget.

But he'd come back too late anyway. His father, as if to spite him for making the effort, died before they even started the drive down from Chicago.

"I enjoyed the tour of the city," Cynthia told Shawna. "Cincinnati's beautiful. All the hills, and the river. And such interesting buildings—Tom took me to see Union Terminal. I just love those old Art Deco buildings ..."

"Hey, Shawna, is all Dad's stuff still out in the garage?" Tom broke in. The two women looked at each other, and a look passed between them. He saw Cynthia give a small shrug to his sister.

"I haven't had a chance to clean anything out of there yet,"

Shawna said. "It's all still the way he left it, I'm afraid. Like the house."

"I'm going to take a look. I'll be back in a bit."

He turned and went out the front door again. Behind him, he heard the conversation start again. "Here, let me give you a hand with all this, Shawna ..."

The garage was in much the same shape as the house. Hinges protested as Tom pulled open one of the two wide, wooden doors. He blinked into the shadows lurking inside, feeling relief as he saw that the ruin of the Corvette no longer sat there. The knot inside his gut eased, even though he'd known from Shawna that his father had finally given up his dream of restoring the wreck and had the Corvette towed to a junk yard just a year ago, when he'd been told that the cancer was terminal.

The garage looked as if no one had used it in years anyway: cobwebs laced the workbench and scattered tools and hung in shabby curtains from the roof beams. Tom had to brush them aside as he searched for the light switch alongside the door. He flicked the switch; a dim overhead bulb flickered into life in response. The place looked no better in the light, but he could see what he'd come to see. For as long as Tom could remember, his father had kept all his old license plates: they were nailed to the support beams of the garage like trophies, a barrage of letters and numbers, all the varying styles of plates that had come and gone over the years. He scanned them now, the interior fist clenching his stomach again.

And twisting hard as he saw it: 251 GHU. It was a rear plate only, bent and scraped, and the decal sticker in the lower right had the date 1992 on it: the year he'd crashed the car. The year before he'd left.

He returned to the house. The two women looked toward him as he hovered near the front door, his hand in his right pocket, curled around the Prius' key. "Look, he said, "I know I said I'd help with this stuff, but there's something I have to check out."

He could see the disappointment in Shawna's face; the concern on Cynthia's. "I thought ..." Shawna began, then stopped. She looked toward Cynthia.

"This is important?" Cynthia asked him. Tom nodded. "Then

go on," she told him with the hint of a smile. "I'll stay here and help Shawna."

Tom glanced at Shawna; she nodded. "Thanks," he told them both. He kissed Cynthia, hugged Shawna, and left.

oOo

The shabby **TEMPORALLY FULL** sign was still up at the garage when he arrived. He eased the Prius into the garage, took the ticket that was spat out at him at the gate, and entered. He circled up the ramp, watching the cars. Yes, as before, they seemed to become older as he rose. When he saw the red Corvette still snuggled in its space, he felt his vision shimmer, as if with a sudden dizziness.

251 GHU. The license seemed to shout to him. Tom stopped the Prius just behind the Corvette, unbuckling and getting out to crouch at the back bumper. The decal in the lower right corner was dated 1992. Tom shook his head. Looking around—there was no sign of anyone about—he went to the driver's door. *"Never leave anything in your car worth stealing, boy, not unless you want trouble."* His father's words. *"Then you needn't bother locking it either—that means no one's going to smash your window or ruin the door trying to get in."*

Tom tried the door; it opened. He slid behind the seat, inhaling the familiar scent of leather, polish, and the unfiltered Camel cigarettes his father always smoked, putting one hand on the four-speed stick shift and the other on the leather-wrapped steering wheel. It all felt as he remembered it, down to the fact the seat was slightly too far forward for him, set for a smaller man.

A man like his father.

Tom reached over to the map slot—there was no glove compartment—pulled out the registration card for the vehicle and scanned the name and address typed with a faded ribbon on the lines there: *Roger Finnigan, 121 Nansen St.* ... His father's name; his address. For a moment, the interior of the car swirled around him, fluid, and he had to close his eyes, pressing the card stock of the registration hard between his thumb and forefinger.

This isn't possible. This can't be. He caught his upper lip in his teeth until the vertigo passed, and opened his eyes again. The name stubbornly remained. He tossed the card back into the map slot.

His father had always been a man of habits; that was one of the minor traits that had driven a wedge between them. Tom was habitually late; his father was punctual to a fault, kept to his routines meticulously, and would become unfathomably (to Tom, anyway) enraged if those routines somehow fell apart. He left work every day at 5:30. He was always home by 6:00, as long as traffic didn't interfere. Tom glanced at his phone: it was 5:10 now. He slid out of the Corvette's seat and went back to the Prius. He'd wait. If this was somehow, miraculously, his father's car, if this wasn't an indication of a psychotic break on his part or a terrible prank by someone, then his father would be coming here in a few minutes.

Tom didn't know what would happen then, what he could possibly say in that impossible moment, in such an impossible second chance. He only knew that he had to stay, had to be here to find out.

He waited until 5:30.

5:45.

6:00.

In all that time, there was no activity in the garage at all. No one came to any of the cars. No other cars moved on the ramps. He was alone.

At 6:10, Tom heaved a sigh. He reached into the bottom glove compartment of the Prius and found the notebook and pen Cynthia had shoved in there. With the notebook propped against the steering wheel, he wrote a letter to his father.

Dad, it began simply, but once he started, everything came tumbling out from under the pen: his anger and resentment, all the pent-up emotions from their estrangement, the regret that they'd never reconciled, that he hadn't been able to be there at the end, the wish that sometime, somehow, they might have reached out to each other and worked their way through the pain to some understanding.

Dad—I wish you could have known how I felt, how much all

this hurt me as much as it might have hurt you. I wish you knew how much I regret all that wasted time.

It was 6:35 as he finished. Wiping at his eyes, he tore the pages from the notebook and folded them. Going back to the Corvette, he opened the driver's door again and put the folded note on the leather passenger seat. He stood there for several minutes, just looking down at the car, at the letter. *This is stupid. This isn't his car,* can't *be his car. This is a delusion. You're on the edge of cracking up, and the longer you stay here, the worse it's getting.*

Back in the Prius, he stared again at the Corvette, which stubbornly refused to vanish. Then he put his foot on the brake, pressed the power button, and put the car in gear.

He drove away.

oOo

The next day was interminable. At the funeral home, he stood with Shawna and Cynthia as a shuffling line of his father's friends, old neighbors, and former co-workers shook their hands and muttered meaningless platitudes about how much they were going to miss Roger.

Miss him? I ran away from him. That's what he wanted to tell them through the forced smile.

At the cemetery, with Cynthia's arm linked tightly through his and Shawna standing at his other side, they watched as the priest spoke a few words about someone who was a stranger to Tom, then intoned a blessing over the casket. Tom looked more at the headstone at the head of his father's open grave, the family name *Finnigan* carved on a ribbon with roses at either end; on one side: *Camille G, Feb. 12, 1951 - Sept. 9, 1984,* on the other *Roger A., June 1949 -* with the death date still blank. Centered beneath both panels: *Married June 15, 1974.* Shriveled flowers drooped in the vase below his mother's name; Tom wondered who'd put them there, and when.

Afterward, the funeral director dismissed the onlookers to allow the workers to place the casket in the waiting hole. "You okay, Tom?" Cynthia asked him.

"Not really," he said, honestly. "Look, I feel like I'd like to be alone for a bit. Shawna, could you give Cynthia a ride back to the house? You guys go on. Just give me a few minutes, and I'll come out and help you guys finish sorting through things."

Cynthia's hand stroked the shoulder of his suit coat. "Are you sure, darling? I could stay with you, and we could just sit quietly if that's what you want. Here or wherever."

He took her hand and brought her to him, hugging her hard and kissing the top of her head. "Thanks," he husked out, "but no. I just … I just want to have some private time. I'll be okay, I promise."

Her green-blue eyes lifted to regard him, searching his face. Then she rose up on her toes and kissed him. "If that's what you need," she said. "We'll be waiting for you. Got your cell?"

He nodded. "I do, and it's on. See you soon …"

He watched Cynthia and Shawna walk away with the rest of the small knot of well-wishers. He leaned against a tree on a small rise above the grave, staring without really seeing as the funeral home staff gathered up the flowers and wheeled the now empty casket carrier back to the hearse. They drove away as the cemetery workers winched the casket slowly down into the grave, removed their equipment, and directed the backhoe operator to move the earth back into the grave from the mound alongside. They began dismantling the temporary tent over the site.

It was all so ordinary for them. They weren't disrespectful at all, but this was just a job to which they had no personal connection. Twenty minutes later, they too left. Tom walked back down the slope to the new grave, to the raw earth flattened and marked with the backhoe's tracks. He sniffed, looking down at his father's last resting place, but there were no tears. There hadn't *been* any tears, not when he'd been told about his father's impending death over the phone, not when he'd hugged Shawna after they first arrived, not when he saw his father in the casket, looking like a waxen stranger on the satin cushions, not during the funeral ceremony. Yes, the grief had threatened a few times, but he'd been able to hold it back. All he had to do was remember the bad times, the arguments, the fights, and any sorrow was flayed to shreds.

He found himself dry-eyed entirely, staring at the grave, and he wondered why.

He was my father. There should be grief. There should be sorrow. It's bothering me enough underneath that I somehow imagined seeing that goddamn old car of his.

No. ... There was only the simmering, diffuse anger.

That last night, when he came at me and hit me and I realized that I was this close to letting go and beating him in return, that if there'd been a knife or a baseball bat at hand for him or for me, something worse could happen. ... I knew I had to leave.

"The problem was, Dad, that we were too much alike, at least in some ways. At least that's the conclusion I've come to: both of us were too stubborn and too convinced we were right to ever apologize, to try to get past the arguments and fights." The words sounded odd, spoken into the hush of the cemetery. He almost laughed. "God, that sounds maudlin, and you always made fun of people who got all sentimental—which is why I always thought it was so strange that you'd go out and buy that damn Corvette and fix it up." Tom shook his head. "I never understood you. You should have come up to Chicago to visit us; I should have come back to Cincinnati when I first heard you were sick. Now it's too late, and I'm sorry for that, Dad. I really am."

He looked up. The Prius waited for him on the winding blacktop road up the slope. "Goodbye, Dad. Wherever you are, I hope you're finally happy, because I have no memories of you ever being that way."

There were still no tears. His eyes remained stubbornly dry. Tom shook his head and walked up the hill toward the car.

oOo

Cynthia glanced up from the box she was filling as Tom entered, brushing back her hair behind her ear. She'd changed from the dress she'd worn at the funeral to jeans and T-shirt. "Hey," she said softly. "You look exhausted."

"It's been a tough day all around," he answered. He could hear Shawna working in the next room. *All the useless kipple we collect in life. ...* He wanted to say more, to tell Cynthia about watching the final burial and his thoughts at the gravesite, about going back to the garage and writing the note that was undoubtedly sitting in some stranger's car. But he couldn't find a way to start. He just stood there, his hands in his pockets.

Cynthia closed the top of the box she was packing and ran the tape gun over the flaps, the tape tearing away from the roll with a sound like ripping fabric. She laid the tape gun on top and uncapped a permanent marker. He could smell its astringent odor as she scribbled on the lid. "I brought a change of clothes for you, love," she told him. "They're up in your dad's bedroom. I thought you'd want to get out of the suit before you started helping us. Goodwill's coming tomorrow to pick up most of this stuff, and Shawna's taking some of your mother's old china." She handed him an empty box. "Here. While you're up there, you should put anything you want to keep in this."

He nodded. He watched her for a few more seconds, then turned and climbed the stairs to the second floor.

The bedroom was as cluttered and dirty as the rest of the house. The dresser on one side of the room had two drawers open, with clothing and underwear half pulled out as if his father had left it that way after finding what he wanted to wear. The bed was unmade, the pillowcase stained and old, though Cynthia had straightened the covers at the foot of the bed and laid out his jeans, a shirt, and sneakers there. As he changed his clothes, he glanced around. Pill bottles—some open, some not—lined the nightstand. A desk sat across from the bed, piled with papers and bills; Tom could see his father's checkbook on top of one of the piles.

He knew that Shawna had power of attorney for his father; she'd be the one to have to deal with the bills and his checking account.

After changing, he sat on the desk chair, spinning around once lazily. He wondered what Cynthia had thought he might want to take back with them from the room. Certainly not clothing; his father had been shorter and significantly more stout that Tom. The furniture here dated back several decades. None of it had ever belonged to him.

The chair stopped with Tom facing the desk again. He opened

the middle drawer; it was stuffed full with old pencils, pens, rulers, scissors, staples, ancient checking account statements, and the like. He tried one of the pens on a piece of paper—it didn't write. The staples were rusted; the scissors dull with the tips broken off.

Junk. Shabby and decrepit, like the rest of his father's life. He opened the side drawers: papers, bills, folders with scribbled hints as to their contents on top. Then, in the bottom left drawer …

The envelope had "Tom Finnigan" scrawled in pencil, along with his Chicago address, as if his father had intended to mail it to him, but there was no stamp on the envelope. He reached down and plucked it from the pile of old medical receipts on which it rested, turning it in his hand, a plain, undistinguished #10 business envelope. He could feel pages inside. Tearing open a corner of the flap, he ran his finger along the seam to open it. He pulled out the papers inside, held together with a bent paperclip. The paper itself was from a cheap notebook: brown along the edges, brittle, and foxed here and there with splotches, while another thin strip of different and newer paper was folded on top of the main sheets. Tom opened the pages and glanced at the handwriting there.

Stopped.

His own handwriting stared back at him: the note he'd written yesterday. *Dad — I wish you could have known how I felt …*

The paper rattled in his hand as he put it down on the desk. He flipped through the two pages of scribbling to the paper at the back. A different hand had written the words there, dating it at the top: *June 15, 2013*—last year, when his father had finally junked the wrecked Corvette.

I found this while going through the car one last time. Don't worry, Tom. I knew before you told me.

He sat there for several minutes, just breathing and staring at the typically brief note, before pushing away from the desk and rushing back downstairs. Cynthia looked up at him wide-eyed as he half-ran toward the door. "I'll be back soon," he told her. "Don't worry."

oOo

He headed south. Toward downtown.

Toward the garage.

He found himself squinting as he approached the edifice and turned into the entrance. The sign was gone. The wooden barrier of the entrance gate was broken, most of it missing. A grimy temporary booth sat alongside the useless gate, the glass smeared and filthy. A bored-looking teenager sporting dreadlocks leaned out from the booth, setting down his smartphone next to the cash register. "Five bucks," he said, holding out his hand. Ahead of him, the stalls Tom could see were all vacant.

Tom reached for his wallet. "What happened to all the cars?" he asked the kid as he fished out a bill. "The auto show over or something?" The only response was a puzzled shaking of the kid's head. "Yesterday, you were all full," Tom continued in explanation. "Lots of old cars."

The kid stared at Tom as if he'd suddenly grown horns. He didn't touch the bill Tom was holding out toward him. "Mister, this place ain't never been anywhere near full in the two months I've worked here." He waved at the empty spaces beyond the gate. "It looks just like this every damn day. Hell, they're tearing the place down next month for some new office building—which is fine by me. I don't know where you think you were at yesterday, but it weren't here." He glanced at the fiver Tom was still holding out toward him. "You sure you still wanna park here, buddy?"

He wasn't sure. He wasn't sure of anything at the moment. "Take it," he told the kid, who shrugged and hit the register, handing Tom a receipt.

"Park where you want—you pretty much got your pick." He chuckled at his own joke. "Just put the receipt on the dash."

Tom tossed the receipt onto the dashboard and touched the accelerator. There were a few cars on the lowest level, but the vast majority of the spaces were open. He took the ramp up to the next level, the level where the Corvette had been. The garage echoed to the sound of his tires and whine of the engine that kicked in as the car climbed. That level was entirely empty, as was the next one.

He stopped the car, putting it in park in the middle of the lane and hitting the power button to turn off the car. He slumped back into his seat.

The cars were here. We saw them. Cynthia saw them, too, the first time. It was this place, the place where Dad always parked. It had to be.

Except that this place was empty: of cars, of memories. The garage was vacant of life.

There was nothing here. He wasn't even sure why he'd wanted to come here again, what he'd expected to gain even if the red Corvette had still been sitting there. Another cryptic note? Another whisper? A pathway to communicate with his father?

His letter, impossibly aged, and his father's note sat accusingly on the passenger seat.

The Corvette had been there. It had been.

Tom jabbed angrily at the blue power button, watching as the dash lights came on in response. He went to toggle the car into drive, but stopped. The garage outside the window was swimming in his vision, and he sobbed once, hard.

Clenching the steering wheel with white-knuckled hands, leaning back against the headrest, Tom allowed the tears to finally come.

NOTES AND QUERIES
by Juliet E. McKenna

"Thank you." As the last chord of their song echoed around the medieval masonry, Ellie smiled at the mum dropping coins into her guitar case.

She didn't think the wide-eyed toddler in the pushchair had even noticed her, but that was nothing new. Short and dark, even playing a guitar, didn't get a second glance beside tall and golden haired with a voice that turned heads a hundred yards away.

Ellie wasn't complaining. Jocelyn was a good mate and they made far more money busking together than they ever would alone. "Have we got time for another one?"

"Not really. Anyway, there's Callum." Jos nodded to a familiar figure clutching a violin case on the edge of their audience.

"Fair enough." Ellie unplugged her guitar from their portable amp while Jocelyn gathered up the microphone and stand.

"Cheers." Callum hurried forward so no other busker could claim this particular pitch for the next hour.

"Where next?" Ellie scooped their latest takings into one of the paper bags they filched from the supermarket's self-service bread display. She wrote the time and place on the side before zipping the cash inside the black satchel they kept tied to the amp. "By the church?"

Jocelyn hunched her shoulders against the cold breeze. "Someone will be there by now. How about a break and we head for St Michael's at four?"

"Okay." Ellie led the way down the alley across the street toward the cafe they had discovered in their first year. Not an international chain offering students a place to sit with their laptops and drink overpriced variations on espresso, but an old-school greasy spoon favoured by taxi drivers and delivery men, as oblivious to the university as that venerable institution was to the city that housed it.

"If we stay at St Michael's till the last shops shut, we'll make more than we would if we head for the bus station now—"

Ellie held the cafe door open. "You don't have to convince me."

Jocelyn kept a spreadsheet of all their takings, week by week and pitch by pitch. A scientist to her core, she couldn't do anything without gathering and analysing data. So now they knew exactly how to make the best of the designated spots in the city centre where the local council decreed licensed musicians could play for an hour at a time. That gave everyone a chance at the most lucrative pitches and saved shopkeepers from a whole day with a talentless trombone outside their door.

Jocelyn headed for a corner table with their equipment. Ellie propped her guitar against a chair. "Tea or coffee?"

"Coffee, please." Jocelyn unbuttoned her coat and loosened her scarf. The cafe window was misted with condensation as the warmth met the wintry cold outside.

Ellie joined the queue at the counter and smiled at the waitress. "One tea, one coffee and two ham and cheese toasted sandwiches, thanks."

The waitress poured her tea first. While she was tutting over a chipped mug and finding another one, Ellie ripped open two packets of sugar and dumped them into the steaming liquid. It had already been a long, cold Sunday and they'd spent Saturday outside as well. Worth it though, over these weekends in the run up to Christmas.

Well worth it. As the waitress returned with Jocelyn's coffee, she reached into an inside pocket for the bank notes they'd earned. They always tucked those safely away, in case of some gust of wind or a thief trying to snatch some cash.

Ellie handed over a twenty and carefully picked up both mugs with one hand, waiting for her change.

Instead the waitress handed the note straight back, with a

shake of her head and tightened lips. "I can't take this," she snapped. "Not legal tender. Not for years."

"What?" Ellie stared at her.

The waitress showed her the Queen's head before flipping the note over to reveal the moustachioed gentleman on the back. "Elgar? He's had his day, love. Been keeping this under your mattress?" Her sarcasm verged on accusation.

"What? No, sorry." Ellie wondered how she'd ever felt cold. Now she was red-faced and sweating with embarrassment as she put down the mugs and fumbled for her wallet.

The waitress sniffed as she accepted a different twenty, examined it closely and then counted out Eleanor's change. "You want to keep your eyes open. It's not like they've just issued the new notes."

So now the woman just thought she was a fool rather than a fraud. Mortified, Ellie shoved her change into a coat pocket and picked up the mugs. "I'm really sorry. I didn't realise—"

"I'll bring your toasties over when they're done." The waitress looked a little less severe.

"What was that all about?" Jocelyn accepted her coffee.

Ellie grimaced. "We got an old note this morning. She thought I was trying to pass it off onto her."

Honestly, how could she have missed it? Of course she knew Edward Elgar had been replaced by Adam Smith, the last time the Bank of England had redesigned the currency and withdrawn the old notes after the requisite grace period.

Adam Smith, Eighteenth century, Scots philosopher and economic theorist. Ellie was a history undergraduate after all, even if Medieval France was her period.

"Never mind, we can still pay it into the bank, can't we?" Jocelyn shrugged. "Now, shall we mix things up a bit by St Michael's? Do you reckon it's too early for carols?"

"Yes, I do," Ellie said with feeling. "It's barely a fortnight since Halloween."

oOo

Their takings didn't suffer for lack of Christmas carols, Ellie thought with satisfaction as they arrived back at their flat. She dumped the black bag on the table with a solid thud and the muffled chink of coins. Resting her guitar against the sofa, she shrugged off her coat.

"Tea or coffee?" Jocelyn yelled from the kitchen.

"Tea! Two sugars!" Ellie unzipped the satchel and lined the paper bags up on the old oak table, the wood ringed by countless careless students' hot cups. Emptying the first, she began counting pennies.

"Not too much copper." Jocelyn grinned as she set down the mugs. Pulling up a chair, she began searching for tuppences.

They always did it this way; pennies and tuppences stacked in tens and fives, ten stacks making a quid. Then fives and tens, then twenty and fifty pence pieces. Finally, one and two pound coins, all neatly ranked on top of each paper bag showing which pitch had earned them what, ready for bagging up in plastic to take to the bank.

"I can pay this lot in tomorrow morning," Ellie offered. "My first lecture's not till ten."

"Thanks." Jocelyn would be in the lab by nine on a Monday. "Oh, here's a foreigner."

She flicked a battered coin across the scuffed table. Ellie studied the Cyrillic writing.

"Ukraine." She fetched the box they kept on the book case. They had small change from countries as far away as China now. Along with enough Euro to come in handy when they went travelling next summer.

Two months exploring Europe, that's what they were saving up for. No history essays for her, no chemistry practicals for Jos. A chance to forget about the decisions they'd have to make after the summer. When Ellie's mum and dad would be expecting her to take the Civil Service entrance exam or think about teacher training.

Ellie had her heart set on a music course at the local technical college. Just for a year. To learn about production and mixing tracks properly, instead of working it out by herself. Just for a year. She could use the money Gran had left her to pay for the course. She could decide what to do with the rest of her life after that, couldn't she?

Jocelyn had her laptop open and was entering their totals on her spreadsheet. "How did we do for notes? Apart from that old one."

Ellie grabbed her coat and reached into the inside pocket. "Another twenty, two tens and three fivers."

"Then we've earned three hundred and thirty five quid! Okay, where were we playing when we got them?" Jocelyn's hands were poised to enter the data.

Ellie told her, then looked more closely at the ten pound notes in her hand. "Hang on."

Charles Darwin was easily recognisable on one but Jane Austen? She flipped the famous authors over. There was the Queen, on all the money ever since Ellie could remember. Ever since her parents could remember. But backing Jane Austen? The Prince of Wales as King, greyer and craggier than ever?

"Someone's playing silly buggers." She handed over the note.

"What—?" Jos looked up, puzzled. "What is it? A prop from some play? Is drama soc doing science fiction this term?"

"Maybe it's from a game?" Ellie shook her head, disbelieving. "Two duff notes in one day."

"The bank will take that old one,' Jocelyn reminded her. "So we're only down a tenner."

She hit the keyboard with a decisive gesture. Screwing up the fake ten pound note, Jos launched it across the room at the waste paper basket. The stubborn paper was already uncrumpling itself to fall short of the waste paper basket. She ignored it.

"Right, how about firing up your laptop and I'll kick your arse at Battlefield?"

"In your dreams," Ellie scoffed, heading for her room to fetch her computer bag.

oOo

Maybe that hadn't been the best idea. She had thrashed Jocelyn but getting to bed before midnight might have been more sensible at the start of the week. Eleanor yawned as she stood in the bank queue. That was one inconvenience paying in bags of coins; no computerised system to deposit them.

Though someone was having some trouble with the latest modern technology. She watched idly through the window as a weather-beaten, middle-aged man took a sharp step backwards from the ATM. Bemused, he looked at something white in his hand.

The black satchel was dragging at her shoulder. Three hundred odd quid in change was jolly heavy and she already had her laptop in her backpack. She lowered the bag of money to the ground as she watched the unfolding drama outside.

Another man waiting to use the cashpoint wanted to know what the problem was. The first man waved his hands, his gestures eloquent with frustration.

The second man took the wad of white paper and unfolded it. Ellie watched them both shake their heads in mystification. The first man came into the bank, indignant, the paper clutched in his fist. The second man joined the queue for the other ATM. When a woman came up to use the vacant one, he put out a hand and warned her off.

"What's all this rubbish?" The indignant man went straight to the next vacant bank teller and slapped one of the sheets of paper down. "Some advertising stunt?"

"Excuse me! There is a queue." The elegantly dressed woman at the head of the line glared.

"I'm sorry." The hapless clerk tried to share her apology between both customers. "Sir, I'm sure the Enquiry Desk can help you?"

She sounded more hopeful than convinced to Eleanor.

"Thank you." The lady who'd been waiting walked forward and claimed the counter with her sizeable handbag, knocking the crumpled paper to the floor.

An older woman in a smart suit hurried forward from the Enquiry Desk. "Can I help you, Sir?"

"What's all this?" The middle aged man waved the papers still in his hand. "I wanted my money, not some daft leaflets!"

"I'm sure we can sort everything out."

As the suited supervisor ushered the man away, Ellie looked at the piece of paper on the floor. It had landed close enough for her to see a swirl of ornate engraving around old fashioned letters. What on earth was it?

She looked at the queue of eight people. With only three counters open, no one was moving quickly and there wasn't anyone waiting behind her. Darting forward she picked up the paper and reclaimed the end of the line.

Smoothing it out, Ellie frowned. The intricate printing said "Bank of England." Britannia sat there proudly in her draperies, armed with shield and spear, endorsing the promise to pay the bearer on demand the sum of FIVE pounds.

She looked more closely. There was a date. This had been issued in London on 19th March 1932. Ellie rubbed the paper between fingers and thumb. It didn't feel like laser printer paper and it wasn't a standard size she'd ever seen in packets of stationery.

"I tried to take some money out and got this rubbish instead!" The middle-aged man's voice rose in exasperation.

"Could I just see your debit card, sir?" the supervisor asked, placating.

Ellie looked out of the bank window to the other side of the street. That's where they'd been playing yesterday, when they'd got that weird tenner, with Jane Austen and the Prince of Wales on either side. The one Jos had guessed was a prop for a time travel play.

Except it had been incredibly detailed for something only going to be seen from a distance. From what Ellie remembered, the engraving was just as detailed as any of the notes she was about to pay in; all swirls and pinpoints and cross-hatching. There'd even been a silver hologram stamp and the paper had been too stiff to be easily scrunched up and thrown into the bin. Just like a real bank note.

But how could it be real? How could a bank's cashpoint be issuing notes with a king's head on the back? Bank notes from the future?

As that idea formed and lodged in her mind, Ellie's first instinct was to dismiss it. Then she looked down at the white five pound note in her hand. They'd been playing opposite the bank on Saturday when they'd got that old twenty. She remembered that quite clearly. There weren't many people so generous to buskers, no matter how cold it was, however enticing Jocelyn's smile might be.

What if whoever had given them that note had got it out of the same ATM? Bank notes from the past as well as the future?

"I'd better get the manager." The supervisor hurried past.

Two more people got their turn at the counter. Ellie fished out her phone and brought up the web browser, ignoring the polite notice asking customers to refrain from using their mobiles and causing delays.

She searched for images of five pound notes from the 1930s. She compared the picture to the paper she held in her hand. Even allowing for the cramped image on the little screen, it looked exactly the same to her.

A forgery? How could old, fake notes end up in an ATM? Why would anyone do such a thing? She added "fake" to her web search. A moment later she nearly dropped the phone.

Collectors paid *how much* for Second World War forged fivers? Over two thousand pounds apiece? Then she saw how much ordinary old-style five pound notes were worth. She looked at the one in her hand. Two hundred and fifty quid?

"I have to say, these do look genuine to me."

Ellie looked up to see the branch manager had arrived. A man about her Dad's age was leafing through the customer's sheaf of white paper.

"And you're saying you got these out of our cashpoint?"

The weather-beaten man curbed his annoyance with visible effort. "I'm not just saying it. That's what happened." He began telling his story all over again.

Someone behind Ellie coughed pointedly. "Excuse me, love?"

She realised the queue had been moving while she was searching the Net. The next vacant teller would wave to her. She dragged her heavy bag along the floor and looked out of the window. No one was using the ATM issuing the bizarre notes.

"We do have his withdrawal recorded." The supervisor turned the screen of the Enquiry Desk's computer to show the manager.

"Next, please!" A bank teller looked over towards the queue.

Ellie hauled the weighty bag up and headed for the counter. But she didn't set the satchel down and start unloading the coins. She handed over the white fiver instead, gesturing towards the Enquiry Desk.

"That gentleman dropped this." It wasn't her money after all.

She walked quickly towards the door. Not running, not rushing. Not attracting attention. Just someone who'd remembered something she had forgotten.

No one outside was waiting to use either of the ATMs. Ellie looked at the one closest to the door. It still looked as if it was working. The screen showed the usual logo and there were no red warnings over the slots. She took her bank card out of her wallet.

For a moment, she thought the machine wouldn't accept it. The cashpoint had already been shut down. So that was that.

For an instant, she was relieved. It had been a mad idea. Then she realised her hand was shaking so much that she wasn't actually getting the card into the slot. Drawing a deep breath, Ellie concentrated on getting the sliver of plastic into the machine.

The screen asked her for her PIN number. Personal Identification Number number. That unnecessary repetition always seemed so silly to her. She clenched her fists and spread her fingers and entered the digits on the keypad.

What service did she require? Ellie's mouth was dry and her heart was racing. Was she completely insane?

But even if she didn't make any profit, how badly could she lose out? It wasn't just notes from a decade ago that banks would still honour for their face value. Even if she couldn't find a way to sell any white fivers herself, she could just bring them back here. As long as they were genuine. The branch manager seemed to think they were. If they weren't? Well, they'd already had one customer turn up with a handful and ask what was going on. Presumably her notes would be the same as his. They'd have an electronic record of her making this withdrawal. She'd just say she'd used the ATM straight after him and then had to rush off. Late for a lecture or a tutorial. Ellie could play the clueless student just this once.

But what if she got more of that other money saying Prince

Charles was the king? Well that would be immediately obvious. She'd show the weird notes to everyone in the queue and then go straight into the bank with as many witnesses as she could muster. Maybe even force a few tears. A poverty stricken student with nothing to pay the bills. With any luck, some of those notes would have already been brought in this morning, if the machine had been issuing them on Saturday.

Was she prepared to take that risk? Ellie stared at the ATM screen. What service did she require? Cash, with a receipt, just in case she had to prove when and where she'd got fake money, to make sure she got reimbursed. She stabbed the button with a shaking finger.

What amount did she want? Ellie bit her lip. Two hundred pounds. That was her daily limit. She hit the number quickly and the money machine's inner workings whirred.

Lights flashed and the ATM offered her card back. The lower slot clacked open and neatly folded sheets of white paper came out. She felt weak kneed with relief. As she collected the old notes, she looked into the bank through the glass door. Someone else had joined the group at the Enquiry Desk. A man with a toolbox.

Ellie shoved the white fivers deep into her coat pocket. The machine clicked and chuntered and offered up her receipt. She took it with trembling hands and headed for the coffee shop opposite. Not that caffeine would calm her nerves but she needed somewhere to sit down and collect her thoughts.

"A latte, please, a small one." She didn't listen as the barista painstakingly explained the pretentious names they were trained to use instead of straight-forward sizes.

"Do you want that to drink in or to take away?" the girl asked.

"Drink in, thanks." Ellie unzipped her wallet and found she just had enough change of her own to pay for it. She wasn't about to break into the busking money they'd spent so long counting and bagging.

She didn't stop to find any sugar but headed straight for the back and the corner table near the loos. That put plenty of empty seats between her and the other customers. Emptying her pocket,

Ellie unfolded and counted out the white sheets. Five pound notes from the 1930s. Forty of them.

The crisp paper rattled as her hand shook. Could she really get two hundred and fifty pounds for each one?

She realised she had no real idea how anyone went about selling old money to collectors. Eleanor decided she hardly wanted to risk trying to sell them herself through eBay. Through an auction house then, or maybe an antique dealer?

She'd ask around, she concluded, looking for dealers who seemed honest and who asked fewest questions. She'd sell the notes a few at a time, so as not to be too noticeable. A legacy from a grandparent, that's what she'd say they were.

Ellie folded up the fivers carefully and opened the satchel to stow them safely in the inside zip pocket. Forty of them worth two hundred and fifty pounds each? Ten thousand pounds?

She drank her coffee, wincing at the bitterness. Hardly. Whoever bought them off her to sell on would surely take some sort of commission. But even if their cut was twenty percent, she'd still make eight thousand pounds.

More than enough to pay for a year doing that music course. Her parents couldn't possibly argue if she wasn't asking them to fund it or having to dip into her inheritance. That money could stay in the bank until she needed it for a deposit on a flat or something just like Gran had wanted.

As long as these notes were genuine, never mind what bizarre circumstance had loaded them into the ATM. She had better find out, and fast. That two hundred pounds was Ellie's food money for the last weeks of term until she went home for Christmas. If she needed to go back to the bank and get her bank balance corrected, the sooner she did that, the better.

She checked her watch. Nearly ten o'clock. She'd better hurry if she didn't want to miss Doctor Maund explaining the transition from Merovingian to Carolingian kings. She'd have to drag the heavy satchel of busking coins along with her too. There wasn't any chance of taking that back to the flat first.

After the lecture? Ellie drained her tall glass cup and remembered the antiquarian bookseller and print dealer whose shop was tucked away down the alley, a little way beyond the cabbies' cafe. She'd only ever looked longingly at the framed maps of eighteenth century England and Ireland in the window, but surely that was as good a place as any to start asking questions.

Right, that was the plan. She'd go there after her lecture. If the antiquarian said the notes were fakes, she'd go straight back to the bank and hand them in. While she was there, she'd pay in the busking money. Ellie rose to her feet and gathered up the black satchel and her backpack.

She really, really hoped that those fivers would turn out to be genuine...

TEMPORALLY OUT OF ODOR: A FRAGRANT FABLE
by Jeremy Sim

Philip Jackson shrugged uncomfortably in his fake lab coat, his stomach already churning with nerves. He checked his clipboard for the fourth time to make sure he had the right room—Ward 204—and the right patient—Walter Mukerjee, aged sixty-one, nasal. Then he steeled himself and knocked.

He entered without waiting for a response, just like a real doctor would. Inside, a roundish Indian man looked up from the hospital bed, his spherical belly half-obscured by sheets. The man had a mean look about him, but the most striking thing about Walter Mukerjee were the bandages that sat triangularly in the middle of his face, creating a flat white void where his nose should have been. Even to Philip, who dealt regularly with prosthetics patients of all kinds, the effect was quite unsettling.

Philip cleared his throat, a split-second late. "You must be Mr. Mukerjee."

"And you must be one of those imbecile doctors who can't read a clipboard," snapped Mukerjee. "Obviously I'm Mukerjee. What do you want?"

"Uh," said Philip. "Right. I'm Dr. Jackson, one of the prostheticists in charge of your case? I understand you're having an issue with your new nose?"

"Yes, I jolly well am." Mukerjee had a pronounced Indian accent, which combined with the plaster over his nose made him sound like a New Delhi version of Donald Duck. "It's the bloody prototypes." Mukerjee frisbeed a sheaf of papers across the bed, making Philip flinch. It was a gallery of digitally-rendered nose prototypes, the standard set offered by Pfalzer-Grumman.

Mukerjee's face stared angrily up at him, nine per page, each with a different nose.

"Uh, what seems to be the problem?"

"There's not a decent one in the whole stack! They make me look like a clown, or a squirrel. Have any of you plastic surgery freaks ever seen a real nose before?"

Philip flipped through the proofs. There were around thirty noses on display: long, short, bulbous, upturned, et cetera. The techs had actually done a decent job with the skin tone this time. But it was true that none of the noses really seemed to fit Mukerjee. Some of the noses actually came out quite scary on him.

Philip sighed. On normal days he sat in a small gray cubicle in a small gray corner answering calls on the Customer Satisfaction line. It was boring work—and he had limited power to actually help people—but at least it had the advantage of privacy. What he hated most were the personal visits: when a situation called for it, he visited customers while they were still in their hospital beds.

What he was doing today was borderline unethical, really. Mukerjee was unhappy with his nose prototypes. Why? Because Pfalzer-Grumman had such a limited selection of noses. Demand for them was low. No sense spending extra development costs on it, especially at a time when the whole company was scrambling to port their old database into the latest modeling software. Philip's job today was basically to con Mukerjee into being happy with a crappy nose.

"What about this one?" said Philip cautiously. "Personally, I think it makes you look quite dashing. A little like James Bond. The Sean Connery version."

"Rubbish," said Mukerjee.

Philip put on his most charming, yet vulnerable smile. "Remember that these are only two-dimensional depictions of a sophisticated product. Our prostheticists are highly trained, and they've been satisfying customers for over twenty-two years."

Mukerjee's face was like stone.

Philip ran his hands through his prematurely thinning hair. He sat down. "You know, I'm pretty new at the company, and I haven't actually seen the guys fab a nose prosthetic yet. But they do a pretty good job with everything else. Glass eyes, ears, nipples. Especially nipples. Give us a long weekend and we'll pop out a nipple like nobody's business." He forced a smile. "Hey," he said, as if noticing the third page of proofs for the first time. "Prototype 6D looks natural. I think it might actually come out well in final."

"No," said Mukerjee. "That one is creepy as hell. I told you, I've been over them again and again. If some of them looked alright, I wouldn't have called you in here. Do I look like a vain man? I just don't want to look like an imbecile for the rest of my life."

Philip closed his eyes briefly. The sad part was that Mukerjee was right. Of course he should be entitled to a nose that he was pleased with. It was a pretty important part of his face, after all. And if he wasn't happy with Pfalzer-Grumman's noses, he should be able to take his business to a company with a wider selection. But that wasn't how it worked. Mukerjee's insurance was partnered with the hospital, who had an agreement with Pfalzer-Grumman. Part of Philip's job was to make sure the customer never saw that.

Philip's stomach gurgled. He often got stomach pains on the job, especially when he had to deal with tense situations like these. His psychiatrist said it was a byproduct of his social anxiety, a holdover from a traumatic childhood. Philip suspected that if this continued much longer, he would need to pay an urgent visit to the restroom.

He could only think of one way of helping Mukerjee, a kind of corporate loophole. It meant long explanations to all his supervisors and a lot of extra paperwork, but his stomach was aching now, and he didn't want to be in this room any longer with this old, disfigured man who hated him. If he wrapped things with Mukerjee up now, he wouldn't have to come back after his toilet trip.

"You know what?" said Philip. "I just had a conversation with a researcher at a partner firm of ours, and he was telling me all about this new technology they're developing for custom nasal prostheses, using a quantum scanning procedure. They use your DNA to reconstruct your nose from scratch. 101% of your old nose back, they say."

That was literally what it said on the cheap-looking pamphlet Philip had received that morning, stuck in his company mailbox under a pile of memos and a take-out menu for the local Thai place. It was for a company called Nasex, obviously one of those biotech popups that sprung up around the area like weeds. Guys who thought they could rule the world with two technicians, a 3D printer, and a pirated copy of AutoCAD. But the companies had their uses. If Pfalzer-Grumman outsourced a job to them, they could almost certainly get it done for cheap. And obviously the Nasex guys had no corporate leverage: they *had* to offer some kind of foolproof guarantee to stay in business. If Mukerjee wasn't happy, Pfalzer-Grumman could make them sweat for it.

Mukerjee was mumbling something about incompetence and rotting in hell. Philip cut him off. "So what do you say we give the new technology a shot? It's got promise, likely going to be the new thing in our field. If you end up hating the prototype, contact us and we'll take it back. You won't be locked down to anything. At the very least it'll give you more options to choose from."

Mukerjee seemed to be assembling a response.

"I'll have the nurse come in for a blood sample. That's all they need for the prototype. Kind of amazing, when you think about it." Philip stood suddenly, clutching the clipboard in front of his chest like a shield. "I'll touch base with you in a couple weeks. It's been a pleasure meeting you, Mr. Mukerjee."

He needed the bathroom, fast. He was glad when the heavy door to Mukerjee's room stood between him and that awful, noseless gaze.

oOo

Three weeks later Walter Mukerjee sat alone in an empty visiting room, waiting for the nurse to return. His palms were sweating.

How had he let it come this far? Just a week ago they had mailed a sample to his house, a crude hunk of plastic that came with a disclaimer saying that it was only a low-res approximation of the final product. A final product they would apparently create from his DNA, using some sort of "quantum" wizardry. Whatever that meant. It was frightening, technology these days.

But the nose had looked alright. Better than any in the first batch. It actually reminded him of his old nose: before the car accident, before everything.

"Ana, what do you think?" he had asked the ceiling that evening, the sample nose lying on his chest like a tiny mammal. Would she approve of him getting a new nose? Or would she dislike the falseness of it? Surely she would have wanted him to look like his old self again. But would she be sad, feel like he was moving on without her?

He knew such thoughts were silly. But they had been married for forty years, and the nose was his first major decision without Ana's input. It felt wrong. He'd lost a nose and a wife in the crash, and apparently only the nose could be replaced with a prosthetic. He was surprised by the smile at his own joke, the pinpricks of tears in his eyes.

But in the end he had said yes to the prosthetics company. The irreversible *yes*: it meant his new nose would enter production, and except for a little fine-tuning and adjustment it was his new nose for life.

He hadn't been ready for that level of finality. But he was getting tired: of the isolation, the stares from strangers, the pointing, the laughter.

He shifted uncomfortably on the wax paper.

A gentle knock sounded at the door and the nurse entered. She had a tiny cardboard box with her, much smaller than Walter had anticipated.

"Here it is!" she said, in the tones of someone introducing a two-year-old to a new teddy. She fumbled with the box and pulled open the lid.

Inside the box, resting on a velvet-lined mold, was his nose.

And it *was* his nose; there was no mistaking it. Flaws and all, down to the pores. A perfect replica: the mottled skin, the slight asymmetry, the color, everything. It couldn't have been done any better. Over the last couple weeks he had almost gotten used to the skull-like slits in his face. Now he knew what he had been missing.

Walter's throat tightened. He felt his face go hot. He looked at the nose for a moment, taking in every detail, relief washing over him like a wave.

"Let's try it on, shall we?" said the nurse. She was compassionately tactful, touching him on the shoulder to turn him toward the light. For an instant, Walter was glad that she was treating him like a two-year-old.

She took out a small, brown bottle. "This is the non-toxic adhesive you'll be using to affix your nose," she said, brushing a cold liquid onto his face. "You can think of it as face glue. It lasts about three days; you'll be able to take your nose on and off for showers and such without reapplying. And it's completely safe. If you notice the adhesive getting a little weak, just dab a little more on."

With the air of an enthusiast tacking on the final part of a model airplane, she pressed the nose straight onto his face. She held his chin and tilted to look at him from several angles.

"It looks fantastic. Honestly. We usually recommend that new prosthetics patients consider wearing eyeglasses to give their face a more unified look—kind of hides the falseness, you know? But I don't think that'll be necessary for you. Have a look."

She held up a hand-mirror and Walter looked.

The nurse was right. It was extraordinary. It was miraculously, magically, perfect.

It was as if the accident had never happened at all.

oOo

"What do you mean it doesn't smell right?" asked Philip Jackson two days later. He held the phone cradled to his ear, and he was struggling to hear Walter Mukerjee's voice over the bustle of the office. "You mean it smells like plastic? That's a common issue with new prosthetics, I'm afraid. The smell goes away after a couple of days. I'd suggest rinsing it with soap and warm water and letting it air dry for an afternoon." He listened intently to Mukerjee's reply, scrunching his face to make out the thickly-

accented words. "I'm sorry, could you repeat that?" Someone had
started the copy machine, which stood ten feet from Philip's
desk. "Ah, Christ," he muttered. "Listen, Mr. Mukerjee. Let me
come pay you a home visit. Yes. I've got your address right here.
I'll be there in half an hour."

He hung up. Today was just one thing after another. That
morning, the boss had called them all into the conference room
for a meeting, where he'd announced that Pfalzer-Grumman had
just concluded negotiations and would be merging with
Oppenthorp Medical at the end of the month. The resulting
company would be called Pfalzer-Grumman-Oppenthorp. A buzz
of constant chatter inundated the office today, and nobody was
getting anything done. It put Philip seriously on edge.

Just as well that old man called, Philip thought, as he grabbed
his coat.

"So let me get this straight," he said an hour later, seated in
one of Mukerjee's faded armchairs. Mukerjee had gruffly
presented him with a cup of tea, which now sat steaming on the
coffee table between them. Philip had taken a sip and
immediately regretted it. It was black as ink, and tasted like
Mukerjee had gone about five scoops overboard with the Ceylon.
"You, uhh, experience strange smells when you're wearing the
nose?"

"Yes," said Mukerjee. Without the bandages covering his
nose, the duck-like-quality of his voice had disappeared. His new
nose looked natural, almost frighteningly real. "I smell things that
aren't present. I'll be getting dressed in the walk-in-closet and I'll
smell curry. I'll be taking out the garbage and I'll smell perfume.
And it's not just once or twice. It happens all the time, fifty times
a day. It just doesn't make sense."

"I see," said Philip, eyeing Mukerjee carefully. He instantly
knew that it wasn't an issue with the prosthetic. Mukerjee had a
neurological problem. His brain was associating smells as a way
of dealing with emotional trauma. He had heard of cases like this,
like when soldiers relived the smells and sounds of mortar shells.

"It's not in my head," said Mukerjee scathingly, as if he had
heard Philip's thoughts. "Do you think I didn't think of that? I
went for a day without the prosthetic. No weird smells. The

instant I put it on again, I smelled Christmas trees. I took it off again—the smell disappeared. Does that sound neurological to you?"

Philip hesitated. It could still be neurological. Maybe Mukerjee's subconscious was only triggered when he put it on. "Well, you've got the nose on right now. What are you smelling?"

Mukerjee sniffed a few times. "I think it's a car. It smells like I'm in a car. But it's hard to say."

Philip kept silent.

Mukerjee made a condescending noise. "Look, I can see you don't believe me. Let me prove it to you."

"Okay. How?"

"Aren't you the doctor? We're going to be scientific about this. First, you blindfold me. Make sure I can't see a thing. Then you're going to take this sample nose they sent me"—he produced a rubberized prototype from a box—"and my prosthetic"—he pulled off his nose and pressed it into Philip's hand—"and press whichever one you want to my face. They feel and smell the same, so I won't know which one it is. Give them a sniff if you don't believe me."

"No thanks," said Philip quickly. Something about the idea of holding someone else's nose in his hand and smelling it made his stomach twist. "I'll take your word for it." He shook his head skeptically. "Pass me that handkerchief."

He took the offered handkerchief, folded a nice, thick blindfold and looped it over Mukerjee's head. He tested Mukerjee by flicking a finger in front of his face. No reaction.

"Okay. Here's the first nose. You ready?" He held the two noses, the sample and the real prosthetic, in his hands.

Mukerjee nodded.

Philip pressed the sample against Mukerjee's nose-holes.

"No smell," said Mukerjee immediately.

"Okay, good," said Philip. He retracted the sample, waited a moment, then pressed the same nose back to Mukerjee's face. "How about now?"

"No smell."

"Okay, good."

Philip had been rubbing the other prosthetic, the real one, against his palm to warm it up. In one motion, he pulled the sample away and replaced it with the warm prosthetic, as if he had hesitated a bit in lifting the sample off.

But Mukerjee noticed immediately. His face changed and he said, "It's not a car anymore. I smell the supermarket. The freezer section, where they keep tubs of ice cream. It smells cold … like raw chicken. Like freezer burn. I think this is the Albertsons on Woodrow Avenue."

Philip pulled the nose away, his mind reeling. What in the world?

Mukerjee reached up and removed the blindfold. He knew he had proven his point.

Philip let his arm fall into his lap. "I don't know what to say, Mr. Mukerjee. I've never seen one of our prosthetics malfunction like this."

"You still think I'm fooling you somehow."

"No, it's not that. If you like, I can call the hospital, have them recommend a specialist."

Mukerjee stared at him for a full five seconds. His expression grew strangely mournful. "Ah, don't worry about it," he said finally, "I don't want a specialist." He pushed himself up off the sofa, stooping to retrieve Philip's untouched cup of tea. "Better not drink this. I've botched it, I think. It's been a few years since I brewed a cup on my own."

As Mukerjee tottered away to the kitchen, Philip sat thinking. He vaguely remembered reading that Mukerjee's wife had died in the car accident that landed him in the hospital, and felt a surge of pity for the guy. It must be tough. He didn't remember seeing anyone on Mukerjee's visitor log at the hospital either.

Mukerjee reentered the room, but did not sit. He extended a hand to Philip, and they shook. "Well, I feel silly," Mukerjee said. "I don't know what I was expecting you to do. Of course it's not a problem you can fix." He took the prosthetic and pocketed it. "I'll put it on with the glue and everything later. Thank you for coming out here."

"You're very welcome," said Philip, standing to leave. Mukerjee ushered him down the hall, moving slowly. On the way out, Philip noticed a couple of interesting photos and knick-knacks scattered around the mantel and the living room. He imagined living in this house alone, mourning a dead wife. It was unfortunate that elderly people ended up in situations like these.

Adjacent to the door stood a small wooden table, an ornate little place to drop keys and mail. On it stood a pair of grotesque Indian dolls. The male figure wore a tiny turban, made of colored silks, and the female wore a baglike dress made of what looked like red napkins. A tiny golden ring glittered in her nose. It made Philip suddenly sad.

"You know," said Philip, as he slipped into his shoes. "It can't hurt if I come back in two weeks to check in on the problem. Maybe you could start keeping a diary of the smells. We could go over the entries together. I'll come here and we can do it in the sitting room. Just make sure to write down all the relevant information: time, place, description of the smell. You know what I mean?"

Philip stepped out the door. He turned to shake Mukerjee's hand again, and was surprised to see that Mukerjee had not moved. He was loitering back near the table with the dolls. His nose-holes glared like a skull's.

Then Mukerjee twitched and wiped a self-conscious hand on his shirt. "No ... no, that won't be necessary. I'll be fine on my own." His voice hid a tremble of emotion as he moved to close the door. "Thank you for offering, though."

oOo

8 a.m., wrote Walter Mukerjee, pressing the nib of his pen into the notebook. *Coffee smell. Folgers?*

He put the pen down and sniffed the air again. It was a rich, wafting kind of smell, the kind of fragrance that pierces through to your sleeping brain in an instant. He glanced out the window. The sky outside was gray, and dewdrops collected on the freezing windowpanes. An instant ago he would have called it gloomy. But the coffee smell, so tangible and ... *real*, made the fog almost comforting. It was so strange. When he'd first smelled it, he'd actually gone down to the kitchen to check if the coffeemaker had started up on its own. It hadn't.

He inhaled deeply, leaned back in his chair, and closed his eyes. Was that the smell of buttered toast?

God, there really is something wrong with me, he thought.

8:15 a.m. Buttered toast, he wrote.

He sat like that, alone, for the next several hours, identifying and transcribing smells. He had always had quite a sensitive nose. It was why he and Ana had eventually settled on things like her taking out the trash every Tuesday, despite the fact that it was supposed to be the husband's job. His mother would have given him hell for it. And they had gotten into more than a few fights when Ana had left something too long in the fridge and couldn't smell it rotting.

He shook his head, trying to clear the heavy ache in his chest. He missed her. He wished he could just turn and see her, reading, or bustling about the living room like she used to. The emptiness in the house now was like slow agony. He wished he could tell her how sorry he was, for picking stupid fights. His biggest regret was saying no to adopting a child after their son Pradesh had come out stillborn and the doctor said it was probably best for her not to try again.

Sometimes he thought he even smelled her in the house still, that curious mixture of lemon and cumin that was uniquely her. Or he caught a whiff of her shampoo, the kind that smelled like apples.

But he was getting distracted. Already a couple of strange smells had gone by unidentified. He bent over the notebook again.

By afternoon, the first page was full. *Shoe leather*, it read. *Cleaning solution. Trees. The smell of wind off cold water. Grocery store. Chinese restaurant.*

At around 4 p.m., he decided to test something. He went to the kitchen, opened the fridge, and unwrapped a block of orange cheddar. He took a deep sniff.

Nothing. No smell at all. Instead, he smelled fresh, outdoor air with a hint of automobile exhaust.

He reached up and peeled his nose off. He tried the cheese again. This time, the sharpness of the cheddar almost made his eyes water. Interesting.

The rest of the evening went by in this way. He'd sit in the study with nose on, pen at the ready, and daydream about Ana and the accident until a new smell hit him. He'd record the time and smell, put the pen back down, and repeat the process.

Walter smelled bedsheets and tepid air around 8:30, when he usually went to bed. He closed the notebook, deciding that it was as good a time as any to call it a night. He had not spoken to a single person or gone outside all day.

A smell hit him, so intense and familiar that his chest tightened instantly. He froze, half in his chair and half out, not wanting to move lest the smell disappear. He took long, careful breaths, savoring each note like a relapsed smoker. A horrible, warm, sweet feeling welled up inside him, spreading from the pit of his stomach out into his arms and fingers and toes.

The smell was of lemons and cumin, with the slightest hint of clean sweat and warm cloth. It smelled like laundry, like chai tea, like mint mouthwash, like Pantene conditioner. It smelled like comfort and stability, like fullness and life. There was even the slightest hint of incense, the exact flavor of which had been imprinted on his brain since the day he married her, forty long years ago.

He sat back in his chair. He opened the notebook.

9:00 p.m., he wrote. *Ana.*

oOo

By the third day, it was clear to Walter that the smells coming to him had a certain logic to them. He always smelled the ignition lighter on the stovetop before smelling food. He always smelled the outdoors before the characteristic smell of his car.

By the fourth day, he had figured it out. He was smelling the smells of someone else's life. A person who woke up to Ana's brewed coffee in the mornings, had toast and butter, went to the park and the grocery store with her, cooked curries with garlic and turmeric and coriander in the evenings, sat on the couch with her, and got into bed with her at night. All these places had their own specific smells, which were as clear and distinct to him as the colors of the rainbow.

His nose, he realized with slow amazement, was living a life where the accident had never happened.

A life where Ana was still alive.

And what a world it was. He could smell her all the time now, pick out her indistinct scent from a bouquet of other odors. She was always there, her fragrance an undercurrent. And the more he tried, the more he paid attention, the more information he could pick out of this secret timeline, this universe he could access only through his nose.

Sometimes, if he closed his eyes and concentrated, he convinced himself that he could hear Ana's humming, hear the mechanical *click* as she switched on the water boiler or the honk of the spray bottle as she misted her plants. But then he'd open his eyes, and it would be clear that he was only imagining the sounds. Smell was all he had. And he'd see the empty house around him, feel a sinking in his belly, and retreat beneath the covers again. In his smells, he was somewhere else—in a taxi; in a library, the books musty and brown around the edges; at a pizza restaurant, a drugstore, a parking garage, a doctor's office. One morning he smelled the distinct smell of frying grease and cotton candy; he was confused until he went to the computer and found that there was some kind of arts festival going on.

He'd crawled back into bed, closed his eyes, and went to the festival with Ana.

It was really possible that she was alive somewhere, he thought. Somewhere out there. In the blackness of time. It all sounded very science fiction-y, but the proof was right here, wasn't it? Right under his nose. He thought back to the accident, how after that truck had plowed into them he had lost consciousness and woken up two weeks later in the hospital. A doctor had told him the horrible news then, that Ana hadn't made it. He imagined that in this alternate timeline he had woken up to Ana beside him, leaning over to wipe his forehead with a warm, wet cloth. It was possible. He could almost feel it.

Maybe the road of reality had forked there, at the time of the accident, and in one of the forks Ana lived and in the other she died. Maybe the quantum nose that they had made him was somehow accessing this other timeline.

The only problem now was that Walter was stuck in the wrong one. The wrong world, the wrong universe, the wrong fork. He didn't want to be here. He wanted to be *there*.

He wanted to talk to someone about it, explain his theory to them. He tried calling up the manufacturer of his prosthetic, a company called Nasex. He got an answering machine. He tried again on two other occasions, with the same result. He tried at Philip Jackson's company, but the frustrated receptionist said something about a corporate merger and not knowing Philip's new extension. After a while, he gave up. He was too tired to summon the energy anyway.

oOo

Walter pulled himself out of bed. The clock read 1:26p.m. What day was it? It was afternoon, but he still felt tired. How long had he slept? Last night Ana had made a delicious fish curry, and Walter had enjoyed the smells of hot jasmine rice and red wine and something else that smelled a little like fireworks. They'd gone to bed late, past midnight. He wondered what the occasion was.

He limped to the bathroom sink, his bones hurting. He washed his face in front of the mirror. He toweled himself off and looked at himself for what was probably the first time in a week.

He was shocked. Where his face had been pudgy before, round and healthy, he was thin, with grayish, sunken cheeks. His bones hurt, and he felt weak. All he wanted to do was curl up back in bed.

He hobbled into the kitchen. When was the last time he had eaten? He couldn't remember. He smelled foods all the time, but had he actually eaten real food in the last few days? His mind seemed foggy.

He opened the fridge, gazed at its bare contents, and selected a shrunken apple out of pure fatigue. He sat down at the dining table and took a small bite of skin. He chewed and swallowed. He took another.

Pointless. What good did it do him to sit here alone at his

dining table eating a shriveled apple? Nobody cared. Nobody even noticed him in this reality; his existence went utterly unacknowledged. Nobody cared if he lived or died. A wave of sour hopelessness bubbled up from somewhere, and he set the apple down. He rested his forehead on the table, his stomach convulsing with hunger.

He was still there four hours later, sleeping with his cheek against the table, when the doorbell rang.

oOo

"Come on, old man," murmured Philip Jackson, standing outside Mukerjee's door. "Answer."

He heard movement inside the house, faint and ponderous. Then the door cracked open.

"I've been calling you all morning," said Philip. "Did—Holy hell, what happened to you?"

The man who opened the door was recognizably Mukerjee, but shrunken. He looked almost skeletal: cavernous eyes, yellowed cheeks, messy thin hair.

"Left my phone somewhere," mumbled Mukerjee, leaving the door open for Philip. He led him into the kitchen. "Want tea?" Mukerjee slumped into a chair, as if he had used up all his energy just walking to the door.

"Thanks, I'm good. But hey, listen. Are you feeling alright? You look a little …" Philip trailed off.

No response from Mukerjee. Not even a twitch. His head lolled sideways.

Philip felt his heart jump. *Holy crap, he's dead*, he thought. He grabbed Mukerjee's wrist and was relieved when he felt the old man's pulse thudding weakly against his fingers. His mind raced. He had to call someone. A doctor. An ambulance.

He had just whipped out his cell phone to dial 911 when Mukerjee grimaced, pulled his arm away, and muttered something.

Philip's thumb hovered over the number 9. "What did you say?"

This time the word was audible. "Hungry."

oOo

Walter was dreaming of food. Ana must be cooking something delicious. It smelled like … eggs. Scrambled eggs. And ketchup. That was strange. Ana hated ketchup.

He was sprawled face-down on the kitchen table. He breathed in, savoring the smell. *Oh, Ana.* He shifted in his chair.

His foot trod on something squishy.

He cracked an eye open and looked down. It was his nose. He had just stepped on his own nose. Something about that made him want to laugh hysterically. Instead, a weak chuckle forced itself out, followed by a set of choking coughs. But something was wrong. If his nose was on the floor, it meant that the food smell …

"Hey, you alright?"

Walter opened his eyes. The young doctor, Philip Jackson, was standing in his kitchen, wearing an old green apron that sported several wine-colored stains. He was holding a spatula. Something was sizzling on the stove behind him.

Walter blinked. "What—"

But Philip slid a plate of food in front of him. A runny mess of eggs and ketchup, with a half-melted block of cheddar cheese on the side.

"I, uh, couldn't find anything else. You haven't got much food in the fridge. But eat it." Philip forced a fork into his hand.

Walter stared down at the plate and its miserable pile of eggs. He looked up at Philip. He looked down again. Maybe it was the tiredness, or the weakness in his body, or the sight of that ratty old apron, but emotion flooded into him like burning wine. With shaking hands, he lifted a forkful of glorious, glorious food into his mouth.

oOo

For the next ten days, Philip didn't leave Mukerjee alone. After work he'd pick up a couple of burritos or a sandwich from the food truck outside the newly-renamed Pfalzer-Grumman-

Oppenthorp building, zip across town to Mukerjee's house on his way home, and watch to make sure Mukerjee ate.

The man was seriously depressed. It seemed to Philip that Mukerjee spent twenty-three hours a day in bed, only venturing out to answer the door when Philip knocked. Then he'd slump into a chair in the kitchen and wait to be fed.

But he did eat. And he seemed to be growing stronger. On the third day, he wore a weak smile when he opened the door to let Philip in.

On particularly gloomy afternoons, Mukerjee would tell Philip stories about Ana, anecdotes and memories from long ago. He spoke with tears in his eyes, and sometimes when the emotions got too intense he would reach up and snatch his nose off, rocking back and forth in his chair while the tears streamed down and around his nose-holes.

Philip had intended to refer Mukerjee to a psychologist, but he kept putting it off. He didn't exactly know why. Maybe it was because he got a strange sense of satisfaction seeing Mukerjee wolf down the food he brought every day, seeing his outlook grow gradually sunnier. It was like taking care of a baby bird. There was something powerful about taking a person's well-being into hand, weighing options, and executing changes. Philip had been working in customer service for ten years and never once experienced it.

He showed up late in December, two months after the beginning of his after-work visits. Over the past weeks, he'd arrived several times to find Mukerjee hunched over the stove, surrounded by horrible, acrid clouds of burning curry spices. On those days they ate their burritos out on the patio, while the house aired out. But finally it seemed that Mukerjee had mastered a simple, odd-tasting curry recipe, topped with fried egg.

He was glad that Mukerjee was managing his own meals. It meant that Philip didn't need to visit *every* day, especially now that work was getting rougher. But there were days when he just felt like it: after a long afternoon of dealing with people it was good to go sit on the beat-up armchair in Mukerjee's living room, eat a slowly-expanding roster of strange Indian food, and talk. The old man always welcomed a chat.

Hearing stories from Mukerjee's life, all the heartaches and triumphs of sixty-one years, made Philip see his workday stresses in a new light. He was reminded that life was short and fragile, that everything could change at a moment's notice, that the road could fork when you least expected. For some reason it made it harder for the old social anxiety to sink its claws in.

oOo

They played chess one day deep in winter, using an old wooden set they'd pulled out of Mukerjee's garage. The pieces were faded, the knights' features barely visible.

As they played, Philip aired out a long string of complaints about his coworkers. He'd been recently promoted to supervisor, and the frustration of trying to teach the proper customer service attitude was too much for him sometimes. Mukerjee would nod periodically and make a move, pinning one of Philip's rooks or capturing a pawn. Then Philip would have to pay attention for a while, and they would sit in silence while he extricated himself from the newest threat.

Halfway through the evening, a soft thump made Philip glance up. Mukerjee's nose had fallen off. It had landed on the chessboard, next to a pawn. It looked like a small, brown mushroom.

The old Indian man reached over, took the nose between thick, wrinkled fingers and moved it to the side of the board, beside the captured pawns and bishops.

Then, the interruption dealt with, Philip and Walter returned their attention to the game and continued to play.

About the Authors

CHRIS BARILI has been writing since he was fourteen, and writes in multiple genres including fantasy, science fiction, horror, western, and paranormal romance. His fiction has appeared on *The Western Online* (as T.C. Barlow), on *Quantum Fairy Tales*, and in the anthologies **These Vampires Don't Sparkle** and **Zombiefied Reloaded** by Sky Warrior Books. Later this year, his work will appear in a third Sky Warrior anthology, **The Dragon's Hoard**. He is pursuing his Masters of Fine Arts in Creative Writing, Popular Genre Fiction, with Western State Colorado University in Gunnison, CO, graduating summer of 2015. Follow Chris at www.facebook.com/authorchrisbarili.

SOFIE BIRD writes speculative fiction in Melbourne, Australia, in between programming, glass sculpting and paying the bills as an editor and technical writer. She is a graduate of the Odyssey Writing Workshop, and has published poetry in the Australian periodical *Blue Dog*. This is her first fiction sale. She maintains a website at sofiebird.net, and you can follow her on twitter: @sofie_bird.

DAVID B. COE/D.B. Jackson is the award-winning author of eighteen fantasy novels. As D.B. Jackson (www.dbjackson-author.com) he writes the *Thieftaker Chronicles*, a blend of urban fantasy, mystery, and historical fiction. As David B. Coe (www.davidbcoe.com) he writes the *Case Files of Justis Fearsson*, an urban fantasy published by Baen, and has also written a dozen epic fantasy novels. He is a co-founder and regular contributor to the Magical Words blogsite (magicalwords.net). Follow him on Twitter at @DavidBCoe and @DBJacksonAuthor.

LAURA ANNE GILMAN is the Nebula award-nominated author of **Silver on the Road**, Book 1 of *The Devil's West*, as well as the *Vineart War* trilogy and the *Cosa Nostradamus* urban fantasy series (including the forthcoming novella **Work of Hunters**). Ms. Gilman also writes mysteries under the name L.A. Kornetsky. You can find her on Twitter as @LAGilman, and at www.lauraannegilman.net

AMY GRISWOLD is the co-author (with Melissa Scott) of the gaslamp fantasy/mystery novels **Death by Silver** and **A Death at the Dionysus Club** from Lethe Press. She has also written several *Stargate* tie-in novels from Fandemonium Books, including the upcoming **Murder at the SGC**. She can be found online at @amygris and amygriswold.livejournal.com.

ELEKTRA HAMMOND emulates her multi-sided idol Buckaroo Banzai by going in several directions at once. She's been involved in publishing since the 1990s—now she writes, concocts anthologies, reviews movies for tabloid.io & edits science fiction for various and sundry. When not freelancing or appearing at science fiction conventions, she travels the world judging cat shows. Elektra lives in Delaware with her husband, Mike, and the well over a dozen cats of BlueBlaze/Benegesserit catteries. She can be found on Facebook/G+ (Elektra Hammond), Twitter (elektraUM), LiveJournal (elektra), and building up her website at www.untilmidnight.com

New York Times Bestselling author **FAITH HUNTER** writes fantasy in several subgenres: the urban fantasy *Skinwalker* series, featuring Jane Yellowrock, a Cherokee skinwalker; the post-apocalyptic *Rogue Mage* series and RPG, featuring Thorn St. Croix, a stone mage; and the upcoming *SoulWood* trilogy featuring Nell Nicholson Ingram, a woman who can siphon off the magic of others and is drawn into solving paranormal crimes. Faith writes mystery and thrillers under the name Gwen Hunter.

When she isn't writing, Faith likes to make jewelry, run whitewater rivers (Class II and III), and RV with her hubby and their rescued dogs.

SUSAN JETT lives in an old wooden farmhouse in New Hampshire with her husband, son, and an old barn full of books. Also, a woodstove and lots of smoke detectors—some of which sometimes go off in the middle of the night for no good reason. She regularly blogs at www.susanjett.com and occasionally tweets under the name @JettSusan. Just in case you want to be among the first to know if her smoke alarms ever decide to take on Novikov's self-consistency principle, or her house burns down …

GINI KOCH writes the fast, fresh and funny *Alien/Katherine "Kitty" Katt* series for DAW Books, the *Necropolis Enforcement Files*, and the *Martian Alliance Chronicles*. She also has a humor collection, *Random Musings from the Funny Girl*. As G.J. Koch she writes the *Alexander Outland* series and she's made the most of multiple personality disorder by writing under a variety of other pen names as well, including Anita Ensal, Jemma Chase, A.E. Stanton, and J.C. Koch. She has stories featured in a variety of excellent anthologies, available now and upcoming, writing as Gini Koch and J.C. Koch. Reach her via: www.ginikoch.com

STEPHEN LEIGH, who also writes under the name S.L. Farrell, is a Cincinnati author who has published twenty-eight novels and over fifty short stories. His most recent novel is **The Crow of Connemara** from DAW Books, March 2015. Stephen's work has been nominated for and won awards within the genre, and he been a frequent contributor to George RR Martin's "Wild Cards" series. He currently teaches Creative Writing at Northern Kentucky University, and is a frequent speaker to writers groups. He maintains his web site at www.stephenleigh.com, and you can sign up for his newsletter there.

SEANAN MCGUIRE writes things. It is difficult to make her stop. When she is not writing things, she can be found in haunted corn mazes around the world. Some of them may be near you. Seanan lives in a creepy old farmhouse in Northern California, which she shares with two abnormally large blue cats, a collection of dolls even creepier than the house, and a lot of books. Find her online at www.seananmcguire.com

JULIET E. MCKENNA is a British fantasy author living in the Cotswolds. She has loved history, myth and other worlds since she first learned to read. She has written fifteen epic fantasy novels, from **The Thief's Gamble**, beginning *The Tales of Einarinn* to **Defiant Peaks**, concluding *The Hadrumal Crisis* trilogy. In between novels, she writes assorted diverse shorter fiction, reviews for web and print magazines and promotes SF & Fantasy through genre conventions, teaching creative writing and commenting on book trade issues. Most recently she's been exploring opportunities in independent digital publishing, re-issuing her backlist as well as bringing out original fiction.

LAURA RESNICK is the author of the popular *Esther Diamond* urban fantasy series, the epic fantasy *Silerian* series, and many short stories. "The Spiel of the Glocken" was inspired by the history of her new home town, Covington, Kentucky.

CHUCK ROTHMAN has been writing science fiction and fantasy for over 30 years, with stories in *Asimov's, Fantasy and Science Fiction, Analog, Daily SF, Strange Horizons,* and multiple anthologies. His novels, **Staroamer's Fate** and **Syron's Fate** are available from Fantastic Books and on Amazon.com. He's been involved in running the Albacon SF convention since 1996. He owns a crockpot and lives in Schenectady with his wife Susan Noe Rothman and can be found on the web on Facebook and at sites.google.com/site/chuckrothmansf/.

STEVE RUSKIN's stories have appeared in *Mad Scientist Journal, Steampunk Trails,* and the anthology **Avast, Ye Airships!** He is an historian of science and technology, focusing on the Victorian period. He has been a university professor, a mountain-bike guide, and a number of things in between. In addition to fiction he has written for publications ranging from the *American Journal of Physics* to the *Rocky Mountain News*. He lives in Colorado. Visit him online at steveruskin.com.

EDMUND R. SCHUBERT is the author of the novel, **Dreaming Creek**, and some 45+ short stories, about half of which are collected in **The Trouble with Eating Clouds**. Recent publications include an audio-story in *IGMS* and stories in **Big Bad 2** and **Temporally Out of Order**. He's currently in his ninth year editing the online magazine *InterGalactic Medicine Show (IGMS)*, also producing three *IGMS* anthologies, and editing and contributing to the non-fiction book, **How to Write Magical Words**. Schubert still insists, however, that his greatest accomplishment came during college, when his self-published underground newspaper made him the subject of a professor's lecture in abnormal psychology. Learn more at: www.EdmundRSchubert.com

JEREMY SIM is an American writer living in Berlin, Germany. He loves curries, fantasy novels and video games, especially the kind with lots of menus. He stubs his toes on furniture with frightening regularity. Find him online at www.jeremysim.com or on Twitter @jeremy_sim.

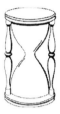

About the Editors

PATRICIA BRAY is the author of a dozen novels, including **Devlin's Luck**, which won the Compton Crook Award for the best first novel in the field of science fiction or fantasy. A multi-genre author whose career spans both epic fantasy and Regency romance, her books have been translated into Russian, German, Portuguese and Hebrew. She's also spent time on the editorial side of the fence, co-editing **After Hours: Tales from the Ur-Bar, The Modern Fae's Guide to Surviving Humanity**, and **Clockwork Universe: Steampunk vs Aliens** with her frequent partner-in-crime Joshua Palmatier. Patricia lives in a New England college town, where she combines her writing with a full-time career as a Systems Analyst, ensuring that she is never more than a few feet away from a keyboard. You can find her on Twitter as @pbrayauthor, or visit her webpage at www.patriciabray.com

JOSHUA PALMATIER is a fantasy author with a PhD in mathematics. He currently teaches at SUNY Oneonta in upstate New York, while writing in his "spare" time, editing anthologies with fellow zombie and co-editor Patricia Bray, and founding the anthology-producing small press Zombies Need Brains LLC. His most recent fantasy novel **Shattering the Ley** (July 2014) starts a new fantasy series, although you can also find his *Throne of Amenkor* series already on the shelves. He is currently hard at work writing **Threading the Needle**, the sequel to **Shattering the Ley**, and designing the kickstarter for the next Zombies Need Brains anthology project. You can find out more at www.joshuapalmatier.com, www.benjamintate.com (yes, he committed pseudonym), or at the small press' site www.zombiesneedbrains.com. Or follow him on Twitter as @bentateauthor or @ZNBLLC.

Acknowledgements

This anthology would not have been possible without the tremendous support of those who pledged during the Kickstarter. Everyone who contributed not only helped create this anthology, they also helped solidify the foundation of the small press Zombies Need Brains LLC, which I hope will be bringing SF&F themed anthologies to the reading public for years to come ... as well as perhaps some select novels by leading authors, eventually. I want to thank each and every one of them for helping to bring this small dream into reality. Thank you, my zombie horde.

The Zombie Horde: D-Rock, David K. Mason, Jen Warren, William R.D. Wood, J V Ackermann, Stephen Ballentine, trit, Duncan & Andrea Rittschof, Deirdre M. Murphy, SharlzG, Rosemary Edghill, Pat Hayes, Nathan Turner, Brian Quirt, Gary Newcomb, Kaia Gavere, Heidi Cykana, Sabrina Poulsen, Melissa Shumake, Samuel Lubell, Liz Justusson, Catherine Gross-Colten, Craig Strong, Misha Dainiak, Hisham El-Far, Roy Romasanta, Evaristo Ramos, Jr., Christopher Northern, Jaime C., Todd V. Ehrenfels, Jay Watson, Mandy Stein, Andy Miller, J C Jones, Nicole Wolfe, Becky LeJeune, Robin Allen, Liz Harkness, Bo, Michelle Lutz, Janet Oblinger, Heidi Berthiaume, Rachel Sasseen, Gina Freed, Rick Dalby II, David Perlmutter, Sofie Bird, Joel Zakem, Ron Oakes, Tim Marquitz, April Steenburgh, Sheryl, Aaron Canton, Cathy Green, Mike Skolnik, Marie Angel, M. DeWorken, Galit A., Joey Shoji, Christopher Mangum, Pam Blome, Kerry aka Trouble, Evil Kitten, Jessica Meade, Max Kaehn, Ashley Oswald, Rory Hart, Brenda Cooper, Jen Edwards, Ruth Stuart, Mark Kiraly, Ellen Kuehnle, Katherine Malloy, Regis M. Donovan, Kristie Strum, Carla Borsoi, Kristi Chadwick, Yankton Robins, D. Taylor-Rodriguez, Nick Watkins, Jessica Reid, Stephanie Cheshire, Jason Lenox, Michael Nichols, Russell Martens, Julie Frost, Keith West, Michael Roger Nichols, Jerrie the filkferengi, James H. Murphy Jr., Brad Roberts,

Christa, Jerel Heritage, K. Gavenman, Sara Glassman, Robert
Gilson, Juli, William Silvia Jr, Rylee Akard, Scott Drummond,
David Drew, Patrick Dugan, Sarah Coldheart, Mary Spila, Svend
Andersen, Lisa Kruse, Aristhosthenes and Jeff, T.Rob, Jonathan
Jordan, Amy Nerenberg, George Mitchell, Jonathan S. Chance,
Thorsten Lockert, Casey C Clark, Carol Guess, Kat & Dan, Tina
M Noe, Patti Short, L. E. Doggett, Beth aka Scifibookcat, Dino
Hicks, Brian, Sarah, and Josh Williams, Beth Vrabel, Jean Marie
Ward, Evenstar Deane, Jason Palmatier, Elaine Tindill-Rohr, Ron
Wodaski, Ragnarok Publications, Rachel Blackman, Mark
Newman, W Converse, Matt Wagner, Larisa LaBrant, Greg
Dejasco, Amelia Smith, Laura Davidson, Andrew Arminio,
Mariada George, Ian Chung, Merav Hoffman, Lennhoff Family,
Becky Boyer, Rae & Henri K, Alexander Smith, Sidra Roman,
Mary Alice Wuerz, Debbie Matsuura, Sheryl R. Hayes, S. Baur,
Ed Ellis, Karen Haugland, Cynthia Porter, Brian Y Ashmore,
Jenn Mercer, Ann Lemay, Jona Fras, Jay Zastrow, Tom B,
Steven Mentzel, Keith Hall, Amanda Johnson, Adora H, Arne
Radtke, Lisa Padol, Jenn Bernat, Mikaela, Thomas Zilling, Kim
Vandervort, Elektra, Gavran, Tsana Dolichva, Michael Bernardi,
Matthew & Amy Nesbitt, Jeff Coquery, Michele Fry, Robert
Maughan, Punky, Annika Samuelsson, Leah Webber, JoanneBB,
Alysia Murphy, Louise Lowenspets, J.P. Goodwin, Zuhur Abdo,
Jolene 'Bob' Taylor, Simon D, William Hughes, penwing, Catie
Murphy, Royce Easton Day, Fred and Mimi Bailey, Julia
Cresswell, Colette Reap, Ben "Zhaph" Duguid, Bas de Bakker,
Catherine Farnon, Wayne L McCalla Jr., Lesley Smith, Liz
Pittman, Paul Bulmer, Tatsuaki Goh, @solardepths, Kevin
Winter, Brian Nisbet, Danielle Hall, Joyce Haslam, Peter Donald,
Kristine Kearney, Rivka, Gabe Krabbe, Diana Castillo, Pete
Hollmer, Deirdre Furtado, Kari, Tiago Thedim Dias, John Green,
Sarah Stewart, Smashingsuns, Robert Early, Jeff Gulosh, Fred
Dillon, Anne Burner, Darryl M. Wood, Keith Jones, Iain Riley,
rissatoo, Peter Hentges, Gary Phillips, James Spinks, Bill and
Laura Pearson, Colleen Reed, Norman Walsh, Mark Webb, Brian
Brunswick, Ian Harvey, Paul V, Heather Fagan, David Perkins,
Rebecca M, Eagle Archambeault, Jake, Chrissie, Grace &
Savannah Palmatier, Tara Smith, Deborah Blake, Jenn Ridley,

Darrell Grizzle, Kaitlin Thorsen, Emily Leverett, David J Fortier, John T. Sapienza, Jr., Wolf SilverOak, Shawna Jaquez, Kurt, Arkady Martine, Axisor, Sarah A., Deanna Stanley, Ty Wilda, James Weber, Jen Woods, Lesley Mitchell, Steven Halter, Lesen Arms, Michael Feldhusen, Loni Marie Addis, Hugh, Cheryl Preyer, Gail Z. Martin, shmoo, Ryan Young, Herefox, M@ Senne, Bill mcGeachin, Ted Brown, Elizabeth Kite, Jennifer Berk, Larry Sanchez-von Guttenberg, Tory Shade, Dina S Willner, Karen Chinetti, Cora Anderson, Adriane Ruzak, Anne Marie W., Gary Vandegrift, Mogepy, Kelsie Covington, Sally Novak Janin, sydney sandberg, Keith E. Hartman, Joelle M. Reizes, Lexie C., Laurie, Maggie Allen, Catherine Barth, Kelly Babcock, A.J. French, Gammelor Goodenow, Shannon Kauderer, Brook West, T. England, Michael Abbott, Giana Tondolo Bonilla, Emy Peters, Jami Nord, Margaret St. John, Tom Carpenter, Sandra Komoroff, Lori Parker, Melanie C. Duncan, Andrew and Kate Barton, Gary Ehrlich, Joshuah Kusnerz, Jason Hargenrader, Doug Eckhoff, E_bookpushers, Jessica Rydill, Keri Mills, Johnathon Otworth, Steve Lord, C. Joshua Villines, Krystina Harrington, Melissa Tabon, Peter Young, Revek, Hans Ranke, Andy Clayman, Eleanor Russell, Jules Jones, Jenny Barber, Derek Hudgins, C Budworth, Morva Bowman & Alan Pollard, Charles Scott, Remer Speaks Jr, catherin nelson, Gina D'Amigo, sam murphy, Christine Swendseid, Michael Carroll, Jennifer Della'Zanna, Hamish Laws, Lirion, Jill Baum, Deborah, Anna McDuff, Beth Tiffany, Jeffery Lawler, Olna Jenn Smith, Chan Ka Chun Patrick, Megan E. Daggett, Capt. Stuckey, Epiphyllum, Tibs, Missy Gunnels Katano, Karen Fonville, PK, K Gendall, Margaret S. McGraw, Alexander Pendergrass, Flights of Fantasy Books & Games, Jon K.G. Allanson, Laura, Louisa Swann, Colin A Fisher, Catherine Sharp, Shawn Marier, Nick D, Tammy Mabire, Mandy Wultsch, Daniel s, Kristin Evenson Hirst, Kenny Soward, Kerri Regan, Damon and Jenna Bratcher, K. M. Strawser, Kevin Niemczyk, Park, Tracy Benton, Forrest Austin, Kriatyrr, Victoria Traube, Catherine Nelson, Orla Carey, james_